PRAISE FOR WILLIAM J. COUGHLIN:

"Coughlin wrote taut and suspenseful novels of the legal system before Scott Turow ever lifted a pen."
—*Washington Times*

"Coughlin knows his stuff!"
—*Playboy*

"Coughlin is a consummate storyteller."
—*Library Journal*

"Coughlin keeps you burning the midnight oil to the very end."
—*Kirkus Reviews* on *In the Presence of Enemies*

"A convincing legal thriller."
—*Publishers Weekly* on *In the Presence of Enemies*

"*Shadow of a Doubt* has much of the atmosphere and intrigue of *Anatomy of a Murder* and a humdinger of an ending . . . A great read."
—Scott Turow

"Coughlin's spellbinding grasp of the courtroom held me on the edge of my seat until the last page."
—William J. Caunitz

"It's a scorcher with a shock conclusion that will leave the reader breathless."
—Liz Smith on *Shadow of a Doubt*

Also by William J. Coughlin

THE HEART OF JUSTICE

WILLIAM J. COUGHLIN

St. Martin's Paperbacks

THE HEART OF JUSTICE

Copyright © 1995 by Ruth Coughlin.

Library of Congress Catalog Card Number: 94-3783

ISBN: 0-312-95551-0

Printed in the United States of America

St. Martin's Press hardcover edition/February 1995
St. Martin's Paperbacks edition/December 1995

10 9 8 7 6 5 4 3 2 1

THE HEART OF JUSTICE

PROLOGUE

They had just finished making love when the telephone rang. She was lying in the crook of his arm, luxuriating in the warmth of the late afternoon sun slanting through the floor-to-ceiling windows on the wall opposite their bed.

They hadn't bothered to draw the curtains. Her country house—their house now—stood high on a hill, surrounded by a vast expanse of rolling meadows, woods, dairy grazing pasture. They both loved the view of the sunlight glinting on the pond just below the house, and beyond that, several miles to the west across the Hudson River, the Catskill Mountains. Except for the sparrows twittering in the newly budding branches of the birch tree that reached to the third-story bedroom window, they had absolute privacy.

The phone rang again.

"Leave it," he said drowsily. "Let's sleep a while. Whoever it is will call back."

But the ringing had already dissipated her sense of peace and well-being. An unanswered phone always made her nervous. What horrible news might be awaiting her at the other end? Few people had the private number in the country. The staff in New York, of course, but they had instructions to call only in the event of emergency.

A few close friends, none of whom knew she was here for the weekend.

"It might be important," she whispered.

He tightened his arm around her naked body, wanting her to lie with him, to savor their pleasure for as long as possible.

"Stay here," he murmured, snuggling against her.

"I'll be right back," she promised, and slipped out from under the comforter. Shivering from the chill air of the unheated room, she tiptoed next door to the library and picked up the phone on the sixth ring.

"Hello?" she said, hugging herself to get warm.

"Hope. I figured I'd find you there. We need to talk," said a deep voice at the other end.

"Jordan?" She wrapped herself in the knitted afghan that lay across the love seat and settled into the rocker. She shivered again, though not from the cold. He was the last person in the world she wanted to hear from.

"You took your time getting to the phone. I trust I didn't catch you at an awkward moment."

She imagined his mouth twisted in a leer. "We were just outside in the garden," she lied. "Jordan, how did you get this number?"

He chuckled again. "Directory assistance."

"It's unlisted," she told him. She glanced out the window and saw that two deer, a fawn and a doe, had come to graze by the pond. Columbia County, much of New York State, in fact, had been overrun with deer. The farmers and the weekenders were united in their complaints about ruined crops and decimated gardens. People were nervous about catching Lyme disease, and the local papers were full of warnings and advice. Hope understood that the deer were a problem. But she loved their shy, gentle grace and welcomed their appearance as some sort of good omen.

"You gave me the number yourself, don't you remember?" said Jordan. "Way back when we were screwing, before you were a respectable married lady."

Hope winced. Trust Jordan Crandell to use the foulest possible language to describe the very short-lived affair they'd had when she was newly divorced and too susceptible to a man's interest in her. She'd managed to forget a lot of the mistakes she'd made during that period, including the specifics of sleeping with Jordan.

What a terrible time that had been: a messy, highly publicized divorce, and six months later, the sudden death of her father, whom she'd adored and tried so hard to please all her life. When Jordan had called to pay his condolences, she'd stupidly accepted his invitation to dinner. She'd been flattered by his attention, even though she'd known him since they were children. Back then he was the shortest, runtiest kid in the crowd, the one who always had to run to catch up with the gang, who got chosen last for teams, got picked on most, had to beg to be included in their games.

He was a born loser. Who would have guessed that Jordan Crandell, who easily could have been voted least likely to succeed, would grow up to be one of the richest men in America? Who would have believed that he would become one of the country's most aggressive and successful corporate raiders?

He was still short. Not even his specially constructed elevator shoes could bring his height above five feet four. But thanks to the several hours a week he spent with his personal trainer, he was no longer a skinny little runt. He was bulked up, bulging with muscles as toned as a world-class athlete's, and he had worked with a voice coach to lower his pitch to an intimidating bass growl. Almost totally bald, he could well have afforded a transplant. He scorned such artifice, however, bragging that bald men had higher testosterone levels and brought more to bed than their hairier rivals.

For old times' sake, because she'd taken pity and paid attention to him when no one else would, Jordan considered her a friend. He didn't have many, though his calen-

dar was crowded with appointments for lunch and dinner.
And in an odd sort of way, Hope was fond of him. He was
most of the things she admired least in a man: insecure,
demanding, driven, vulgar, and vengeful. But out of respect for their shared past, she tolerated his failings and
overlooked his indiscretions, even going so far as to defend him publicly within their intersecting social circles
when the chorus of disapproval got too loud.

He appreciated her loyalty. He sent her roses on her
birthday, offered her investment tips (none of which she
ever followed, because she already had more money than
she knew what to do with), made uncharacteristically
generous contributions to the charities she supported.
The one and only time she had asked him for a favor, he
had readily exerted his far-reaching influence and pulled
the necessary strings.

Now, she cursed whatever crazy impulse had led her
to use his connections.

"How's the newest addition to the Federal Court system?" he asked. "Keeping you satisfied? Because if he's
not—"

"Paul's fine," Hope cut in. "We're very happy. As a
matter of fact, we were just getting ready to drive over to
the village before the grocery closes."

Jordan snorted. "Don't you know that's why God gave
rich people like us servants? To run our errands. And it's
only five o'clock. You have plenty of time."

"This isn't New York City, Jordan," she said. "We're
in the country. People eat dinner at six and go to bed by
ten."

"You wouldn't catch me wasting my time in that hell-
hole. But I guess you know I didn't call to talk about
cows or pigs or whatever the fuck people talk about up
there. Have you 'fessed up to Paul? Shared with him that
little package I sent you?"

She thought she heard a floorboard creak. Glancing
nervously in the direction of the bedroom, she lowered

her voice. "You're bluffing, Jordan. There's nothing there you can use to hurt Paul."

"Just watch me, Hope. I could have him brought up on charges, destroy his career. The evidence all points directly at Paul. It's so touching, isn't it, how Paul stepped in to save the family's honor?"

"You don't know that, Jor—" she began.

"Goddamnit, Hope! Don't be naive!" His voice boomed out at her. "The point is, I cashed in some very important chits for you and the Honorable Judge Paul Murray. All I'm asking for is a little payback. Paul's no dummy. He couldn't have gotten as far as he did before you came along without sucking up to the right people. He knows damn well how the system works."

"I'll see what I can do." She tried to placate him.

"This is no big deal. My lawyer says the other side is just blowing air. He'd probably rule in my favor anyway. All I'm looking for is a little insurance policy. By the way, you ought to call my girl at the office and make a date for the three of us to have dinner. I've got the best French chef in town working for me now. Stole him from Périgord. They hate my guts over there, but I'm eating like a goddamn king. Okay?"

"Sounds lovely. I'll check my calendar," she said, thinking she would rather walk on coals than have dinner with Paul and Jordan Crandell.

"Be sure you do," he said, and the line went dead.

She put the phone back and walked over to the window. The deer were gone now, vanished into the woods at the edge of her back lawn. The wind had picked up, and the pond was ruffled with waves. She was glad they had nowhere to go this evening. She had lied to Jordan about the trip to the grocery. They had everything they needed for dinner—French bread, all the ingredients for the lemon chicken and risotto they would cook together, fixings for salad.

She crept back into the bedroom. Paul was fast asleep,

one arm extended across her side of the bed, as if he were reaching for her. A restless sleeper, he'd kicked off most of the quilt, baring his shoulders and back. At forty-seven, he was in good shape, lean and muscular, thanks to regular workouts at his health club. He still had a full head of dark wavy hair, with only a hint of gray around the ears.

She'd thought of the Kennedy men the first time she'd met him. He had the same rugged Irish features, toothy grin, and bright blue eyes. Waking up next to him in bed their first morning together, she had told him so, and he'd laughed. Apparently, she wasn't the first woman to draw the comparison.

"Their looks maybe," he'd said, his ruddy cheeks turning redder. "But not their connections."

His roots were strictly working-class Irish.

She'd been born into tremendous wealth but felt she had nothing to show for her thirty-seven years. She admired his ambition and had wanted to help him in whatever way she could. Only later had she begun to understand the depths of his pride in having earned each of his achievements by dint of his own hard work.

He was an excellent judge. Everyone said so: his friends, his colleagues, even *The New York Times* in an editorial that praised his nomination to the federal bench. Only the timing had been off. Paul himself had been taken by surprise. A person could only fantasize about one day becoming a Supreme Court Justice, but the chance to serve as a Federal Court judge was a dream within reach. Still, he hadn't expected the honor to come his way so soon. He'd been prepared to be patient, to wait until the groundwork had been laid. Then, suddenly, the prize was his.

Sharing his excitement, Hope had been sure she'd done the right thing to help him win it.

But on this mid-May afternoon that was slowly sliding

into dusk, she wondered about the wisdom of her decision. As she pulled the cover over him and bent to kiss the back of his neck, she couldn't push away the fear that she had made the biggest mistake of her life.

ONE

"SHE'S LOVELY, ISN'T SHE?"

Paul Murray pulled his gaze away from the dark-haired woman who stood across the room, surrounded by a small knot of admirers. He chuckled with ill-concealed embarrassment. "Was I being that obvious?" he asked.

"Hope Scott," said Drew Abrams, a fellow committee member. "As if you needed me to tell you her name. I stared, too, the first time I saw her."

Paul glanced back at Hope Scott. The pictures he'd seen of her in newspapers and magazines hadn't done her justice. She was simply dressed in a black silk skirt, short enough to reveal a stunning pair of legs; a matching black silk jacket; a simple cream-colored blouse that managed simultaneously to show off her shoulders and be discreet.

Taller than he'd imagined, she carried herself with the erect posture and grace of a dancer. Her head was tilted back slightly, exposing a long, thin neck that Modigliani would have loved to paint. Her lips were set in a half-smile. Paul wondered what was being said to provoke that smile. To his surprise, he found himself wishing he were the person provoking it.

"We're damned lucky she accepted Mrs. Osburgh's invitation to join our committee. With her connections and money, the Preservation Society will raise twice the amount we did last year,'' Drew Abrams said.

He nodded in the direction of the food that their hostess, Hallie Neuwirth, had provided for the pre-meeting cocktail hour. "I suggest we sample some of that caviar, then you'll want to pay your respects to our chairperson. I've already done my duty with Mrs. Osburgh.''

Paul followed Abrams to the buffet table. Most of the planning committee's meetings were long on talk, short on food or drink. But Hallie Neuwirth, whose arbitrageur husband was newly rich, hadn't yet mastered the old money's rigid social code. Her walls were covered with expensive art, her apartment filled with museum-quality furniture, and her table weighted down with an endless supply of Petrossian's Russian beluga caviar at $57.50 an ounce. The crowd that ran New York might sniff at such ostentatious displays of affluence, but they were happy to feast at her expense.

Hallie Neuwirth was grateful to be a part of that crowd. The Municipal Preservation Society, dedicated to the protection and restoration of landmark buildings, was one of the city's most prestigious organizations. The fourteen people who had gathered on this rainy October evening to plan the next fund-raiser were an eclectic mix of the old guard and the nouveau riche. Paul didn't fit into either category. Nevertheless, as a justice of the New York State Supreme Court, he brought a certain cachet to the committee's letterhead.

The benefits were mutual. Paul needed the committee as much as it needed him. Despite his impressive-sounding title, he could only strain his neck looking up the judicial ladder at the far more exalted state Appellate Court, the Court of Appeals, and Federal Court. But it took a great deal of influence to get elected to the bench. His progress depended on the continued support of the men and women who made things happen in the city.

Paul had clerked for a year right out of law school,

then spent sixteen years at Goodstein & Carney, first as an associate, then as a partner. He had no regrets about giving up a lucrative corporate practice. As a judge, he could make a difference about how the law should be interpreted. The route to the bench had led him into local clubhouse politics, charitable organizations, appointments to influential committees. He had cultivated the right friends, people like Connie Osburgh, the sixty-year-old doyenne of the Municipal Preservation Society, who were willing to dip into their pockets to help him get elected.

Mrs. Osburgh seemed to have taken a special liking to him. She smiled and patted the sofa, inviting him to sit down next to her. In her tidy pageboy, beige cashmere sweater, tweed skirt, and comfortable oxfords, she looked more like a boarding school housemother than a society grande dame. In taste and dress, Mrs. Osburgh was ultra-conservative. Standards had to be maintained. But she prided herself on being open-minded about people like Paul Murray. He was such a gentleman, so bright and well mannered one would never guess his background.

"You're looking well, Paul," she said.

"Thank you, Mrs. Osburgh. As are you. Did you have a pleasant summer?" Paul asked.

Mrs. Osburgh beamed. "Marvelous. You've never been up to our place in the Adirondacks, have you? You must come some weekend next summer. We have such fun there, and I'm sure my husband would adore meeting you."

He had heard about the Osburghs' Adirondack retreat, which she had inherited from her mother. The log cabin lodge and five outbuildings were set on hundreds of acres of virgin forest, in an area so remote that all the supplies had to be brought in by canoe. Electricity was provided by a primitive generator that regularly broke down, but the Osburghs didn't seem to mind the inconvenience.

"And speaking of meeting people," she went on. "Have you been introduced yet to Hope Scott? She's a darling girl. Her mother and I were such very great friends, poor thing."

Paul couldn't tell whether Mrs. Osburgh was clucking over Hope or her mother. "Oh, Hope! Do come over here and meet one of my favorite judges."

Hope Scott extricated herself from the conversation and came to join them. Face to face, Paul saw that her features were less than perfect: her large green eyes a tad too far apart, her mouth overly generous, her forehead perhaps too prominent. None of that mattered. In ancient times, he thought, a man would have gone to war for such a woman.

He stood up to greet her. She was almost his height, five nine, and she stared directly into his eyes as she extended her hand. "I'm glad to meet you, Judge Murray."

She spoke so softly he almost had to strain to hear her.

"I feel as if I already know you. I followed the Banning trial last year, and then of course I read the piece about you in *The New Yorker*."

Ordinarily, he would have been flattered by her interest. But she could hardly have missed hearing about the case, a tragic story of child abuse and murder that had dominated the media for weeks.

"My fifteen minutes of fame," he said. "Overall, I think I prefer my privacy."

She smiled, not the half-smile he'd noticed earlier, but a grin that seemed to bubble up from some inner spring of amusement. "Fame does have its price," she said. "Believe me, I ought to know."

A passing waiter stopped to offer them wine. She took a glass for herself and handed one to him. "To privacy." She clicked her glass against his. "A rare and precious commodity."

He smiled then, too, remembering that she'd had to put up with a lifetime of photographers snapping her picture, of newspapers and magazines reporting her every move.

"Touché," he said. "And please, call me Paul."

"Paul." She repeated his name slowly, as if she were trying to decide whether it suited him. "All right, I will. Does that mean we're going to be friends?"

Her tone was casual, lilting. She was flirting with him, but he told himself it meant nothing. A woman like Hope Scott could have any man she wanted. She flirted out of habit, not interest.

"Well, I certainly hope so," he said awkwardly.

His wife had been dead almost two and a half years, but he'd only recently begun seeing other women, most of whom he met through friends who made no secret of their wish to see him remarried. "You'll love her, she reminds me so much of Helen," they invariably assured him.

None of them seemed to understand. He didn't want someone who reminded him of Helen. The resemblance—real or imagined—would only serve to remind him of what he'd lost.

No one could replace his wife of almost twenty-five years, but he wasn't about to become a monk. And though he never would have believed it, the cliché was true: Time did heal wounds. Perhaps not all of them, but enough that he was enjoying life again. He dreamed of Helen less frequently, and some mornings he caught himself humming as he dressed for work.

But he was a rank amateur at playing the dating game. The rules had changed since he'd met Helen at a college mixer during the fall of his freshman year. In this new age of sexual equality, women often offered to pick up the tab. They didn't wait for him to phone, but pursued him openly, calling with invitations to the theater or the opera or brunch.

One woman, an interior decorator whom he'd taken to dinner, had later sent him a note with her card: "I don't think we'd make good lovers," she had written in her neat parochial school penmanship. "But please keep me in mind the next time you redo your apartment."

Her blunt approach had felt like a punch in the stomach. When had women learned to be so direct? Thinking it over, he realized her method had a lot of merit. Both of them led busy, complicated lives. Why waste time mouthing niceties they didn't mean? Still, he didn't understand how she could have been so certain about not being lovers. He hadn't even kissed her goodnight.

"I'd adore some caviar," said Hope. "Nobody ever eats anything anymore. The women all want to be stick-thin like Connie Osburgh, and the men are too busy talking deals to stop long enough to put food into their mouths. Do you like to eat?"

Paul laughed as she took a plate, then spooned caviar and sour cream onto the delicate blini pancakes. "I *love* to eat." To prove his point, he helped himself to a plate. "I make a point of doing it at least three times a day."

"Hello, Blair." She waved at another committee member before returning her attention to him. "Chinatown has some wonderful Vietnamese restaurants, just a few minutes away from the courthouse." She took another bite of blini, then carefully wiped a trace of sour cream off her lips with a cloth napkin. When she smiled, he noticed for the first time the tiny dark beauty mark just to the left of her bottom lip.

Her eyes danced with amusement as the silence between them stretched to the point of awkwardness. Finally, he realized that she was not going to be the one to break it. She was waiting for him to respond . . . to invite her to lunch? Could that possibly be what she had in mind?

Somehow, it was hard to imagine Hope Scott negotiating the wall-to-wall crowds that packed Chinatown's sidewalks at lunchtime. He'd been to a couple of the Vietnamese restaurants there. The food was excellent, but the ambience was noisy and rushed, hardly the quiet elegance she must be used to at Le Cirque or Lutèce or wherever she normally dined.

"Hope?" Hallie Neuwirth swooped down on them, tapping Hope's arm with her perfectly manicured nails. "Mrs. Osburgh's about to start the meeting, but she wants to ask you something first. Will you excuse us, Paul?"

"Of course." He nodded, wondering as Hallie steered her away how a woman like Hope Scott kept herself amused. *A woman like Hope Scott . . .* He should probably stop thinking of her as some sort of generic brand, when actually he had very little sense of what she was about. Except that she apparently liked caviar and Vietnamese food and seemed to have a keen sense of humor, he really didn't know her at all.

He wished he could change that. He didn't know if he dared.

"Trust me on this one, gentlemen. I can smell a good business deal, and this particular merger has the full-bodied aroma of a vintage Burgundy."

George Osburgh III sat back in his leather armchair and smiled at Winthrop Harding, Jr., and Harry Matheson, his fellow trustees for the Sanford Scott Trust. A waiter silently cleared the remnants of their lunch from the table. In a moment, coffee would be poured from the eighteenth-century silver server that Osburgh's great-great-grandmother had received as a wedding gift from the governor of New York. Chocolate chip cookies and fresh fruit would be offered for dessert. Then, if all went according to Osburgh's plan, the three men would agree to invest some portion of the late Sanford Scott's considerable fortune in Jordan Crandell's discretionary fund, to be used for his next big move on the corporate battlegrounds.

Four times a year, the trustees met here in the private

dining room of Osburgh & Bartlett, the Wall Street investment banking firm founded by Osburgh's grandfather in 1902, to make decisions regarding the Scott Trust. The quietly elegant room, with its gleaming mahogany surfaces and Bavarian cut-glass chandelier, seemed an appropriate setting for their discussions. The man who had entrusted them with the administration of his estate had been raised by a father who celebrated the potential of commerce and a mother who appreciated beauty and elegance.

More importantly, the connection between the Scotts and the Osburghs went back two generations. Scott's grandfather had done business with George Osburgh's grandfather, whose stern-faced portrait glared at them from its place of honor above the mantel. George Osburgh and Sanford Scott had known each other since boyhood, when their families had summered together on a tiny island off the coast of Maine. Later, they had been roommates at Groton, and their friendship had continued during their years at Harvard.

In theory, the three trustees' votes each carried equal weight, but Osburgh was the only one of them who had called Sanford Scott by his childhood nickname, Sandy. He was the first person Hope Scott had phoned when her father had keeled over and died of a heart attack on the fourth hole of the Castle Pines Golf Course. When Osburgh said, "I think Sandy would have liked this idea," his colleagues tended to see it his way.

Yet the controversial proposal he had brought to the table on this rainy autumn day was meeting with deep opposition. An astute businessman, Osburgh had felt their resistance from the moment Harry and Winthrop walked into the room. The Bobbsey twins, as he had contemptuously dubbed them. Harry was the managing partner of the venerable New York law firm, Langley & Dunlap. Winthrop had parlayed his family's commercial real estate holdings into an empire that included a liquor

distillery, a 20 percent interest in a major European hotel
chain, and a part ownership in one of America's largest
canned food companies.

But as far as Osburgh was concerned, they were idiots,
Sandy's idea of a bad joke, the kind he'd played on Osburgh since they were boys. The two men even looked
alike, both conservatively dressed in Brooks Brothers
pin-striped suits, their cheeks flushed and their eyes
bright from too much wine at lunch.

Osburgh always made sure they had plenty to drink.
He himself rarely drank, never smoked, ate a strictly low-
fat diet, and exercised religiously. His maternal grandfather had been a Methodist minister who preached tem-
perance and lived to celebrate his ninety-seventh
birthday. Osburgh was determined to surpass him, and at
sixty-four looked a good ten years younger. He was tall
and broad-shouldered, and he was proud of the fact that
he weighed only five pounds more than he had when he'd
earned his varsity letter as a linebacker at Harvard.

"George, I can't see how you could possibly justify
this move," said Harry.

His sideways glance at Winthrop confirmed what Osburgh had suspected, that they'd already discussed the
proposal between themselves and rejected it.

"Starwares is ripe for the plucking. Somebody was
bound to come after them, and Crandell believes that his
company is a logical fit for Starwares' long-range goals.
If Crandell succeeds—and he hasn't failed yet, I don't
need to tell you, gentlemen—he stands to make himself
and us a lot of money."

"Us?" Winthrop peered at Osburgh above the rim of
his coffee cup.

"Us . . . the Scott Trust . . . ," Osburgh said impatiently. He gestured at Crandell's proposal, a copy of
which they'd each received earlier in the week. "Have
you gone over the figures?"

Harry Matheson pulled a cigar out of his inside jacket

pocket and tapped it against the table. Osburgh knew Matheson resented the "no smoking" rule that was strictly enforced on the premises of Osburgh & Bartlett. He could have made an exception for Harry Matheson but pointedly chose not to.

"The figures look damn good, George," he said. "But this isn't the sort of thing in which we would normally involve ourselves. And Crandell's one hell of a tough customer. Do you really think you could trust him?"

"Langley & Dunlap would happily represent Crandell if he came knocking at your door. You'd take his money. Are you opposed to giving him some of ours as an investment that would be handsomely repaid? Honestly, Harry, if you had your way, we would bury the Scott Trust money in New Jersey."

"It's not *ours*," Winthrop reminded Osburgh, helping himself to another cookie. "It's Hope Scott's. We merely administer the trust on her behalf. The question we have to ask ourselves is, how would Sanford Scott feel about backing Crandell in what could be a very risky venture?"

"Dammit, Winthrop!" Osburgh slammed his fist on the table. "Sandy Scott was no saint! He was a hard-nosed businessman who made money by taking risks and backing winners."

And say what they might about the man, Jordan Crandell was a winner. He was also totally ruthless and arrogant beyond words. Osburgh's grandfather would have called him a scoundrel, and he would have been right. Crandell bought and sold companies and accumulated money as easily as other men purchased new ties or shirts.

In a recent profile in *Vanity Fair*, the writer had called him "a Great White corporate shark." Upon hearing the epithet, Crandell had reportedly chuckled over the description and begun humming the theme song to *Jaws*.

Just this morning, Osburgh had breakfasted with him at Crandell's fourteen-acre estate in Westchester County, an hour north of the city. He had pledged the trust's involvement in the takeover fight, in return for which Crandell had promised a 20 percent stake in the newly formed corporation. He had also made certain other promises, applicable only to Osburgh, contingent upon the success of the takeover. These guarantees, of course, had not been included in his proposal, and Osburgh saw no reason to disclose them to Matheson or Harding.

Sandy Scott would have approved. He had thrived in the no-holds-barred wheeling and dealing atmosphere of the eighties. The legend that had sprung up around his memory had him standing firm against the army of junk-bond-financed corporate marauders who had forever altered the face of American business. Osburgh knew better. Had Sandy lived a year or two longer, he would have no doubt been among the major players. But there was no point in correcting the picture of Scott as the last of the old-fashioned corporate executives. The image was good for the trust. And what was good for the trust was good for George Osburgh III.

He signaled the waiter to pour him another cup of decaffeinated coffee. Then he said, "The terms of Sanford Scott's trust documents make our duty clear: not only to preserve the corpus, but to increase it. If Crandell succeeds—and we have every reason to believe he will—we could make millions."

Osburgh was sure that Harry, who still held to the old-fashioned notion that only honorable men should be admitted to Wall Street and the kingdom of God, had instigated the opposition to Crandell. But over breakfast, Crandell had described in some detail how some years back he'd agreed to prevent Winthrop Harding's name from appearing in a very messy sex-scandal story that had run in one of his newspapers. "He owes me big," Crandell had said, going on to make a couple of suggestions about how to remind Harding of his debt.

It was time to call Harding's bluff. "I don't know

about you, Win, but I think that we three are powerful enough to *whip* Crandell into shape,'' George said, lightly emphasizing certain key words as Crandell had instructed him. ''Hell, we might even be able to *dominate* the situation to such a degree that we'll have him kissing our *boots*. Anyway, this is just a one-shot business deal. We're not *handcuffed* to him for life.''

Harding's face turned noticeably pale, and his fingers shook so badly that coffee spilled all over his fingers.

Son-of-a-bitch, George thought. So Crandell hadn't been lying. George never would have guessed that Win had it in him.

''Perhaps the proposal does have some merit,'' Harding said uneasily. ''It's incumbent upon us to carry on as Sanford Scott would have himself if he were still alive, and he was a risk taker. Normally, of course, I would never approve of investing the trust's money in a take-over battle, but this is Jordan Crandell we're talking about.''

Matheson's cheeks were mottled with angry red splotches as he glared at the defecting Harding.

''There's no way in the world I would vote yes,'' Matheson said tightly. ''Investing in Crandell is playing with fire, and the game's too dangerous for my blood. I can't imagine what you two gentlemen are thinking. Such a move would absolutely put us in breach of our fiduciary duties.''

Osburgh clenched his fists beneath the table. This proposal meant more to him than the two men could ever imagine. Still, he consoled himself that though he would have preferred to get their support, he could move forward even without their votes. He was the one who administered the trust on a day-to-day basis, moving the money around, singlehandedly making all but the major financial decisions. He was sure that between Crandell and himself, they would figure out how the Scott Trust could reap the benefits of Crandell's upcoming deal.

But he wouldn't soon or easily forget Harry Matheson's self-righteous recalcitrance.

"Very well," he said, struggling to conceal his fury. "Let's move on to the next order of business. But you're all wrong about this investment, Harry. It is a game, but hardly as dangerous as you might imagine. And money is just a way of keeping score."

JORDAN CRANDELL HAD done his homework. His team of researchers and private investigators had amassed hundreds of pages of data on Eric Lynch, the ultimate computer nerd whose software systems were fast gaining dominance over the computer industry. As usual, Crandell had spent hours reading through the documents, underlining important points, making notes on file cards that his secretary then entered into his notebook computer.

Crandell had long ago discovered that knowledge equaled power. He used information to get what he wanted, whether in his business or personal life, which were inextricably linked. Corporate stock, a new image, a controlling interest in a company, four-star cuisine, beautiful women, real estate, expensive wines—they were all commodities to be acquired and dispensed with whenever it pleased him.

Now he wanted Starwares. He'd never wanted anything so badly in his whole life. He was obsessed with the dizzying array of possibilities to be gained from a merger between his Summit, Inc., media empire and Eric Lynch's titanic corporation. He knew everything there was to know about Starwares' founder and chairman, including the fact that he was a highly skilled chess player. Crandell liked that about Lynch. He, too, enjoyed a good game of chess. He was ready to make his first move.

Normally, he would have invited the CEO onto his turf in order to grab the home field advantage. But gaining Lynch's confidence demanded a more subtle strategy.

Lynch had to be persuaded that Crandell was coming as a starstruck suitor, wooing him with the corporate equivalent of a dozen long-stemmed roses and a box of Belgian chocolates. It would be easier that way to catch Lynch off guard and capture his king.

Starwares was headquartered in Heber City, Utah, a dusty cowboy town set in the middle of the Wasatch Mountains thirty miles southeast of Salt Lake City. Crandell had flown in to Salt Lake on his corporate jet the previous evening, arriving just as the sun was setting over the Great Salt Lake. His meeting with Eric Lynch was scheduled for 8:00 A.M. Now, as his driver sped south along the I-80, Crandell reviewed what he'd read about Lynch and the company he'd founded in what would have been his senior year at MIT, had he stayed there long enough to graduate.

Lynch had two great passions in life—creating ever more complex computer software systems, and skiing. His college roommate, a Mormon from nearby Provo, had brought him west to ski at Park City, and Lynch had immediately felt at home. In the fifteen years since he'd first settled in Heber City and become the local hero, Starwares had grown into the area's major industry, employing some ten thousand people. Lynch owned a house at the top of the slopes in Sundance, the exclusive ski resort and film institute that Robert Redford had lovingly carved out of the walls of the Sundance Canyon.

He was a millionaire many times over, one of the wealthiest men in America. He was also on the forefront of creating software with which to travel the information highway of the twenty-first century, the coming revolution in the communications industry. Crandell was determined to ride that highway right alongside Eric Lynch.

Lynch was hunched in front of his computer monitor, eating a doughnut, when Crandell was ushered into his office. "He's expecting you," the secretary said in a low voice. "The best thing to do is sit down and wait. In a few minutes, he'll notice you're here."

Crandell glanced at his watch. It was eight o'clock. He was exactly on time. With anyone else, excepting the President of the United States, he would have insisted that the meeting begin as scheduled. Making someone wait was a ploy he'd often used himself, but never with one of his corporate equals. His fellow CEOs would have been insulted by such a cavalier approach. But Lynch, by anyone's definition, was a certified genius who didn't operate by standard business rules.

Crandell knew he was lucky to have gotten in the door. He unbuttoned his coat jacket, sat back, and watched Eric Lynch as he gazed at his monitor.

Ten minutes passed. Finally, Lynch grunted and looked up. He blinked his eyes, gazing blankly at Crandell as if he were just waking up from a deep sleep.

"Jordan Crandell. It's a pleasure to meet you." Crandell leaned across the desk to shake Lynch's hand. Lynch looked very much as Crandell had expected: a good ten years younger than his thirty-five years, dressed in khaki jeans and a creased denim workshirt, his brown hair falling over his eyes, his face pale from being indoors for too many hours at a stretch.

By the beginning of December, a brief six weeks away, the slopes would be covered with snow and Lynch would be tan again from his daily runs down the mountains. He'd have no time then for discussions of mergers. Crandell had been advised to make his presentation brief and to the point. With that in mind, he cut to the chase. "I don't know if you've had a chance to read the proposal I sent you—"

"Of course I read it," Lynch broke in. "I may look like a nerd, but I'm not an idiot. I run a multimillion-dollar corporation, which is precisely why you're here, isn't it?"

Silently cursing himself for his poor opening gambit, Crandell smiled gamely. "I'd never take you for an idiot, Eric, if you don't mind my getting down to a first-name basis, and I meant no offense. Okay, so you've looked at all the facts and figures. I'm not going to screw around trying to tell you that Summit is a great company, which we are, or why I think we should join forces. I believe we'd make an excellent fit, highly profitable for all concerned. You're obviously at least somewhat intrigued, or I wouldn't be here. But you must have questions. So, ask me anything. I'm free for as long as you are."

"Yeah, you're right. I do have questions. You want a doughnut?" Lynch held up a half-filled box of doughnuts from the 7-Eleven.

"Thanks, no." Crandell shook his head. His stomach felt queasy at the thought of eating the rich, oily doughnuts so early in the morning.

Lynch chose a chocolate-glazed cruller. Between bites, he ticked his questions off on his fingers. "Number one, what can you do for Starwares that I can't do for myself? Number two, let's say I can work with you and your people, what's to stop other guys from coming after Starwares once they hear we're in play? Number three, how much do you really get about this brave new world of the information highway? Number four, why'd you come all the way to Heber yourself? Why didn't you send the investment bankers around to sniff out my reaction?"

He finished off the cruller and contemplated the box, as if deciding whether to eat another one. Then he said, "Mr. Crandell, I'm great with systems, not very good with people. I figure you're either dumb or really smart. You tell me. Which is it?"

TWO

PAUL COULDN'T GET her out of his mind. The day after the landmarks meeting, in the middle of a pretrial hearing regarding a problematic narcotics raid, he suddenly remembered the beauty mark next to Hope Scott's lower lip. He imagined himself touching it with his index finger, then touching her lips, then kissing her. The image caught him by surprise.

He wanted to see her again. He felt the cold hand of guilt—his Irish legacy, he thought. The Irish would feel guilty about being admitted to heaven. He tried to absolve himself. Helen had teased a promise out of him that he would find someone else to share his life. She would have hated the thought of him sitting alone in their apartment on a Friday night, reading last month's *Law Journal* and drinking a beer while he heated up the chicken his housekeeper had left in the refrigerator.

He stayed up too late and fell asleep watching an old Humphrey Bogart movie. He dreamed of Helen, the same dream as always: She was twenty again, the girl with the neat blond flip and dazzling smile. She was wearing her blue gym suit and running toward him. His heart filled with love and wonder that this magical girl could be his.

He reached over to wrap his arms around his wife and nestle into her back and neck. But the space where she should have been was empty, the sheets cold and unrumpled. Swimming toward wakefulness, he opened his eyes and stared at the TV set. A lean, muscular, leotard-clad woman with short-cropped hair was screaming at him to stop the insanity.

"Okay, I'll stop," he muttered, groping for the remote control. But what could be more insane than falling for Hope Scott?

Wide awake now, he got up, made coffee, and retrieved *The New York Times* from his front door. Through his open window overlooking Park Avenue, he could hear the garbage trucks making their early morning rounds. The sky was clear, the air soft. It was seven o'clock on what promised to be a glorious October day. He had a squash date at noon, a lot of hours to fill until then. He went through the newspaper, paid his bills, read a memo from his law clerk. At ten o'clock, he pulled out the list of names, addresses, and phone numbers that had been distributed at the committee meeting.

Hope Scott lived on Fifth Avenue. He guessed from the number that her apartment was only a few blocks away from him, probably at 63rd or 64th Street. He must have passed the building hundreds of times on his strolls through the neighborhood. He stared at her name on the list, and in good lawyerly fashion reviewed the facts he knew of her life.

She had inherited one of America's great industrial fortunes, a fortune that had been increased many times over by her father, Sanford Scott. But her family's wealth was not the only reason for Hope Scott's fame.

People magazine had named her one of the top ten "faces of the future" when she turned eighteen, the same year she'd been the season's reigning debutante. At twenty, after posing for a series of controversial lingerie ads shot by fashion photographer Horst, she had almost been disinherited by her father. She'd managed to redeem herself, however, and graduated with honors from

Bryn Mawr, then gone off to London to study economics. The life of the graduate student must not have suited her, for suddenly she was back in the United States, auditioning for roles in Hollywood, showing up in Aspen with Warren Beatty, jetting off for long weekends in New York, Saint-Tropez, or Mustique.

Paul knew all of this because Helen, an otherwise sensible woman, had breathlessly followed Hope Scott's well-chronicled adventures. When she eloped in her mid-twenties with a professional ski racer, Helen had correctly predicted that the marriage wouldn't last long. By the time the racer left her for a younger woman, Hope's father was dead and she seemed to have lost her need to keep the tabloids in business.

Her name still appeared in the gossip columns. But these days, she was best known for serving on various charitable boards and for appearing around town with a succession of New York's wealthiest, most powerful men. Paul had seen her interviewed not long ago by Barbara Walters after the Blanche and Sanford G. Scott Foundation had donated three million dollars to the Children's Defense Fund.

"You could have your pick of the field," Barbara Walters had gushed. "It's been six years since your divorce. Why haven't you remarried?"

"Why should I?" she'd replied. "I already have everything I could possibly want."

Barbara Walters had looked skeptical. "Perhaps you just haven't met the right man."

"Have you, Barbara?" Hope had shot back, and the interview moved on to another topic.

She would most likely be out of town, gone to the Hamptons or Connecticut for the weekend. He cleared his throat and quickly punched her number, expecting to get the maid or an answering machine. Hope answered the phone herself on the second ring.

"Hello," he said. "It's Paul Murray."

"Hello, Paul." Her voice was warm and welcoming. "You sound surprised to hear me. Did you mean to call someone else?"

"No." He laughed, deciding to tell the truth. "I never expected you to answer your own phone."

"Ah, well," she said, sounding amused. "It's the houseman's day off, the maid just eloped with the chauffeur, and the cook's in the scullery, peeling potatoes. But I don't want to bore you with my problems. How are you?"

"Fine, thanks." He cast around for a jokey response. Failing that, he got right to the point. "Look, I know this is short notice, but I was wondering whether by any chance you're free for dinner tomorrow evening."

"As a matter of fact, I am."

He smiled at the phone. "Great! I don't know what you like to eat, besides caviar and Vietnamese, but—"

"Do you mind if I make a suggestion?" she interrupted him. "I've been craving sushi, and I know a wonderful place not far from here that rivals some of Tokyo's best."

He smiled again. "Sushi would be great. But I'm a fairly recent convert to the cause, and you sound like an expert. You may have to help me out with the order."

"My pleasure. Oh, Lord!" She interrupted herself. "I have lunch today with Aunt Connie and Uncle George . . . the Osburghs? I don't dare be late, and I'm not even dressed yet. Will you pick me up tomorrow? Around seven all right?"

"Seven's fine."

She said goodbye and hung up.

Paul put down the phone and noticed that his palms were slick with sweat. He felt as nervous and exhilarated as a teenager about to go out on his first date with the most popular girl in the class.

LEW VALENTINE WAS famous for being a workaholic. Early in his career, he had earned a reputation as a go-getter, someone who just didn't know how to relax. He *had* to work harder than everyone else at Valentine Industries. He was the boss's kid. Now, at fifty, he was the boss, but he still worked six and a half days a week. Sunday mornings from nine to twelve-thirty he spent with his wife and three children. Then it was back to business—meetings at the office, or more frequently, games of golf and tennis that were meetings masquerading as sport.

He'd brought the company a long way from its modest beginnings as Electrical Outlets, the small, New Haven–based chain of appliance discount stores established by his father. Rising through the ranks from stockboy to chief executive officer, Valentine had taken the company public, then moved across the face of corporate America like a video Pacman, gobbling up a fiber-optics company, a high-tech medical company, and the nation's second largest cellular phone company, among many other acquisitions.

Earlier in the year, he had sold off the medical company for a pretax profit of a billion plus dollars. The money had been burning a hole in his wallet. Interest rates were down. He was ready to go shopping again. More than a few company officers and their investment bankers had been knocking at his door, peddling their wares, offering him a veritable banquet of corporate goodies. He let them in, listened, and nodded to show his interest.

His father, who'd won and lost a fortune at the race track, had taught him to play poker. In college, he'd made enough money at the game to buy himself a brand-new Thunderbird convertible. Rule number one, his father had drummed into him, was never to tip his hand. He'd already targeted his next acquisition. For anyone who had half a business brain, it should have been as obvious as a billboard in the middle of Times Square. But as far as he knew, no one had figured it out yet, which suited Valentine perfectly. He had no stomach for a bidding war that would send the price of an already expensive property soaring way beyond its worth.

For precisely that reason, he'd agreed to the interview with Kurt Zelmanski of *The Wall Street Journal*. The *Journal* had generally treated Valentine kindly in the past, and with good cause. He'd always done well by his stockholders.

"Confuse the enemy," his father always said. "Keep 'em guessing."

There were two ways to do that: pay too much money to his public relations firm—or talk to Zelmanski. He invited the reporter up to his house in Connecticut. He'd give him a couple of hours of his time, offer him a drink, introduce him to the family, send him on his way. A profitable use of a Saturday afternoon.

When Zelmanski appeared at his front door, he looked much younger than Valentine had expected, a broad-faced kid with a crewcut and a mouthful of teeth, who probably hadn't even hit thirty yet. Valentine was disappointed. Couldn't they have sent him a seasoned veteran? The fun was in the challenge. Faking Zelmanski out would be a piece of cake.

"Come on in," Valentine said. He led the way up the winding double staircase to two leather couches that faced each other in front of the fireplace in his office. "So, Mr. Zelmanski, you mentioned something about doing a profile on me. I'm afraid I make for very dull copy. You may regret driving all the way out here to see me."

"I doubt that," said Kurt Zelmanski, who already knew a great deal about Lew Valentine. His trained reporter's eye took note of Valentine's casual Saturday afternoon attire: the V-necked burgundy sweater, the perfectly tailored Brooks Brothers pants, the Bally loafers. But beneath the expensive clothes, Valentine looked like an average suburban Joe, with thinning hair combed sparsely across his scalp, bags under his eyes, a slightly protruding pot belly, and nails chewed down to the quick. Lew Valentine was one nervous guy.

"How about a drink? Coffee, designer water? Something stronger?"

"I'm fine, thanks." Zelmanski held up his pocket-sized tape recorder. "Do you mind? I find it much easier than trying to take notes and ask questions at the same time."

Valentine shook his head. "Not at all. Remind me, if we have time, to show you around the grounds. Just don't ask me the names of any of the flowers. My wife's the gardener. Well, what would you like to know?"

"As I mentioned when we spoke on the phone, we're thinking of doing a fairly long piece on you and your company. I've already read the clips about how you got started, what you've done with the company, that sort of thing. You're a real American success story, Mr. Valentine."

"One of many," Valentine said, waving away the compliment. "I was lucky. My father put together a rock-solid company. He pointed me in the right direction. I just followed his finger."

"You did a lot more than that," said Zelmanski, who just last week had discovered that Valentine and his father hadn't spoken for the last twelve years of the old man's life. "You've turned Valentine into one of the country's biggest cellular phone companies. Where do you go from here, Mr. Valentine? You've got some spare cash to play with. What are you going to do with it?"

"I've been weighing my options. A lot of attractive offers have crossed my desk lately. I've passed them along to my numbers people to do their analysis, then I'll make my decision based on their recommendations."

"Anything in particular strike your fancy?"

"If you were dating three or four women at once, would you let it get around that you thought one of them had nicer tits—pardon my French—than the others?"

Valentine slapped his knee, then he said quickly, "On second thought, I'd rather you didn't use that particular quote. I'm a happily married man. What I can't say in front of my wife or kids, I don't say in print."

"Uh-huh," Zelmanski said noncommittally.

A buddy of his at the *Palm Beach Post* had sworn on a keg of beer that according to their Palm Beach housekeeper, the Valentines had a very open-ended take on marital fidelity. Zelmanski figured the arrangement was what kept Valentine such a happily married man. His buddy had offered to put him in touch with the housekeeper, but Zelmanski was in no rush. Valentine's personal life was his own business, unless it affected his business life.

"What about computers?" he asked.

"Computers?" Valentine gnawed at his thumbnail a moment, then folded his hands in his lap.

"Computers linked directly to your worldwide cellular phone system. The mind boggles at the possibilities, doesn't it?"

"I suppose so." Valentine stood up and went over to the bar. He poured himself a glass of mineral water with a wedge of lime. "You sure I can't give you something to drink?"

"Okay, I'll have the same as you." Zelmanski watched Valentine pick up the Pellegrino. "I heard that Jordan Crandell flew out to Utah this week," he said.

"Crandell likes to travel. Utah's a beautiful state. You ever been there?" His face a mask, Valentine brought the drinks over to the couch and handed one to Zelmanski.

Zelmanski ignored Valentine's question and posed his own. "A little early for skiing, don't you think?"

"What are you getting at, young man? Why should I give a damn about Jordan Crandell's frequent-flyer mileage?"

"I can think of only three reasons why Crandell would have gone out there," said Zelmanski. "One, he's suddenly gotten religion and decided to join the Mormons. Two, he's pitching a movie script to Robert Redford. Three, he's taken an interest in Starwares. If I had to bet, I'd put my money on door number three, and I doubt he was talking to Eric Lynch about getting a good deal on accounting software.''

Valentine picked the lime out of his glass and sucked the juice out of it. ''Didn't you say you wanted to do a piece on me? If I'd known you were coming to talk about Crandell, I'd have given you his office number and saved us both the time.'' He glanced at his watch. ''It's getting late—''

''I'm sorry,'' Zelmanski said quickly, almost managing to sound apologetic. ''I'll be blunt. I've been watching you and Crandell for a long time now. You're about the two cagiest players in the arena today. My guess is you're both hungry for a piece of Starwares. But what I haven't yet figured out is whether you've made your move or whether Crandell got there first.''

Valentine threw back his head and roared with laughter. ''You remind me of that board game I used to play with my kids. Clue, I think it was called. The punchline always went something like this: 'Col. Mustard killed the butler in the library with the candlestick.' Keep turning over those cards and moving around the board, Mr. Zelmanski. Eventually, you might just come up with the right scenario.''

''Okay.'' Zelmanski smiled. ''I guess I'll have to do exactly that, since you're not even going to give me a hint about your plans. But seriously, Mr. Valentine, I'm a reporter, not a detective. I don't write a story until I get my facts confirmed. So if I'm right about you—and if I'm telling you anything new about Crandell—remember, you heard it first from me. Call me anytime, day or night.''

Valentine nervously jiggled his knee. Zelmanski had served him even better than he'd anticipated, but he had to get rid of him fast. If the reporter was right, Valentine couldn't waste another second playing games. He had to get hold of his lawyer and his bankers and move up the schedule. There was no fucking way Crandell was going to win this fight.

He stood up, tried to curb his impatience. "I will call you, Mr. Zelmanski, if I have any news. And you feel free to do the same. You got balls. I admire that. But the kind of questions you're asking me come dangerously close to looking for insider information. Watch out for that, Zelmanski. It can be hell on the career."

THEY HAD DRINKS first at Hope's apartment, which took up the entire tenth floor of the building. It was as elegant as he'd expected it to be, but somehow also managed to feel comfortable and homey.

"I'll show you the rest another time," Hope said as she brought him into the living room. "I don't want to overwhelm you on your first visit."

"How long have you lived here?" Paul asked, staring out the window, which faced Fifth Avenue and over-looked Central Park. The lights in the buildings on the other side of the park winked at him through the twilight. From this vantage point, the city had never looked or felt so romantic.

"I grew up here," said Hope. She handed him a glass of wine. "My father left me the apartment when he died. Of course, I redid it when I moved in. My father's taste was rather more formal than mine. Sometimes I feel silly, living alone in eighteen rooms. But it's my home, and I love the view, especially now, when the trees are turning such glorious colors."

"When I was growing up in Brooklyn, my mother would sometimes bring me to the Metropolitan Museum. She loved the Impressionists, I loved the mummies. Afterwards, we'd always take a walk down Fifth Avenue, and I'd stare up at those buildings. They were so grand, so much more impressive than anything in my neighborhood. And I'd wonder, what kind of people lived in them?''

Hope smiled. ''You make it sound as if we were raised on different planets. Didn't you ever see me waving at you from my bedroom window?''

''Well, now that you mention it. . . .'' He smiled, too, as he tried to imagine her as a young girl. He realized, suddenly, how much he liked Hope Scott. Whatever assumptions he'd made about her were quickly falling away. She was so different from any woman he'd ever met before—and yet he felt as comfortable with her as if they'd known each other for years. He felt something else with Hope that had been missing from his life for far too long, the excitement that came from being in the presence of a very attractive woman and knowing he might soon be making love to her.

The feelings persisted during the cab ride to Kansai, the restaurant on East 53rd Street off Lexington Avenue where she'd booked them a reservation. Sitting next to her, their thighs touching as the cabbie swung around a corner, he remembered the particular taste and smell of sexual desire. He wanted her, and the way she held onto his hand for seconds longer than necessary when he helped her out of the cab told him she wanted him, too.

The maître d' at the pleasantly unpretentious restaurant greeted Hope and showed them to a table toward the back of the room. They were quickly brought a small bottle of hot sake and a plate of steamed shrimp dumplings.

''Kansai is one of New York's best-kept secrets,'' Hope said, pouring soy sauce into the little bowl that had appeared along with the dumplings. ''A friend of mine who was visiting from Japan first brought me. I'm terrified that the place will get discovered by the *Times* restaurant critic, and then there'll be lines out the door.''

A waiter appeared to take their order.

''Sushi?'' Hope asked.

Paul nodded. "You're the expert. I'll follow your
lead."

She ordered for them both, salmon, tuna, sea urchin,
octopus, mackerel. Paul sat back and watched her consult
with the waiter, both of them nodding and smiling as the
waiter scribbled her choices on his pad. "And whatever
else Mishio recommends tonight," she said finally, before turning her attention back to Paul. "So, have you
always wanted to be a judge?" she asked as she un-
wrapped her chopsticks and started on the dumplings.

He followed her example and dipped one into the accompanying pungent yellow mustard, then into the soy
sauce. "I always wanted to be a lawyer. I come from a
noisy Irish family that was forever arguing about politics
and the law, whether justice could be had for all, rich or
poor . . . that sort of thing."

"Was your father a lawyer?"

"I was the first person in my family to graduate from
college. My father was a bricklayer, like my uncles and
grandfathers. I worked my way through Yale and did well
enough to get into the law school. During my second
year, Bobby Seale, the Black Panther, was being tried for
murder. My criminal law professor suggested I go over
to the courthouse and observe the trial. Have you ever
served on a jury?"

She made a face. "The most boring three days of my
life."

"Unfortunately, too many people agree with you. But
I was fascinated by the whole process, and the judge's
role was what intrigued me the most. He had so much
responsibility, so much power. He seemed to be carrying
on his shoulders the weight of all that legal theory and
precedent."

Paul laughed. "You have to understand. I was just
twenty-three years old and the product of a Jesuit education. I was easily awed then by tradition and ceremony."

"But no longer?"

"Actually," he said, remembering how the familiar everyday rituals had kept him going through the most difficult times after Helen was gone, "probably now more than ever."

As if she had read his mind, she said, "Did your wife die suddenly?"

It was still painful for him to talk about Helen's death. He sat back and slowly sipped the warm wine. "She was sick for five months. I don't know which is worse—a sudden, unexpected death when you don't get the chance to say goodbye, or watching someone you love get steadily weaker and weaker."

"My mother died when I was ten," Hope said. "She was on her way to Bendel's, crossing Fifty-Seventh Street, when a car slammed into her. She died instantly. My headmistress took me out of art class and broke the news. I've always thought it so ironic that my mother should have been heading for Bendel's, of all places. My father never approved of her shopping there. Too trendy, he used to call it."

They stared at each other, surprised by the serious turn the conversation had taken. Hope poured herself a fresh cup of sake. "I'm sorry. I didn't mean to get so morbid. Oh, good, here's our dinner. We can gracefully change the topic."

The sushi was the best he'd ever tasted. Following Hope's example, he abandoned the chopsticks and used his fingers to pick up the slippery morsels of raw fish and vinegar-soaked rice. Between bites, they chatted about movies, theater, and books, their conversation flowing as easily as if they were old friends. But beneath the surface, he could sense the electricity building between them, a sexual current that got sparked each time her eyes met his.

The room had filled up since they'd arrived, the Japanese customers greatly outnumbering the Americans. Although the clientele looked prosperous and well dressed, they were far from being the glamorous publicity seekers whose names regularly appeared in the society pages. Occasionally, someone brushed past them, but no one seemed to give Hope a second glance. She was well protected here from intrusive stares or autograph hunters, an anonymous face in the crowd enjoying her dinner.

Yet he'd often seen her photograph in the Sunday *Times* next to the descriptions of recent fund-raising benefits. He'd had to attend his fair share of such events himself. Some were more amusing than others, but mostly they were rather dull affairs that usually drew the same moneyed set. Which was the real Hope Scott, he wondered—the jeweled and begowned woman flashing a smile at the camera, or the woman across from him, dressed in a sweater and pants as simple as anything Helen might have worn?

Their talk turned to skiing, which he'd tried only a few times and had never much liked.

"Did you ever ski out west?" she asked, and he remembered that she'd been married to a professional skier and lived in Aspen.

"Helen was from Vermont. We'd go up to visit her family, and she'd coax me onto the slopes, but I never took to it. Too much trouble. All that equipment and having to wait on line for the ski lift."

"You had a good marriage, didn't you?" She stared at him, wide-eyed, as if daring him to tell her the truth.

He nodded. "I went up to Northampton in October of my freshman year for a Yale-Smith mixer. We met that night, hardly dated anyone else for the next four years, and got married three weeks after graduation. We were lucky. We had no idea who we were or what we were doing, but somehow we managed to make it through the rough spots."

"I envy you," she said. "I got married for all the wrong reasons, and it was a disaster from day one. I was almost relieved when Brett walked out. I don't know why we stayed together as long as we did. He'd been cheating on me for years. That's why we never had kids. I didn't respect him enough to be the father of my children.''

The unspoken question hung in the air between them: And you and Helen? This was painful territory, one he'd not had to venture into for so long that he'd lost the weapons he'd once used to defend against the hurt. He could have ignored the issue, moved on to more neutral ground. But he felt something important happening between the two of them, and he wanted to match her honesty with his own.

''We wanted to have children,'' he said slowly, groping to find the right words. ''But there was a problem. We went through all sorts of tests and procedures, but nothing worked. I wanted to adopt, but Helen wouldn't hear of it. If she couldn't conceive her own child, she didn't want to raise someone else's. She was a teacher, so her life was full of children. That became enough for her.''

Hope spoke very quietly. ''What about you?''

''It was a loss for me. I'm the oldest of six, I always imagined having a big family of my own. It was one of those rough spots I mentioned before. But then life goes on, and you find other rewards. I have lots of nieces and nephews. I spoil them as much as I can.'' He hesitated a moment, torn between betraying a very private secret and needing her to know the whole truth.

''The problem was Helen's. Today, there would probably be any number of solutions. But this was almost twenty years ago. . . .'' His voice trailed off. ''I don't know why I'm telling you all this. I'm not usually so open with someone I've just met.''

''Nor am I,'' she said.

She seemed about to say more but fell quiet as the waiter appeared to clear away the dishes.

When he was gone, she said, ''Normally, I'd suggest you come up to my place for coffee and dessert, but I have an eight A.M. class tomorrow.''

Once again, she surprised him. "You're a teacher?"

"A student. I'm getting a master's in urban studies at Columbia."

"I'm impressed. Do you get extra credit for joining the Preservation Society?"

She laughed and shook her head. "I wish. To be honest, I wasn't keen on joining yet another committee. It's a cause I believe in, but I'm overbooked as it is. But it's hard to say no to Aunt Connie. She's my godmother, and her husband George is an administrator of the trust that controls my family's money."

"Well, whatever the reason, I'm glad you said yes."

"And I'm glad you called yesterday. I was hoping I wouldn't have to wait until the next committee meeting to see you again."

They smiled at each other, a tacit promise for the future, communicated in a language in which only they were fluent.

He reached for the check and pulled his wallet out of his jacket pocket.

"I'll let you pay for dinner tonight," said Hope. "But next time I pick up the check, okay?"

He laughed, amazed as always by the brave new world of dating customs. "Okay. Just as long as there is a next time."

"There will be," she said. "You can count on it."

WHEN THE OSBURGHS dined alone at home, they ate off trays in front of the giant-screen television set in the library. Connie Osburgh had initially objected to installing the set among all of her father's vellum-bound books, some of them first editions of seventeenth- and eighteenth-century masterpieces. But as she got older, her eyes got weaker, and she had to admit there was something to be said for watching her shows on a screen big enough that she could see all the details.

Melrose Place was her favorite. She adored Heather

Locklear, the pretty blond girl who was the star of the show. Young, bright, and full of mischief, she reminded Connie of her daughter Julia at that age. She'd said so once to George, but he'd scoffed at the comparison.

Nevertheless, he humored her. He tried to leave their Wednesday nights free so she could watch the program, since she'd still not accepted the notion that one could tape a show, then watch it later on video. More often than not, he sat with her during the hour-long episode, reading the paper as he kept one eye on the set and muttered under his breath about the messes some people got themselves into.

Connie liked having his company. What with all their commitments and obligations, it was rare that they had any free hours together. Not that they had all that much to talk about, but the lack of conversation didn't bother her. After forty years of living with George, she had few illusions left about what to expect from marriage.

She had no complaints. They'd raised three wonderful daughters, all of whom had married well and given them six grandchildren, with another on the way. They'd been spared any scandal or unpleasantness of the sort that too many of their friends seemed to be suffering of late.

Connie knew that other women envied her. And with good reason. Certainly, she and George had their share of troubles. What family didn't? Their oldest daughter, Dosie, had flirted with radical politics back in the early seventies, a passing phase, thank goodness. And Flip had once been caught smoking marijuana in her dorm at Emma Willard. But all in all, they'd been very fortunate.

Whatever passion she'd felt for George as a young bride had disappeared long ago. They slept in separate bedrooms, which suited her perfectly. She was a night owl who liked to stay up late reading, whereas he preferred to be asleep by ten-thirty so he could get to the office by eight. Their arrangement had gone on for so many years that she'd all but blotted out the circumstances under which George had removed himself to the guest room across the hall.

He'd cheated on her. Another woman might not have been as understanding. But at her mother's urging, she had promised to forgive him, in return for which he'd vowed never again to humiliate her or bring shame upon their families' good names by being unfaithful.

Despite his promise, she'd felt then—and her mother had agreed—that his sin could not go altogether unpunished. Hence his exile to the guest room, presumably until she could rid her mind of that horrifying image of her husband in the arms of some cheap floozy. They never again spoke of the incident. It was as if it hadn't occurred. But she hadn't invited George back into their bed, and he hadn't asked to be admitted.

People always remarked on what a loving, affectionate couple they were. She herself felt they were as close to being a perfect match as one could find. Same background and breeding, mutual interests, mutual worldview. George was the love of her life. She said so unequivocally whenever she was asked. His every mood, expression, and gesture were familiar to her. She wished only that her single friends—most especially poor, dear Hope—could achieve the same happiness and satisfaction she had in marriage.

But something was bothering George tonight. He had hardly touched the broiled chicken that Cook had prepared just the way he liked it. He'd snapped at the maid because Gristedes had been out of his favorite brand of frozen yogurt, which was hardly poor Martha's fault. He'd kept silent during the national news, instead of arguing aloud with Peter Jennings, as he normally did. His eyelid was twitching, a sure sign that he was upset.

At moments like these, Connie wished George were more of a drinker. A glass of scotch or wine could soothe the troubled soul, help the mind to wander down creative pathways that might lead to a solution. She herself enjoyed a good strong drink or two before dinner. The merit of alcohol was one of the few areas where she and George disagreed.

Discreetly checking her watch, she saw that forty-five minutes remained before *Melrose Place* began. Plenty of time to coax him into a better humor. Pushing the "mute" button on the remote control, she said, "What's wrong, dear? You seem irritated. Is the market down?"

George Osburgh turned and smiled at his wife. There were days when he hated her so much he understood how sane men committed murder. He'd started hating his wife on their wedding day. Watching her walk up the aisle of St. Bartholomew's Church on her father's arm, dressed in her mother's antique lace gown, his head pounded like a metronome with the question: *What have I done? What have I done?*

He'd been a good husband to her, except for having continued to break his promise not to sleep with other women. She'd caught him just once and kicked him out of their bed. It was no great loss. She was a dried-up old stick who'd never enjoyed sex, no matter what he did to turn her on. She wouldn't have known what an orgasm was if it had thrown itself in her path, waving a red flag.

Finding other women to go to bed with was as easy as crossing Wall Street. In the glory years of the eighties, he'd just about worn himself out fucking all those women. But then the government had started going after the major players, and the Street had sobered up. He'd gotten more careful, because these days the newspapers printed any damn thing they wanted, and he did have a certain image to uphold. And then Nancy had come to work for him, and for the first time, he'd wished he could get a divorce.

"Nothing's wrong, dear," he said, wondering what she saw when she looked in the mirror. Didn't she care that she hadn't gotten laid in almost two decades? Or that she was still having her hair done at Elizabeth Arden in the exact same style her mother had worn fifty years ago?

Connie wagged a skinny index finger at him. "Come, come, George. I know you too well to believe that. You're downright peevish this evening. Are you upset that I'm going to Sissie's for the weekend?" She sighed. "I should never have said yes to her. If only you two were better pals."

He forced a smile and patted her hand. "Nonsense, Connie. I'm perfectly fine about your going to Southampton."

The thought of her gone for two days, affording him the opportunity to spend long uninterrupted hours with Nancy, had sustained him during his meeting today with the examiners from the Securities and Exchange Commission. If she changed her mind and stayed in the city, he couldn't be held responsible for his actions.

"Julia called today to see if you'll come to church with her and the children on Sunday. She says little George is begging for his Poppy to take him to the zoo. We thought perhaps lunch at Serendipity and the zoo afterwards?"

"Perhaps," he said. "I'll have to check my calendar. I may have a meeting on Sunday with Jordan Crandell."

Connie pursed her lips and frowned. "Ugh, Jordan Crandell. He's such a dreadful person. So very much *not* our kind. Must you do business with him?"

"I'm afraid I must." He laughed, a short, dry bark that drew a quizzical glance from Connie. "Whatever his shortcomings, he's a brilliant businessman."

He was also the means to Osburgh's salvation, the potential redeemer of his financial soul. Although he was not a particularly religious person, Osburgh still retained a childlike belief in the power of faith. Crandell's offer of a finder's fee in return for a loan from the Scott Trust was the answer to his prayers.

Of course, he had transgressed, committing the sins of avarice and theft. But he was only human, and therefore imperfect. He had suffered greatly for his wrongdoings. Haunted by his fear of being found out, he had lain awake nights, fretting about how to repay the money he'd illegally borrowed from the trust.

The newspapers were like ravenous sharks, circling the waters downtown in search of the next big story. They'd gorged themselves on Boesky, Milken, and Drexel Burnham. But the pickings had been scarce of late. Even Donald Trump had cleaned up his act. They were hungry for fresh blood. They needed headlines. The slightest hint of a financial discrepancy could send them into a feeding frenzy that would spell ruin for him and his entire family.

THREE

I WANT A mean, dirty son of a bitch!''

Walter Spaulding, vice president and general counsel of Valentine Industries, massaged the back of his neck with one hand and held the in-flight phone in the other.

"Are you listening, Walter? Or am I talking to myself here?'' yelled Lew Valentine.

"I hear you, Lew. A mean, dirty son of a bitch,'' echoed Spaulding.

Next to him, seated on the aisle in the first-class section of the Boeing 747, his wife Marilyn rolled her eyes. Lew Valentine paid her husband a salary handsome enough to support two homes, more clothes than she could wear in one lifetime, a nanny, a maid, Manhattan private school tuition, a BMW, and a time-share condo in Vail. But that didn't mean she had to like the man. He was the devil, a monster masquerading as a person. He drove Walter crazy, calling him at all hours of the day and night, snapping his fingers to do his bidding like a dog dependent on his master's goodwill for a bone or a biscuit.

She especially disliked him now for ruining their long-planned vacation in Spain.

"Can't it wait?'' she'd wailed, after Valentine had tracked them down at the private villa they'd rented and summoned her husband back to New York less than twenty-four hours after they'd arrived. "You've got fourteen goddamn lawyers working under you in that department. Can't you just this once tell him to ask somebody else's advice?"

"Not if I want to continue being head of that department," Walter had said, reaching for his suitcase.

Marilyn had cried and carried on, accused Walter of being spineless, threatened to divorce him if he didn't stand up to Valentine.

They'd caught the first flight out of Barcelona.

Valentine had instructed Walter to call him from the plane. Marilyn was drinking champagne with her breakfast of scrambled *huevos*. Walter was trying to placate his enraged boss, who was blaming everyone from Walter to the kid in the mailroom for not keeping up to speed on Starwares.

"Who told you about Crandell going to Utah? Was it a reliable source?"

"Fuck who told me!" Valentine screamed into the phone. "You said you were on top of the situation. If this is your idea of minding the store, I better goddamn well hire a goddamn watchdog."

"More champagne, *señora?*"

Marilyn nodded yes to the flight attendant. At least they were getting good service. The only other first-class passenger was the young Japanese man across the aisle. Dressed in an Armani suit, he sat cross-legged with his eyes closed and his hands resting on his knees, his palms open to the ceiling.

"We have our feelers out to Lynch," Walter said wearily. "For all we know, your source could be a plant, one of Lynch's own men trying to jack up the buying price."

"If this guy's a plant, then I'm Dolly Parton. And let me tell you something, Spaulding. I'm looking down at my chest and I don't see any tits." Valentine chuckled. "That's a good one, huh?"

"Yeah, pretty funny, no tits."

"Whose tits? I thought he was pissed off at you," Marilyn whispered to her husband. She held up her glass, offering him some of her champagne. "Can't you get off the damn phone? The movie's about to start."

Walter mouthed shut up to his wife. If Valentine was still looking for a laugh, the situation hadn't yet tilted out of control. "Look, Lew," he said. "Even if Crandell's been to Utah . . . hell, even if he's already tried to get into bed with Lynch, we're still in good shape."

"Oh, yeah? How do you figure that?" growled Valentine.

"Did you look at that latest set of numbers we worked up for you?"

"What the hell do you think I did?"

"Then you know we have some room to play there, and we've got solid backing from the banks if we need it. I hear that Summit's fourth-quarter earnings are flat. Crandell may have trouble raising the cash."

"Jordan Crandell is a goddamned pirate. I'm not looking for a bidding war, but I'll do whatever it takes to stop him. You just make sure all our legal bases are covered."

The Japanese man across from them hadn't stirred from his cross-legged position. His expression was serene and untroubled. Spaulding guessed that the man was meditating and wondered how many years it would take for him to achieve a similarly tranquil state of mind.

"It shouldn't be a problem," he tried to soothe Valentine. "Nobody knows takeover strategy better than Goodstein & Carney. They've done well by us in the past."

Valentine snorted. "Well, look to the future, Walter. Crandell's got a trail of footprints that leads to every one of the top law firms in the city. Those guys are all in bed with each other. I want an outsider. Like I said before, I want him mean and tough and fearless."

"Do you have someone in mind?"

"The guy from Michigan."

Valentine's voice in his ear felt like a jackhammer, pounding at his brain. Bands of pain gripped his forehead and temples. "The guy they call the Michigan Assassin? Bernard Odette? He's a killer. Sure, he damn near ruined General Motors and Gulf Oil, but he's a throwback to another era, more con man than counsel."

"He sounds perfect."

"I hear that half the corporations in America have him on their payroll. He does nothing for them, but they pay his fees as insurance that he won't appear against them. It would be a conflict of interest for a lawyer to sue his client."

"So?"

Spaulding shifted his weight, reached into his pants pocket, and pulled out the small pillbox that held his aspirins. "What kind of an ethical lawyer would agree to such an arrangement? He's like a legal Al Capone, selling protection."

"Do you think Crandell has him on the payroll?"

"I doubt it. Crandell thinks he's Superman. Invulnerable to everything except kryptonite."

The flight attendant was back, handing out headsets for the movie. Marilyn dangled a pair in front of Walter. He shook his head. She glared at him.

"I want someone who can run Crandell up a tree and hang him, if necessary," said Valentine. "I don't give a damn if he's an ax murderer. I want Odette. Get him."

"He won't come cheap," Spaulding warned. He put two aspirins on the back of his tongue and swallowed hard.

"Walter, we're on the *Titanic* and we've just hit the iceberg. Frankly, I don't give a shit how much it will cost to patch the hull. We can afford him. Put it another way: we can't *not* afford him."

Spaulding sighed. "I'll call him as soon as I get back to New York."

"You call him as soon as I hang up. It'll save you from having to listen to Marilyn kvetch about how I ruined her vacation." Valentine was still laughing when he broke the connection.

Walter smiled at Marilyn. He hadn't eaten any breakfast, and the aspirins were clawing at the lining of his stomach. "Lew sends you his best."

"That bastard," said Marilyn.

THE COLUMBIA UNIVERSITY campus was crowded with students who were eager to revel in an autumn day that felt more like July than October. Business was booming for the ice cream vendor stationed in front of the gates at Broadway and 116th Street. The Frisbee players were competing for space with undergrads flying kites in front of Butler Library. Children from the Morningside Heights neighborhood toddled cheerfully across the lawn as their mothers stood chatting alongside their strollers.

Lured from her library carrel by the sunshine and balmy weather, Hope Scott lay down on the grass and tried to concentrate on her reading.

Many of her friends thought she made an unlikely graduate student. She had applied on a whim. The surprise discovery had been how much she enjoyed being a student again. It gave her a sense of purpose and direction, both of which had been conspicuously absent in her life for too long.

She liked the discipline required to get up for early morning classes, complete the reading assignments and papers, study for midterms and finals. Examining the economic, social, and political currents of the urban environment—and trying to find some solutions to its ills— forced her to think in a way she'd forgotten she could. But this afternoon, it was hard to absorb the equations of urban economics when all she wanted to do was close her eyes, raise her face to the warm sun, and daydream about Paul Murray.

Some mornings she woke up, looked in the bathroom mirror, and saw herself getting old. A network of tiny lines was beginning to form under her eyes. It was visible only under the brightest lights, but it was there, a road-map of her future.

She wasn't too concerned about losing her looks. She had inherited her grandmother's fine bones and healthy skin, and she had her pick of the top plastic surgeons, if she chose to go that route.

But she worried about turning forty, about missing out on the chance to have children because she hadn't met the right man to share her life. The men she knew were all like her father—too absorbed in themselves and their money games to discover who she really was. Or else they were fortune hunters, more attracted to her wealth than herself.

Paul Murray was different. He loved his work, but he had a life outside the courtroom. He seemed genuinely interested in her, asking questions that felt sympathetic rather than intrusive.

Putting her book aside, she rested her head in her arms and gave herself up to a romantic fantasy in which Paul was cast as the male lead. Their mouths were just about to meet in a passionate kiss when she was startled back to real time by two passing Barnard girls.

"He's *sooo* cute, isn't he?" said one, giggling over her ice cream cone.

"I think he's really got a thing for you," said the other.

Hope smiled as they strolled away. The feelings were the same, at nineteen or thirty-seven. In high school, she and her friends had chanted, "He loves me, he loves me not," as they'd slowly stripped the petals off daisies. She'd had her fair share of crushes. She had even made the mistake of marrying one of them. Rather than make the same mistake twice, she'd stayed single. But her feelings for Paul were different from anything she'd ever experienced before.

"Playing hookey?"

Hope turned over to greet the young woman standing over her. "Hey," she said to her friend Yvonna Carter.

"Hey, yourself. How are you ever going to get a job and support yourself, lazing around like you do?"

Yvonna always teased her about her inheritance, and Hope loved her for it. They'd met the year before, when they'd worked together on a model city for their urban development seminar.

"We should be sitting by the river, drinking margaritas. So what's happenin' that's new and different?" Yvonna said, popping a piece of gum into her mouth and dropping down next to Hope.

Of mixed Vietnamese and black background, Yvonna had cocoa-colored skin, chocolate brown eyes, and black hair that she wore in long braided cornrows. Her exotic beauty and long, slender legs had helped launch her career as a runway model, but her personal style ran more to T-shirt, jeans, and cowboy boots than to high-fashion designer outfits. At age ten, she and her mother had been reunited with her American father, who lived in Oakland, California. Her practical, street-smart attitude was tempered by the remembered echoes of tinkling Buddhist prayer bells.

Hope propped herself up on one elbow and posed the questions she'd been mulling over. "Let me ask you something. Do you believe in love at first sight?"

"Only if it's Denzel Washington." Yvonna laughed. "Why? You think you got a case of it?"

"I met this man. We've been out once, and I'm seeing him again this weekend."

"And?"

"I think I want to marry him," Hope said, giving voice for the first time to what she hadn't dared say aloud to anyone else.

Yvonna peered at her wide-eyed over the top of her sunglasses. "Tall, dark, and handsome?"

Hope laughed. "Yes, yes, and yes."

"Then go for it, honey," Yvonna said, cracking her gum.

"That simple?"

Yvonna shrugged philosophically. "Why make life complicated? Do you love him?"

"I think so. I don't know. I've only known him for a week."

"Give it another week and you'll know for sure," Yvonna advised. "How is he in bed?"

"We haven't gotten there yet."

"Ah! The missing piece of the puzzle."

"No, it's more than that," Hope said slowly. "He was happily married for a long time, until his wife died a couple of years ago."

"And you're afraid of competing with a ghost."

Hope nodded. The truth was exactly that simple.

"In Vietnam, we had many ghosts," said Yvonna, looking wistful as she did whenever she spoke of her homeland. "I was such a scared little kid. Then one day, my mother taught me that all you have to do is face them down, say 'boo!,' and they disappear."

"You make it sound so easy," Hope said skeptically.

"Trust me, girl. It works."

LEW VALENTINE HAD dispatched Walter Spaulding in a company limousine to meet Bernard Odette at La Guardia and bring him back to the office. He was more than a little curious to meet the character who was known as the Michigan Assassin. He'd already had a taste of the man's high-handed style. Odette had dictated the circumstances of their initial exploratory meeting with the same passion and precision normally applied to hammering out the terms of a takeover agreement.

Odette's negotiations, conducted with Spaulding, had alternately maddened and amused Valentine. The man was obviously a lunatic. But Valentine couldn't help but wonder: If he could fight so hard about matters as trivial as how and when he would be reimbursed for his first-class travel arrangements, how much more zealous might he be in the heat of courtroom battle?

Valentine glanced at the clock on his desk. Assuming Odette's flight had come in on schedule, the men were due any minute. He stood up and restlessly paced his enormous, sleekly contemporary office. The floor-to-ceiling windows of the thirty-fifth–floor corner suite in the General Motors Building gave him a bird's-eye view of Central Park and the upper Manhattan skyline. On a clear day, he could see past the New Jersey Palisades on the other side of the Hudson and all the way north to the far reaches of the borough. Today, however, the sky was gray and threatening, the visibility limited. But Valentine was oblivious to both the view and the weather conditions. His mind was fixed on one thing only—besting Jordan Crandell in his bid for Starwares.

The buzz of the intercom startled him back to the present. "Mr. Spaulding and Mr. Odette are here to see you, sir," his secretary announced.

"Give me five minutes," he said.

Making people wait, even when they were on time and he was ready for them, was one of his favorite management tactics. He sat down behind his desk, closed his eyes, and visualized success, as he and his wife had learned to do from the New Age therapist he had on retainer.

Success was a front-page headline in *The Wall Street Journal* that read: "VALENTINE INDUSTRIES SCORES STUNNING COUP OVER SUMMIT." Concentrating, he imagined the lead paragraph, which credited his vision and tenacity. The therapist had instructed him to make the vision as detailed as possible. In his mind's eye, Valentine enlarged the point size of the headline and gave the story a byline: "By Kurt Zelmanski."

He took a deep breath and felt the aura of victory

glowing around him. Adjusting his tie, he buzzed his secretary. "Send them in."

As if escorting visiting royalty, Spaulding ushered
Bernard Odette into the office and made the introductions.

Valentine was startled by Odette's youthful, brash,
good looks. He had expected an older man, someone who
looked like he'd had some experience in the boardrooms
and courtrooms. Odette seemed too young to have had
the managements of so many major corporations cower-
ing at his feet, begging for mercy.

Odette appeared to be only in his early forties. He was
tall, lean, and deeply tanned, with carefully sculpted, jet
black hair. His face, long and angular, seemed more
suited to a dashing young actor than to a corporate lawyer. Valentine's discerning eye noted Odette's obviously
expensive clothes, which were tailored with a touch of
Broadway flash. Not for him the conservative pin-striped
suit and white shirt look that was favored by the white
shoe Wall Street attorneys.

"Nice to meet you," Odette said. He extended his
hand, showing off a large diamond on his well-manicured
right pinky. His grip was firm, his voice a vibrant bari-
tone trained for courtroom performance.

"Likewise. Please, make yourself comfortable," said
Valentine, having already decided to conduct the meeting
from behind his desk rather than inviting Odette to join
him on the more informal couches in the conversation
area.

Odette seemed completely relaxed and at ease as he
settled into his chair. He shot the monogrammed cuffs of
his silk shirt. The initials, too large to be in good taste,
caught Valentine's glance.

"Handmade," Odette said, noticing the gaze. He ex-
tracted a gleaming gold cigarette case from his suit jacket
and lit up a cigarette with a matching gold lighter. He
smiled. "One of my many vices."

Valentine's nostrils twitched in displeasure. A reformed smoker, he disliked the smell. "I hope you had a good trip."

"Good enough."

"And I presume that Mr. Spaulding briefed you on our situation?"

Odette's smile flickered off as if a switch had been thrown. He fixed his pale blue eyes on Valentine. "Yes. You had your heart set on screwing the sexiest girl in the class, only to find out that Jordan Crandell may already have gotten to first base with her."

"That's a rather crude take on the situation, but you've got the idea."

Odette looked around for an ashtray. Valentine quickly shoved a crystal paperclip holder across his desk as a substitute.

"Jordan Crandell usually gets what he wants," Odette went on. "My guess is, you folks have good reason to be nervous."

"We hardly need you to tell us that."

"How true. You're obviously aware of the extent of your problems, or I wouldn't be here, would I?" said Odette, sounding amused.

"Precisely," Valentine snapped. "Now, Mr. Odette. You're known to be among the country's handful of pre-eminent takeover experts. What would you suggest we do?"

Odette drew on his cigarette, then slowly exhaled. "Abraham Lincoln is one of my role models. He was a hardworking country lawyer who outsmarted the big-city boys and got further than anyone had a right to expect he would. One of his favorite maxims was, 'Time is a lawyer's stock in trade.' Are you familiar with that particular maxim of his, Mr. Valentine?"

"I can't say that I am," Valentine said icily.

"You manufacture and sell cellular phones, among many other products. My stock in trade, the commodity

I sell for a living, is advice, and appropriate legal action predicated on that advice. You're asking for my advice, but you haven't paid for it yet.''

Barely controlling his anger, Valentine drummed his fingers on his desk. "Jesus! Do you think we're going to cheat you out of your fee?''

Odette chuckled. "I got burned once, never again.''

"What's your hourly rate?'' Valentine said, forcing himself to be calm.

"You want to rent me for an hour or two?'' Odette shook his head. "This is a complicated matter. Your company stands to risk a substantial amount of money. I'll agree to represent you, but only if I'm granted sole responsibility for the entire matter. I don't like committees, and I hate to work in tandem with other lawyers, no matter how gifted they may be. In other words, gentlemen, I'm either the whole show or I take my ball and go home.''

Valentine looked from Odette to Spaulding. The expression on his face was one of incredulity.

Spaulding shrugged imperceptibly. Odette had been Valentine's bright idea, not his. The streets of Manhattan were crawling with arrogant, egocentric corporate lawyers, but none of them came even close to Odette.

"You're pretty convinced that Crandell did go to Utah to meet with Eric Lynch,'' Odette went on. "I'd be inclined to agree with you. It would be easy enough to find out for certain. If you take the worst-case scenario and assume he's already spoken to Lynch, you need me. And even if he's not yet made a bid, chances are he will. At the risk of repeating myself, Mr. Valentine, you need me. No doubt about it.''

The image of his visualized *Wall Street Journal* headline flashed through Valentine's mind. In his thirty-year career, he had only once failed to acquire a company he wanted. Crandell had yet to come in second. He was determined to even the scorecard. Defeating Crandell would be tantamount to knocking out the class bully.

"I'm sure you know that Jordan Crandell never gives up," Odette continuted. "That's the secret of his success. He won't accept any compromises. He won't be deterred by any of the roadblocks you throw up. We're not talking about a quick day or two in court. He'll come after you like a crazed animal. He'll do whatever he has to to win. We'd have to play the same game."

"We're prepared to go all the way," Valentine said firmly.

"Easy to say now. No one's looking over your shoulder, second-guessing you. The pressure comes later, from the stockholders, other officers, the newspapers. Are you prepared to bet everything on the outcome? You'd be taking enormous risks, both corporate as well as personal."

Valentine had heard enough. "Odette," he said, "maybe your news coverage isn't so good out there in Michigan, because obviously you don't know sweet fuck-all about me. I'd sell my grandmother if that's what it would take to acquire Starwares and beat out Crandell. Now, I believe we were discussing your fee."

Odette smiled and lit up another cigarette. "If the scenario plays out as I expect it to, this case could occupy my time for at least a year, maybe more. I would be risking my hard-earned good name and reputation. You're not the only one who has a lot to lose."

"Cut the sales pitch, Mr. Odette," Valentine growled. "Name your price."

"The sales pitch, as you put it, is really a statement of how my price is arrived at. This will be no small skirmish, but a major corporate war."

Valentine could see why Odette was such a formidable opponent. He was as relentless as a hard rain. "What's your fee?" he repeated.

"You're not hiring Bernard Odette. You're hiring the Michigan Assassin, an image, if you will. Judges will sit up and pay attention, newspapers will run features, your stockholders will be assured you have retained the best there is. In other words, there's a lot to this package besides a superb trial lawyer.''

Valentine folded his arms across his chest and stared silently at Odette. He wasn't going to ask him again.

Odette smiled. ''I require a flat fee of three million dollars.''

''What!'' Valentine exploded.

Odette held up a warning finger. He wasn't finished. ''Plus a three-million-dollar bonus if we win, and your company, because of my efforts, completes a successful merger with Starwares.''

''That's ridiculous,'' Valentine sputtered.

Odette's smile widened. ''I'll also want a four-bedroom apartment in Manhattan during the duration of the action. And you would have to meet all my expenses, personal and legal, including the salaries of whatever household staff I might have to hire during my stay in New York.''

Valentine could feel his cheeks grow red with anger. ''What the hell do you take us for? That's the most outrageous—''

''You think so!'' Odette's deep voice snapped like a cracking whip. ''I have a mansion in Grosse Pointe that's run by a staff of six. Do you think I'd give up the comfort of that for any extended period of time in order to live in a Manhattan hotel, no matter how nice? I am a millionaire, several times over, all of it earned because I do what you want and need better than anyone else in the country. Under the circumstances, I'm probably selling my services rather cheaply.''

Valentine studied the man. ''Then why do it? Why take the risk?''

Odette's expression turned solemn. ''Jordan Crandell is the most shameless buccaneer in the history of American business. He makes J. P. Morgan look like a Little Leaguer. If I defeat him—and I will—my value will go sky-high. And my standing as a giant killer is fixed for all time. Besides, Crandell and I share one thing in common. I, too, am a fighter. And this one will be to the death. *A morte.*''

Valentine sat back, impressed in spite of himself. Working with Odette wasn't going to be easy. But it would be fun to watch Crandell take his licks. Odette was more than a legal gun for hire. He was a samurai warrior.

''We agree to your terms, Mr. Odette,'' he said. ''The case is yours.''

THE AMERICAN AIRLINES jet slowed over Canada, hanging back until the approach pattern for Detroit's Metropolitan Airport was less congested. The aircraft had passed over Lake Erie and approached the heart-shaped Lake St. Clair, the northern route into Detroit.

Bernard Odette sat by himself in the first-class section, looking out at the endless clear sky as he idly swished the last of the bourbon about in his glass. The flight attendant had made a pest of herself, mistaking his easy manner for an invitation. She was pretty, but there was an indefinable hardness about her, like a veteran who had seen too many battles. She was older than the other attendants on the flight. Odette guessed that she was husband-hunting, and he presumed she considered him a good prospect.

He sipped the last of the bourbon, taking the half-melted ice cube into his mouth and chewing on it. The Valentine case presented a challenge. He'd not had many lately. He had established such a fierce reputation that no one wanted to fight him anymore. The money kept rolling in, but he hungered for real combat. Now he had his opportunity.

The prospect of a chance to bring Jordan Crandell publicly crashing down was exciting, almost sexual. He could hardly wait to begin.

He glanced down. They were flying above the islands known as the St. Clair Flats. Sailboats, tiny toys from this altitude, dotted the water, their skippers trying to get in some autumn sailing before the ice made boating impossible.

The plane began to descend.

The attendant smiled and took his glass. Her fingers touched his and paused for just a moment. Her eyes were fixed on his.

"Thanks," he said.

Her answer was a seductive look and a slight squeeze of his hand. Then she was gone. He put up his small tray table and checked his seat belt.

As a young lawyer, he had had his fill of flight attendants. The game had been fun then. Now, every woman seemed to want something more than a quick roll in the hay and an expensive bottle of champagne with dinner.

The Valentine case would also afford him a chance to rid himself of Beverly. They had lived together for just over a year. He had even briefly considered marrying her, but then the small annoyances had begun. She was intelligent, which was part of the problem. At first, he hadn't realized what a manipulating bitch she was. She had masked her maneuvers, but slowly the pattern emerged, despite all she did to conceal it.

She didn't want to love him. She wanted to own him, then train him to suit her own ideas of what he should be. He liked himself just as he was. He'd gotten there a long time ago, and he had no intention of changing his ways, even for a woman as incredibly sexy as Beverly.

The airplane flew over the industrial belt northeast of Detroit. Huge factories, each a mile square, extended to the horizon. Slowing up as the wing flaps dropped, the plane came in over the I-94 interstate, touching down neatly on the runway. Odette reached for his briefcase. His chauffeur would be waiting for him outside. He hoped Beverly would not be waiting with him.

He sighed. Beverly was a great lay—he would miss that. Dumping her would be a slow process. She would probably want to quit her executive position at Ford and follow him to New York. He would dissuade her, pleading that his work would be too all-consuming, that they'd have no time to see each other. He'd let her live in his house for a while, perhaps occasionally come visit her. Then he'd arrange to have the place redecorated. She'd have to move out.

That would end it. No angry words, no scenes. He wondered why he so loved the battle of the courtroom, but dreaded personal confrontation. There were lots of women in New York. Saying goodbye to Beverly would be a slow, quiet process, but it would be painless. At least for him.

FOUR

THE HOUR WAS getting late. Paul was aware that the jury was growing restless. He couldn't blame them. The case was a difficult one, a suit brought by Ethan Grant, the former president of Sunset Pictures, charging the corporation that had recently acquired his parent company of violating his stock option agreement with his ex-employer. The jurors were struggling to make sense of complex securities accounting methods, as well as the intricacies of the takeover fight itself.

The windows had been thrown open, but the courtroom felt hot and stuffy. The handful of journalists and other spectators were barely able to stifle their yawns. Even the lawyers looked bored as the witness on the stand, a financial analyst, droned on in a nasal monotone about the value of the securities on the day the plaintiff had been fired, compared with their value on the day the deal had been completed.

Taking advantage of a pause in the testimony, Paul decided to adjourn the proceedings.

"It's almost five o'clock," he said. "I'd prefer to finish questioning the witness tonight, but the mind cannot absorb what the seat cannot endure."

There was a ripple of appreciative laughter. The defense attorney, having almost finished his cross-examination, opened his mouth to object, then quickly changed his mind. No sense in alienating the members of the jury who were already gathering up their pens and papers.

"We'll adjourn until tomorrow," said Paul. "As usual, I will remind you all not to discuss the facts of this case amongst yourselves or with any of your friends and family. I'll see you here tomorrow morning, nine A.M. sharp."

He stepped down from the bench and left the courtroom through the door that led to his private chambers. Once inside, he loosened his tie and hung up his robe, a gift from Helen some birthdays ago. The sleeves were beginning to fray. He knew he should buy a new one, but for silly, sentimental reasons he kept putting off ordering it.

His law clerk poked her head into his office. "Do you need me for anything?"

Naomi Bowman was a bright, ambitious woman in her late twenties who was blessed with a photographic memory that enabled her to crank out legal memos with the speed of light.

He waved her away with a smile. "Get going before I change my mind," he said, and turned to the briefs that had been submitted by the opposing counsels.

He made notes as he turned the pages, jotting down citations of cases that he wanted to read in full. Occasionally, he wondered whether he wasn't more suited to the bookish world of an appellate judge. But the courtroom still presented new challenges. One day, perhaps, he'd get bored and want to move on. For now, he was content with his work.

He'd become so engrossed that he missed hearing the knock on his door and didn't look up until a familiar voice startled him out of his concentration.

"I trained you too well. It's the public who's paying you now, not the client. Don't you ever go home?" Jesse Rubin stood in the doorway, regarding Paul with the proprietary gaze of a proud parent.

As a first-year associate at Goodstein & Carney, for no
other reason than that he'd written a law review article
about unfair pricing practices, Paul had been assigned to
the trade regulation department, headed up by Jesse
Rubin. It was considered hardship duty. Jesse was a tough
taskmaster who demanded nothing short of perfection.
He ran his department as if it were the legal world's
equivalent of Marine boot camp, with himself as the chief
drill sergeant.

Paul's first few months at the firm were a nightmarish,
mind-numbing grind. As a lowly associate, he alternated
endless hours of legal research with all-night marathons
drafting briefs. It was no accident that Goodstein & Carney regularly ranked among the top ten New York firms
for billable hours. The pay was good, but the firm got its
money's worth out of its employees.

With the prospect of partnership dangling before him
like the apple in the Garden of Eden, Paul did whatever
was asked of him and then some. Sensing that Paul
shared his same hunger to learn and succeed, Jesse had
ridden him especially hard. On more than a few occasions, Paul had come close to storming into Jesse's office
to quit. But the ultimate rewards had been well worth the
effort. Jesse had taught him how to write an airtight brief,
introduced him to important clients, assigned him to
high-profile cases, groomed him for the ultimate prize of
partnership.

Over the years, as their relationship evolved, Jesse and
his wife had initiated a friendship with Paul and Helen,
and Paul had come to think of Jesse almost as a second
father. But it had been several months since they'd seen
each other, and Paul realized with a pang how much he
missed his former colleague, who was now one of the
firm's three managing partners.

Waving him a welcome, Paul said, "What brings you
to the courthouse, counselor? A sudden burst of curiosity
about how the law actually works?"

"With all due respect, Your Honor, I've already forgotten more about the law than you ever knew." Jesse grinned as he lowered his oversized frame onto Paul's couch.

For as long as Paul had known him, Jesse had been engaged in a losing battle between his sweet tooth and his waistline. Bakeries and candy stores called to him like the sirens tempting the sailors of old. He owned a roomful of state-of-the-art exercise equipment and paid a small fortune each year for membership at a health club near his office. He ignored the equipment, avoided the club, and kept on indulging himself.

Making himself comfortable, he unbuttoned his suit jacket and said, "I had a meeting with the mayor at City Hall, so I decided to drop by to say hello."

"The mayor's asking you for advice? I didn't think things were going that badly for him."

"He needs help persuading the corporations to stay in the city. Everybody's looking across the river at the lower rents in New Jersey. His tax base is wasting away before his eyes. I told him I'd see what I could do." Jesse pointed to the business section of the *Times* that lay on the couch next to him. "You got yourself one hell of an interesting case there."

"Yeah, and every bit as complicated as you can imagine. I feel for the jury. To be honest, I was surprised that your litigation department isn't involved on either side."

Jesse ran a hand through his thatch of curly white hair. "Ethan Grant wanted to hire us, and we almost said yes. But we're already representing one of the banks that funded the takeover. We decided that the potential for a perceived conflict of interest was too great."

Paul smiled to himself. Such a decision was so typical of Jesse. A sliver of memory from one of Paul's first days at Goodstein: Jesse Rubin presiding in the conference room over the newest group of raw recruits, delivering his traditional lecture on legal ethics, the one that always began with, "I don't care what goes on at other law firms, but we at Goodstein & Carney hold to the highest possible moral standards."

The associates listened and solemnly took notes, then laughed behind Jesse's back for trying to play God. Several months later, the story broke that disbarment proceedings had been initiated against a fifth-year associate at one of Wall Street's most prestigious firms. He'd consented to his client's secret request that he withhold key documents from a government regulatory agency during the discovery stage of a landmark antitrust case.

The Goodstein associates stopped laughing. They shivered in their offices, imagining a similarly ignominious end to their legal careers for no reason they could guess at other than greed or wanting to curry favor with a client.

Whatever else Goodstein & Carney might be accused of, its ethics had never been questioned, either in a court of law or within the gossipy, close-knit world of New York's top law firms.

Paul smiled. " 'Perceived conflict of interest.' Those words are emblazoned on my brain. Do you still give the same lecture? From a judicial point of view, I like your thinking on that."

"You ought to be grateful," said Jesse, shrugging off the compliment. "This is just the kind of case that has your name written all over it. If one of our people were involved, you might have been asked to recuse yourself."

"Maybe, though I think I've been gone long enough that I'm not still thought of as one of your boys." Paul winked. "Of course, I appreciate that as usual you're looking out for my best interests."

"You got that right. How about doing me a favor in return? Teach my second-year securities course at NYU next semester so I can head up the Mayor's Commission."

Paul hesitated. His schedule was already tight, with not

much room to spare for another commitment. Teaching a course would mean having to prepare lectures, marking papers and exams, meeting with students. Yet he strongly believed that judges couldn't stay cloistered in the confines of the courtroom, and the idea of having some kind of influence on the next generation of lawyers was tempting. Beyond those more philosophical considerations, he hated to say no to Jesse, who rarely asked anything of him.

"Let me think about it, okay?" he said finally.

"Sure," said Jesse, pulling himself up from the couch. "As long as you call me next week and say yes." He checked his watch. "Damn. I'm supposed to meet Molly for dinner at eight, and I have to go back to the office first. By the way, we want you to come to Shelter Island with us this weekend."

Molly was a successful commercial realtor, but Paul felt she had missed her true calling as a matchmaker. "Who else is going to be there?"

Jesse laughed. "I always said you were one smart lawyer. So sue us for wanting you to have a life again."

"Thanks, but as it happens, I not only have a life, but I already have plans for the weekend."

"You call this living?" Jesse pretended to twirl a nonexistent mustache and did a decent imitation of Groucho Marx as he backed out the door.

Chuckling as he picked up the brief he'd been reading earlier, Paul thought about how much he missed spending time with Jesse and Molly. He particularly missed the easy companionship he and Helen had developed with them, despite the age difference between the two couples. They'd had great chemistry as a foursome, playing energetic games of tennis and sailing Long Island Sound. Once, they'd even gone flat-fishing for a week in the Florida keys, consuming prodigious quantities of beer in direct inverse proportion to the number of fish they'd let get away.

How would Hope fit into the vacuum that had been created by Helen's death, he wondered, absentmindedly doodling on his legal pad. What would they think of her? And the most intriguing question of all, why did he care?

He forced himself to concentrate and worked for another hour until his stomach began growling with hunger. Gathering up his papers, he suddenly changed his mind and left them stacked on his desk instead of bringing them home in his briefcase. He was too tired to work anymore this evening, he decided, as he turned off the lights and closed the door to his office.

The hallway was quiet, deserted except for one lone guard whose footsteps echoed loudly on the stone floor as he made his rounds. " 'Night, Your Honor," he called to Paul.

"Goodnight, Ed."

Normally, the heavily trafficked corridors were filled with the sounds of people in trouble, people bearing petitions, lawyers conferring in the corners, babies crying in their parents' arms. The State Supreme Courthouse was a census taker's dream, a cross-section of New York's citizenry, an equal opportunity environment where drug dealers rubbed elbows with whiplashed accident victims, corrupted cops, and cuckolded husbands. The atmosphere was permanently scented with the aroma of anxiety, fear, anger, and a dash of hope.

The elevators were slow, even at this hour. While he waited, he peered over the railing at the rotunda that was the first-floor heart of the Art Deco-style building.

The courthouse had been built at the tail end of the Depression, but somehow money had been found to create an opulent monument to the law, embellished with rich wood paneling, intricate ornamental metalwork, and stained-glass windows. The artisans employed by the Department of Public Works had created a circular, multipaneled mural on the ceiling of the rotunda that celebrated justice through the ages.

Paul often spent a few moments at the end of the day gazing up at the mural, admiring the colorfully detailed portraits of historic lawgivers and legal figures from Hammurabi, Moses, and Justinian through the eighteenth-century English legal writer Sir William Blackstone and U.S. Supreme Court Chief Justice John Marshall. Tonight, however, his mind on other, nonjudicial matters, he left without stopping, hurrying down the long, shallow flight of stone steps to the quiet street below.

WHILE SHE WAITED for Paul to arrive at her apartment, from where they would be leaving for the weekend, Hope replayed in her mind the conversation she'd had the night before with her aunt Grace.

The phone had rung just as Hope was getting into bed. Thinking it might be Paul, she grabbed the receiver. Her heart sank when she heard a woman's voice and realized it was Aunt Grace, calling from Palm Beach.

"Hello, darling. Just calling to check in."

To check *up* would have been closer to the truth. Grace was a busybody who tried to keep tabs on Hope under the guise of being concerned about her only brother's only daughter.

"Hope," she said, her voice rising in excitement, "I know it's rather late, but I simply had to call you. I've just come from a dinner party where I met the most marvelous man for you."

Hope sank back against the pillows. A dinner party meant that Grace had been drinking, which accounted for the high-pitched tone and the slurred words. "Marvelous man" meant someone who was rich, blandly good-looking, not very bright, and hopelessly dull. She closed her eyes and pictured her aunt's dream date: a blond, pedigreed Ken doll dressed up in black tie, carrying the keys to the vault that held his family's fortune.

"His name is Charlie Piggott. The family's originally

from Boston, but he lives in Los Angeles because he's a film producer of some sort. He said he'd never met you, but I thought perhaps you might know him. Do you, Hope?''

"No, Aunt Grace."

"Well, it doesn't matter, because he's coming up to New York next month. I gave him your name and number and said he was to be sure and call you."

Hope picked up the remote control and flicked on the television set that sat in the cabinet across from her bed. She pressed the "mute" button and channel-surfed, searching for an image that would distract her while Grace prattled on.

"Please, Aunt Grace, I wish you wouldn't give people my number without asking me first."

"I'm doing this for your own good, Hope," said Grace, sounding hurt. "I'm sure that if you could meet someone suitable—"

"I may have a candidate of my own," Hope blurted out, trying to stave off yet another of her aunt's haranguing speeches about the need for her to find an eligible prospect.

She regretted the words as soon as they were out of her mouth. Given such a golden opportunity, Aunt Grace immediately thrust her foot in the crack of the door that opened onto her niece's personal life.

"Not that awful Jordan Crandell?" she tsked.

Now, Voyager was playing on the American Movie Classics channel. A sucker for old-fashioned tearjerkers, Hope had already seen it ten, maybe fifteen times. Bette Davis and Paul Henreid were gazing soulfully at each other, getting ready to smoke a cigarette together. Their love was so pure, so poignant. She badly wanted some of that for herself.

"Jordan Crandell's just a friend, Aunt Grace. I know better than to marry him."

"Thank goodness you still have a shred of common

sense left. From what I hear, he's a terrible person who seduces every woman he meets. He may charm some people, but I remember him as a scrawny little boy whose nose never stopped running. Does his nose still run all the time?''

"No, Aunt Grace. He found himself a good allergist, and that problem's been taken care of.''

"Well, I still think marrying him would be a disaster.''

Hope reached for a tissue. Even without the sound, the movie made her cry. "We agree about that, at least,'' she said, wiping away the tears that were trickling down her cheeks.

"Tell me about this man you've met. Do I know him?''

"No.''

"Hope. What are you up to? Who is he?''

"He's just a person, Aunt Grace.'' She sniffled. "He's from New York.''

Grace's tone sharpened. "His *family*, Hope.''

Paul Henreid stuck two cigarettes in his mouth and lit them both. On anyone else, it would have looked stupid, but after what he'd been through in the movie, Hope was ready to forgive him anything.

"He doesn't have a drop of blue blood in his veins, I'm afraid. He's Irish Catholic, from Brooklyn.''

"Not a goddamned Kennedy!'' Aunt Grace sounded truly shocked.

"No, Aunt Grace,'' Hope quickly reassured her. "Not even a poor relation.''

"What does he do?''

"He's a judge.''

"Money?''

"Enough to live comfortably, I think. I haven't seen his tax returns yet, but I'll send you a copy as soon as I do.''

"Oh, Hope, don't be so damned naive,'' Aunt Grace clucked. "It may amuse you to play with people not of our class, but marriage is out of the question. What's that old saying? 'Mating a wolf and a dog never works for long.' You should know that.''

"That's not a very nice analogy, Aunt Grace. He's a wonderful man, a widower who's smart and kind and interesting."

There was a deep sigh at the other end of the line. "I know better than to tell you what to do. You've never followed my advice. You're just like your mother that way. But I must say that from your description, this man sounds wholly unsuitable. He wouldn't fit into our world, Hope, and you know it. I hope it's not too late for me to be giving you this warning."

"Do you mean, have I slept with him yet?"

"Hope!" There was a long pause, followed by another, deeper sigh. "If only your dear father were alive. I assure you, he'd know how to handle you."

"I'm sure you're right, Aunt Grace," Hope said, as Bette Davis uttered the most self-sacrificing line in movie history: *Don't ask for the moon—we have the stars.*

To give up so much love for the sake of honor . . . she wondered whether, if ever confronted with it, she would be capable of making such a choice.

"Of course I'm right. But please, won't you at least have dinner with Charlie Piggott? The two of you have so much in common. You're not getting any younger, you know. What's that awful vulgar expression I hear on TV all the time? Oh, yes . . . your biological clock is ticking, Hope. I'd hate for you to be deprived of the joys of motherhood simply because you haven't been diligent enough about finding a husband."

Hope grabbed another tissue, this one to stifle her laughter. Aunt Grace was a less than credible expert on the joys of motherhood. She couldn't spend more than half an hour in the same room with her daughter Miranda without getting into a vicious fight, which was probably why Miranda had moved to San Francisco with her two young children.

As for her son Walker, they hadn't spoken in three years, not since his third wife had divorced him after catching him in bed with twin sisters who hadn't yet reached the age of consent. Money had bought Walker his way out of a jail term for statutory rape, whereupon he'd relocated to Italy, and Aunt Grace had announced to the family that she'd washed her hands of him until he learned to control himself.

The temptation was great, but Hope chose not to remind Grace of her failed filial relationships. Instead, as politely as she could manage, she said, "Thank you for your concern, Aunt Grace."

"You know I'm only watching out for your happiness, dear. So please, think twice before you get yourself into a tawdry affair with this judge person. Promise?"

"Yes, Aunt Grace, I promise," Hope said dutifully.

"Good. And do try to come down for Thanksgiving, won't you? It's so important to spend these holidays with one's family, don't you think?"

"I'll try, Aunt Grace," Hope lied, having no intention of being anywhere near Palm Beach at Thanksgiving. "I'll speak to you soon."

She slammed down the receiver, turned off the television, and settled into bed. But the call had annoyed her so much that she stayed awake for what seemed like hours, staring into the darkness, fuming at her aunt's horrible, small-minded comments. Finally, when sleep refused to come, she switched on the lamp, climbed out of bed, and went into the library to pour herself a glass of brandy. Curling up in her favorite armchair, she slowly sipped the drink and stared out at the quiet, lamplit city below her window.

Aunt Grace was insufferable. Given the choice, she would have opted to control Hope's every move. Fortunately, she only rarely left Palm Beach, so most of their contact was confined to the telephone; but even from that distance she was often able to wound Hope where she was most vulnerable.

She was still hurting the next day when Paul showed up exactly on time to drive up to the country.

"Hello, you're very punctual," she said, when the maid showed him into the living room.

He was dressed casually, in a plaid sports shirt, faded blue jeans, and a leather jacket. Though it didn't fit her image of a judge, he looked even more handsome than she'd remembered.

He kissed her, a friendly peck on the cheek that left her hungry for much more. "It's such a beautiful day that I couldn't wait to get out of the city."

She bent her head to rearrange a bouquet of flowers that were already perfect. Trying to sound as if she were teasing, she said, "And here I thought you couldn't wait to see me."

"That, too," he said, so seriously that she believed him.

Her car was waiting for them in the driveway under the protective eye of the attendant who'd been hired by the building's co-op board for that express purpose. Paul watched with thinly veiled amusement as Hope's houseman loaded her overnight case, a cooler, and several bags of food into the back seat of the car.

"I could have done that myself," he said, after the houseman had wished them a good weekend and gone back into the building.

Hope blushed. Some things she took for granted, without stopping for a second to consider how her lifestyle might look to people who hadn't grown up as she had. Was this what Aunt Grace had meant about mating dogs and wolves?

"Oh, well." She pointed to the medium-sized canvas bag slung over Paul's shoulder. "You can throw that in back with my stuff."

It was a magnificent day, precisely the crisply clear autumn weather that Hope had been wishing for ever since she'd invited Paul up to her house. The forecasters

had officially proclaimed this weekend the best one of
the season for viewing the fall foliage at its peak. Already
at 11:00 A.M. the temperature had risen to sixty degrees
and was supposed to get up to the mid-seventies by the
afternoon.

Hope had suggested they go for the day and bring a
change of clothes along in case they decided to spend the
night. "It's no fun driving the Taconic in the dark, and
there's plenty of room," she'd said, all the while imagining the two of them lying in each other's arms in her bed,
while a fire crackled in the fireplace.

Saturday traffic thinned out once they were beyond the
Saw Mill River Parkway and heading north on the Taconic. In the two weeks since she'd last traveled this way,
the color of the leaves had dramatically changed. The
trees on either side of the road glowed in the sunlight,
alternating hues of red, yellow, gold, and purple so deep
and bright they seemed almost unreal.

As before, conversation flowed easily between them,
until they fell into a comfortable silence, drank in the
scenery, and listened to Mozart on the CD player.

She'd driven this route so often in the past five years
that every bump in the road, every exit sign and turnoff
felt like a familiar and much-loved friend. The Taconic
was a twisting, narrow speedtrap of a highway from the
point at which they picked it up in suburban Westchester
County until just beyond Pawling, the midway mark in
the two-hour trip. There, in rural Dutchess County, the
road gradually grew wider and flatter as the elevation
rose and the vistas expanded. To their left were the gently
rolling Catskills, to their right the Berkshire foothills, ex-
tending east and north into Connecticut and Massachu-
setts. On either side, the open fields were dotted with
herds of cows and weathered barns that stood out against
the crystal-clear sky with the varnished brilliance of an
eighteenth-century English landscape.

Red Hook, Pine Plains, Ancram, Hudson . . . the names

of the towns called out to Hope, verses in a poem that ended at the exit for Hillsdale, where they turned east onto Route 23. She'd driven this road by accident the first time, having taken a wrong turn while visiting friends who owned an estate in Germantown, overlooking the Hudson River.

That day, too, the weather had been Indian summer warm and sunny, and she'd been in no particular rush to reach her destination. She'd given herself permission to get lost along the pretty country roads that snaked off Route 23, passing tiny villages where historic Hudson Valley homes were surrounded by trailer parks and split-level developments. Eventually, she'd emerged at a crossroads called Craryville, which consisted of a white clapboard Methodist church, a defunct gas station where an old-fashioned ''Drink Coca-Cola'' sign flapped in the breeze, a sagging liquor store, and a yuppie food outpost that went by the name of Random Harvest.

She needed a house within easy driving distance of Craryville. That fact had hit her with the force of revelation. It had taken several months of exploring the area, but finally she'd found what she'd been looking for, a battered hilltop one-hundred-fifty-year-old farmhouse, separated from its neighbors by thirty-five acres of what once had been a working farm.

She'd retained as much as she could of the original structure, and spent a fortune on additions and renovations that tripled the square footage. It was the best and most extravagant investment she'd ever made. *Architectural Digest* had heard about it from the builder and asked to do a feature on the house, but she'd turned them down. It was her secret hideaway, the place she shared with only the handful of people who mattered most to her. And now Paul.

Just before they reached her turnoff, they stopped at the roadside stand where she often bought locally grown fresh fruit and vegetables. They loaded up with a jug of

cider, a basket of slightly tart Northern Spy apples, a
bag of sugared pumpkin donuts, the last of the season's
tomatoes, and a lopsided pumpkin. Then they drove another ten minutes up the steep, winding hill that ended at
her driveway.

"Must be hell to negotiate in the winter," Paul said as
he stepped out of the car. And then, "Wow!" as he took
in the two-story house and the sweeping panorama. "It
goes on forever, doesn't it?"

She smiled. "Every time I look, I notice some new
detail that I haven't seen before. We can go for a hike
later, if we're in the mood. But first come see the house,
and then I thought we'd have some lunch. Are you
hungry?"

"Starving. What's on the menu?"

There was cold shrimp salad, goat cheese, gravlax and
capers, a couple of crusty baguettes and a chilled bottle
of wine.

"Are you sure there's enough?" Paul asked, chuckling, as he helped Hope wheel the portable serving table
outside onto the westward-facing patio that caught the
afternoon sun.

"I had in mind a simple picnic, but I guess I got carried away," Hope said, joining in his laughter.

"I approve of your choices. This sure as hell beats the
soggy tuna sandwiches I got when I was a kid taking day
trips to Rockaway Beach."

She nodded at the wooden patio table. "We can eat
there or spread a blanket on the grass."

"Oh, a blanket on the grass, by all means. This is a
picnic."

While they ate, she pointed out some of her favorite
trees, and told him about the roses that bloomed in early
June. "My caretaker helps me with the garden, of course,
and I also have a terrific young woman who comes by
three or four times a week. But when I'm here, I do a lot
of the pruning and weeding myself."

A trio of persistent bees, enticed by the last of the asters, dahlias, and chrysanthemums that bordered the patio, buzzed about their heads. From somewhere far in the distance they could hear the growl of a tractor. A light breeze rustled through the fallen leaves. Otherwise, the air was still and quiet.

A squirrel darted out of the bushes, stopped for a moment as if to appraise them, then scurried off to search the grass for food.

"Well," said Paul, clearing his throat.

Hope turned to look at him, and he forgot what he wanted to say. Their unspoken desire hung between them like a ripe cluster of grapes, waiting to be picked.

He felt almost feverish with excitement as he leaned over and kissed her. Her lips were soft and full, and her mouth tasted of apples. She fell back against the blanket and drew him down against her, her hands clasped against the back of his neck as their mouths met again. Her skin felt smooth as velvet, and she offered herself to his touch as willingly as a flower opening its petals to the sun.

He pulled off her shirt while she unbuttoned his, exploring each other with mouths and fingers. Moaning softly as he caressed her breasts with his tongue, she pressed her hand between his legs and tugged impatiently at his zipper.

He fumbled to undo it himself. "Here on the grass?" he asked, his breathing gone ragged with the need to be inside her.

Her eyes were wide and hungry. "If that's all right with you."

It was much better than all right. He had never wanted any woman so badly in his life. Making love with her, their bodies moving together in a natural rhythm both fierce and tender, was about as close to perfect as he ever might have imagined.

If only it could last forever.

*   *   *

JORDAN CRANDELL LEANED back in his chair and propped his Gucci shoes up against the windowsill. Ten floors below, a bitter cold November wind swirled scraps of garbage, shriveled leaves, and sheets of discarded newspapers along the mostly empty sidewalks of West Broadway. The tourists, daunted by the inhospitable weather, had moved their sightseeing indoors to the fashionable art galleries, trendy clothing stores, and flavor-of-the-month bistros for which SoHo had become famous. Occasional drops of rain spattered against Crandell's window. A major storm was predicted before evening, with a flood watch for low-lying areas.

Crandell cradled the telephone against his ear and lit a cigarette.

"What happened to the money I sent you last week?" he asked his fifteen-year-old daughter, Rowena.

"It's so expensive over here, Daddy. I tore my best jeans and I had to buy another pair. Usually I keep a little for emergencies, but this time I'm really desperate."

Crandell expelled a lungful of smoke. "Why don't you ask your mother for an advance?"

"Oh, Daddy!" Rowena giggled seductively. "You know Mother. She's as tight as Scrooge. Like she's totally incapable of parting with a penny. I wouldn't want to waste the transatlantic call."

"And you were pretty sure this call wouldn't be a waste of money?"

"Daddy"—her tone was sweet and coquettish—"I know I can always count on you. So like I need about five hundred dollars."

He wondered whether she was back on drugs. The last time, before he'd sent her off to school in Switzerland, he'd had to go to a series of therapy sessions with her, a drain on his time that he could ill afford. But he didn't want to say no. She was his only child, basically a good kid, and he could afford to spoil her a little bit.

"I'll send you three hundred."

"Oh, c'mon." Her tone turned petulant. "You're like one of the richest men in the world. It said so in *People*."

"Don't believe everything you read, Rowena. I'll wire you three hundred dollars and not a penny more."

"Oh, Daddy. Thank you, thank you, thank you. I promise I'll be more careful from now on. You'll see."

"I'd better see," he growled. "Or you'll be back in New York so fast your pretty little ass will quiver."

Rowena giggled. "Don't worry, Daddy. I'll be good. Love you. 'Bye."

He hung up the phone. She was a conniving little vixen, as pretty as her mother had once been, and just as dumb. With any luck, in a couple of years some sharp-eyed Harvard B-School whiz would snap her up, rightly expecting Jordan Crandell's helping hand to be part of the arrangement.

He was willing to negotiate a reasonable deal in order to keep her happy and somebody else's responsibility.

He stubbed out his cigarette and glanced at the pack on his desk, which he'd opened this morning on his way downtown. Seven were missing. That was too many, dammit. He was trying to cut down, but without much luck. A friend had suggested hypnosis, and Crandell thought perhaps he would make an appointment, at least find out how the process worked.

The trouble was, he enjoyed smoking, just as he enjoyed a couple of dry martinis and a thick, juicy sixteen-ounce sirloin served medium rare with a plate of cottage fries. There were too few pleasures in life, and one by one they were being deemed hazardous to his health. Jesus, even getting laid could be deadly these days.

Lighting another cigarette, he shook his head at the thought of dying over a piece of ass. As far as that went, he exercised some control. He got himself checked regularly and made certain he was well protected. But getting laid sure as hell wasn't as much fun as it used to be, not like the good old days, when he fucked any sweet thing that crossed his path.

Now that he was just a couple of birthdays short of forty, he was even beginning to toy with the idea of getting married again. There were a couple of interesting prospects, both of them models he'd met around town. Or maybe he'd work something out with his old friend, Hope Scott. She was great in bed, smart, and good-looking enough that he never felt embarrassed about showing up with her on his arm. Of course, she was getting on a bit, and women never wore their age as well as men. On the other hand, he chuckled, at least with Hope Scott he would know she wasn't marrying him for his money.

He hadn't spoken to Hope in a while, he realized. He picked up the phone to call her just as his secretary buzzed him.

"What?" he said, annoyed by the interruption.

"Eric Lynch on line two."

He'd been calling Lynch at least once a week since their meeting in Utah. Sometimes Lynch took the call, sometimes he didn't. This was the first time he'd initiated a conversation himself. Crandell punched the button on his phone console. "Eric, always good to hear from you. What can I do for you?"

"Lew Valentine wants to meet with me, Mr. Crandell."

He picked up his pen and printed the words "Lew Valentine" on a piece of paper. "Tell him you're not interested."

"Who's to say? Maybe I am."

Reminding himself that Lynch only looked like an innocent kid, Crandell began scoring a tight grid of black lines through Valentine's name. "How's the skiing?"

"Still too early for snow, Mr. Crandell. Which is why I thought I should come to New York next week, talk to Valentine, see how his offer stacks up against yours."

"Valentine's a jerkoff with no vision for the future. He can't do diddly for you, Eric. Trust me on this."

"I owe it to my shareholders to hear what he has to say, and I was thinking of coming east anyway to spend Thanksgiving with my parents. How's the weather in New York?"

Crandell swiveled in his chair and stared out the window. The rain was coming down steadily now, blown sideways by the wind. He watched as a pedestrian standing in front of the downtown branch of the Guggenheim Museum across the street struggled to keep her umbrella upright. Suddenly, it folded inside out, carrying her along like Mary Poppins.

"It sucks," he said, half-expecting to see the woman go sailing off above the building. "Listen, Eric, I've been talking to my bankers. I may be able to sweeten the deal a little bit. Is that what this is about? Another dollar a share? Because what I have in mind for us goes way beyond money."

"Talk to me, Mr. Crandell."

He could hear Lynch typing at his computer keyboard while he delivered his sales pitch, spinning an image as elegantly intricate as a spider's web of the extraordinary technological offspring to be produced by a marriage between Summit and Starwares. It was nothing he hadn't said before to Eric Lynch, but he intuitively sensed that Lynch enjoyed having him repeat his spiel.

The clicking sound continued even after he stopped talking. He wondered whether Lynch had heard a word he'd said. Of all the company heads he'd ever dealt with, whether in friendly mergers or hostile takeovers, Eric Lynch was the most difficult to read. To say that he was sending mixed signals about his interest in a merger of their two corporations was a gross understatement. Lynch was as mercurial as the weather on a tropical island— sunny skies one moment, rain the next.

"Did Valentine happen to mention who's representing him?"

"He didn't say and I didn't ask," said Lynch.

On the line beneath the inked-in box where he'd written Valentine's name, he scrawled, "V's lawyer? Get name."

"Mr. Crandell, I'll come clean with you."

And about fucking time you did, Crandell thought. "Please, go ahead."

"I have my own personal reasons for not being keen to do a deal with Lew Valentine. But I have to at least give him the courtesy of a hearing, if you get my drift."

He would have liked to hear more about Lynch's reasons, but no further details were forthcoming, and he knew better than to ask. Lynch's admission was about as helpful as a quick swipe of a damp cloth on a dingy mirror. The details of the image revealed in the glass were no less murky than before.

"I understand, Eric. But be careful what you say to Valentine. He's no fool," Crandell warned.

"Nor am I, Mr. Crandell. Nor am I."

It irritated Crandell that Lynch consistently refused to call him Jordan. Why, he wondered, whenever he analyzed the myriad pieces of data that comprised the impending merger. Lynch's use of his last name seemed to betoken the existence of other unknown factors that might influence their deal. Unknowns made Crandell nervous. He didn't want any last-minute surprise rabbits pulled out of Lynch's hat.

"I tell you what, Eric," he said. "Since you're going to be in New York, I'd love for you to come by the office, meet some of my top people, get to know us a little better. Are you familiar with the city at all? We're headquartered in SoHo."

"SoHo? That's kind of different, isn't it? I always picture you guys gazing down at the rest of the world, wheeling and dealing in the rarefield atmosphere of your midtown skyscrapers."

"That's not my style. SoHo suits me better. I acquired the building fifteen years ago when I took over Salter

Publishing. My editors like working in this neighborhood, and if they're happy, I'm happy."

"Okay. Sounds like a good idea. I'll be back in touch once I'm more clear on my plans."

"Excellent," said Crandell. "In the meantime, I'll put together a tentative schedule, to be adjusted to your convenience, of course."

"Yeah, sure. Send me an E-mail, Mr. Crandell. You have my number."

Crandell hung up the phone and rubbed his palms together in anticipation. Eric Lynch was about to see New York as he had never seen it. Crandell would give him a dog-and-pony show that would make Lynch forget all about Valentine or any other would-be bidders. By the time he left the city, he might even be calling Crandell by his first name.

He had his work cut out for him. Suddenly, the day seemed less dreary. He would have to cancel his four o'clock meeting with the president of his magazine division. No big loss. The details of magazine publishing bored him. His job was to look at the big picture and steer the company on a course of continued expansion.

He buzzed his secretary. "Get me George Osburgh."

She was back on the line a minute later. "He's gone to lunch, Mr. Crandell. I left word for him to call back."

"Then get me Rick Major and tell him I have a job for him."

Another few moments passed, then, "He's at lunch, too."

"Goddamnit!" Crandell barked. "I pay that shmuck a fat check every week so that when I need information, he's there to get it for me. When he calls back, Donna, you be sure to tell him how many résumés I get from unemployed private detectives. Hell, I don't even want to talk to the guy. You tell him he's got to the end of the day to find out who's representing Lew Valentine."

"Representing him on which matter, Mr. Crandell?"

"What the hell do you care? Just tell him to get me the goddamn information. And Donna? Order me a grilled chicken salad, and you can order something for yourself, too. Then bring your steno pad in here. Some of us have to earn our salaries."

While he waited for her, he mentally made himself a list of the other people he needed to speak to that afternoon: Warren Breed and Bradley Fisher, whose investment banking firm of McCreedy, Mellor & Company was representing him in his negotiations with Starwares. Ken Wolch, the head of the corporate department at the law firm of Kraft, Wolch, Morad & Hathaway. Jack Borden, his chief financial officer. Bebe Weiss, the editor-in-chief of *Pastiche,* Summit's upscale consumer magazine.

And Hope Scott.

FIVE

"OBJECTION, YOUR HONOR!"

William Elmendorf, the counsel for the plaintiff, had been jumping up from his seat all morning, objecting to the questions posed by the defense attorney, Marion Beck.

"What now, Mr. Elmendorf?" asked Paul.

A heavyset man with a bad rug, a bulbous nose, and a ruddy complexion, William Elmendorf had previously exhibited an unfortunate tendency to ramble during the arguments he'd presented on behalf of his client, the advertising agency of Drummer, Bean & Watson. He'd seemed curiously ill-prepared as he sought a temporary injunction preventing a breakaway group of Drummer, Bean employees that had constituted their own boutique agency within the larger shop from either hiring away any of their former associates or accepting any accounts that had previously done business with them at Drummer, Bean.

Ironically, in spite of Elmendorf's muddled, poorly organized presentation, Paul had felt compelled to rule in his favor. Documents had been discovered that cast some doubt on the claim made by the dissident group of copywriters and art directors that they had no intention of soliciting Drummer, Bean employees or clients. Paul had

issued a temporary injunction, then set aside a week to
ten days to hear testimony from the people now working
at the newly formed agency of Quigley & Newman to
determine whether they'd been lured away by their former associates.

Paul glanced at the copy of the witness list that lay on
his desk. At the rate they were proceeding, the hearing
could stretch well into a third week. Glaring over his bi-
focals at William Elmendorf, he tapped his foot impatiently behind the wooden barrier of the bench.

"Ms. Beck is leading the witness, Your Honor," Elmendorf said. "I fail to see how her line of questioning
could possibly—"

"Mr. Elmendorf," Paul broke in. "We've already
been down this particular road of yours three times in
the last hour. Each time you've raised the objection, I've
overruled you. Aren't you beginning to grasp the futility
of your thinking in this regard?"

"But, Your Honor. . . ." Elmendorf was nothing if not
persistent.

"Overruled, Mr. Elmendorf. And don't make me say
it again. You understand?"

"Yes, Your Honor." The lawyer's cheeks flushed an
even brighter red as he resumed his seat and leaned over
to whisper something into the ear of Drummer, Bean's
general counsel, who was seated next to him.

Paul bit his lip to keep from grinning. He would do his
best, as always, to render a ruling that was fair and impartial, but he couldn't ignore the uncanny resemblance between Elmendorf and Bozo the Clown. He nodded at
Elmendorf's opposite number. "You may proceed, Ms.
Beck."

He knew Marion Beck, who was more or less his contemporary, from his days at Goodstein & Carney. The
first woman to make partner at Langley & Dunlap, she
was a slim, attractive blonde who felt secure enough
about her status at the firm that she'd exchanged her for-

mer uniform of severely cut dark suits for softer and much more flattering clothes that made her the bright spot in an otherwise drab courtroom.

She was an excellent litigator, a much better choice of attorney than William Elmendorf, who seemed to have floundered into legal waters far beyond his depth and was now, belatedly, reaching for a life preserver in the form of his constant stream of objections.

"Thank you, Your Honor." She smiled at him, and he wondered whether it was true that she'd recently begun having an affair with Harry Matheson, the managing partner at Langley & Dunlap. He hoped not. Matheson was a tight-assed patrician snob who didn't look like he'd be very lively in bed. Marion deserved better.

"Ms. Russell," she said, picking up where she'd left off before Elmendorf's objection, "was the memo you received on the morning of October 14, signed by Joseph Quigley and Robert Newman and stating their resignation, the first you knew of their departure from the agency?"

"Absolutely." Jenna Russell, a creative director newly employed at Quigley & Newman, nodded her head of tight black curls. "I was totally shocked. At five o'clock the day before, I had a meeting with Joe about a TV commercial I was working on. The next morning"—she snapped her fingers—"Pouf! He's gone."

"How did their leaving personally affect you?"

"I think Joe Quigley is a genius. I've done my best work under his direction. It was devastating to think that I'd have to start reporting to somebody new. I swear, I actually lost my appetite, I was so upset. Now that's serious!"

Marion Beck smiled. "I can imagine."

Paul listened and took notes as Jenna Russell continued answering the questions. She was a good witness, credible and articulate in her responses. Joe Quigley and his associate Robert Newman clearly commanded a high degree of admiration and loyalty from their staff. It remained to be seen whether the memo found in Robert Newman's desk drawer listing the names of many of their employees and clients was proof of their intent to undermine Drummer, Bean, or merely a wish list of the people they'd want to join them at their new address.

It was the kind of case Paul relished, touching on complex issues such as the rights of ownership, definition of assets, and managers' fiduciary responsibilities. Having the chance to weigh and rule on such points was one of the reasons he enjoyed presiding over civil cases.

The map of white-collar crime had changed in the last decade, its contours shifting in response to the volcanic eruptions of junk-bond-financed corporate takeovers and leveraged buyouts. From the vantage point of his judge's bench, Paul had watched with mixed emotions the metamorphosis of the American business community. Like a discontented child forced to sit on the sidelines, a voice inside him had intermittently whined, "I want to play, too." Cases like *Drummer* v. *Joseph Quigley* were finally giving him a turn at the bat.

Marion Beck consulted her notes. "No further questions, Your Honor," she said.

"Your witness, Mr. Elmendorf," said Paul.

He poured himself a glass of water as William Elmendorf stepped up to the microphone. Why, he wondered, with all the top-notch legal resources available to them, had Drummer, Bean selected a second-string player to lead their team?

Elmendorf's blunders only made Paul's job more difficult. He had to curb his annoyance and guard against the temptation of deciding the case on the basis of which attorney gave a better performance, rather than on its merits. The odds were better than even that whatever his decision, an appeal would be filed. Paul was determined not to give his colleagues on the appeals court level any room to find fault with his conduct or interpretation of the law.

There were plenty of mediocre judges, and a handful who were worse than mediocre, presiding over courtrooms throughout the state. Some, thirty- and forty-year veterans, were verging on senility. Others were tough-minded and knowledgeable, but so sure of their superior expertise that they too often used the bench as a bully pulpit, trying to teach by example how a case should be argued. Still others allowed their prejudices to inform their decisions.

They were all the bane of a system that functioned only as honestly and effectively as its practitioners. After six years in the courtroom, Paul had few illusions left about the inviolacy of judicial conduct. The checks and balances were limited. Judges, almost by necessity, tended to close ranks in order to protect their own.

"Ms. Russell," said William Elmendorf, leaning against the podium, "previous to their rather abrupt departure from Drummer, Bean, did either Joseph Quigley or Robert Newman ever discuss with you your long-range employment goals?"

Jenna Russell wrinkled her brow in concentration. Then she replied, "Yes, I suppose you could say so. About six months ago, at my annual salary review, Joe did ask me what I imagined myself doing in two years."

"And you told him what, Ms. Russell?"

"That I wanted to continue as a creative director, but with responsibility for some of our larger, more important accounts."

"Did Mr. Quigley indicate whether that would be a possibility for you?"

She nodded. "Yes. He said there was opportunity for advancement and that he and Bob were quite pleased with my performance thus far."

"So he dangled in front of you the very tempting carrot of advancement if you continued to work for him and Mr. Newman?"

"Objection, Your Honor!" Marion Beck declared.

"Mr. Elmendorf is interpreting the facts for the witness."

An easy call. "Sustained. Please rephrase the question, Mr. Elmendorf," Paul said.

"Did you feel a sense of loyalty toward Mr. Quigley?" Elmendorf amended.

"Yes, I did. He's very highly regarded in the advertising business. He's like a mentor to me."

"A sense of loyalty such that had he told you he was leaving and asked you to keep quiet about his intention, you would have done so?"

"I guess so. But he *didn't* tell me."

"No indication, no advance warning whatsoever?"

She shook her head. "No."

"So his memo dated October 14 was the first you knew of his departure from Drummer, Bean?"

Paul's annoyance got the better of him. "Mr. Elmendorf, you don't seem to be listening to Ms. Russell's answers," he snapped. "She already testified to that point."

Elmendorf glanced at the sheet of paper in front of him, thus missing the angry gaze turned on him by Drummer, Bean's general counsel. "Sorry, Your Honor," he said. "If I may have just a moment to double-check my facts. . . ."

"Go ahead, Mr. Elmendorf, but we don't have all day," Paul said wearily.

Justice would be served in his courtroom, no matter how incompetent her standard-bearers.

BERNARD ODETTE HAD begun to assemble his New York staff, assessing the weaknesses and strengths of each candidate, relying on his inner sense of how each candidate might function under pressure. Loyalty was particularly important. Billions of dollars were at stake. Buying or planting a spy was not uncommon in these knock-down corporate battles.

Odette had already screened two secretaries and a paralegal, conducting the interviews in the luxurious Trump Tower apartment provided him by Valentine Industries, according to his specifications. For the next several months, the apartment would serve as his home as well as his base of operations. He anticipated that his life would be so consumed by the potential legal action that such an arrangement would save precious time.

The last woman he'd interviewed, an experienced middle-aged legal secretary, appeared to be uncomfortable with the prospect of working in his home. She had excellent qualifications, but he'd had to reject her out of hand. There was no room to observe the normal proprieties or niceties. If he had to dictate stark naked in the bath, so be it. His secretary would have to adjust.

Each of the people he hired would have to realize that he or she was enlisting as a foot soldier in a corporate war. They wouldn't be wearing uniforms, and no real blood would be shed. But they would be engaged in battle nonetheless, and as their commanding officer, he demanded utmost obedience and unswerving commitment to the cause.

Autumn was a difficult time of year to find choice young lawyers. He needed someone to back him up—someone smart and driven who could make routine court appearances and handle the bulk of the research. Most of the prime candidates had already been snapped up by the big New York law firms that competed frantically every year for the crop of new lawyers coming out of the Ivy League law schools. The rest were either clerking or working at smaller firms or for the government.

But Odette didn't want any Ivy Leaguers. He preferred the city or state school graduates like himself, the scrappers whose advancement wasn't cushioned by family money or connections. They knew what life was about, and they were accustomed to clawing their way upward to get what they wanted.

He not only respected but needed such toughness. The big firms could keep their legal scholars and socially graceful shmoozers. He wanted the fighters, and the hungrier the better.

Catherine Riznicki, the applicant seated across from him, had graduated from the City University of New York Law School in Queens. Earlier, he'd looked over her résumé and found it interesting enough to put a tiny check in the upper left corner.

She was a short, heavyset young woman, neither pretty nor ugly, with high Slavic cheekbones and slightly slanted eyes that glared at him with the impudence of a Siamese cat.

"Your grades leave something to be desired, Ms. Riznicki," he said as soon as she had introduced herself.

She didn't miss a beat. "I worked nights all three years of law school. I didn't make Law Review, but I didn't fail anything either. I wanted to pass all my courses, and that's what I did."

He'd memorized her résumé. There was no reference to her place of employment. "What kind of work did you do?"

"I was a waitress and barmaid," she said evenly.

He liked that. No apologies made, none necessary. "I presume you did your studying during the slack times?"

She laughed, and her smile softened her features. "At the joints where I worked, there was no slack time. I could have found easier places, but less business means smaller tips, and I needed the money."

"Are you married?"

They both knew he wasn't supposed to ask about marital status. If she objected to the question, he would immediately eliminate her. But she only shook her head. "Divorced. I married another law student. I thought he would help put me through school, and he thought I would do the same for him." She smiled again, wryly. "Turns out we were both hustlers. We handled our own divorce, the first case for both of us. He found a sweet little thing from Philadelphia whose parents had money and married her. The father helped land him a job with an uptown firm. That shows what a plan and persistence can do.''

Odette laughed. ''Tell me about your legal experience.''

''I have a job with two small-time negligence lawyers. I carry their bags and look up the law for them. Frankly, I can make more money waitressing. I was considering going back to being a barmaid when I heard you might be hiring. So here I am.''

Odette liked to surround himself with attractive women. It was good for his morale. But Catherine Riznicki looked more like a linebacker, though her smile invited a man to take a second glance. Still, he sensed she had just the qualities he was looking for.

''This is a short-term job, no future as such, you understand?'' he said.

''Long hours and plenty of action. Is that the deal?''

''That sounds about right.''

''And the money?''

''What are you making now?''

She shook her head. ''Not nearly enough. If there isn't a future, there has to be money.''

''What figure did you have in mind?'' Odette enjoyed negotiating, and the process served also to test the girl's intelligence.

''If I tell you, Mr. Odette, and it's too low, you'd consider me a fool. And if it's unrealistically high, you'll show me the door. Either way I lose. You're offering the job, so you must have a figure in mind.''

''I do.'' She was shrewd. Another trait he admired. ''Three thousand a month. The job will last for approximately eight months to a year, perhaps longer.''

She shook her head. ''That's not nearly enough. Not if you want me to put in lots of overtime, which I expect to do. You should be offering at least double that.''

"Perhaps, for someone with some experience. But you've only been a lawyer for a few months, you don't even know yet if you passed the Bar exam, and what you've done for those two ambulance-chasers hardly qualifies you for corporate work."

"You're right. But you won't find anyone experienced, at least not around Manhattan, who will work those hours for that kind of money. Not unless they're desperate."

"You sound desperate," he said, lighting a cigarette.

"Not desperate enough to sell myself short." She waved the smoke away with her hand.

"Do cigarettes bother you? I don't provide a smoke-free environment."

"I worked in a bar, Mr. Odette. I think a smoke-free environment is anti-American. Six thousand a month sounds about right to me."

"I can't afford it."

She laughed, a great big belly laugh that even made him smile. "Oh? The notorious Michigan Assassin is hired by Valentine Industries to handle a billion-dollar case, and you want me to believe that you can't afford to pay me what I'm worth? Give me a break, Mr. Odette. Given what you stand to make on this deal, six thousand is a more than fair figure."

"Suppose you aren't worth it?"

"Then you'll fire me."

"If I hire you, you'll earn every damn cent of that money."

"If you hire me, I intend to."

Odette nodded. "When could you start?"

"Tomorrow."

"Won't you have to give notice?"

Her eyes narrowed again. "The older of my two employers is almost eighty. He can't weigh more than a hundred pounds soaking wet, but he has the hots for me. Every time I turn around, I feel the old goat's bony hand on my behind. I told him I would quit if he didn't stop.

I'd hit him except that he's so frail I'm afraid I might kill him. I didn't mind so much when the old geezers in the bars used to do it; at least they tipped. All I get now is a lot of passionate wheezing. I have every reason to leave without notice, and they both know it.''

He chuckled at her description. ''And if I took similar liberties?''

''You won't,'' she said, smiling. ''You can have any woman you want. You wouldn't waste your time grabbing my overly wide bottom. And if you did, I wouldn't be afraid to crack you. You look like you could take a punch.''

Odette chuckled again. He'd made up his mind to hire her. She was precisely what he was looking for, and she would probably give him a laugh or two when he needed it. ''Five thousand a month with no bottom-pinching. Take it or leave it.''

''What about health insurance?''

''Look, Ms. Riznicki—''

''Mr. Odette, this is the real world. You may not have to worry about such petty details, but I do.''

''You could be losing out on a great opportunity.''

''And you could be losing out on a great employee.''

''Five thousand, five hundred, and that's the bottom line.''

She stood up and extended her hand. ''Okay, boss. What time and where do I start?''

''Tomorrow morning, eight o'clock, right here, Ms. Riznicki.''

''My first name is Catherine, but everyone calls me Rizzy. I'd feel more comfortable if you did, too.''

He stood up, towering over her. ''I hope I'm right about you, Rizzy.''

She grinned up at him. ''You just made the sharpest deal of your career, Mr. Odette.''

A BLIZZARD OF incandescent stars glittered against an ink black sky. Millions of miles below, present but unseen in the darkness, the harshly jutting peaks of the Wasatch Mountains reached heavenward, awaiting Utah's first snowfall of winter. Until then, the dun-colored slopes were quiet and bare, the surrounding towns empty of skiers. The proprietors of the area restaurants and souvenir shops kept themselves occupied refurbishing their establishments while monitoring the forecast on the Weather Channel.

"Think snow!" urged the bumper stickers on many of the four-wheel drive vehicles belonging to the local residents. Normally, at this time of year, Eric Lynch would have been doing just that, thinking of snow, imagining the feel of the superfine, waist-high powder under his skis. But tonight, as he sank deeper into the relaxing warmth of his hot tub and gazed up through the angled retractable glass roof that covered his home spa, he had matters other than snow on his mind.

He removed his hand from the water and pressed first one, then another of the buttons on the panel that was set in the outer rim of the hot tub. The room went dark, and the adjoining panes of glass above his head slid approximately four feet apart. He inhaled deeply. The sharp bite of the fall mountain air felt cool and refreshing against his face.

Winter was coming. Eric had decisions to make that would affect the entire future course of his business. The pressure was on, but he had always flourished under pressure. He smiled at the shadowed mountains that surrounded him, thinking that no one could have predicted he would accomplish as much as he already had.

His mother taught history at a Providence, Rhode Island, high school, the same one he himself had attended. His father was an accountant. Though good with numbers, he possessed no special talent that would account for his son's singular ability to solve the most elaborate computer problems, a form of genius that almost seemed a gift of the gods.

And yet, like Avis, he was only number two in the industry. As hard as he tried, he was still chasing number one, the world's preeminent computer virtuoso. "That guy from Seattle" was the label he gave his chief rival, when he was forced to refer to him. Though not a superstitious person, Eric Lynch didn't like to *think* the man's name, much less speak it aloud.

A major cash infusion would make all the difference. The information highway was no longer a visionary's pipe dream—it was being built, one labyrinthian software code at a time, its only boundaries the ownership of cable rights and the limits of the human imagination. With the right partner, Starwares could very well overtake the guy from Seattle in the race to dominate computer technology.

But who was Starwares' Mr. Right? Jordan Crandell or Lew Valentine? Or some other as yet unknown candidate who might prove to be the perfect match? How to decide among such an embarrassment of choices?

He closed his eyes and saw himself as a small child, waiting on the sidelines to be picked for a Saturday afternoon game of tag. A remembered rhyme popped into his mind: *Eenie, meenie, minie, mo. Catch a tiger by the toe. If he hollers, let him go. My mother says to pick Y-O-U.*

The phone rang, interrupting his reverie. He opened his eyes and waited for the machine to pick up the call. A few moments later, the message was broadcast over the housewide loudspeaker system.

"Hi, Eric," came his mother's voice. "Your dad and I are wondering whether you're coming home for Thanksgiving. Ruthie, Bob, and the kids will be with us . . . but I already told you that, didn't I? Well, give us a call when you have a minute. We're hoping to see you."

Reminding himself to phone his parents, he reached for his can of Coke and took another sip. He hadn't been back east in months. It would be good to see his family and spend the holiday with them. He would stop in New

York for a couple of days, meet with Crandell, hear what Valentine had to say.

A successful merger was as much about chemistry as it was about the numbers. From what he knew thus far of Crandell and Valentine, neither was his ideal mate. There were pros and cons on both sides; but maybe perfection was too much to ask for, except when it came to writing software codes. Introduce the people factor into any given equation, and suddenly there were all kinds of uncontrollable variables. Those variables were one of the reasons he was still single. He didn't like to take chances on women any more than he did on a merger.

Of course, in theory, the decision would ultimately depend on the vote of Starwares' board of directors. But without Eric Lynch, there would be no board. He had no doubt that the directors would vote to merge with whichever corporation he wanted.

He had written some of his most dazzling programs while racing to meet a deadline that almost anyone else would have considered impossible. Now he needed a deadline in order to make his choice. By the time he returned from New York, he would know whose bid he wanted to accept.

THE FIRST TIME she had married, Hope had endured endless weeks of anticipating Brett's proposal. He'd finally popped the question just as they were stepping off the chairlift at the top of one of Aspen's most difficult runs.

"Yes, of course," she'd breathlessly replied, and then suddenly, he was whizzing past her down the mountain, screaming with what she'd assumed was unabandoned joy that she'd agreed to be his wife.

It was hard to imagine Paul resorting to such melodrama. Nor could she imagine herself passively waiting for him to propose. Though she'd known him only a short while, she was convinced, as surely as she'd ever felt anything in her life, that they were meant to be together. She wanted formal recognition of that fact—a wedding ceremony, a ring on her finger, the privilege of introducing him as "my husband, Paul Murray." She wanted, while there was still time, the chance to have his baby.

But was that what he wanted? She decided to swallow her pride and simply put the question to him.

The limousine that was taking them to a premiere benefit performance by the New York City Opera was stuck in traffic two blocks away from Lincoln Center. At 6:40 P.M., the height of rush hour, the Upper West Side north-south thoroughfares were crowded with bumper-to-bumper cars, taxis, and buses. Tired commuters vied for supremacy of the road with hungry Broadway theatergoers, anxious to grab a bite to eat before the curtain went up at eight.

Hope and Paul were already ten minutes late for the pre-performance cocktails and first course of dinner, the rest of which would be served at the New York State Theater after the last curtain call. But Hope was unaware both of their lack of progress and the cacophonous din of honking horns. Gazing out the side window, tinted gray to shield them from curious glances, she noticed only the stream of pedestrians on the sidewalk just a few feet away from the car. Many of them were couples: young and old, straight and gay, laughing or fighting or holding hands as they slowly sauntered by or rushed quickly past. Always couples.

The limo inched forward, reaching the intersection of 65th Street and Columbus Avenue just as the light turned red.

Paul glanced at his watch. "Should we get out and walk?"

"Maybe we should get married," she said, astounding them both with her non sequitur.

"Are you serious?"

Losing her nerve, she quickly backtracked. "I don't

know what made me say that. It's probably a bad idea—''

"No. I think it's a good idea," he said, taking her hand. "I'm just surprised it occurred to you."

She felt the blush rise in her cheeks as he stared at her. "I guess I'm not as unconventional as I might seem." She shrugged, not knowing what else to say.

He smiled. "I thought you didn't want to marry again. That you already had everything you wanted in life."

That dumb Barbara Walters interview. She couldn't believe he'd seen it. She remembered how she'd squirmed so uncomfortably under Barbara's skeptical gaze.

"Turns out I was wrong," she whispered. "I never thought I'd meet the right man. And then I did."

"I love you," he said, moving closer to take her into his arms.

"I love you, too," she said, just as the light changed.

The limo shot across Broadway and turned left into the standing lane in front of Lincoln Center. The harried driver, grateful that they'd finally arrived, put the car into park and got out to open the back door for his passengers. He grinned as he caught a glimpse of them, oblivious to the world, wrapped in each other's embrace.

Miss Scott was a nice lady. He didn't know the judge very well, but he seemed like a standup guy, not a creep like so many of the men he frequently chauffeured around town.

Hope pulled away first. "Is that a yes?" she asked Paul.

"It's a yes if you'll have me," he said.

Hope smiled at the driver. "Wish us luck, Ken," she said. "We're getting married."

He reached out his hand to help her out of the car. "Congratulations, Miss Scott. And to you, too, Judge Murray. You're a lucky man."

"No," said Hope. "*I'm* the lucky one."

* * *

"IF YOU'LL JUST follow me, Mr. Crandell."

Michael Hill, the associate producer assigned to greet Jordan Crandell, ushered him into the green room where guests of Charlie Rose's public television show waited their turn to appear before the cameras.

"Charlie will be by in a few minutes to say hello. In the meantime, please help yourself to tea, coffee, Perrier, fruit, whatever. I think you know Mr. Valentine—"

"Jordan," said Lew Valentine, who had just gotten up from the couch to pour himself a cup of coffee. "Always a pleasure."

Jordan Crandell nodded. "Likewise."

How ironic, he thought, that they both should have been asked to participate in Charlie Rose's roundtable panel on the future of telecommunications and the cable industry. He'd committed himself to appear on the program weeks ago. Now here he was, face to face with his rival, about to discuss the very topic that was probably uppermost in both their minds.

Crandell smiled as Valentine sat down with his coffee. He'd never much trusted or liked Lew Valentine, and now that Valentine was trying to steal Starwares away from him, he liked him even less. But he forced himself to make a show of affability. The pretense of warmth might help him ferret out some bit of information that could prove useful.

"What's new, Jordan?" Valentine asked. "It's been a while."

"Not too much. What's up with you?"

Valentine shrugged. "The usual. Keeping an eye on the market. Trying to turn a profit."

Crandell wondered whether Valentine was aware of his own interest in Starwares. Though it wasn't yet public knowledge, they certainly knew enough people in common that word could have leaked out to him. Crandell's attorneys and bankers were bound by confidentiality, but such information easily found its way into the rumor pipeline. He could think of at least two people on his board of directors who would have trouble keeping their mouths shut even for the sake of national security.

Valentine was a tricky bastard, slippery as a water moccasin and twice as deadly. But he was nowhere near as smart as he gave himself credit for, and he was getting cocky. According to Crandell's sources, he'd fallen into the dangerous habit of believing his own press releases.

Crandell smiled, thinking that he'd already outmaneuvered Valentine by personally going to visit Eric Lynch. Just today, he'd received confirmation that Lynch would be coming to New York and was willing to devote the better part of a day to meeting with him and his people. Ignoring the "No Smoking" sign on the wall, he pulled out his cigarettes and removed one from the package. "Do you mind?" he asked.

Valentine shook his head. "So where's the rest of the gang? I understand they've got us facing off against one of Gore's Beltway bureaucrats, and a couple of computer nerds from Silicon Valley."

"Anyone worth knowing?" asked Crandell.

"I guess that depends on your rating system. Bill Gates is off somewhere in Africa or Hawaii. Their second choice was Eric Lynch. But it would take a lot more than a spot on Charlie Rose to pull him away from Utah, if you know what I mean."

Crandell kept a poker face. Valentine was on a fishing expedition, angling for information. According to Rick Major, Summit's private investigator, Valentine had recently retained Bernard Odette to represent him, and Odette was putting together a temporary New York staff. It didn't take much brainpower to deduce that Valentine had hired the infamous Michigan Assassin because he was gearing up for all-out warfare. The question was, how much did he know?

"We took a look at Starwares last year, ran some numbers, but ultimately decided to pass,'' said Crandell. ''The fit didn't feel quite right.''

Valentine nodded. ''I hear that Lynch is difficult to deal with and impossible to please. He's like one of those little high school virgins who'd cocktease you to death, then run screaming to Mama when you tried to score. There's no percentage in starting up with him.''

''Oh, sure,'' Crandell agreed. ''No percentage in that whatsoever.''

A large round clock on the wall, similar to those Crandell remembered from his grammar school days, loudly ticked off the seconds. He smiled at Valentine, who returned the smile and said, ''Utah's a nice place. My wife thinks we should buy a ski house in Deer Valley. You ever been out there?''

''Funny you should ask.'' Crandell drew on his cigarette. Valentine was putting him on notice that he'd heard about his trip. It was his move. ''I was in Utah just last month. Beautiful country.'' He looked off into the distance, as if recalling the splendors of the state. ''Terrific people, those Mormons. They still give you an honest day's work for their pay. No wonder Eric Lynch located there. I wanted to check out his setup, but he couldn't or wouldn't see me.''

He leaned forward to put out his cigarette in a cup of coffee someone had left behind on the table. ''Like you said, he's difficult to deal with.''

''Right,'' said Valentine, staring speculatively at him.

''Doesn't Johnny Carson have a place in Deer Valley?'' asked Crandell, trying to draw out the match.

''Yes.'' Valentine abruptly changed the subject. ''My wife wanted to know if she can call you,'' he said. ''She's got a bug up her ass about raising show dogs and was hoping you'd give her some pointers.''

Crandell pictured Rennie Valentine, a tense, perfectly coiffed woman with an overly eager smile, trying to make friends with a pair of frisky puppies. It was hard to imagine her romping in the grass with them, as he often did with the two prizewinning Belgian sheepdogs he kept at his weekend home in Westchester County. But it couldn't hurt to do Valentine a favor, or to make a friend of his wife.

"By all means, I'll talk to her," he said expansively, taking out one of his business cards. "I can introduce her to my trainer. He used to be with the Israeli Army canine corps."

Valentine pocketed the card. "Thanks, I owe you one."

The door to the green room opened. "Gentlemen," said Michael Hill, walking in behind a stunning ash blond woman in her early thirties. "I'd like to introduce you to another of our panelists, Madeline Kline, who's with Vice President Gore's task force on the future of the information superhighway. Ms. Kline, Lew Valentine and Jordan Crandell."

Crandell eyed the young woman, whose long, shapely legs were shown off to advantage by her above-the-knee-length black skirt. He was a registered Republican, but if Madeline Kline was typical of what Clinton and Gore were bringing to Washington, he might be inclined to support the Democrats in the next election.

"Delighted to meet you, Ms. Kline," he said. "I'm a big supporter of Al Gore. He's got a damn good agenda. Make a fine president one day. I'm looking forward to our discussion, as is my friend Lew Valentine here."

"I'm glad to hear it, gentlemen," said Madeline Kline, helping herself to a glass of orange juice. "It's a fascinating topic. As a matter of fact, I brought some reports with me that I'd love to share with you."

Valentine smiled. "Jordan and I were just now talking about still-to-be-defined regulatory problems posed by the information superhighway, weren't we, Jordan?"

Crandell nodded and managed to look interested. But his mind was elsewhere, far from this television studio where the man who was sure to be his chief competitor was making a play for Madeline Kline.

All the pieces were in place. No one—not even Lew Valentine—could stop him now. Victory only waited on Eric Lynch's assent and the team of lawyers who would take over the courtroom and eviscerate the Michigan Assassin.

PAUL HAD ASSUMED that Hope would want a traditional church wedding. But faced with the questions of how, when, and where, she surprised him, as she so often did.

"I know how it works," she said. "You start small, just a few close friends and family. Then suddenly, you remember all the people who'd be insulted if you didn't invite them. Before you know it, your guest list is so long you have to hold the wedding in St. Patrick's."

Paul thought of his large, extended family and chuckled. "And you still end up insulting someone or another."

It took them less than an hour to work out the details. They both agreed they wanted to keep it simple and low-key. Paul would ask one of his colleagues to perform a double-ring civil ceremony in Hope's living room on the Wednesday before Thanksgiving, with Yvonna and the Rubins as witnesses, if they were available.

"Are you kidding?" roared Jesse Rubin, when Paul broke the news to him. "I'd fly back from the moon to act as your witness."

Yvonna's reaction was similar, though pitched in a higher key. Hope had to hold the phone away from her ear as Yvonna yelped with excitement. When she calmed down enough to speak, she insisted on getting the Rubins' phone number, so she could coordinate the post-wedding brunch with them.

"You don't have to do that," said Hope.

"I want to do it," Yvonna said, her tone so stern that Hope didn't dare argue.

They were lying in bed, lingering over the Sunday *Times,* when Paul brought up the question of a prenuptial agreement. He'd presided over too many vicious divorces in which the partners used money as a weapon not to believe that in certain cases, a prenuptial was a necessity.

Hope made a face. Money was an uncomfortable area for her, one they hadn't talked much about. There were any number of bothersome questions that they'd already had to resolve. Where to live, for example. She'd been to his apartment, which was gracious and warm by most standards, but utterly modest compared to hers. When she suggested he move in with her and sublet his place, Paul had smiled and said, yes, he thought that made the most sense.

When they went out to dinner or to the theater, they'd fallen into the habit of taking turns paying the bill. She happily would have covered everything but knew he would never permit such an arrangement. He'd told her that his judge's salary, which was low compared to what he would have been earning as a corporate lawyer, was supplemented by investments he'd made while still a partner at Goodstein & Carney. Nevertheless, there was obviously a huge financial disparity between them. It was an issue they couldn't ignore forever.

"But I hate the whole idea of beginning our marriage by talking about the possibility of divorce," she protested, looking up from the crossword puzzle, her green eyes filled with reproach. "I don't need to be protected by a legal document. I trust you. You're not a fortune hunter."

"It's as much for my protection as yours," he said. "Some of the cases I hear involve major corporations. I need it in writing that I have no legal rights to your money, and that I have nothing to do with the investments made on your behalf by your trust."

"But I don't even know how my money's invested," she said.

He looked shocked. "Don't you read their statements?"

She shook her head. "There are no statements."

"They have to send you quarterly reports, information about their investments, something. . . ."

His voice trailed off as she continued to shake her head. "It's a blind trust."

"Come *on*. Nobody except the President has a blind trust."

"I know." She sighed, remembering the day her father had summoned her to his office to discuss the trust he had set up to handle the family's affairs after his death. "My father was very old-fashioned. Money was men's business. He had no use for the women's movement, what he used to call 'those damned women's-libbers.' He certainly wasn't about to let me have the slightest say in how the family's money was invested. God! He could be so damn stubborn!"

Paul put down the newspaper and stared at her. "Do you know the names of the trustees?"

"Of course. They were good friends of my father. Winthrop Harding, Harry Matheson, and George Osburgh."

He was impressed. "Your father chose well. They're highly respected businessmen, all of them."

Relieved that the matter was so easily solved, she tapped her pencil against his arm. "So if it's a blind trust, we don't need a prenup, right?"

"Wrong. Is Harry Matheson your lawyer?"

"Yes."

"I think you should call him first thing tomorrow morning and have him draw up an agreement."

She felt pushed by him—an old, familiar feeling from her childhood that made her all the more resistant to his request. Her father had tried to tell her how to run her life. Did Paul think he could succeed where Sanford Scott had failed? Was she now, only days before their wedding, about to discover that beneath his wholly reasonable exterior lay hidden the soul of a dictator?

Crossing her arms against her chest, she asked, "Did you and Helen have any kind of prenup?"

He smiled, remembering those long-ago days, and shook his head. "When Helen and I got married, we hardly had a bent sou between the two of us. It would have been ridiculous."

He glanced at her and saw her distress. His voice softened as he went on. "Look, this has nothing to do with how we feel about each other. I love you, Hope. I would never want anything to come between us. But as a sitting judge, I want to minimize even the semblance of a conflict of interest. Otherwise, I could be forced to recuse myself from too many cases that would interest me."

She uncrossed her arms, her reluctance slowly giving way to the force of his logic.

"All right," she said crankily. "I'll have them draw up the agreement. But I still don't like it. I don't like it one damn bit."

"I don't like it, either," he said, slipping his arm around her. "But it's a very small price to pay for getting married. And I promise that once it's signed, we'll stick it in a drawer and never have to think about it again."

SIX

$\mathbf{K}$RAFT, WOLCH, MORAD & Hathaway was universally accepted as the most daring and imaginative of the brash midtown Manhattan law firms that specialized in litigating the takeover wars. Ken Wolch, the firm's chief strategist, had devised many of the arcane legal maneuvers that had figured in the bitterly fought cases of the mid-eighties. The firm had represented Jordan Crandell since his earliest sorties on the corporate battleground, and both sides had benefited from the relationship.

Kraft, Wolch charged Crandell astronomical fees for their services. Crandell paid the bills without complaint, secure in the knowledge that he could call on their expertise at any hour of the day or night. Wolch, a blond, curly-haired man in his mid-fifties with a gap-toothed grin and a deceptively mild manner, headed up a team of crack litigators who remained on perpetual standby alert, ever ready to provide service and counsel for their preeminent client.

The news that Lew Valentine had retained Bernard Odette had brought a smile to his lips. Wolch and Odette were old friends and legal adversaries who had gone head-to-head too many times to count in courtrooms across the country—from New York and Wilmington, Delaware, to Chicago and San Francisco. He was looking forward to their next encounter and hoped that Crandell was right about the coming battle.

For the meeting with Eric Lynch at Crandell's headquarters, he was accompanied by his number-two man, Byron Babcock. A product of New England prep schools and Harvard, Babcock was himself a formidable courtroom opponent, with a touch of the gutter fighter about him that Crandell found very reassuring. His presence this morning was more a matter of window dressing than necessity. Ken Wolch could easily handle whatever problems Lynch might raise. But Babcock, who had the fierce eyes of a habitual competitor, was also an avid skier. He spent several weeks each winter out west and could be depended on to talk sports with the eccentric Lynch if there was a lull in the conversation.

Eric Lynch had arrived alone, without a single one of his lawyers or investment counselors. Babcock had raised a questioning eyebrow in Wolch's direction, as if to say, What's with this guy? Was he putting us on? But Wolch and Crandell, who were more familiar with his habits, knew that Lynch had been thoroughly prepped by his people in advance of the meeting. With his remarkably retentive mind, he didn't need to travel with a retinue. Whatever was worth remembering would be duly and accurately reported to all concerned as soon as he returned to Heber City.

After a quick tour of Summit's offices, Crandell brought Lynch over to his private conference room, where they were joined by the two lawyers, along with Warren Breed and Bradley Fisher, as well as Summit's general counsel, Marty Wagner, and its chief financial officer, Jack Borden.

Ken Wolch began by summarizing the major issues of the proposal that Lynch had received some weeks earlier. Then he got down to specifics.

"As you know, Summit is offering to pay sixty-five dollars a share with nine thirty-five of that in cash for each of Starwares' shares outstanding, which I believe are currently trading at fifty dollars.''

Wolch looked over at Breed and Fisher for confirmation of the numbers. The two investment bankers nodded, and Wolch went on. ''As Jordan has already discussed with you, Summit is proposing a merger between our two companies, such that Jordan would be the controlling stockholder of the combined company and you would retain the title of chief executive officer of Starwares.''

As Wolch continued with his presentation, Crandell kept a close watch on Lynch. It was difficult to tell whether he was paying attention, because his gaze kept shifting about the room, moving from the very impressive art that hung on the walls, to the view through the window of the historic cast-iron building across the way, to an area in the middle distance beyond Wolch's head.

He was holding a pen in his hand, but the only use he'd put it to thus far was to draw a series of uneven overlapping circles intersected by arrows that filled up most of a legal pad page. Crandell caught himself wondering whether the circles had a hidden meaning, some kind of computer code perhaps that only Lynch and his closest associates could understand. He quickly dismissed the thought. Lynch's peculiarities were making him paranoid. He had to remember that they both stood to gain from the deal.

Starwares' stock was undervalued at its current price. Valentine had already expressed his interest in the company. If Lynch didn't agree to Summit's terms, Valentine and ten other suitors were bound to come after him. Before Lynch left today, he had to be persuaded that Summit would be the best possible fit for his company.

Wolch finished going over the broad strokes of the plan. ''Any questions, Mr. Lynch?'' he asked.

Lynch nodded. ''Let's keep going, though. I'll save them until you're done.''

Warren Breed took over next to discuss the proposal

on a point-by-point basis, including a review of the financing sources.

Then it was Lynch's turn. He shuffled his papers and leaned forward on his elbows. He ran his fingers through his hair. He chewed on the end of his pen.

Jordan Crandell glared at him, fast losing patience. Lynch was like an unruly schoolboy, daydreaming in class, refusing to take notes, throwing metaphorical spitballs at the teacher. The guy wasn't even dressed properly, for Chrissakes! What kind of self-respecting businessman showed up for an important meeting in a sports jacket, wrinkled pants, and a shirt with fraying cuffs and a stained collar?

"Well, here's how it sounds to me," Lynch said finally. "I'm looking for seventy dollars a share, which means you have a distance to go to meet my price. The money's an important issue, but my far more overriding concern is that I not lose control of my company. I can't be expected to come to you—" he gestured across the table at Crandell—"to get approval for every expenditure or creative decision. And what if you suddenly decide you don't like me? I built this company from scratch. I don't want to wake up one morning to discover that I'm out of a job."

He paused, as if expecting an argument, and stared at Crandell, who smiled grimly. In fact, Crandell was far more interested in Lynch's reaction to his meeting with Lew Valentine than in whatever objections he was raising. Thus far, today, everything was going exactly as he had planned it. But Valentine's offer might be the wild card that could screw up his deal. The key was for Lynch to leave Summit's office today firmly convinced that striking a deal with Lew Valentine would be the worst mistake of his life.

It was time to bring on the dancing girls in the person of Bebe Weiss of *Pastiche,* who'd been asked to join them for lunch and strongly encouraged to discuss with

Lynch the joys of working for a hands-off boss like Jordan Crandell. Normally, Crandell would have reserved a table for the group at one of the nearby restaurants, Il Cortile in Little Italy, Bouley or Chanterelle in TriBeCa. But Eric Lynch was a case unto himself. No doubt about it.

"We can talk about the problems you raised, Eric," he said. "But I'm getting hungry, and this seems like a good time to adjourn for lunch. There are a couple of places nearby that serve overpriced pasta and plates of salad with kinds of lettuce you've never heard of before. Or we could order in some deli sandwiches. What's your preference?"

Eric Lynch smiled for almost the first time that morning. Food was not a subject he gave much thought to. He didn't understand the appeal in slavishly following each new culinary fad or rushing to audition yet another trendy restaurant. When he sat down to a meal, he was looking for nourishment, not a dining experience. Nor was he a connoisseur of fine wines. Usually, he was too preoccupied even to taste what he was eating or drinking. But he did have a weakness for corned beef and pastrami, and good deli was impossible to find in Utah.

"A corned beef on rye would make my day," he said, grinning.

Crandell reminded himself to think about giving Rick Major a raise.

The investigator's report on Lynch was proving to be as accurate as it was thorough. Major had stressed that Lynch was a man of simple tastes, not one to be impressed by fancy restaurants, limousines, or any of the usual perks that Crandell and his colleagues accepted as their executive prerogative. "On infrequent visits to New York, Lynch has been seen at the Carnegie and Stage delis," Major had written. "Associates note his fondness for corned beef."

The assorted overstuffed sandwiches with sides of cole

slaw, pickles, potato salad, and deli mustard had been
ordered from the Stage Delicatessen well in advance of
the meeting. Maintaining the pretense that the choice of
menu was a last-minute decision, Crandell buzzed his
secretary. "Deli sandwiches all around, Donna. Make
sure they send plenty of whatever else comes along and
some sodas."

Then he turned back to Lynch. "A couple of other
people from my staff will be joining us for lunch. When
they heard you were coming by, they expressed an interest in hearing what you had to say about the future of
computers and interactive information exchange."

"I hope I'm not speaking out of school, but Jordan
mentioned that Lew Valentine had also expressed interest
in Starwares," said Ken Wolch.

Lynch nodded. "I met with Mr. Valentine yesterday,
as a matter of fact."

Crandell lit up a cigarette. "Did he try to sell you his
usual bill of goods?" he asked, trying to keep his tone
light.

Lynch shrugged. "He had some interesting things to
say."

"How much do you know about Lew Valentine, Mr.
Lynch?" said Jack Borden.

"What's your point, Mr. Borden?"

"That if you're looking to retain your autonomy, Lew
Valentine is exactly the kind of guy you want to steer
clear of. He may sound convincing, and he's certainly
very good at making promises, but his record speaks for
itself. He's taken a slash-and-burn approach to every
company he's acquired."

Crandell sat back and nodded his agreement. Ken
Wolch caught his eye and smiled. They'd anticipated
most of Eric Lynch's objections and had already worked
out a more generous agreement that seemed likely to
overcome any hurdles he might throw up.

They, too, wanted Lynch to continue running Starwares. What good was the company without him? But Crandell was in no hurry to unveil the revised agreement. The longer he waited to trot it out, the greater his concession would seem to Lynch, who might then be willing to come down somewhat on the price.

Summit would win by appearing to lose, which was, after all, the key to any important negotiation.

THE OSBURGHS LIVED in a nineteenth-century, five-story townhouse in Gramercy Park, formerly the home of a New York mayor who happened to have been a cousin of Connie Osburgh's father. Her parents had bought the house for her and George as a wedding present. Now, with the children all grown and gone, it was far too large for just the two of them. But Connie couldn't bear the thought of leaving the only place she'd lived in as a married woman.

She said so to Paul in a very quiet voice, as if she were sharing a deep secret with him, as she showed him through the formally appointed receiving rooms on the first floor.

"I can understand how you feel," said Paul.

He gazed up at the bas-relief detailing on the fourteen-foot ceilings in the sunroom at the back of the house, which overlooked the rear garden. The house felt like a setting out of an Edith Wharton novel, a trip back in time to another era, to a far different New York. To his uneducated eye, the furnishings looked old and extremely expensive— English antiques and faded Aubusson rugs spread over darkly polished wood floors. The windows were hung with tightly drawn heavy brocade drapes. Very little street noise intruded upon the Osburghs' privacy, as if the drapes provided insulation against the contemporary world which stopped short just outside the Osburghs' front gate.

"I'm very pleased for you and Hope," said Connie Osburgh. "But we could have had a darling little wed-

ding with no trouble at all. It was really very naughty of
Hope not to let us know in advance.''

She had already let Hope know she was rather miffed
that Hope had arranged a wedding without inviting her
and George. She'd long since gotten over her beloved
goddaughter's ill-starred elopement. Hope had been just
a child; she hadn't known any better. But she, Connie,
had been responsible for introducing Paul to Hope, and
Hope had never even told her that they were seeing each
other.

Not to mention that surely, this time, Hope could have
shown some consideration for her family and friends who
were so eager to share in her joy. Surely she should have
understood that a proper church wedding with a lovely
reception afterwards at one of the clubs would have given
them all an occasion to celebrate.

Hope had been given a similar lecture by her aunt
Grace. ''I'm sorry, Aunt Connie,'' she said meekly,
shuddering at the thought of what Grace and Connie
would have had her do in order to get married.

''Ah, well, never mind,'' Connie Osburgh had sighed.
As long as Hope was happy. Paul Murray was a dear,
sweet man. And at Hope's age, she could understand not
wanting to wait too long to get married.

She would do something in their honor in January or
February perhaps. Now, of course, between Thanksgiving and Christmas, it was impossible to get everyone together. But at the very least, she and George had insisted
that the newlyweds come for dinner. George hadn't even
met Paul yet. She was sure they would get on famously.

A warm fire was burning in the living room where
Hope sat chatting with her uncle. George Osburgh stood
up when his wife and Paul reentered the room. ''My dear,
something to drink? Paul? What can I get for you?''

''A martini, George,'' said Mrs. Osburgh. She smiled
at Paul. ''I do like a good martini before dinner. George
has never learned how to mix them properly, but fortunately, we have a houseman who does them just right.''

"I'm not much of a martini drinker," said Paul. "But I'll take a scotch if you have it."

"Scotch it is." George Osburgh poured the drinks and helped himself to a glass of tonic water.

"Has Hope been telling you all about the wedding?" asked Mrs. Osburgh.

Hope moved over so that Paul could sit next to her on the couch. "I thought I'd wait so you could hear about it, too."

"I was just saying to Paul that it was too silly of you not to let us make the wedding for you. We're quite expert at it after marrying off three daughters."

"My aunt Grace would never have forgiven me. Doing it ourselves seemed the best solution."

Connie Osburgh sniffed. "Well, you know how I feel about Grace. . . ." Her voice trailed off as she realized that Paul wasn't yet sufficiently of their crowd to hear such an intimate revelation.

"Shall we have a toast?" asked her husband.

"Yes, of course, dear. What a good idea."

He raised his glass. "Our very best wishes for happiness to you both."

"May your marriage be as filled with love and commitment as ours is," added Connie Osburgh, beaming with pleasure, her little pageboy fairly bobbing.

"Thank you," Hope and Paul murmured in unison.

They clicked glasses all around as the Osburghs' houseman came in with a plate of canapés.

"You must try some of these, Paul," insisted Connie Osburgh. "Perhaps Hope told you that I'm famous for my canapés."

Hope had warned Paul about her godmother's sawdust hors d'oeuvres, which were inevitably offered along with the drinks. The best thing to do was to take a couple and swallow them quickly, she'd said.

"Now you promised you'd tell us about the wedding," Connie Osburgh reminded Hope. "Who officiated? Anyone we know? What did you wear? Did you have any kind of a honeymoon?''

"Oh, Aunt Connie, Uncle George doesn't want to hear about this," said Hope, taking one of the proffered deviled eggs and melted cheese bits.

"That's quite all right, Hope," said George Osburgh. "I'm used to girl talk. Why don't you and Connie visit for a bit, while your husband and I get acquainted? All right with you, Paul?''

"Of course, sir." Paul caught the mischievous gleam in Hope's eye as he followed George Osburgh to the twin armchairs placed on either side of the bay window at the far end of the living room. She had predicted that as her father's oldest friend and trustee of his estate, George Osburgh might well feel an obligation to behave *in loco parentis* and take him aside for a private talk.

"Isn't it a little late to inquire after my intentions?" Paul had asked her.

Hope had smiled. "Better late than never, I suppose. I suspect Harry Matheson told him you signed an agreement, which should reassure him. But he'll want to make sure you're one of us." She had giggled then and said, "Thank God, you're not. That's one of the reasons I love you. But I would never say so to Uncle George."

"Another scotch?" the older man asked him now.

"No, thanks." He knew it behooved him to make a good impression on George Osburgh, and Hope had said that Osburgh only rarely drank. Though he wouldn't have minded a second, Paul decided he would do better to decline.

"I hear good things about you," Osburgh said. "My wife speaks well of you, but more importantly, so do some of my business associates."

"Thank you, sir. I know my decisions aren't always popular in the business community, but I do my best to be fair."

"So I'm told." Osburgh chuckled. "I may as well admit that I checked up on you."

Paul smiled. "I expected as much."

"Hope's a wonderful girl. She and her father didn't always see eye to eye, but he loved her very much. He entrusted me with her well-being. I just want what's best for her."

"I wish I'd had an opportunity to meet Mr. Scott. Hope's told me a lot about him. It's a loss for me not to have known either of her parents."

"Tell me about your family," said Osburgh.

Paul guessed that although George Osburgh already knew a great deal about his family, he wanted to hear Paul's description of them. The Murrays weren't old New York stock, but he was proud of them, and he had nothing to hide.

"I grew up in Brooklyn. My parents were working-class Irish immigrants, and we didn't have much money. But they were determined that we would succeed. They pushed us all to get an education, to get ahead, to move up in the world. Unfortunately, they're both dead, but I'm still close to my sisters and brother." Paul grinned. "They haven't met Hope yet. My sisters are all vying for the privilege of throwing us a party."

"Are you the only lawyer?"

Paul shook his head. "One of my sisters is an assistant district attorney on Long Island, and another one works for a law firm in Manhattan. Numbers three and four are a teacher and a full-time mom. My brother has his own security consulting firm in Connecticut."

"Not a cop in the lot." Osburgh chuckled.

"The old Irish connection? In fact, my brother was a cop for several years, but the pressure gave him ulcers. He took early retirement and went into business."

"What about you, Paul?" asked Osburgh. "Where do you see yourself five years from now?"

Paul glanced across the room at Hope. He wished he could catch her eye, so she could rescue him from what was beginning to feel more like a job interview than a friendly get-acquainted chat. But she was deep in conversation with Connie Osburgh, who appeared to be listening raptly to Hope's account of their wedding.

"Five years from now I'll have three more years to go on my judge's term," he replied. "I'll be teaching a course at NYU next semester. If I like it enough, maybe I'll start doing that on a regular basis, as well."

George Osburgh downed the rest of his tonic water and signaled the houseman, who was standing at a discreet distance by the door, to bring him another. "No higher aspirations than those? I'd have thought a man of your considerable talents might at least see himself serving on the Court of Appeals."

He paused while the houseman brought him his drink, then waited for the man to move away. "In fact," he said, "from what I understand, you could be in the running for a federal judgeship. Is that something that would interest you?"

An appointment to the federal bench was one of Paul's great ambitions, but he rarely gave it much thought. Such a judicial plum had to be earned, and he didn't feel he'd sufficiently been in the public eye or presided over enough high-profile cases to warrant being chosen for the job. It was kind of George Osburgh to suggest the possibility, but he had to be misinformed.

"I'd consider that an enormous honor, but it's too soon," he began. "Perhaps by the time I finish serving my term—"

"Nonsense!" scoffed Osburgh. "You've already served . . . what, six years?"

Paul nodded.

"Why wait another eight? You're already fairly well known and highly thought of in the right circles. Marrying into the Scott family certainly hasn't hurt your cause. Or had you not given that any thought?"

He peered at Paul over the top of his glass, as if daring him to deny that he'd considered the professional benefits to be gained from his marriage.

Paul was well aware that the world into which Hope had been born was as fraught with customs, intrigues, and suspicions as a medieval English court. Like a knight of old, he would have to pass certain tests before being deemed worthy of his lady's hand. George Osburgh had thrown down the gauntlet. Ritual demanded that he take up the challenge.

"With all due respect, sir, I won't pretend I don't know the value of having the right connections," he said, choosing his words carefully. "I've worked hard to make my name known among the right people in order to get where I am today. But the one and only reason I married Hope is because we love each other. Beyond sharing a wonderful life together, I have no expectations."

His response was met with several moments of silence as George Osburgh stared frostily at him. Then his expression softened. Paul guessed that he'd passed the first and most difficult test.

"You'll do fine, Paul. I'm pleased with Hope's choice," he said. "Who knows what else the future holds in store for you?"

ERIC LYNCH SWIVELED his chair and gazed out his office window. Thick grayish-white stormclouds hung low in the sky, promising soon to deliver the snow that was already falling at the top of the mountains just to the west. The forecast was calling for two to three inches in Heber City, six to eight at the higher elevations. With any luck, in another few days the slopes would be packed with enough snow for skiing.

It would have been great to get out there this afternoon for a couple of runs down the mountain. Normally calm, today he was feeling the strain of the ongoing negotiations with Jordan Crandell. Despite following his regular daily exercise routine of swimming laps and working out in his home gym, he felt tense and jittery. Wheeling and dealing held no excitement for him. He wanted matters settled so he could get back to work.

He fiddled with the winter landscape paperweight a friend had brought back from Switzerland, thinking that the meetings in New York had been very instructive. Possibly there were other companies—more desirable, more suitable—that might be interested in allying themselves with Starwares. But they remained to be heard from, and he wanted to move quickly, before he lost even more ground in his race to the top.

No marriage was ideal, but it was better than living alone, his mother had told him over the Thanksgiving holiday. She'd been speaking literally, urging him to find the right woman to share his life. But she could have been talking as well about a business relationship. Jordan Crandell was far from the ideal mate, but compared to Lew Valentine, he seemed to be the lesser of two evils.

Valentine had been every bit as arrogant and pretentious and crude as Lynch had expected. He had bragged about his private fleet of ten corporate jets, his private collection of Ming vases (paid for out of corporate funds), and his recently renovated offices. He'd even gone so far as to quote the prices on some of the French and English antiques that had been purchased for the headquarters at a cost of twenty to forty thousand dollars apiece.

For lunch, Valentine had taken him to Le Cirque, where the entrées began at $29.00. Lynch had stared in disgust at the menu. What a waste of money that could have gone instead into new product development. In between bites of a wild partridge and red cabbage confit, Valentine had tried and failed to refute his reputation for dismantling or downsizing almost every company he'd acquired. He'd offered no new information, no surprises. The only good thing to have come out of their meeting was that it had given Lynch a bargaining chip to throw down onto Crandell's table.

The chip seemed to have served its purpose. Crandell had begun to sweeten his offer almost as soon as Lynch had listed his objections. He'd continued to move the offer closer to acceptable over the course of their negotiations.

Eventually, he had agreed to give Lynch a fifteen-year management contract that guaranteed him the right to continue as Starwares' CEO. The contract also included a golden parachute clause, in the event that his contract was terminated, that was worth six times his future salary plus a commitment to pay any adverse tax consequences. Yesterday, Crandell had finally conceded Lynch the right, under certain conditions, to buy back 100 percent of the company.

The revised proposal addressed his concerns about maintaining control and offered close to everything Lynch and his board had wanted. All that remained to be resolved was the issue of price. Summit had raised its bid by three dollars a share, to sixty-eight dollars. But that was still two dollars short of what he was looking for.

They'd been dickering back and forth for days now. Several of his directors had suggested he take the sixty-eight dollars. They were concerned that Crandell would get fed up and walk away. Lynch thought otherwise. He sensed the force of Crandell's appetite for this takeover. He was like a hungry man, stretching out his arm for the plate of food just beyond his reach.

The question was, could he trust Crandell? He still didn't know. But he thought he could work with him. That was a beginning.

"Yo, Eric!" Bruce Einhorn, Starwares' chief comptroller, strolled into the office and leaned against the doorjamb. "Are you ready to hear some good news?"

Lynch took a deep breath, trying to contain his excitement. "Give it to me."

Einhorn, an ex-hippy with a ponytail and two earrings, flashed him a thumbs-up signal. "Crandell came up with seventy on the nose. I was sweating plenty at the end, but you were right about him. I talked tough, and he finally caved in."

Lynch triumphantly pumped his fist in the air. "I had a feeling he'd come through for us. He knows that even at seventy, we're still a bargain." He grinned at Einhorn, whom he'd met long ago at a math camp where Bruce, six years his senior, had been one of his counselors. "Congratulations. This is going to be great!"

"Not so fast," cautioned Einhorn. "We have to talk to the board, and the investment banking boys have to perform due diligence."

"I don't see any problem there, do you?"

Einhorn shook his head. "We've already examined Crandell's financing. It all checks out. He's a solid citizen."

Lynch grinned again. "A solid citizen with a hankering for a computer company. Seventy a share . . . I like it. I like it a *lot.*"

"So will our shareholders," said Einhorn, smiling. "I see nothing but smooth sailing from here on in."

"I think I'll give Crandell a call to offer my congratulations," Lynch said, reaching for the phone.

"Sounds good." Einhorn threw him a jaunty salute. "I'll catch you later."

"Right." Lynch speed-dialed Crandell's private number. The now-familiar voice of Crandell's secretary Donna came on the line.

"Hello, Mr. Lynch. He'll be right with you."

"Eric! Good to hear from you," boomed Crandell a second later. "Congratulations. You got yourself one hell of a deal."

"You got yourself one hell of a company," said Lynch.

Crandell laughed. "Well, I always say that you don't have a good deal unless both parties walk away winners. When's your board meeting?"

"Next Tuesday. I don't foresee any difficulties. If I'm happy, they're happy. We can issue a press release as soon as we get approval."

Crandell chuckled. "My friend Lew Valentine's going to have a coronary when he hears about this."

"I guess he's gonna be pretty pissed off." Lynch turned the paperweight upside down and watched a flurry of tiny white flakes blanket the painted Alpine village. "I told him we weren't for sale."

"You're not. This isn't a sale. It's a long-term strategic alliance that's necessary for both of us to keep up with the competition."

"That sounds good, but do you think Valentine's going to buy such semantic distinctions?"

"Probably not. Even before you went to see him in New York, he'd hired himself one of the biggest legal cannons around, a heavy hitter out of Detroit named Bernard Odette. The guy's armed and dangerous."

Lynch wasn't worried. "We can handle them," he said confidently. "My lawyers already started drawing up the merger agreement we discussed, including the amendment to the poison-pill clause."

"Excellent." Crandell was momentarily silent. Lynch could hear him puffing on his cigarette. Then he said, "I'm curious about something. In one of our conversations, you mentioned that you had personal reasons for not wanting to get involved with Lew Valentine."

Lynch glanced outside again. The snow was beginning to come down now, thick wet flakes that were sticking to the sidewalks and road. He closed his eyes and imagined himself soaring down the side of a mountain, surrounded by silence and an endless field of pure white snow. There were few experiences that matched that thrill. Sex, maybe. Solving a particularly stubborn coding problem. Putting to rest a very old grudge.

"Years ago," he said, "when I was in high school, I got a part-time job at an Electrical Outlet store in Providence. They gave employee discounts on most of their merchandise, and I had my heart set on buying my own stereo system. My second week there, who should walk

into the store but Lew Valentine himself. I was waiting
on a customer . . . an older woman, recently widowed.
You know the type?''

"Oh, sure," said Crandell.

"She kept asking me the dumbest questions about a
TV set she was thinking of buying. Did the remote control really work? Would she need a new antenna? Did I
think she would prefer an extra-large screen? I mean,
how the hell was I supposed to know what she'd prefer?
But I figured she was lonely and just wanted someone to
talk to, so I tried to be as polite as possible and answer
her questions. Meanwhile, Valentine's standing a few
feet away, openly eavesdropping, and I'm pretty nervous,
because he's the boss's son, and I'm so new on the job.
But hey, it says in the employee manual that the customer's always right, service is everything, and I'm trying to
give this woman good service, right?''

"Of course," Crandell said.

"Finally, she leaves, without buying the goddamn tel-
evison set. Valentine points his finger at me. 'You,' he
says. 'Come over here. I was watching you just now . . . ,'
as if I didn't know. But I figure, okay, here comes the pat
on the back. Then he says, 'You spent too long with her.
Any idiot could have figured out she wasn't a serious
buyer. You're wasting my time and money.' ''

Lynch paused, feeling his rage and humiliation as if
the incident had occurred only yesterday.

"Then what happened?" asked Crandell.

"Then he fired me."

"You're kidding!"

"He goddamned fired me," said Lynch. "I hated the
guy then, and I still hate him today."

"Let me get this straight. You're saying that you blew
off Valentine because of something that happened twenty
years ago?''

"I blew him off because he's a scumbag who spends
billions of dollars to buy a company, then pillages his

newly acquired assets to help pay off his debts. He has
no more idea how to treat a partner than he does a customer. One thing you should know about me. I have a
long memory, and I don't forgive easily.''

"I'll remember that, Eric," said Crandell.

"Good," said Lynch. "Because so far, it's a pleasure
doing business with you, Jordan."

AT HIGH NOON, Lew Valentine was alone in the middle of
a Kenyan jungle, armed with a Holland and Holland royal
rifle and a custom-made Loveless hunting knife. Since
well before sunrise, he had been stalking the huge and
majestic lion that now stood sniffing the air just thirty
yards away from him. This particular animal was a legend among the Kenyan hunters and scouts who roamed
the territory. No human being could capture or kill it,
they said. This lion was too clever, too elusive, too powerful ever to be tracked or brought down.

Lew Valentine knew he could do what no other man
had succeeded in doing. He had found the lion. Now he
would kill it. He raised his rifle, took silent and painstak-
ing aim. The lion, sensing movement, turned its head in
his direction and growled. Valentine's heart was hammering at an unnatural rate. He could feel the rush of
adrenaline coursing through his body.

He tightened his finger around the trigger. In another
moment, the lion would be dead.

A bell shrieked. As if in slow motion, the lion leaped
into the air, ready to pounce at his throat.

Valentine screamed. He bolted awake, his heart pounding so fast he had to gasp to catch his breath. The phone
next to his bed shrilled again, the shrieking bell from his
dream.

"What the fuck?" he groaned, struggling to sit up
against the pillows.

"Lew?" His wife, curled up at the far end of their
super king-sized bed, murmured in her sleep. "The
phone. . . .''

"I got it, I got it," he muttered and grabbed the receiver.

Calmer now that he was awake, he glanced at his clock and saw that it was 5:30 A.M. Jesus! Who the hell was calling him at this hour?

"Yeah? Hello?" he growled.

"Mr. Valentine?" It was a man's voice, not immediately recognizable.

"Who is this?" Valentine demanded.

"Mr. Valentine, I'm sorry if I woke you up. It's Kurt Zelmanski from *The Wall Street Journal*. I don't know if you remember but I interviewed you some time back and—"

"I remember you, Zelmanski. Why the hell are you calling me in the middle of the night?"

"I'm at my office, Mr. Valentine. I just heard that Jordan Crandell is about to become Starwares' majority stockholder. I wondered if you'd care to comment."

"Bull-fucking shit!"

"Is that your comment, Mr. Valentine? Can I quote you?"

Valentine's wife turned and glared at him. "Lew! Watch your mouth! I'm trying to get some sleep here!"

"No, you can't quote me!" Valentine hissed into the phone. "Hold it a second."

He threw back the covers, hurried next door to his study, and shut the door. "You're misinformed, Zelmanski. Eric Lynch told me himself that Starwares wasn't for sale," he snapped.

"When was that?" asked Zelmanski. "Was it in the context of any discussions you were having about a possible merger with Starwares?"

"Never mind about that. Tell me what you know."

"Starwares' board approved the merger as of six o'clock last night. The press releases are going out this morning. What's your next move? Will you be making an offer for Starwares yourself?"

Valentine noticed that the skin around his thumbnail was raw and bleeding from having been picked at. Though Crandell's move wasn't altogether unexpected, he should have been more prepared. He'd been caught with his pants down, and he didn't like the feeling one bit. He was furious with himself. He was even angrier with Lynch and Crandell.

He'd know the whole story in a couple of hours, but in the meantime, he wanted to get as much as he could out of the reporter. "What else do you know, Zelmanski? Tell me something interesting, and I'll give you a quote you can splash across the front page."

Zelmanski laughed. "Fair enough. I hear that Lynch turned out to be a much tougher negotiator than anyone would have guessed. Crandell's paying through the nose. Seventy dollars a share."

Valentine quickly calculated his projected numbers. He could have gone—was prepared to go—higher. There'd been some vague whisperings that Crandell had overextended himself last year when he'd bought into one of the baseball expansion teams, that he'd lost money on a joint venture with AT&T. He might not have as much room to play as was commonly perceived. As he himself could.

"Here's something for you to think about," he told Zelmanski. "Crandell's financing."

"What about it?"

"Where's it coming from? How is it structured? How high can he go if another player enters the field?"

"Are you that other player? And are you implying he could have a problem?" Zelmanski's eager tone betrayed his excitement.

"You can quote me on this, Zelmanski," Valentine said. "At seventy dollars a share, Jordan Crandell is leaving himself wide open for a serious bidding war. As far as I can see, this is in no way a done deal."

"That's it?" Zelmanski sounded disappointed.

"Call my secretary after eight-thirty. She'll put you in touch with my attorney, Bernard Odette."

Zelmanski whistled. "Odette, huh? This is going to be more fun than I thought."

"For you, maybe. But not for Jordan Crandell." Valentine yawned. He needed a cup of coffee, and his personal trainer was due to show up in less than an hour. "I'd tell you to phone anytime, but you've already taken that liberty. Keep in touch. And call Odette."

"Count on it," said Zelmanski. "Thanks, and enjoy your day."

The line went dead.

"Fuck you," said Valentine. He yawned again, at the same moment that the timer on his one-cup coffee machine clicked on. He grabbed the milk out of the refrigerator next to his desk and punched in Odette's Michigan number. Waiting for Odette to pick up, he suddenly remembered a fragment of a dream. Something about hunting a lion.

The closest he'd ever come to seeing a lion was on the photography safari he'd taken two summers ago. The guide had mentioned the possibility, but no lion had ever materialized.

The phone was answered on the third ring. "Odette speaking."

"You're up," he said.

"Of course I'm up. It's nearly six o'clock."

"Starwares is going to announce a merger with Summit this morning. I want to move fast. I'm sending one of my planes to get you. My secretary will be in touch as soon as she has the flight information. Call me from the plane."

"Right," said Odette and hung up.

The coffee had just finished brewing. Valentine poured a cup, added milk, and glanced at his daybook. The date at the top of the page caught his eye, and then he remembered. It was his father's birthday. Good old Lionel. He would have been eighty-one today. Or was it eighty-two? He couldn't remember anymore.

Gulping down the coffee, he thought about what a bastard his old man had been. Tight-fisted, critical, close-minded. They'd argued endlessly about expanding the business, and plenty of times Lionel Valentine had pissed him off so badly, he'd felt like killing the guy.

But he had to hand it to Pop. He'd taught him a lot about how to run a company. "It's a jungle out there," he used to say. "You got to hunt down your competition, then go for the jugular. Kill the sons-of-bitches before they kill you."

Happy birthday, Pop, he thought. *I sure hope you're paying attention, because those sons of bitches are about to get their fucking heads blown off.*

THE DOOR TO Bernard Odette's Trump Tower apartment swung open even before Kurt Zelmanski had a chance to ring the bell. Standing in wait for him was a plain-faced, solidly built young woman. She briefly scrutinized him, then flashed a smile that made her look almost pretty.

"Mr. Zelmanski? C'mon in. Mr. Odette's on the phone, but he'll be with you in a couple of minutes," said the woman, who could have passed for one of his cousins.

He peered at her, liking what he saw. "Kurt Zelmanski," he said, shaking her hand and following her inside. "And you?"

She grinned again. "A fellow 'ski,' huh? Catherine Riznicki's the name, but everyone calls me Rizzy."

Zelmanski glanced around Bernard Odette's New York base of operations and whistled. The place was done up all in bronze, marble, and velour. It was overpowering, to say the least, and far more sumptuous than what he would have imagined for a temporary war room, even if the commanding general was the Michigan Assassin, leading Lew Valentine's troops into battle.

He glanced at the partial view of the East River and Queens and ran his hand across the surface of the gleaming mahogany coffee table. "Jesus! This guy sure knows how to live. What's a nice Polish girl like you doing in a joint like this?"

"It's just a humble law office. We defend the poor and downtrodden capitalistic classes. My boss sleeps on a cot in a dingy back room."

"And I'm the last king of Tasmania," he said. He took a quick glance at her hands and saw that they were bare of rings. A good sign. "Where's the living legend? I have an appointment."

She pretended to scratch her head. "Who is it you work for again? The *Enquirer*?"

"May God strike you dead for that. I'm one of the principal writers for *The Wall Street Journal.*"

"You're too young," she said.

His youthful features fooled them every time. "Older than you, child," he said, guessing that she couldn't be more than twenty-five. "Although I admit to only thirty-eight fun-filled years."

"And probably a houseful of little Zelmanskis, I bet."

Was she digging for information or just making conversation? "My, aren't you the nosy one? But to satisfy your curiosity, I am single and with no children that I know of. Are you interested in my body, by any chance?"

She burst out laughing, and he was hooked. "Are you rich, Kurt?" she asked.

"No," he said mournfully. "Not on my reporter's salary."

"Then I'm not interested." The phone rang. She picked it up, said "Yes?" then, "Okay, I'll bring him right in."

She crooked her finger. "Let me introduce you to someone who is rich."

"Too bad you're not interested," he said, admiring her

from the back as he followed her down a long, marble-floored hallway. "You have a nice strong body, good for plowing and making babies. You'd be the queen of Cracow, you know that?"

"My knees are suddenly weak from such romantic talk," she said, glancing at him over her shoulder.

She led him into the first large room off the hallway, which he guessed usually functioned as a bedroom but had been turned into Bernard Odette's plushly furnished office. The Michigan Assassin was smoking a cigarette and talking on the phone at what had to be one of the biggest desks he had ever seen.

"I want that yesterday," Odette was saying as they came in. Then he slammed down the receiver and extended his hand.

"This is Kurt Zelmanski," said Rizzy. "Watch him. He claims to be Polish."

"Sit down, Mr. Zelmanski," said Odette, pointing him to a chair.

"Kurt, please," he said.

"Okay, Kurt it is."

"Would a tape recorder inhibit you?" he asked. "It bothers some people."

Odette shook his head. "No problem. But I assume you'll shut it off if I want to say something off the record."

His response was voiced as a command rather than a question.

"Sure," Zelmanski agreed.

"Join us," Odette said to Rizzy. "You might learn something, and you can make sure the little machine is off when he says it is."

Zelmanski laughed. "You're not the trusting type, obviously."

"Not in this business," said Odette. "Now, what can I do for you and *The Wall Street Journal*?"

He turned on his tape recorder and set it on the table

between them. "You know that I spoke to Lew Valentine yesterday morning."

"Very *early* yesterday morning, as I understand."

"I thought he should be the first to know about Starwares and Summit."

Out of the corner of his eye, he saw Rizzy struggling to suppress a grin.

"How considerate of you," Odette said dryly. "I assume you read their press releases yesterday."

"Oh, sure. All that talk about the deal being an 'irrevocable marriage' that could not be 'torn asunder.' What do you make of it?"

Odette rolled his eyes. "What a crock. You'd think they might have hired themselves a savvier public relations firm. I could have found them someone in Detroit for a quarter what they're probably paying those crooks." He stopped to light a cigarette with a gold, engraved lighter. "But that's not what you came to discuss with me. Speaking substantively, I'd say that Mr. Crandell and Mr. Lynch won't be celebrating any anniversaries together. That's one so-called happily married couple that better start thinking annulment."

"Mr. Valentine implied that maybe Jordan Crandell's financing wasn't what it should be," said Zelmanski.

Odette pointed to the tape recorder. "Turn that off."

Rizzy leaned over to check that he had complied. Odette waited until she said, "It's off." Then he asked, "What exactly did Mr. Valentine tell you?"

Early in his career as a journalist, Zelmanski had learned to pay close attention not only to what an interviewee said, but also to his or her facial expressions. A twitch of the eye, a frown, a pulsing vein in the forehead, an upturned lip could reveal much about what the person was thinking or feeling.

Odette's face disclosed nothing, however. His expression remained even and calm. Nevertheless, he sensed a change in the atmosphere. Had he told Odette something he didn't yet know? Far more likely, Valentine had spoken out of turn, and the financing issue was a key point in his defense strategy that Odette wasn't ready to disclose.

"He didn't say much, except to raise some questions that he thought might be worth my considering."

"No doubt they were interesting questions, well worth pursuing." Odette brushed an almost invisible piece of lint off his trouser leg. "By both of us. More than that I'm not prepared to say at the moment. Do I make myself clear?"

"Is that for attribution?"

"Absolutely not." Odette chuckled. "I'll sue your goddamn ass if you quote me directly. But I'm not worried. I think you're smart enough to know you'll get a lot more out of me down the line if you dig for your own dirt instead of asking me to spoonfeed it to you. I liked what you did last year with that story about the phony securities profits scheme."

Zelmanski was flattered that Odette had matched the story to his name. "Yeah, thanks, I had a good time with that one."

"Believe me, you'll have an even better time with this if you don't jump the gun."

Zelmanski nodded. He got the point. "Can we turn the machine back on?"

"Yes," Odette said. "Now, for the record, what is it exactly you want to know?"

"Did Lew Valentine have any discussions with or make any overtures to Eric Lynch prior to the announcement of his merger with Summit?"

"As a matter of fact, Mr. Lynch did meet with Mr. Valentine in New York toward the end of November to explore such a possibility. Mr. Valentine had judged their meeting to be very positive and hopeful, so he was shocked and dismayed when Mr. Lynch subsequently phoned him from Utah to say that Starwares was not for sale."

"You were hired by Valentine in October, weren't you?"

"Yes, that's right."

"You're a heavy hitter. Was Valentine preparing for a tough fight even in advance of his meeting?"

Odette again motioned for him to turn off the tape recorder. Then he said, "You know the answer to that. You were the one who told Valentine about Crandell's trip to Utah in the first place. Listen, Kurt, I'm a busy man, and I assume you are, too. So let's not waste any more of our time. Ask me something you don't already know."

The Michigan Assassin was living up to his reputation. Zelmanski nodded his assent and resumed taping.

"With all due respect, won't Valentine be somewhat disadvantaged because you may not be as familiar as the opposition's attorneys with the New York courts?"

"Rizzy," said Odette, "take a good look at this young man."

"Yes?"

"He appears to be bright and well informed, does he not? Yet it turns out he's a total idiot."

Rizzy gazed solemn-faced at Zelmanski. "You think so, boss?"

"How else to understand such a question?"

She shook her head. "It's truly puzzling."

"Hey, it's a fair question," Zelmanski objected. "I know you've tried a few cases in New York, but it's not your regular stomping grounds."

Odette exhaled a mouthful of smoke. "I could argue and win a case on Mars if I had to, make no mistake about that. But in terms of jurisdiction, we'll probably file whatever motions are necessary in Federal Court. That would eliminate any so-called edge the local boys might have over me. Now, I presume you need a good quote to hang your speculations on, right?"

"Blunt and insulting, but true enough."

"Okay, listen up. This confrontation is more than just

another takeover battle. Jordan Crandell is a thief who
thinks he can get away with corporate murder. If he wins
this battle, the whole concept of business ethics will be
as obsolete as buggy whips.''

Zelmanski was about to ask him why he thought Jordan Crandell was any worse a crook than his client, but
before he had the chance, Odette looked at his watch.
"I'm sorry," he said. "I wish I had more time, but I
have a conference call scheduled in two minutes. If you
want another interview, just get in touch with Rizzy, or
we can do it by phone."

"Thanks, I'll do that," Zelmanski said.

"I'll show you out," said Rizzy.

He waited until they got to the door. Then he said,
"He's an interesting guy, your boss. But I'm even more
interesting. We really should get better acquainted. I bet
we have a lot in common."

Rizzy put one hand on her hip. "Are you asking me
for a date?"

"I knew you were a smart girl the minute I laid eyes
on you."

"That's smart *woman*, Mr. *Wall Street Journal*, and
you better believe it. So, are you angling for an inside
source?"

"Nope," he said cheerfully. "How about dinner, tomorrow night? I know a place in the East Village that
makes an outstanding potato pirogen."

"*I* make an outstanding potato pirogen," she said.
"Make it Indian and you're on."

"Indian it is. I'll call you tomorrow," he said and
walked away whistling.

Could be that Santa Claus was coming early this year.

SEVEN

Hope smiled a greeting at Jordan Crandell as he made his way toward the table he'd reserved for them at La Grenouille. He waved at her, then stopped to chat with four men, who were all similarly dressed in pin-striped suits, rep ties, and red suspenders. Another man hurried over to shake his hand. Jordan Crandell was a star. People wanted to know him. Do business with him. Be seen with him. Be him.

A tabloid gossip columnist was sitting a few tables away. Hope watched him watching Jordan, to see whom Crandell was joining for lunch so that he could drop their names in his next day's column. She saw him smile with satisfaction as Jordan approached. Earlier, the columnist had been eyeing her speculatively. Today was obviously his lucky day. Jordan Crandell tête-à-têting with the newly-wed Hope Scott Murray was a hot little item, rife with potential for speculation and innuendo.

"Sorry I'm late, Hope," he said when he finally reached their table.

Hope knew his tardiness was as carefully calculated as his measured progress through the flower-filled room. His tacit message was loud and clear. He'd called her a couple of months ago, just after she'd met Paul, to make a date. Something in his voice had warned her that he might have been suggesting more than an invitation to dinner. As politely as possible, she had put him off, pleading too many commitments just then, but perhaps in a couple of months when her calendar cleared up.

He understood, he'd said brusquely. His schedule was also tight.

She'd sensed his feelings were hurt. Whatever he had become as an adult, quite likely he would never get over being the little kid with the runny nose whom nobody wanted to play with.

Perhaps she should have mentioned Paul then, but it had felt too soon to be talking about him. Most of her life was lived so publicly that she had relished keeping their involvement a secret. Now, of course, their marriage had been featured in all the New York papers. The *Star* and the *Enquirer* had plastered her on their front pages. *People* had covered them in a two-page spread, for which the writer had dredged up all the tired old stories about her family and her youthful escapades.

Accustomed to such coverage, she had been concerned about Paul's family, friends and colleagues. He'd assured her that most of them would be tickled to see him getting so much publicity. Judges had such stodgy images. He didn't mind basking in the reflected glory of her fame.

She wondered whether Jordan had been offended that he'd had to read about their marriage in the newspaper like everyone else. As a wedding gift, he had sent them an exquisite Limoges snuff box in the shape of a heart, which must have cost him a fortune. The accompanying card had read, "Best wishes and much happiness," rather a formal expression, she had thought, to accompany such a sentimental present.

He'd sounded cool at first when she called to make a lunch date, and to offer her congratulations on his latest deal, which was garnering almost daily newspaper attention. She'd guessed that he was hurt, perhaps, strange as it seemed, even jealous. But she knew he'd get over his pique, if indeed that was what he was feeling. He couldn't afford to lose her as a friend. He didn't have very many.

She offered her cheek for a kiss. "Please, don't apologize," she said. "I know how busy you must be. I wish you'd have let me come down to your neighborhood."

"Don't be silly," he declared. "I like coming up to midtown, and I pay my driver extra to make sure we don't get caught in traffic."

Their waiter appeared with menus and a wine list. "Something to drink, sir?"

"Hope?" said Crandell.

She shook her head and pointed to the glass of Chardonnay she had ordered while she was waiting. "I'm fine for now."

"I'll have Glenfiddich, straight up," he told the waiter. "We'll order wine with lunch."

"Oh, Jordan, I don't think I should," she protested. "One glass in the middle of the day is about my limit."

"I insist. This is a celebration. For both of us. But I do have a three-thirty meeting, so let's decide what we're eating and get that out of the way."

The waiter brought Crandell his drink and they ordered: grilled salmon fillet with beurre rouge for her, sweet and sour venison with truffles for him. "Is red all right?" he asked.

She nodded, having already decided that she would drink only one glass.

"We'll have a bottle of the Chambertin," he said.

"An excellent choice, Mr. Crandell." The waiter smiled his approval and left to place their order.

"Well," said Jordan. He raised his glass. "To a long and happy marriage."

They clicked their glasses and sipped their drinks. Then she said, "You deserve a toast, too. To your success with Starwares. Everyone's talking about what a marvelous coup this is for you."

He smiled smugly. "It *is* an excellent opportunity. Lynch is a strange guy, but he's brilliant. I figured him out and snapped him up."

"Is Valentine any real threat to you?"

He flicked his hand, as if waving away the possibility. "Do I look worried? What about you, though? All I know about your new husband is what I read in *People* magazine."

She didn't believe him for an instant. A contributing editor from *Pastiche* had left messages for both Paul and her, requesting interviews for the article she was writing about the two of them. The editor must have done some preliminary research, and Jordan had likely read at least part of her file on Paul. The article might even have been his idea.

"He's a wonderful man. . . ." She shrugged. "I don't know what else to tell you about him."

"You didn't know him very long before you got married, did you?"

"Jordan." She laughed. "You sound as if you're accusing me of some terrible crime. Put it this way. It was enough time for me to be sure that we belong together."

"Sally and I got married six months after our first date. What a disaster that was."

"You were barely old enough to vote when you married Sally," she told him. She picked up her wineglass, saw that it was empty, and took a sip of water instead. "Jordan, you're reminding me awfully of my aunt Grace. Has she put you up to giving me a scolding?"

He gulped down the rest of his scotch. "No, of course not. You couldn't pay me to speak to your aunt Grace. I was just making conversation."

The waiter arrived with the wine. They fell silent as he ceremoniously uncorked it, poured some for Crandell to taste, and presented him with the cork.

Crandell sniffed the bouquet and took a sip. "Good, very good," he pronounced.

The waiter beamed, as if he himself were receiving Jordan Crandell's nod of approval.

"You were saying?" Crandell broke off a piece of roll and looked at her.

The wine was delicious. Drinking it, she finally began to warm up after the frigid eleven-block walk downtown from her apartment. What had she been saying? She couldn't remember.

"How's Rowena?" she asked, trying to decide how and when to bring the conversation around to the real purpose of the lunch.

"She's a gorgeous little pain in the ass, just like Sally. Spends money like her, too. She'll bankrupt me before she even gets through high school." He chuckled at the absurdity of such a notion, then went on, "She's coming home in a couple of days for Christmas, and if I'm lucky she'll hook up with her mother for the rest of the holiday. She's too much for me to handle. Do yourself a favor, Hope."

"What's that?"

"Don't ever have kids. They're too much responsibility, and you don't need the headaches."

She was spared having to come up with an answer by the waiter, returning with their food. He arranged the plates in front of them, then poured them each another glass of wine. "Can I get you anything else, *Monsieur* Crandell?" he asked.

"Not now, André," he said, and turned back to her. "Are you staying in town for Christmas?"

"I think so. Paul usually spends it with his family, so this will give me a chance to meet all of them."

"Irish, aren't they? How quaint, a real Irish Catholic celebration."

"You *have* been talking to Aunt Grace," she said.

"Hell, I'm just kidding. How's the fish?"

"Excellent as always."

She looked around. Though almost every table was

full, the noise level was low, except for an occasional burst of raucous laughter. She knew, or was at least acquainted with, more than a few of the people in the room. Most of them had a similar look about them, a look she recognized when she saw herself in the mirror. They seemed sleek, confident, well cared for. Money was no object. Power was their currency.

"Jordan, I need a bit of advice," she said.

"I'm delighted. Advice is my stock in trade."

"I'm sure you know that Paul is on the State Supreme Court," she began, recalling what George Osburgh had told her the night she and Paul had been to his home for dinner.

Crandell nodded.

"I know he enjoys his work, and of course everyone thinks he's doing a marvelous job."

She stopped, her nerve failing her. Often, in the years since she'd become aware of what it meant to be Hope Scott, she had pulled strings or used her connections to raise money in support of a good cause. But she had never asked for any special favors for herself, nor cultivated friendships because of what that person might be able to do for her.

Now that was about to change. Her uncle George had persuasively explained how helpful she could be to Paul in his career. Paul, Uncle George had pointed out, was so obviously talented that he was bound to advance. That could take time, however, and why should he waste the years when she could easily provide him with a shortcut through the process?

Uncle George's argument made good sense, and she valued his opinions. They disagreed, of course, about politics, and sometimes he could be awfully stuffy and limited in his thinking. But he also understood the waves and currents of professional advancement. And above all, she believed that he had her best interests at heart.

Yet a small inner voice urged caution. She kept recalling Paul's insistence on the prenuptial contract. He was determined that their financial interests be kept separate, so that no one could charge him with conflict of interest or marrying her for her money. Still, this was something she wanted to do . . . could do . . . for her husband. She would swear Jordan to secrecy. He owed her that much.

"Yes?" he prompted her.

She played with the stem of her wineglass, noticing that it was almost empty again. "What would you think of my trying to help Paul get an appointment as a Federal Court judge?"

"Is that something he wants?"

She nodded. "He's mentioned it as a possibility at some point in the future." Suddenly, she felt guilty, discussing her husband behind his back. "He doesn't know I'm talking to you about this. I don't want him to know. Ever."

"No, of *course* not," he murmured understandingly. "Go on."

"Well, is that something you or anyone else we know could perhaps, ah, facilitate?"

"Poor Hope." He laughed. "This is really terribly difficult for you, isn't it?"

"How can you tell?"

"You look so miserable. Listen to me. I get at least thirty calls a day from people who barely know me asking for favors. You and I grew up together. We're practically related. If you can't turn to me, who can you turn to?"

Her head was swimming. Despite her good intentions, she had drunk too much wine. He was right, though. She had known him all her life and had no illusions about his dark side. But she also knew he would never unleash it against her.

"Do you know how a person gets to be a federal judge?" he asked.

"Yes," Hope replied, if a bit tentatively. Uncle George

had explained it to her. "He or she has to be recommended to the President by a senator. The President's appointment is subject to Senate confirmation."

"You've done your homework. I like that," he said approvingly.

"Do you think you could help Paul get a recommendation?"

"It's possible. I believe there are two vacancies right now in the Southern District, which includes Manhattan and the Bronx. One of our illustrious senators was just telling me the other day how grateful he was for my contributions to his campaign. I don't think he'd be averse to a suggestion for the court, especially if the person I'm recommending has an excellent track record."

This was even better than Hope had wished for. She couldn't wait to see the look on Paul's face when he got word that he was under consideration.

She reached over and squeezed his hand. "Jordan, thank you so much. I appreciate whatever you can do. Can we keep this strictly between the two of us?"

"Of course. It's my pleasure, Hope," he said. "You're giving your husband a very wonderful wedding present. I only hope he appreciates it."

THE AMSTERDAM CLUB had been established in 1843 by a well-heeled group of New York bluebloods who traced their lineage back to one of the original thirty Dutch families that had settled New Amsterdam under the auspices of the Dutch West India Company. During the early 1970s, in order to survive the cost of operating such an establishment in Manhattan, the club had been forced to extend eligibility to anyone wealthy enough to afford the substantial one-time initiation fee and equally substantial annual dues.

This was not to say that any old millionaire could buy his way onto the roster. An applicant had to be nominated by no fewer than ten members in good standing, and he could be denied membership if two or more members voted against his admission. George Osburgh belonged, of course, as had his father and grandfather, by dint of having been descended from an original founder. Among his earliest memories was a birthday party for his grandfather that had been held in one of the club's stately private rooms. He felt almost more at ease at the Amsterdam than he did in his own home.

He loved its hushed atmosphere, the utter respect with which each member was treated by the staff, many of whom had worked there for decades. The club was housed in a building on West 11th Street that had been built in 1876 and still retained the gracious charm and dignity of that period. The walls were hung with portraits of the founders, alongside paintings by John Singer Sargent and Thomas Eakins. A double marble staircase dominated the center hallway and spiraled up to a library on the second floor, beyond which was the main sitting room where Osburgh often stopped off after work for a cranberry juice and soda or a pot of tea.

He had suggested that Jordan Crandell meet him at the Amsterdam, rather than at his office, precisely because he knew that the club set a certain tone, one that could prove useful in the discussion he was about to have with Crandell. He also suspected that Crandell, who already belonged to both the Union League and Downtown Athletic clubs, coveted an invitation to join the Amsterdam. As yet, no one had seen fit to submit his name to the membership committee. It would not hurt Osburgh's cause for Crandell to be reminded of what could be his, should they reach a mutually satisfactory arrangement.

He'd arrived early for their meeting, in order to enjoy a cup of his specially stocked Earl Grey tea and a few minutes of peace at the end of what had been an extremely hectic day. The market had been fluctuating all week, with interest rates seeming to be on the way up again. And there were rumblings from the Justice Department of increased antitrust activity that could wreak havoc with some of the takeover deals his firm was currently handling.

At home, Connie was gearing up, as usual, for Christmas: sending out cards to all their friends and relatives; buying gifts; "planning" the Christmas dinner menu, which never changed from one year to the next; inviting the grandchildren over to bake cookies. It was always wonderful to see his daughters and their children, but otherwise he couldn't summon up much enthusiasm for the festivities. He would rather be spending the holiday with his mistress and executive vice president, Nancy Ames.

He sighed, thinking of Nancy. He felt more tired than normal this afternoon; dispirited even, which was unusual. The tea was not having its customary reviving effect. He considered ordering a scotch, then rejected the idea. He needed to keep his wits about him. Jordan Crandell would drive a hard bargain. He couldn't afford to falter or slip up in any way.

Here came Crandell now, briskly crossing the room, rubbing his palms together, as if he were savoring some delicious possibility, or perhaps simply warming them from the chill.

"Goddamn cold out there, isn't it?"

"My wife tells me the *Farmer's Almanac* is predicting a harsh winter," said Osburgh, as the waiter approached.

Crandell ordered a scotch, Osburgh his cranberry cocktail. A bowl of tiny cheese crackers was brought for them to munch on. They exchanged pleasantries until their drinks were delivered and the waiter had left them alone.

Then Crandell said, "I assume you've been tracking my deal."

Osburgh nodded. "Valentine didn't waste any time."

"That was no surprise. We're on top of it. Lynch hates Valentine. He'll fight that bastard for all he's worth."

"What do his directors have to say, now that Valentine's come in with eighty-five dollars a share?'' Osburgh asked the question that had been uppermost in his mind since that morning, when the news had flashed across the Dow Jones ticker in his office.

"Fuck 'em,'' said Crandell. "They're a bunch of pussies. They'll do whatever Lynch wants.''

Osburgh grimaced. He'd never understood why intelligent people had to resort to vulgarities to express themselves. His employees knew better than to use foul language in his presence. But he couldn't very well reprimand Jordan Crandell, so he said only, "I hope you're right. I know a couple of his board members. I'm not sure they're as pliant as you've been led to believe.''

"Never mind about them. Let's talk about us,'' said Crandell, helping himself to a fistful of the cheese crackers. He gulped back the scotch and signaled the waiter to bring him another.

"Well,'' Osburgh began, then interrupted himself as Ken Wolch came into the room and spotted Crandell. "What's *he* doing here?'' he demanded.

Crandell chuckled. "Don't look at me, George. I sure as hell didn't invite him. I guess even Amsterdam Club members occasionally require the services of Kraft, Wolch. He's a damn good lawyer. You ought to get to know him.''

Osburgh bit his tongue and watched Wolch make his way over to them. Ken Wolch was an upstart, a clever corporate ambulance-chaser who'd had to strike out on his own because he hadn't been able to get himself hired by any of the Wall Street firms.

"Ken,'' Crandell was saying now, "I don't think you've met my friend George Osburgh.''

Osburgh flushed. Partner, perhaps. Friend, never. Jordan Crandell's impudence had to be the Lord's punishment for the one stupid mistake of his career that had brought him to this moment.

"George.'' Wolch nodded. "I know you by reputation,

of course. Jordan, call me later at home. I've got a couple of interesting ideas I want to run by you. Good to meet you, George.''

Osburgh hardly bothered to conceal his disdain as Wolch walked away.

"George," said Crandell, laughing again. "Wake up and smell the reality. It's firms like Kraft, Wolch that are winning all the battles these days."

"That doesn't mean I have to like them," Osburgh sneered.

"Sure, have it your way, George. So, as we were saying. . . ." Crandell leaned forward and lowered his voice. "Are you in or out?"

Osburgh sipped the last of his juice and put down the glass. "It's complicated, as you might imagine," he said slowly. "We would need to work out the terms very carefully. I can't have any exposure whatsoever on this thing."

"You and me both, pal."

"You understand that these are rather extraordinary circumstances."

"George," Crandell broke in, "cut the crap. I don't give a rat's ass why you suddenly find yourself short two million dollars. I could make some educated guesses. It must be very frustrating to hold the keys to the Scott strongbox and not be allowed to help yourself to some of the goodies. There's so much to go around. Who's going to miss a million here or there? Certainly not our sweet, trusting little Hope."

It took a supreme act of self-control not to react. Every fiber of his being ached to punch Jordan Crandell in the face. The horror was how close Crandell had veered to the truth.

All through the eighties, Osburgh had watched with a mixture of contempt and envy as the arbitrageurs made millions with their greedy games of risk, betting their hunches on possible takeover bids. Once, at a dinner party, he had been seated across from Ivan Boesky, the most famous of them all. In spite of himself, he had listened, enthralled by the arbitrageur master's tales of his trade.

Sometimes, the arbs lost. More often, they won. All that was required were nerves of steel, a pile of startup money, and a keen sense of the market.

Or a pipeline into a source of inside information.

Most of the arbs knew better than to seek out tips from him. Osburgh & Bartlett was considered a bastion of rectitude among some of the more upstart firms that had provided the financial fuel for the takeover decade. Nevertheless, his acumen was respected, and occasionally the calls had come, delicately probing for hints. He had let the callers know, in no uncertain terms, that he would not abide such attempts to subvert the system.

Then the stormy nineties came roaring around the corner, bringing an end to Reaganomics. The boom towns collapsed under the weight of the recession, the land values plummeted. Yesterday's sure things were today's financial disasters. Even the most astute investors found themselves scrambling to cover their losses.

Osburgh & Bartlett survived unscathed. The Scott Trust experienced not even the slightest tremor. But to George Osburgh's horror, he himself took an enormous hit. A savings and loan in which he had invested heavily went belly up. His balance sheet showed a deficit of four million dollars. He simply couldn't afford to be that deeply in the red.

George didn't know where to turn for help. He had always been an intensely private man, brought up to rely on his own resources to work out his problems. Besides, he dared not confide in even his most trusted confidants, for fear that somehow word might get out that he had lost his touch. That kind of rumor could prove lethal to him and his firm.

The solution presented itself in the form of a feared

hostile takeover, by a British industrialist, of a Michigan-based food products company. The company was represented by the investment firm where one of his son-in-laws worked. The son-in-law, a reticent man who became garrulous to a fault after a couple of drinks, mentioned that his firm was exploring a possible white knight rescue attempt by a much larger food company. ''It's going to be a heck of a battle, but one way or another, they're going to be sold,'' he had said.

Grasping at the information as if it were his lifeline back to solvency, Osburgh quietly borrowed money from the Scott Trust and bought forty thousand shares of the Michigan company's stock through a third-party broker in Chicago. By his highly educated calculations, he estimated that once the merger went through, his profits could go as high as five million dollars—enough to repay his unsanctioned loan from the trust and cover his previous losses.

His relief was short-lived. The white knight lost interest, and the food company decided instead to buy back the Brit raider's stock. The company was taken out of play, and the price of its stock fell below its original market value. George Osburgh woke up one morning to find himself further in debt to the tune of two million dollars. The money had all been borrowed from the Scott Trust.

Alone in his bedroom, he lay awake nights trying to figure out how to extricate himself from near ruin. If he'd been reluctant before to disclose his predicament to anyone, now he was even more determined that nobody must ever know. He lost his appetite and grew noticeably thinner as he worried about the inevitable day that the auditors discovered the discrepancy and traced the missing funds back to him.

During the course of one especially dark night of the soul, after a birthday party for his favorite grandson attended by the entire family, he decided that suicide was the only answer. He would call the doctor, get a prescription for sleeping pills, find out how many he needed to take to achieve the desired effect.

His mind made up, he slept better that night than he had in months. The next day, the first call of the morning came in from Jordan Crandell. He had an idea he wanted to discuss, a way for both of them to make some money, and he wanted to know whether Osburgh was interested.

They'd had several meetings, many conversations. He'd found himself sinking deeper into the muck of Crandell's illicit scheme. He tried to reassure himself that no one would be hurt by their machinations. Indeed, only good could come of it. Nevertheless, now that he was on the verge of sealing his deal with Crandell, the Methodist minister's voice of his maternal grandfather thundered in his head: One wrongdoing begets another, and yet another after that.

He'd never been a quitter, yet now he yearned to flee this room, flee his life and the sordid circumstances in which he was trapped. In a million years, he could not have imagined that he would ever have arrived at such a point. Thank God his father was not alive. The most honorable, upright man he had ever known, his father would have discerned at a glance the shameful stain that lay beneath George's irreproachable facade.

"Spare me your conjecture," he snapped at Crandell. "Why I need that money is my business. All that should concern you is whether we can reach an agreement."

Crandell threw back his head and laughed so loudly that several members turned to glare at such a breach of decorum. Mortified by his guest's ill-bred behavior, Osburgh grimly set his lips and waited for Crandell to explain the source of his amusement.

"Don't you think it's a little late for *whether* we can reach an agreement?" asked Crandell, still chuckling. "I'd say we're already down for the count. I came here to negotiate your fee for lending me a chunk of the Scott Trust change to help fund my Starwares deal."

"Shh!" Osburgh hissed. He glanced around quickly, checking to see if Crandell had been overheard. "Can't you be more discreet?" he demanded sotto voce.

"You're being paranoid, George. Nobody's paying any attention to us," said Crandell. Nevertheless, he lowered his voice. "All right, then, here's what I propose. You lend me a half billion, borrowed short term from Scott. Upon completion of my deal with Starwares, I pay you three million—"

"Three?" Osburgh sputtered. "That's absurd! You'll have to do better than that, Crandell, for what you're asking of me."

Crandell tapped his fingers against the mahogany tabletop. "Give me a number," he said finally.

"Ten million."

"Now *you're* being absurd. I can't go any higher than four and a half."

Osburgh shook his head. "It's not worth my while at that number. I need six at the minimum."

Crandell snapped his fingers. "Six it is," he said.

Osburgh opened his mouth to bid the number higher, then abruptly changed his mind. His grandfather was preaching again in his head, reminding him that greed was one of the seven deadly sins. Six million would allow him to recoup his loss and replenish the Scott coffers. There was no need to profit from his ill-gotten gains.

He nodded his agreement. "Very well. I can live with that. But what if you lose to Valentine? I don't want a contingency basis for my fee."

"Read my lips," Crandell growled. "I'm not going to lose to Valentine. You can take that to the bank along with your six big ones. Now, have you made any progress with Harding and Matheson? Any chance at all they'll agree to lend me the money?"

"No." Osburgh left it at that, preferring not to describe to Crandell the extremely heated discussion he'd had with his fellow trustees when he'd recently raised the

subject again. Harry Matheson had even mentioned the
words "breach of fiduciary trust." He'd not gone so far
as to make any accusations against Osburgh, but he'd
come uncomfortably close.

"It's probably just as well. Anyway, I already figured
out how we're going to do this."

Osburgh frowned. He'd had about as much as he could
take for one day of Jordan Crandell. Besides, Connie was
out for the evening at one of her committee meetings. If
he left now, he might still catch Nancy at the office. They
could go back to her apartment for a quick bite and whatever else might follow.

"I'm sorry," he said. "We'll have to save that for another time. I have another appointment, and if I don't
leave immediately, I'm going to be late. Do you mind?
You can order yourself another drink on my tab, if you'd
like."

"Thanks, I think I'll do that. And just my luck, I see
someone over there I need to talk to."

"Fine." Osburgh reluctantly extended his hand to
shake Crandell's. "I'll hear from you, then."

"You bet," Crandell said cheerfully.

At six o'clock, the room was filling up with bankers,
lawyers, and some of the city's top corporate executives.
Jordan Crandell hailed a waiter, ordered his third scotch,
and sat back to survey the scene. He counted at least
twelve people with whom he socialized or did business
on a regular basis; most of the others he knew by name.
The man he wanted to see—New York's senior senator—
was standing by the door, gladhanding each new person
who entered the library.

Crandell considered walking across the room to say
hello, then decided to wait for the senator to come to him.
It would happen sooner or later, and he was in no great
rush to leave. He slowly sipped his scotch, rolling the
liquid around his tongue, savoring the sharp sting of the
aged alcohol. His lunch the other day with Hope Scott

had left him feeling slightly melancholic. The image of her face, glowing with happiness, kept coming back to haunt him.

He wasn't fool enough to think he was in love with her, but too late he realized he'd taken comfort from her unmarried state. As long as she was single, he could believe he'd have her if and when he wanted. Now, thanks to Paul Murray, that option was closed to him, at least temporarily. He felt the loss as keenly as if he'd actually been wooing her. He should have known she was ripe for the plucking and moved faster.

He was furious with himself for missing the opportunity, angry at Paul Murray, whom he'd yet to meet, for getting there first. She was an asset in any social situation, a beautifully polished gem that by rights belonged to him. He had always admired the way she quietly dominated a room. It was nothing she deliberately said or did that made people flock to her, yet she drew them like a magnet. He should be sharing that force field with her.

Crandell almost laughed aloud, thinking of her in bed with her straitlaced Irish Catholic judge. That couldn't be much fun. Rick Major hadn't yet finished his full-scale investigation of Murray, but so far, according to Major, it seemed the guy had been totally faithful to his wife. Even as a widower, he'd hardly screwed around. Crandell shook his head. What a waste of a man's best years! What a waste of Hope's time.

He'd told Major he wanted the full report on Murray by the end of next week latest. He had no doubt there'd be some dirty secret lurking in a dark, long-forgotten corner of Murray's past. There wasn't a man—or woman—alive who hadn't once done something that was better off forgotten, and he was eager to see what indiscretion Judge Paul Murray kept hidden from the rest of the world.

In the meantime, however, he'd promised Hope he'd get her judge a promotion. What the hell? It was an easy favor, worth his while to call in a chit if it made her happy, and, more important, obligated to him.

He glanced again at the senator, who this time looked his way and nodded, as if to let him know that yes, he'd gotten Crandell's message. A moment later, he was crossing the room, smiling at anyone who met his eye.

"Jordan!" he said, greeting him warmly. "You're looking well."

"Senator," said Crandell. "This is a well-timed surprise. Have a seat."

The senator checked his watch. "Just for a minute. I'm waiting for Hamilton Wilcox. Sorry I didn't get back to you, but I was in committee meetings most of yesterday. What can I do for you?"

Crandell frowned. "One of my lawyer friends mentioned a disturbing fact to me the other day."

"Oh, really?" The senator shifted in his chair, preparing himself for bad news.

"Are there really four vacancies on the federal bench right now? That seems an awful lot, considering that the court calendars are so crowded."

The senator sighed. "It's true, I'm afraid. But I have one of my staff members working up a list of candidates to present to the President."

"Why the delay?"

"You'd be amazed how difficult it is to find qualified people."

"Would you take it amiss if I made a suggestion?"

The senator narrowed his eyes. "Jordan, I'm known for my liberal positions. With all due respect, I couldn't in good conscience recommend any of your antediluvian legal friends."

Crandell chuckled. "Of course not. Your junior colleague will take care of that when the time comes. As a matter of fact, the man I have in mind is practically a card-carrying liberal. For all I know, you two are from the same county, maybe even related."

"Oh?" The senator raised a bushy eyebrow. "You're full of surprises, Jordan. Who is this possible long-lost cousin of mine?"

"Paul Murray. He's a Supreme Court judge, sitting in Manhattan. Used to be a partner at Goodstein & Carney. He's well connected, has an excellent reputation."

"Murray. Why do I know that name?"

"He's newly wed. To Hope Scott."

The senator grinned. "Ah, yes," he said. "Thanks for the tip. I'll see what I can do."

PAUL MURRAY GENTLY put down the phone and stared across his office at his framed law school diploma. Doctor of Jurisprudence, Yale University Law School, class of 1970. The words were spelled out in Latin, printed on the sheepskin parchment in large ornate lettering. It was his mother who had insisted on framing the document, carefully carrying it by train to a store in Boro Park that she usually deemed too expensive. But not this time, not for her Paulie's diploma.

No one, not even Helen, could understand the distance he'd traveled to earn that degree. Two of his sisters had also graduated with honors from law school, one from NYU, the other from Fordham. But he'd been the first, the oldest, the trailblazer. The one who'd carried on his shoulders the weight of all his parents' hopes, dreams, and fantasies for what America could mean for their children.

What a heavy weight that had been. He'd almost forgotten the pushed-down anger and resentment he'd felt all through his youth when his parents had urged him to do better, try harder, be smarter, set an example. Sometimes, he just wanted to be. But that wasn't good enough for the firstborn son of Agnes and John Murray.

They'd been so proud of him. He would always remember the day his father had reversed their roles and asked him for help. He'd done what he could—enough, as it turned out, to solve the problem and set things right again. After that, John Murray had increasingly turned to him for advice, a peculiar changing of positions in a family where his father's word was the unquestioned law.

His mother had died two years after he'd started at Goodstein & Carney, but his father had lived to see him make partner and get elected to the bench. If only he were alive today. He would have been the first person Paul would have called to share the news he'd just received.

Was it too sentimental to think of going out to the cemetery on Sunday to visit their graves? It was almost Christmas, his mother's favorite holiday. Perhaps he'd call Patty, the sister to whom he'd always felt closest, to ask if she would join him.

But first he wanted to call Hope. He dialed their number, trying to think where she might be at this hour. Then she picked up, and his face creased in a smile. He still got excited by the sound of her voice. For the umpteenth time, he marveled at his great luck in meeting such an extraordinary woman.

"Hope," he said, hearing the tension in his tone.

She must have heard it, too, because she said, "What's wrong? You don't sound quite yourself."

"No, nothing's wrong," he quickly reassured her. "But something odd just happened. I got a call from Washington. I'm being recommended as a candidate for the federal bench."

"Oh, Paul! How marvelous!" she exclaimed.

"It's a real honor, a lifetime appointment by the President of the United States. George Osburgh and I were just talking about it when we went to dinner there. But I don't get it. People usually spend years waiting and maneuvering for such an appointment. Now it's mysteriously fallen into my lap like a golden apple."

"It's no mystery to me. You're very talented, everybody says so. And you've done your share of clubhouse politicking."

"Still," he said, "I don't have that kind of clout. Do you suppose your uncle George could have something to do with this?"

"Oh, I don't think so. But what if he did? You deserve this job."

"All judges worry about hidden obligations. You have to. People are always looking to hook you over to their side."

"Paul, what's that cliché? You don't look a gift horse in the mouth. Stop worrying about how or why it happened, and enjoy the honor."

"Okay, you're right." He laughed. "I have to admit, I'm pleased."

"Pleased? You should be thrilled. I'm going to take you to dinner tonight. We have to celebrate."

"Dinner's fine," he said. "But let's wait on the celebration. I've only been recommended. The President does the actual nominating. Then, I suppose, I'll have to appear before the Senate Judiciary Committee, and the full Senate has to confirm me. I'm a long shot. This might never happen."

She tsked into the phone, in an unwitting imitation of his mother. "Darling, don't be such a pessimist. Of course you'll be confirmed. Can we talk later? I have to run to class."

"Of course," he said. "I love you."

"I love you, too."

He replaced the receiver and stared again at his diploma. He tried to picture himself sitting in front of a microphone, responding to senatorial questions, just as he'd seen happen during various televised hearings. Hope would be there with him, lending him moral support and an air of excitement to the hearing. He wondered what they would ask him, how deeply they would delve into his background, who would be his ally, who his opponent.

Then the image changed. He was seated at the bench

in the Federal Courthouse, just down the street from
where he was now. He was wearing a new robe, purchased in honor of his promotion. He tapped his gavel,
signaling that court was in session. Signaling that a
whole new era in his life was about to begin.

EIGHT

HOPE PERMITTED HERSELF a tiny smile of satisfaction as she glanced around her living room. Usually, she preferred to entertain in small groups at a sit-down dinner around her dining-room table. But on this occasion, she and Paul had invited sixty-five guests for a Sunday evening buffet supper, with informal seating at the rented round black granite cocktail tables that were scattered throughout the living room and dining room. The buzz of conversation punctuated by occasional bursts of laughter assured her that on this blustery March night, people were glad to have been invited for the dual celebration of the Murrays' marriage and the confirmation of Paul's Federal Court appointment. The party was an unqualified success.

Low crystal bowls filled with white starburst lilies had been placed on empty surfaces about the apartment, and their delicately sweet fragrance wafted through the air as she moved from room to room. The mood felt festive, thanks in part to the pianist who was playing Cole Porter songs on the Steinway in the living room.

The previous month's Senate hearings had gone quickly and easily. After the confirmation had been announced, so many people had called to offer congratulations and ask when they were going to get to meet the new appointee that Hope had decided to have a party and make the necessary introductions.

Most people had already helped themselves to the cold lobster salad, baby lamb chops, smoked salmon, and grilled vegetables, and were now getting down to the business of socializing. The various disparate groups seemed to be getting along. Jesse Rubin appeared to be charming Connie Osburgh; Yvonna Carter was sharing a joke with Paul's friend Lawrence Amdel, the judge who had performed their marriage ceremony; and Paul's brother, Jimmy, was deep in talk with her aunt Grace, who had flown up specially from Palm Beach for the occasion.

Jimmy, the baby of the Murray family, was a leprechaun lookalike with an upturned nose, crinkly blue eyes, light red wavy hair, and a belly that was starting to show evidence of a few too many beers. According to Paul, he was the spit and image of their father, and his sisters still doted on him, even though he was thirty-four years old, married, and a successful businessman.

She wondered what Jimmy and Aunt Grace could possibly be discussing so intently and then immediately guessed the answer—security systems. Aunt Grace was an absolute maniac about security. No doubt as soon as she'd heard that was Jimmy's field, she'd begun picking his brain, attempting as always to get something for nothing. If Jimmy wasn't careful, he might find himself overhauling Aunt Grace's entire system at a fraction of his usual rate.

"Wonderful party," said Molly Rubin, coming up to give her a quick hug. "Have you eaten anything yet?"

"Thanks, I'm fine." She smiled. "Have you seen Paul?"

Molly pointed down the hall to the library. "He got cornered by Hallie Neuwirth. Shall I go rescue him?"

She shook her head. "Maybe she had some Preservation Society business to discuss. He'll extricate himself if she goes on too long."

"All right, then," said Molly. "I'm going to talk to Winthrop Harding about some of my rental properties."

As Hope made her way into the dining room, checking to see that nobody lacked for anything, she became aware that Jordan Crandell's duel with Lew Valentine for possession of Starwares was a major topic of interest for many of those present.

The contest between the two financial titans had dominated the front pages of both the *Times* and *The Wall Street Journal* since just before Christmas, when Valentine had thrown himself into the fray with a merger bid of eighty dollars a share, ten more than Crandell's offer. A week later, Eric Lynch had issued a statement that he had no intention of talking to Valentine without first receiving a breakdown of his financing sources. Valentine responded to Lynch's thinly veiled insult by giving an interview to Kurt Zelmanski of the *Journal* in which he pointed the finger back at Crandell and raised his own questions about Crandell's financial stability.

The salvos had flown back and forth as the two companies continued raising their offers, upping the ante like rival bidders at a hotly contested auction. It was anyone's guess to what fiscal heights the battle might still yet soar, and the ongoing drama had captured people's attention. Even Hope, who rarely gave more than a quick glance to the business section, found herself following the story. She had invited Jordan Crandell to the party this evening. His secretary had left word that he'd be delighted to join them, but then he'd telephoned on Friday and said an emergency had come up and he had to be out of the country for the weekend. His secretary would be calling to arrange dinner for the three of them in another month or so, once the Starwares matter was settled.

Hope was in no hurry to have that dinner. She knew Jordan Crandell was too smart to mention anything about his involvement in Paul's appointment. Still, she preferred to wait until Paul became more used to the idea of

himself as a federal judge. It was only a matter of time
before he would realize what everyone else already
knew. That he deserved the promotion and would bring
honor to the position.

Assured that everything was under control in the dining room, she made her way down the hall, stopping to
chat with several guests until she reached the library,
where she found Paul and Hallie Neuwirth.

"Hallie, darling, I was just coming to find you," she
said, noticing the look of relief on her husband's face.
"Connie's in the living room, and I didn't want you to
miss her."

"You're too sweet," said Hallie. "And so is your dear
husband. The two of you are just the most adorable couple." Blowing them kisses, she hurried off to find Connie
Osburgh.

"Phew! That woman certainly can talk!" Paul nudged
her into the library and shut the door. He nuzzled her
hair, inhaling appreciatively. "Mmm, you smell wonderful."

"We should get back to our guests," she said, smiling
as she folded herself into his arms.

"Not without a hug and a kiss to fortify me."

She gazed into his bright blue eyes. "Is it that awful?"

"Not at all. How are you? Do you feel all right?" He
gently rubbed her stomach as she leaned in to kiss him
again.

"I've never felt better."

They grinned at each other, rejoicing in their delicious
good fortune, savoring the news of her pregnancy. That
was the third reason they had to celebrate, one that was
still too new and private to share with their guests.

There'd been no good cause to worry that she couldn't
conceive, except that she was in her late thirties. Nevertheless, she had somehow expected that it would take
them months of trying and disappointment until she got
pregnant. She had received the results of the test over

the phone during a recess in Paul's confirmation hearing.
Hope had floated from the phone booth in the Senate
building back to the hearing room, where Paul was waiting. The grin on her face immediately told him what he
was hoping to hear.

By the time the Senate voted to confirm his appointment a week after the hearings, she was feeling the symp-
toms of her pregnancy. She wasn't about to complain
about the morning sickness and exhaustion that everyone
promised would pass by the end of the first trimester. She
wouldn't care if she were sick the entire nine months she
was pregnant. What mattered was that she and Paul were
going to have a baby. Within the short span of five
months, she had suddenly been granted everything she
could have wished for in life.

"EIGHTY-THREE DOLLARS A share?" roared Jordan Crandell. "There's not a chance in hell Valentine can make
good on that!"

Eric Lynch, Bruce Einhorn, and Jack Strawn, Starwares' chief counsel, exchanged glances as Crandell's
voice, amplified on speakerphone, reverberated off the
walls of Lynch's office.

"You don't have to scream, Jordan," said Lynch. "We
can hear you perfectly at normal voice level."

"Where the hell is that money supposed to be coming
from?" Crandell asked, lowering his voice only slightly.

"Altdir Communications is in for eight hundred million dollars," Einhorn replied.

There was silence at the other end.

"Jordan? Are you there?" Lynch said finally.

"Son of a bitch," said Crandell. "When's your board
meeting?"

"Next Monday."

"That's only four days away. You guys got to get yourselves organized."

Lynch stood up from his desk. Einhorn and Strawn,

seated on the couch, watched as he began to pace the
room. They had spent most of the day closeted with their
lawyers and bankers, poring over a long-term analysis
that compared the relative merits of the two deals. Valentine had also supplied them with four binders filled with
financial information, the intent of which was to prove
that his proposal for a merger was fiscally viable.

"You have that backwards, Jordan," Lynch said. "It's
you guys who have to get organized if you're going to
stay in the game."

"What kind of crap is that? I thought you hated Valentine. Dammit, Lynch! Don't fuck with me!" Crandell
bellowed.

The tension in the office was palpable. Lynch was concerned that he had given away too much by admitting to
Crandell that he didn't want to merge with Valentine. On
the other hand, his attorneys had told him that he was
legally bound to advise Crandell that he would have to
better his offer or risk losing out.

In essence, Crandell had no choice. He had to raise his
bid. The question that only he could answer was whether
he had access to the necessary backing.

Lynch had had his fill of lawyers, investment bankers,
and urgent phone calls from Crandell and Valentine. Na-
ively, he had believed the matter could be settled quickly,
without too many complicating factors. Now, he gestured
impatiently to Einhorn to deal with Crandell.

"We're not fucking with you. We want this deal to
happen, Jordan," said Einhorn, referring to the notes the
lawyers had prepared for him. "We'll do whatever it
takes, but we owe it to our stockholders to negotiate on
their behalf the best possible value for their shares. I'm
sure you can appreciate that."

He looked over at Lynch, who silently signaled his approval.

There was another long silence at Crandell's end.
Lynch could hear him puffing on his cigarette. By now,

he felt as if he knew Crandell—not as he might know a friend, but in the way that he understood the deep inner workings of a complicated programming code whose kinks he'd been asked to untangle.

Crandell wanted Starwares as badly as Lynch wanted his money. Lynch was prepared to help him. He would even go so far as to urge his board to accept a slightly less favorable bid from Summit over one from Valentine. But Crandell had to meet him at least halfway. Otherwise, he would lose his clout and his stockholders would lose money.

"I'll see what I can do and get back to you," Crandell said finally.

"We'll be here," said Lynch.

THE SOUTHERN DISTRICT Federal Courthouse at Foley Square was only a half-block south of Paul's former quarters on Centre Street, but the two buildings felt a world apart. Visitors to both buildings had first to pass through a well-guarded X-ray and security check, but the similarity ended there. In contrast to the hurly-burly atmosphere of the State Supreme Courthouse, the Federal Court was pervaded by a sense of dignity and calm that seemed to befit its more exalted status. The corridors were quiet and uncrowded, and the handful of people standing outside the courtrooms whispered amongst themselves in hushed tones as they waited to be summoned inside.

Riding the private elevator to his third-floor chambers, Paul mulled over the first case that had been assigned to him. In the federal courts, assignments were made by a lottery system. A roll of the wheel had determined that he would preside at the trial of a powerful Chinatown businessman who stood accused of one count of racketeering, three counts of murder, and two each of gambling and heroin trafficking.

His friends and allies described the thirty-five-year-old

Winston Chang as an upstanding leader in the Chinese
community, the president of one of its most prestigious
social clubs, a loving husband and doting father of three
young children. The government claimed he was a cold-
blooded gangster with ties to organized crime who had
ordered the murder of at least twelve people.

To make its case, the government was relying for the
most part on the testimony of several young members of
a Chinatown street gang who had allegedly carried out
the murders ordered by Mr. Chang in order to safeguard
his illegal gambling operations. Two witnesses had already taken the stand. The trial had been proceeding
smoothly until this morning, just before the lunch break.
A high-ranking member of Mr. Chang's tong had been
sworn in as a government witness. Under questioning by
the defense attorney, the man had admitted that he himself had been arrested on a murder charge the previous
year.

The defendant's attorney, Marsha Knight, had immediately asserted that the witness's credibility had been
impeached by the murder charge, which had not previously been disclosed by the government. Paul decided
to call the lunch recess as planned, and invited the attorneys into his chambers for a conference after they returned from the lunch break.

The two lawyers were already present when he took
his seat at the head of the conference table in the outer
room of his chambers. "Ms. Knight, Mr. Leahey," he
said. "Please, let's try to keep this civilized, shall we?"

"Your Honor," said Marsha Knight. An experienced
criminal defense attorney with a ferocious intensity, she
used her youthful looks, short stature, and signature
cherry red lipstick to advantage by lulling witnesses into
a false sense of ease. Now she looked as if she were about
to explode with fury.

"Yes, Ms. Knight?"

"Your Honor, the government has deliberately withheld from us information that could be crucial to our case. If my investigator was able to determine that Mr. Liu had been arrested for murder, surely the government knew as well.''

''Mr. Leahey?'' Paul turned to the assistant U.S. attorney.

''Your Honor,'' said Kevin Leahey, a tall, thin man with prematurely gray hair and stooped shoulders. ''Surely Ms. Knight can't seriously believe that we deliberately kept her in the dark about Harold Liu's arrest record. It came as a total shock to us, as well.''

Marsha Knight scowled. ''Your Honor, I must insist that Mr. Liu be dismissed as a witness because his credibility has been severely undermined. Moreover, I must insist that—''

''Ms. Knight,'' Paul cut in sharply. ''This is my courtroom, and if there's any insisting to be done, I'll be the one to do it. I shouldn't have to point out to you that Mr. Liu's lack of credibility works to your advantage.''

The color rose in Marsha Knight's already bright cheeks, and her lavish sprinkling of freckles stood out like a dalmatian's spots. ''Your Honor,'' she said stubbornly, ''Mr. Leahey's disclaimer notwithstanding, we believe that this shows bad faith and misconduct on the part of the government. Moreover, it leads us to wonder what other information is being withheld from the defense. What else don't we know that could be crucial to our case?''

Kevin Leahey shook his head. ''Ms. Knight is grasping at straws now, Your Honor. She knows her client is guilty as sin, so she has to resort to these cheap tricks to confuse the issues at hand.''

''That's ridiculous!'' Marsha Knight exploded. Her voice rising with each word, she went on, ''My client is a legitimate businessman who's well respected in the Asian community. You have absolutely no evidence of any wrongdoing on his part except for the testimony of those two-bit gangsters you've been trotting onto the stand.''

"Ms. Knight," Paul began, glancing at his watch.

Ignoring his interruption, she jabbed her index finger at Kevin Leahey. "I know all about you Irish Catholic Fordham Law School types. You're the Irish Mafia. You're a bunch of racists who can't tolerate the success of someone like Winston Chang simply because he's Chinese and—"

Paul knew he was being tested, much like a teacher coming into the classroom in the middle of the year. It was essential that he assert his authority before the situation veered out of control. He glowered at Marsha Knight and said quietly but firmly, "Ms. Knight, that's enough. One more word and I'll hold you in contempt. Do I make myself perfectly clear, Ms. Knight?"

"Yes, Your Honor," she mumbled, her cheeks flaming bright red.

"Good," he declared. "Then there's no need for any further discussion. And next time, Ms. Knight, pick your fights more carefully. I may be new to this jurisdiction, but I'm not an easy mark. Be sure to tell that to all your friends in the legal community."

Satisfied that he'd made his point, Paul stood up to go put on his robe. "I'll see you both back in court in exactly ten minutes."

LEW VALENTINE GLARED at the cover of *Pastiche,* which featured a smiling Jordan Crandell amidst a smorgasbord assortment of computers, holding aloft a length of cable wire as if it were the Holy Grail. "Ride the Information Superhighway to the 21st Century" read the caption under the photograph. "Starwares Climbs the Summit."

"I'm going to wipe that shit-eating grin off Jordan Crandell's face if it's the last thing I do," said Valentine, hurling the magazine in the direction of his wastepaper basket.

The magazine sailed pass the basket and landed at the foot of Bernard Odette's chair. Odette picked it up and flipped to the article, where there were several more photographs of Crandell, including one in which he and Eric Lynch were sharing a chairlift up a snow-covered slope in Park City, Utah.

Odette glanced at the piece. He had to hand it to Crandell. The article was a nice example of PR puffery, heavily slanted to portray Crandell in the best possible light. It was written with such skill that most readers would never make the connection between Jordan Crandell, the forward-thinking, benevolent, would-be buyer of Starwares, and Jordan Crandell, chairman of the board of *Pastiche*'s parent company.

"Are you ready to take these two fuckers to court?" Valentine demanded.

Odette rolled up the magazine and neatly lobbed it into the basket. Though he never would have admitted it to Valentine, he was enjoying this case. There'd been a dearth of significant merger suits in the past couple of years, and he'd missed the high-stakes action of a hostile takeover attempt.

He'd been working long hours to formulate a winning argument. Rizzy Riznicki had already proven herself to be every bit as indispensable as she had promised him. He had also made an arrangement with a small New York law firm that specialized in corporate law to hire as many of its associates as necessary to do the extensive legal research and discovery that would lay the foundation of his case against Starwares and Summit. He was close to being ready to file. His arguments were nothing short of brilliant.

Never one to believe in false modesty, he said as much to Valentine, adding, "I'm going to make it so hot for Jordan Crandell and Eric Lynch that they'll hate each other's guts by the time I get through with them."

"Talk to me," snapped Valentine. "Tell me what you've got."

Odette lit a cigarette.

Valentine frowned and buzzed his secretary. "Anita, bring an ashtray in here for Mr. Odette."

They went through the same ritual every time they met in Valentine's office. Odette wondered why Valentine didn't just give up and keep one on hand for him.

He smiled at Anita as she handed him the ashtray. A voluptuous young woman with full lips framed by dimples on either side, she had caught his eye on previous visits when she had flirted shamelessly with him. He hoped that Valentine wasn't sleeping with her, because he planned to invite her out to dinner as soon as his schedule permitted.

Turning his attention back to Valentine, Odette said, "As you're well aware, Crandell and Lynch have been making a lot of noise about the synergism of their two companies. My highly informed guess is that they're positioning themselves to defend their deal as a strategic alliance, rather than as a sale."

Valentine shook his head. "I don't get it. What's the difference?"

"Since Crandell will be coming in as the major stockholder, this can't possibly be viewed as a strategic alliance. Because no matter what Starwares' board members may presently think is in the best interests of their company, once Jordan Crandell has bought up the controlling shares of the stock, he's in the catbird seat. Then it becomes purely up to him to decide what's best for Starwares. I've no doubt whatsoever that the court will see this transaction as a sale, in which case the spoils must go to the highest bidder."

"Which is us," said Valentine.

"Of course." Odette smiled his most cunning smile as he stubbed out his cigarette.

"I like it," Valentine said, leaning back in his chair. He tapped his index finger against his lips. "But it almost seems too simple."

Odette chuckled. "I don't know who you've had working for you in the past, but trust me on this, Lew. I didn't get to where I am today by relying on simplicity. I have eleven lawyers working overtime to research every aspect of every case that has any bearing on our argument. I've got them analyzing the most minute details of whatever's gone down since the very first second you started thinking about buying Starwares."

He lit another cigarette, inhaled, and chuckled again. "I pity that poor guy."

"Who? Lynch? Don't waste your sympathy on him. I was all set to do business with him in a fair and friendly way. He came to New York, cockteased me, then screwed me over. Hell, I even took him to lunch at Le Cirque."

Odette stared over Valentine's shoulder at the bare treetops of Central Park. Just to the north, he could see Wollman Rink, which was dotted with tiny stick figures of those few ice skaters who were hardy enough to brave the subfreezing temperatures.

"Actually," Odette said, turning his gaze back to Valentine, "I wasn't feeling sorry for Eric Lynch. I was referring to the judge who gets assigned to this case. He's going to be drowning in motions."

"These judges don't really bother to read all that paper, do they?"

Odette smiled. "Too many of them leave it to their clerks to do all the work. But there are also those who will read every word."

"So how do we make sure we land the right one?"

Odette sighed to himself, wishing he liked Valentine more as a person. Ultimately, it didn't matter, as long as Valentine paid the bills. But long ago, he had discovered that when a client had a simpatico worldview, the whole process became more enjoyable.

He pulled out another cigarette and flicked his lighter. "We can't make sure. It completely depends on the luck of the draw."

* * *

ARRIVING HOME AFTER a particularly difficult day in
court, Paul was so deep in thought that several seconds
passed before he noticed his key didn't fit his front-door
lock. He tried again, jiggling the key left and right, but
with no success. He turned the handle, thinking perhaps
someone had mistakenly left the door unlocked. It remained firmly shut. He stared at the key, and only then
realized that he'd automatically pulled out the one to his
Park Avenue apartment.

Smiling at his mistake, he fished out the correct key.
"Hope?" he called, as he finally opened the door.

Eleanor, the maid, came out of the dining room, carrying a fresh bouquet of flowers and a vase. "I believe she's
in the second guest room, sir," she told him.

"Thank you, Eleanor," he said, wondering whether he
would ever get used to the presence of the live-in staff
that addressed him as if he were a member of the British
royalty and catered to his every need and desire.

He still couldn't quite accept that Hope's apartment
was now his home. She had offered to do whatever was
necessary to make him feel comfortable there. But he
knew he couldn't explain without hurting her feelings
that tearing down a wall or redecorating a room wouldn't
help his adjustment. He simply needed time to settle in
to his new life.

Yet he was truly and completely happy to be married
to her. And try as he might not to draw a comparison, he
couldn't help but be struck by the differences between
his two marriages. The common denominator was the gut
(and just a little guilty) knowledge that Hope was as right
for him now as Helen had been for him then.

He and Helen had met as kids and grown up together.
The person each had become had been influenced by the
other. Whereas he and Hope were already two fully
formed adults whose dissimilarities were as exciting to
him as their shared interests. As he drove home in the

late afternoons, he looked forward to telling her about his day and hearing how she'd spent hers. He welcomed his impending state of fatherhood. Especially since his new court appointment, he felt his life could not be more complete or gratifying.

The period leading up to his confirmation had been tension-filled. He hadn't realized until the opportunity presented itself just how much he had wanted the federal appointment. Knowing he was under investigation, he had forced himself to review his career and examine all personal or professional decisions through the same critical lens as the senators who served on the judicial sub-committee. There was very little to hide or regret. One short phone call, perhaps, made such a long time ago that it couldn't possibly matter any more in the greater scheme of events.

In the end, the senators had asked him very little of substance. He had worried needlessly about a phone call that ultimately had done far more good than harm.

HE FOUND HOPE drinking a glass of milk, with her feet propped up on a hassock in the guest bedroom that they had already begun referring to as the baby's room. One of her textbooks lay unopened on her lap.

"There you are," he said, coming over to kiss her.

"Cheers," she said. She took a sip of milk and grimaced. "I never did like the taste of this stuff. My mother used to have a devil of a time getting it down my throat. She'd laugh now to see me drinking four glasses a day."

"Cheers." He lowered himself onto the bed, feeling his fatigue. "Have you been studying?"

"Trying to, but I haven't gotten very far. All I can think about is how I want to decorate the baby's room. And whether it's a boy or a girl. And what to name him or her. I've been sitting here all afternoon, worrying about how little time we have left before the baby comes. Oh, God! I look a mess, don't I?"

"You look beautiful," he said, loving the way her hair
had slipped loose from the knot at the back of her head
to frame her face. "And we have plenty of time. There's
absolutely nothing to be worried about."

She frowned and brushed her hair back. "You're
wrong. November will be here before we can even blink.
In the meantime, there's so much to be done—"

"Hope." He leaned over and stroked her arm. "Calm
down, darling. Everything will be just fine."

She burst into tears and buried her face in her hands.

Utterly bewildered, he knelt at her feet. "Honey,
what's wrong? I'm sorry, I didn't mean to upset you."

"It's not you," she said, weeping.

In one of the books on pregnancy they'd bought, he'd
read that women in their first trimester often experienced
emotional mood swings, from great bursts of excitement
and creativity to bouts of depression. But Hope had
seemed purely thrilled by her pregnancy—unless there
were other feelings that she'd kept hidden from him until
now.

"Come, sit with me so I can hold you," he said, gently
pulling her out of the chair and leading her over to the
bed.

She sat huddled in his embrace, her shoulders shaking,
until finally she stopped crying. She pulled a tissue from
the box next to the bed, blew her nose, and looked up at
him. "I'm sorry," she said. Her eyelashes were wet and
fringed with tiny teardrops. "I should never have taken
the call."

"What call?"

"Aunt Grace." She tried to smile. "She called to warn
me."

"But I thought she liked me."

"She does, as much as she can ever like anyone whose
family hasn't ruled New York society since before the
Vanderbilts."

"Ouch. She sets a tough standard. So now she thinks

you should dump me? Isn't it too early for us to split up? We're practically newlyweds," he said, trying to lighten her mood.

She shook her head and now her smile came more easily. "Not for Aunt Grace. She divorced her second husband just after their ten-month anniversary when she caught him in bed with the gardener's assistant. However, it's not us she's worried about. It's the baby. She thinks it's too soon. That we don't know each other well enough."

"Your aunt Grace is one nervous lady. What do you think?"

She giggled. "I think I must be losing my mind if I've started paying attention to her."

"Good. Objection overruled. And next time, I'll have her held in contempt of court."

Her dark mood lifted, she grinned. "Gee, I like being married to a judge. How about dinner at home tonight, just the two of us?"

"Sounds great. I'm kind of tired, and I can't think of anyone I'd rather spend the evening with than you."

"Tough day?" she asked sympathetically.

He nodded. "But interesting. I may as well have been at a tennis match. Both the counsel for the defense and the government's attorney think it's their mission in life to object to everything the other one says. They certainly are keeping me on my toes."

"How much longer will it go on?"

"Oh, another week or so of testimony, then three days to a week for the jury to reach a decision."

"Do you think they'll find him guilty?"

He shrugged. "I don't know. It's a hard call. There's a lot of evidence against him, but he's got an excellent defense attorney who's very adroit at discrediting witnesses. I suspect she'll make a very persuasive closing argument."

Hope took his hand and played with his wedding band,

then spread her fingers on top of his. Her fingers were long and delicate and perfectly formed. His were blunt and splayed like his father's. They were a peasant's hands, strong and capable.

"I'd love to see you at work. How would you feel if I came down and sat in on the trial for a few hours on Thursday?" she said.

"That would be great," he said, pleased by her interest. "But I should warn you, it's not like *L.A. Law.* Some of the proceedings can be very slow going."

"If it gets too dull, I'll amuse myself with erotic fantasies about making love to you in the courtroom."

"I like the sound of that," he said. "Why don't you give me a sneak preview right now?"

She smirked at him. "But we're not in the courtroom."

He got up and crossed the room to close the door. "Then we'll just have to pretend. That's why the good Lord gave us imaginations."

KURT ZELMANSKI PUSHED the save button on his computer and leaned back in his chair. He stretched his arms over his head and yawned. The coffee in his mug was cold, and a half-eaten bagel with a smear of cream cheese looked stale and unappetizing. Suddenly, he realized he was starving and tried to remember when he had last eaten.

He'd ordered the bagel with coffee and a double portion of well-done scrambled eggs about an hour after his editor's call had awakened him out of a deep sleep at noon. It was his day off, for Chrissakes. He'd been up until five writing. The protein in the eggs had helped, but he'd felt logy all day. He squinted at the clock on his VCR. Damn. It was almost eight. No wonder his stomach was screaming for food.

The box of cereal on his counter was empty except for a few shreds at the bottom that he shook into his mouth.

The refrigerator contained nothing but three Heinekens, a pint of souring milk, a bottle of ketchup, a carton of ancient, crusty sesame noodles, and the container of chocolate yogurt that he'd bought back in December when he'd made a short-lived effort to improve his diet.

It was Saturday night, and he was as hungry for company as he was for a good meal and a couple of drinks. Rizzy Riznicki's face popped into his head. He'd mistakenly figured her for an easy lay. They'd been out to dinner twice—Indian food at Curry Mahal on Second Avenue, then pizza at John's on Bleecker Street. She lived somewhere on the Upper West Side. Maybe if he took her to dinner closer to her apartment, he'd have a better chance of taking her to bed at the end of the evening.

What was she doing tonight? He dialed her home number and got her machine. "Leave me your name and number. If I have time, I'll call you back," said the message.

Nice, he thought. Real friendly. "It's Kurt Zelmanski," he said after the beep. "Make time or you're going to end up a horny old maid."

He ran his hand over his chin. He needed a shave and a shower. He needed food and conversation and sex.

Maybe Rizzy was still at work. He punched Odette's number.

She picked up in the middle of the first ring and said, "Hi."

"Hi," he said, glad to have reached her.

"Who's this?"

"It's Kurt. Zelmanski."

"Oh, hi."

He thought she sounded pleased to hear from him but couldn't tell for sure. "I guess you were expecting someone else."

"You're right," she said cheerfully. "I was."

"You're still at work." Dumb, he thought, as soon as the words were out of his mouth. Why state the obvious?

"You're a very observant person. I guess that's what makes you a good reporter."

"What are you doing tonight?" he asked, fishing in his drawer for clean underwear.

"What's it to you?"

"C'mon, Rizzy," he coaxed, "I already know you're a tough nut. Stop trying to impress me. How about some dinner?"

"Well, I suppose I do have to eat," she said grudgingly. "Though I was rather looking forward to the cold fettucine alfredo that my boss brought home in a doggy bag from lunch."

He smiled as he stripped off his clothes so he'd be ready to shower as soon as he got off the phone. "You can have the fettucine tomorrow night, when it's really disgusting. I'd be willing to come up to your neighborhood, if that's easier for you. Do you like Mexican food?"

"It's greasy, fattening, and messy. Ergo, I love it. How about that Mexican restaurant on Columbus and Seventy-Third? It's right around the corner from my apartment."

He liked the sound of that. "Great. Nine o'clock okay?"

"Fine. See you then," she said.

An hour later, panting slightly from having run the last couple of blocks from the subway, Zelmanski hurried into the restaurant to find Rizzy washing down a basket of chips and salsa with a large margarita.

"I couldn't wait," she told him. "Hey, Andy!" she called to a tall, good-looking waiter whom Zelmanski guessed to be an aspiring actor. "A margarita for my friend." Then, belatedly she consulted him. "Yes? Or do you want a beer?"

He grinned. "I like a woman who knows my mind. I've been thinking margaritas all the way up here on the train."

They were both eager to eat, so they concentrated first

on the menus. He grinned again when she ordered the deep-fried beef chimichangas with a side of guacamole. The last three women he'd dated had all been health nuts who ran, worked out, and shuddered at the sight of red meat or fried foods. Rizzy Riznicki had an appetite that matched his own, and he liked a woman who had some heft on her.

"So what's new in the war zone?" he asked, as soon as he'd downed half a margarita.

She studied him thoughtfully as she chewed on another corn chip. "If you're here on business, forget about it. Tonight is strictly R&R for me."

"You know I crave your bod. I was just making conversation," he assured her.

"Oh, sure," she scoffed. "Like you've thought about anything else in the past week besides Crandell, Lynch, and Lew Valentine."

"I have to admit they've crossed my mind. But I already have impeccable sources for my stories. I don't need to stoop to plying you with alcohol and refried beans to get information."

She signaled the waiter, who was evidently a friend of hers. "Hey, Andy. Another round of margaritas, please."

Andy winked at Zelmanski. "Watch out for her. In another hour, she'll have you begging for mercy."

She shrugged, as if mystified by his comment. Then she said, "Besides, for all you know, I could be feeding you false information to confuse the enemy."

"You wouldn't do a thing like that."

"Oh, wouldn't I?"

Andy brought them their margaritas. "On the house," he whispered to Rizzy. She blew him a kiss. Then she picked up her glass and carefully ran her tongue around the rim, licking off the salt.

Zelmanski couldn't tear his eyes away from her tongue. He remembered how it had felt when they'd kissed goodnight on their previous date. Full. Ripe. As tantalizingly sweet as a juicy, height-of-summer peach.

"You've been working your butt off, haven't you?" he said, swallowing hard.

She nodded. "My boss is definitely getting his money's worth out of me. But you won't hear me complaining. My motto is work hard, play hard." She grinned. "And I can't wait to play."

He smiled. She couldn't have made the message any clearer if she'd spelled it out for him. Tonight was the night. And about time, too. "Is Odette almost ready to file?"

"You tell me, if your sources are so good."

"I say he's real close, or you wouldn't have a free evening tonight."

She kept quiet. He knew he'd gotten her there. "I think your boss has a good chance of winning in court," he said.

"No kidding. He's a brilliant lawyer. I've already learned more from him than I did in all three years of law school."

The food arrived. "Anything else to drink?" asked Andy.

The margaritas had kicked in nicely. He was just starting to unwind. "I'll have a Dos Equis with a slice of lime," he said.

"A reporter," Rizzy told Andy. "Thinks he can drink me under the table." She smirked. "Make that two Dos Equis."

By unspoken consent, conversation stopped as they dove into their food. His quesadilla gigante was an impressive-looking tortilla stuffed with beef, beans, mushrooms, and cheese, topped with salsa, guacamole, and jalapeno peppers. He would pay with indigestion in the morning, but tonight he was in pig heaven.

When the beers came, he looked up from his plate and found her staring at him. "You were hungry," she said.

"I didn't eat much today. I got all caught up in researching a story."

"Anything I might be interested in?"

In fact, after endless hours of studying annual reports, following trails of financial investments, trying to find a break in the pattern, he thought he might have hit pay dirt. The potent combination of alcohol and rich food had made him feel relaxed and less guarded than usual. Eager to try out his theory, Zelmanski decided to take a chance and share his suspicions with her. If he was right and he came up with supporting evidence, he would score the biggest investigative coup since Watergate.

"I did find something," he said. "But you have to promise not to tell anyone, not even Odette."

"Cross my heart and hope to die," she said, drawing a cross over her left breast.

He hadn't heard that expression since childhood, and it made him want to trust her all the more. "Okay," he said, leaning forward conspiratorially. "Maybe you remember that when I was interviewing Odette just after Crandell announced the takeover, I mentioned that Valentine had raised a question about how Crandell was financing this deal?"

She put down her fork and nodded.

"Odette wouldn't commit one way or another to that possibility."

"I remember that, too."

"I decided to follow the lead, just in case Valentine knew what he was talking about." He picked up his beer and saw that the bottle was empty.

"Have another," she suggested, raising her hand to get Andy's attention.

"Only if you will."

"Two more, thanks." She handed Andy the empties. "Go on," she urged Zelmanski.

"You swear you'll keep this to yourself?" he said again.

"On my honor as a fellow Slav. We Poles have to stick together, right?"

"Right." He took another few large bites of the quesadilla and washed them down with a long swig of the fresh beer. "So I think Valentine could be right about Crandell's backing. I've spent the last few days reading SEC filings and quarterly earnings reports. I'm no accountant, but I know enough about this stuff to figure out that when two and two add up to three, something's fishy."

She was staring at him, her intense brown eyes alive with interest. "You get enough hard data to back you up, you'll have a hell of a story. Or better yet, get someone inside his company who'll talk to you."

"Does Odette have anything on this?" he asked, hearing himself slur his words. He wasn't drunk, just pleasantly unwound. And still sober enough to try and find out whether her side had anything he could use.

She shook her head, no.

Zelmanski didn't know whether or not to believe her. He wondered whether he had made a big mistake confiding in her. He drank the rest of his beer and decided that the worst-case scenario was she'd get Odette interested in talking to him. Depending on what her boss had, maybe they could even trade information.

"Anything else I can get you two?" Andy asked, coming over to their table.

"Not for me," she said.

"I'm fine," said Zelmanski.

Andy slapped the check down in the middle of the table. She grabbed for it. "This one's on me." She smiled at Zelmanski. "Walk me home," she said, "and I'll invite you in for a coffee and kahlua."

He couldn't help wondering whether it was the research or him that had turned her on.

NINE

I'M SORRY," GEORGE Osburgh said. "I don't understand why this is happening."

His voice trailed off as he closed his eyes and fell back against the pillow.

"It's *okay*, George," Nancy said, pulling herself up to lie next to him. "You don't have to keep apologizing. These things happen."

But not to him. He felt mortified. Was his sudden inability to perform a function of his age? Just last month, his doctor had assured him he was in excellent health, with the cardiovascular system of a much younger man. Yet now, for the second time in two weeks, he had failed to get hard, no matter which of her very excellent techniques Nancy had used to try and arouse him.

It really was unprecedented. And humiliating.

"Do you want some gum?" she asked him, unwrapping a piece for herself.

"No, thank you," he said. He forced himself to open his eyes and face her.

He wished she could have held off on the goddamn gum. She was trying to quit smoking, mostly because she knew he disapproved of the habit. Her therapist had told her that chewing gum was a good substitute for cigarettes, a way to fulfill her oral needs without lighting up a cancer stick.

He appreciated her effort. But as much as he hated the smell of smoke, there was something so cheap and undignified about gum chewing, especially when she did it right after they'd had sex. Or worse, right after they couldn't have sex.

She reached for the bottle of wine in the ice bucket on her bed table and poured herself a glass. "What's wrong, George?" she asked.

"Nothing's wrong."

He sighed. Everything was wrong. First, his huge financial losses. Then, his involvement in Crandell's scheme. Now, his impotence. If only he could relive that moment when his life had begun to unravel. If only he could take a ride in H. G. Wells's time machine and set matters right again.

"My therapist says that very often there's a psychological component to impotence," Nancy said. "Are you having some sort of psychological problem?"

"You discussed this with your therapist?" He stared at her in horror.

She shook her head impatiently. "What's the big deal? It's not as if he knows you. Anyway, he's professionally bound to keep everything I say in confidence. Kind of like a priest in the confessional."

"Like a priest." He swung his legs over the side of the bed and reached for his boxer shorts, which he'd flung on the floor in his earlier flush of optimistic anticipation. He felt so close to Nancy in so many ways that he often forgot she was a lapsed Catholic.

He gazed bleakly at the framed black-and-white photograph on her wall, an original Atget. To think that he was being spoken about during her therapy sessions. It was all he could do not to bury his head in his hands, but he would never want her to see how weak and exposed he felt.

On several occasions during his childhood, he'd mis-
behaved badly enough that his mother had taken a hair-
brush to his bare behind. After all these years, he could
still recall how he'd wept with pain and despair that he'd
brought such shame on himself. He wondered whether
that memory was the sort of thing Nancy talked about
with her therapist. He couldn't imagine what went on in
her twice-weekly sessions. He supposed he could have
asked her. The truth was, however, that he preferred not
to know.

He didn't approve of spending thousands of dollars to
pour one's heart out to some stranger who happened to
have a degree in psychology. What was the point? He
didn't see that Nancy had changed much through the
course of her treatment.

When he'd hired her two years ago, she'd been a
bright, desirable, lively young woman. She was still all
of those things. She had also grown rather more self-
assured, but he suspected that had happened by virtue of
her having done so well at work. And possibly because
of their relationship, if he did say so himself.

Besides, for no money at all a person could confide in
his or her minister or friends. Not about impotence, of
course, which was too hideously embarrassing to be discussed, particularly when it happened during what were
supposed to be the throes of passion with his mistress.

He sighed again, thinking that he did rather wish there
were someone he could talk to, who would listen without
judging him, who would tell him he had nothing to worry
about. Nobody would ever know that he had borrowed a
half-billion dollars from the Scott Trust to pay into Jordan Crandell's specially set up discretionary fund. The
money, plus his fee, would be returned and repaid to the
fund long before the trust's annual report had to be issued. His investment would show a profit. Everyone
would be happy.

"Where are you going, George?" asked Nancy, as he

pulled on his trousers. "Just because you're having trouble doesn't mean you need to hop out of bed and get dressed. There's me, too, to satisfy, you know."

"Of course, Nanny," he mumbled, hoping to mollify her by using the nickname he called her in private. "I was just going to get myself some mineral water."

It hadn't occurred to him that she might want to continue. Of course, there were things he could do to satisfy her, but it all seemed rather pointless now, even in poor taste.

He never thought of Nancy as a feminist, but she was, after all, just thirty-three and a graduate of Radcliffe. She couldn't have avoided absorbing at least a few of the women's liberation notions that must have been tossed about on campus.

Padding off to the kitchen, he asked himself when things had begun to go so terribly awry in his life. His hand was trembling as he poured the glass of mineral water. A small puddle spilled on Nancy's immaculately clean, bleached oak butcher block countertop. He tore off a piece of paper towel to blot up the water and thought about adding a drop or two of scotch to his drink.

Nancy was always urging him to loosen up and have a drink. Maybe just this one time it wouldn't hurt. To calm his nerves and restore his equilibrium.

She kept her alcohol in the cabinet next to the refrigerator. He took out the bottle of scotch and carefully measured a jigger into his glass.

"Bottoms up," he said, staring at his reflection in the gleaming glass door of the oven.

"George?" Nancy called.

The scotch tasted bitter going down. He felt its fiery power begin to work through his bloodstream as soon as it hit his stomach. "Coming, darling," he answered, and hurried to rejoin her in the bedroom.

"I decided to have a drink," he told her, shedding his trousers and climbing back into bed.

"What a good idea." She smiled approvingly and held up her wineglass. "Let's toast. To the cosmic forces that brought us together and keep us together."

The sentiment didn't sit well, but he obligingly touched his glass to hers.

"Are you sure everything's all right, George?" she asked again, leaning on her elbow and contemplating him with her pale gray eyes. "Anything happening at work I should know about? Trouble with Connie or one of the girls?"

"No, no," he assured her. "I'm just tired. I think I need a vacation."

"I wish we could go away together," she said wistfully. "Couldn't you arrange a little business trip for the two of us? Some place warm with a beach, like St. Barts or Hawaii?"

He tried to smile. If only it were that simple. He drained the rest of his drink. Or maybe it was.

The sheet had fallen away from Nancy's body, leaving exposed her perfect pear-shaped breasts. He reached out to touch her and suddenly felt more hopeful. He pulled the sheet back all the way and stared at the rest of her.

Dressed, she was beautiful. Naked, she was magnificent.

She tugged at his waistband. "Ready to try again?"

To his vast relief, his problem was a thing of the past. He quickly got rid of his shorts and rolled over on top of her. "Ready when you are."

KEN WOLCH WOULD normally not have mentioned to Jordan Crandell that he was having breakfast with his old friend, Bernard Odette. But under the circumstances, he had thought it prudent to tell Crandell in advance, rather than risk having his number-one client read about the meeting in Liz Smith's *Newsday* column or on page six of the *Post*.

As expected, Crandell had been hard-pressed to understand how the two opposing counsels would want to share a pot of coffee, let alone break bread together. "You won't find me sitting down any time soon with Lew Valentine," he'd querulously declared to Wolch.

It was Wolch's deeply held belief that Jordan Crandell could have saved himself a pile of money by negotiating with so many of his rivals instead of suing them. However, since much of that money had ended up in his firm's coffers, Wolch kept his opinion to himself. He also ignored Crandell's attempts to persuade him to break his date. Who he dined with was ultimately nobody's business but his own.

He arrived at the Regency dining room exactly on time for their 7:00 A.M. breakfast, although he knew Odette would show up at least five minutes late. Odette was always late. He was even late for court. Once, as a joke, Wolch had bought Odette a Mickey Mouse watch with a huge face and hands. The next time they'd done battle against each other in court, Odette had conspicuously displayed the watch in front of him on the counsel table. Wolch had had the last laugh, however. He'd won the case, then won it again on appeal.

The hostess led him to his table and took his order for coffee. Then he unfolded his *Wall Street Journal* to read what Kurt Zelmanski and his cohorts were saying today about his case. He hadn't got past the first line when he was interrupted by Jesse Rubin, whom he'd known since they'd gone to law school together at Columbia.

"Nice work if you can get it," said Rubin, clapping him on the back. He pointed to the headline which proclaimed: "VALENTINE RUMORED TO SHIFT STRATEGY."

"It's a living." Wolch chuckled. "But there's no need to be envious. The next big one could well be yours."

"Well, I can't say that I envy you when the client is Jordan Crandell."

Wolch grinned. "No comment, counselor."

"We should have lunch. It's been a while."

"As soon as things clear up for me, I'll give you a call. But only if you promise not to bring up the Alumni Fund. I've more than done my bit for them this year, even if my check didn't meet your exacting standards."

"Those three glorious years at law school made you who you are today," Jesse Rubin said, smiling.

"Ha! So it's Columbia that's to blame. Well, I'm afraid your memories are a lot fonder than mine. *I* didn't make the Law Review, if you recall."

"You've managed to pull in a client or two, nonetheless. I'll talk to you soon. My best to Susie."

"Likewise to Molly," said Wolch.

Bernard Odette arrived a few minutes later along with Wolch's coffee.

"Late night?" asked Wolch, shaking Odette's hand.

"I have to keep reminding myself I'm not as young as I used to be. Or as the women who accept my dinner invitations."

"Whatever happened to—"

"Beverly? Her plans for our relationship outgrew mine. It wasn't meant to be." He shrugged philosophically as he scanned the menu. "The hell with my cholesterol count. I need protein this morning. A cheese omelette, bacon, and plenty of rye toast. How about you?"

"I spent last evening with my wife of thirty-one years. I'll stick with my usual, bran flakes and orange juice."

They gave the waitress their orders, then settled back to catch up and gossip about colleagues and mutual acquaintances.

They had their ground rules. The case at hand was off-limits, except in the most general terms. There was to be no trading information, no soliciting a settlement on either side unless one or the other of their clients had indicated an interest in such a possibility. Even so, there was no chance they'd run short of conversation. They knew too many people in common and shared a deep fascination with the multileveled convolutions of corporate law.

"I noticed Jesse Rubin as I came in," said Odette.

Wolch nodded. "He stopped by to say hello. I think he's wishing he were sitting where we are on this one."

"He's done work for Valentine in the past. Probably resents me for moving into his territory."

"Maybe not. Rubin's one of the good guys. I don't know that he has the stomach for such a dogfight."

"Do you?"

"Just try me," said Wolch.

"I intend to. Ah, very good. Here's our breakfast." He picked up his fork and knife and smiled at Wolch. "I really must be getting old. Time was I would have cured what ails me with a Bloody Mary."

Ken Wolch smiled knowingly at Odette. "Forget it, Bernie. I'm not buying your old-timer act. I heard what you did in San Francisco for Western Petroleum. You're still the Michigan Assassin, and you've still got those killer instincts. However, I've got my own unbeatable trump card, and it's called Jordan Crandell. You work for Crandell, you don't lose. Not even to the Michigan Assassin."

Odette's hearty laugh rang out above the low murmur of voices, catching the attention of the other diners seated nearby. "Point taken. So I understand you have several new appointees to Federal District court," he said. "What do you know about them?"

Wolch spooned up the last of his bran flakes and banana. "Bonnie Kerman used to be with the Criminal Division at Justice, and before that she was an assistant U.S. attorney."

"Tall, thin, mid-forties, very self-assured?"

Wolch nodded. "That sounds like her. Then you've got Jonathan Eisenberg. He clerked for Thurgood Marshall, went on to become a partner at Parker & Dunning. A brilliant guy, but rumor has it he's having a bit of a tough time getting used to being on the other side of the bench."

"Who else?"

"Paul Murray," said Wolch. "You should ask Jesse about him. They used to be partners until Murray got himself elected to the New York Supreme Court. He has a reputation for being a nice guy, but don't cross him in the courtroom or his temper shows. I hear he's smart, especially when it comes to corporate and trade reg. He must also be smart about women. He just married Hope Scott."

"I'd like to see myself appointed to Federal Court one of these days," Odette said as he wiped up the remains of his omelette with a slice of well-buttered toast.

"You?" Wolch hooted in disbelief. "You wouldn't be able to keep your mouth shut long enough to let the lawyers make their arguments. And I bet your shirt and suit cost almost as much at that fancy London tailor you patronize as what one of those judges makes in a year."

"Close to," Odette proudly admitted.

Wolch picked up the *Journal* and unfolded it to the article by Kurt Zelmanski he'd begun to read earlier. "Speaking of costs, is Zelmanski on your payroll now? Every time I open up this damn paper, he's quoting you or Valentine, or taking another poke at my client."

Odette shrugged. "I only met him once. He wanted an interview, so I gave it to him. He struck me as an energetic young fellow with a nose for a good story. If you'd like, the next time he calls, I'll give him your number."

"Oh, stuff it, Bernie," Wolch said good-naturedly. "The guy's got my number. He's just not interested in using it. That's okay, though. Despite what you or Kurt Zelmanski may think, this case will ultimately be fought and won in court, not on the pages of *The Wall Street Journal*."

"And may the best man win," said Odette with the smile of a leopard.

Wolch's smile in return went no further than his lips. His bright blue eyes were hard and flat. This was one battle he wasn't going to lose.

"Indeed, may the best man win."

THE ROLLING STONES blared out of the six-foot-tall speakers that stood in the four corners of Lew Valentine's private gym one floor above his office. Valentine was on the StairMaster, dressed in a T-shirt emblazoned with his corporate logo and a pair of black running shorts. His face was bright red and he was sweating profusely. His lips were moving, but the music was so loud that Bernard Odette couldn't make out what he was saying.

Odette cupped his hand to his ear and shrugged to let Valentine know he couldn't hear him. Valentine nodded. He pointed to the sound system behind the treadmill and motioned to Odette to turn down the sound.

Mick Jagger's voice faded to a whisper.

Valentine maintained his pace as he called out to Odette, "Didn't you bring your workout clothes? I thought you were coming to work out with me. I told your girl I have every machine you could possibly want here."

He had left the message with Rizzy. Odette smiled, imagining Rizzy's wrath if she were to know how Valentine had referred to her. "I got the message. Thanks, but I'm not much for machines," he said.

"Great stuff. State of the art," Valentine boasted. "I spared no expense when I put in this gym. I told my board of directors it would be worth every penny to keep me healthy and fit. I couldn't do them much good dead, could I?"

His tone seemed to demand a response. "Not much good at all," Odette agreed.

"I work out every day, either here or at home with my personal trainer. Do you have a trainer?"

Odette shook his head, thinking, hell no. He was getting tired merely watching Valentine.

"You really ought to get one. It's a smart investment. This last year, I already lost ten percent of my body fat and lowered my cholesterol fifteen points. Not too shabby, huh?'' Valentine stepped off the machine and bent over to catch his breath. ''Throw me that towel, would you?''

Odette obliged and wondered, what next? Would Valentine now request that he spot him while he went through his free weights routine?

''So the Starwares board is meeting even as we speak,'' said Valentine, vigorously rubbing himself with the towel. ''How soon do you think we'll hear?''

Odette looked at his watch. Valentine knew as well as he did that when a corporate board met in order to choose between two suitors, the debate could go on for hours. The directors had to be scrupulous in their efforts to determine which was the more advantageous bid.

In this particular case, they would have to weigh Eric Lynch's obvious and stated desire to ally himself with Jordan Crandell against Valentine's substantially more lucrative offer. Though Odette was confident they would eventually vote for the latter, he knew the discussion could be heated and lengthy.

''Utah's two hours behind us,'' he said. ''The meeting was called for nine-thirty, so they've already been talking for over four and a half hours, assuming they kept going through lunch. It's hard to say, Lew. We could hear any minute, or not until tomorrow.''

''Nah!'' Valentine picked up a skipping rope and began jumping in place. ''It's not going to take that long. Want to make a small bet—say, a couple of thousand dollars—that we'll get a call by six o'clock, New York time?''

Odette shook his head. ''Thanks, but no. I make it a policy never to bet with clients.''

''Yeah, especially when you know the client's right.'' Valentine chuckled. ''This one's a piece of fucking cake for those guys, if you'll pardon my French. They *have* to choose us.''

The jump rope thudded against the wooden floor in an

alternating rhythm with Valentine's feet. Odette thought about excusing himself to go have a chat with Anita while her boss was otherwise occupied. Life was too short, he thought, to stand here like an idiot while Valentine amused himself playing children's games.

Valentine was the client, and as much as Odette disliked him, he wasn't worth offending. "Was there something you specifically wanted to discuss, Lew? Or was this visit meant to be more in the nature of a social call?" he asked.

"You lawyers." Valentine wheezed between jumps. "It doesn't matter whether you're from New York or Detroit. You're all so damned uptight. Look at you, standing there with your arms crossed against your chest. I bet you never relax. I bet you don't even know how to have fun."

Odette thought about the fun he'd had two evenings earlier with Anita, who was beginning to be a rather regular feature in his life. He would miss her when the case was finished and he returned to Detroit. But she was all he would miss about this case.

"Fun's all relative," he said, his fingers itching to light up a cigarette.

"Pepper!" Valentine suddenly screamed.

Odette stared at him, mystified, until he realized Valentine must be referring to the double-time speed at which he was now twirling the rope and jumping.

Seconds later, Valentine just as abruptly slackened the pace, then stopped completely and placed his index finger over the pulse point on his wrist. Panting, he said, "One hundred twenty-five beats a minute. Not bad. I'd like to shave off another couple of seconds."

His T-shirt was drenched with sweat, and his hair was matted against his head. He picked up his towel again and draped it around his neck. "Okay, I'm done. Next, a quick shower, and then twenty minutes of steam. You might as well join me. We can talk in there."

"We don't want to miss the call from Starwares," Odette said.

"Anita knows my routine. If I don't answer in the gym, she'll transfer the call to the steam room."

Odette was unenthusiastic about the idea of sharing close quarters with Valentine while perspiration oozed from his pores. He couldn't understand why the man suddenly seemed so eager for companionship. And then the answer dawned on him.

Lew Valentine was scared. For all his bravado, for all his professed certainty about Starwares, he was worried he'd lose the deal. Odette couldn't wait to share the joke with Rizzy. The guy was a nervous wreck. All that running and jumping and heavy breathing were merely ways to keep himself from going off the deep end.

He felt a flicker of compassion for Valentine that passed as quickly as a glimmer of distant lightning in the summer night sky. He, too, hated to lose. But years ago, he'd learned that it made no sense to be afraid of loss. The scent of fear attracted failure the way wild animals were drawn to the smell of fresh blood.

He brought into every case, every conference, every courtroom, the certain knowledge that he would win. On those infrequent occasions when success eluded him, he gave himself the luxury of believing that he could have done no better. That he'd done the absolute best he could. He wondered whether Lew Valentine ever afforded himself that same luxury.

"I don't have a lot of time, Lew. We can talk right here," he said.

"I *pay* for your time, Odette," said Valentine. Then he caught himself. "Sorry. I'm a little jumpy today. The waiting's tough on me. Kind of like when your wife's getting ready to give birth. You have any kids, Bernie?"

Odette shook his head.

"So you don't know how it feels. You sit around for nine months, you and your wife, wondering what's going to come out of there, a normal kid or a monster with two heads and webbed feet. The last part's the worst, when your wife goes into labor. She's crying and screaming and cursing, and you're sweating right along with her and wishing she would hurry up and get it over with. And there's not a goddamn thing you can do to hurry her up.'' He smiled wanly. ''You see what I mean?''

''The waiting's rough,'' Odette said. ''Where's Walter Spaulding? Shouldn't your chief counsel be here for this?''

''Spaulding? You know he's useless. I keep him around for window dressing. So, how about a few minutes of steam? It's great for getting rid of all the toxins.''

''Thanks, but I like to keep my toxin levels as high as possible.'' Odette smiled, in case Valentine was too nervous to realize he was joking. ''Listen, Lew. I need to make some calls, check in with my office. Why don't I wait for you downstairs while you finish up?''

''All right,'' Valentine said, sounding as if he were doing Odette a tremendous favor. ''But don't go anywhere I can't find you, you hear me?''

A bell shrilled loudly just as Odette turned to leave. ''What the hell is that?'' he said.

''The phone,'' said Valentine. ''They fixed it so I can hear it over the music.'' He grabbed the receiver as it shrilled again. ''Yeah? Okay, put them through. . . .'' He glanced at Odette. ''It's Spaulding. He's got Don Voss on conference call.''

Odette nodded. Don Voss was Starwares' outside counsel. This was the call they had been waiting for.

''Go ahead, we're all here,'' said Valentine. ''Walter, could you stop flapping your mouth long enough so I can hear what Don is saying?''

Odette watched as Valentine's face contorted into a hideous mask of fury. ''They what? You're shitting me!'' he screamed into the phone. ''What the hell kind of. . . . That's crap, and you know it! . . . No, you listen to me,

Voss! You tell Lynch he's playing way out of his league if he thinks he can fuck with me. . . . Yeah, you're damn fucking right you'll see us in court. And Voss? One more thing you can tell your boss. He better start hunting for a new job, because he's not going to last five minutes after I take over Starwares!''

Valentine clicked off the telephone handset and glared at Odette. His chest was heaving, and his cheeks had turned bright red again. "They voted against us! Can you believe it?"

Odette was eager to return to his office and speak to Donald Voss himself. But his client, who looked to be on the verge of a heart attack, obviously needed some hand-holding. "What reason did they give?" he asked.

" 'Too conditional.' Bullshit! Altdir's already in for eight hundred million, and I've got phone companies from here to New Mexico lining up to invest with me. And those clowns in Utah are saying my offer's too conditional?"

He stared at Odette, as if daring him to respond. Then he picked up one of his handweights and heaved it across the room. Odette ducked as the weight sailed past him. It thudded against the far wall and fell to the floor, leaving behind a long, jagged scar where it had dented the plaster.

Lew Valentine stared from the crack in the wall to Odette. "I don't care what it takes, Odette," he said, more calmly now. "You win this case for me. I want that company, goddamnit! And nobody, I mean nobody, better get in my way."

IN THE TWELVE years Rick Major had worked for Jordan Crandell, Major had rarely seen his boss as determined to dig up dirt on someone as he was about Paul Murray. Major couldn't figure out what Crandell had going with the guy. Not that it was any of his business. Rick Major got paid to gather information. But for a top-notch private eye, guesswork came as naturally as breathing. Tracking down a lead more often than not meant following his nose and trusting his gut instincts.

Major's work for Crandell took him all over the map. He spent a lot of time in his car, commuting to Manhattan from his home in Rockland County, or driving around the tri-state area to meet with his contacts. He flew a lot of miles, too, every year, which was good for his frequent-flyer plan, not so good for his marriage. In transit, he read a lot of novels, mostly police procedurals, or listened to books on tape. Or he played guessing games, concocting elaborate scenarios about Jordan Crandell's motives.

By now, Major thought he had a pretty good handle on him. But every so often his boss surprised him. His reaction to Major's report on Paul Murray, for example. After weeks of careful research, Major had turned up nothing more serious than a couple of parking tickets that Murray had let go longer than he should have and a tendency to be late paying the bills.

He'd delivered his report to Crandell just before Christmas. That same afternoon, Crandell had summoned him to his office. Expecting a ''Congratulations for job well done, and here's your Christmas bonus,'' he'd found himself instead on the receiving end of one of Jordan Crandell's infamous temper tantrums.

Crandell had picked up the file and flung it at Major, sending Major's neatly typed pages flying all over the desk and floor.

''Dammit! I don't pay you a small fortune to come up with this kind of shit! Nobody's that squeaky clean!'' he'd ranted. ''I don't care what it costs. You find something real on this guy!''

Major had hurried back to his office, thinking dark thoughts about Jordan Crandell and his Scrooge-like qualities. He poured himself a stiff shot of the whiskey he kept in his drawer for just such emergencies and started working the phones. He put out the word to all his contacts: "Keep your ears open and ask lots of discreet questions. We'll make it worth your while."

Three months had passed, and he had come up with nothing. Major was almost ready to do the unthinkable and fabricate some story about Paul Murray's one and only fall from grace. Such a thing went against all the principles he adhered to as a private investigator who believed that the truth, if sought long and hard enough, would always emerge. The consequences, if he were to be found out, were terrible. He could lose his job, possibly his PI's license. On the other hand, he knew Crandell was fast running out of patience.

The rain was beating so hard against his window that he couldn't see across the street. It had been storming for two days straight, the kind of steady downpour that made him think of the story he'd learned in Sunday School about Noah's Ark and the forty-day rains that had brought the Flood. He supposed it was true, as his five-year-old daughter kept telling him, that April showers brought May flowers. But they also made it hellishly hard to navigate the city streets or keep dry as he dashed from one appointment to the next.

His phone rang three times before he remembered that his secretary had called in sick. "Major here," he said, praying that it wasn't Crandell's secretary at the other end.

"Hey, Durante! How ya' doin'? Great day for the fish, ain't it?" Frankie Pollock chuckled in his ear.

It was Frankie Pollock, a bail bondsman in the Bronx, who had given him his nickname, after Jimmy Durante, the legendary comedian whose nose was even bigger and more prominent then Major's. But Frankie Pollock was also an invaluable source, who collected information about people that Crandell wanted to know about the way bees collected honey.

Major pressed the record button on the tape recorder

that was permanently attached to his telephone. "Hello, Frankie, what's going on?"

"Why don't ya' drive on up here and buy me lunch?" Pollock suggested.

Major groaned silently. Frankie must have something to tell him, but the last thing in the world he wanted to do today was take a drive to the Bronx. The trick was to get Frankie to spill the beans over the phone.

"In this rain? The traffic's so bad that I wouldn't get there before dinner."

"Dinner's even better. Anyways, I gotta stick around for Night Court. We could hit the deli on 161st Street. You know, the one around the corner from the Stadium. Or you could bring me something from one of those fancy SoHo restaurants I'm always reading about in the *Post*."

"Tell me what you know, and I'll give you a rain check. It's brutal out there today, Frankie. It's worth a lot to me not to go all the way up to the Bronx."

"It'll be worth even more if you quit kvetching and get your ass up here. If you're still interested in getting something on Paul Murray, this is gonna be good, I promise you," said Pollock.

It better be, thought Major, as he navigated the small river that had formed on the FDR Drive.

On his way from the office, crossing Houston to get on the FDR, he'd stopped at Ballato's for an order of garlic bread and penne with sausage for Frankie. Now, his car reeked of garlic, and the food would probably be ice cold by the time he got to the Bronx. Frankie wouldn't care. His main criterion for enjoying a meal was that it be charged to somebody else's tab.

Just as he'd feared, traffic was creeping, both because of the rain and a rubbernecking delay at the site of an accident just south of the Willis Avenue Bridge.

He'd never understood why New York drivers felt compelled to slow to a crawl and stare at accidents.

Hadn't they ever seen an ambulance before? Were they so starved for thrills that the side of a car that had been squeezed in half like an accordion was enough to make them stop and gape?

He bet they didn't rubberneck at accidents in Montana or Arizona. One of these days, he was going to make good on his favorite threat and leave New York forever. He didn't have to work for Crandell. His skills were as portable as his computerized Rolodex and the telephone. If his wife didn't want to come along, that was her problem.

"Let's keep it moving, folks," he muttered as the congestion finally opened up and he hit the Bronx. After that, it was just a matter of avoiding the potholes on the Major Deegan until he took the 161st Street exit and swung around onto Jerome Avenue and into the closest parking lot.

In spite of his umbrella, he was soaking wet by the time he covered the short distance from the lot to Frankie Pollock's storefront office, conveniently located just a couple of blocks away from the County Courthouse. He waited in the outer reception area while Frankie finished up with a client, a haggard young Hispanic woman with a baby and two toddlers clinging to her legs.

After she was gone, Pollock shook his head as he ripped open the bag of food. "Poor kid. Did ya' get a look at her face? Her husband gave her that black eye and fat lip. But never mind. Her and her sisters scraped together the money to post bail so he can get out and beat her up again. Go figure."

He shrugged and pulled off the lid of the takeout container, then sighed with pleasure. "Italian. My favorite. How about you, Durante? Ain't ya' joining me?"

Major stared in dismay at the chunks of sausage, congealing in the tepid tomato sauce. "I already ate," he said. "So, okay. I'm here, and I brought you lunch. What have you heard?"

"This is gonna cost you more than your standard rate, you know," warned Pollock as he dumped the penne onto a paper plate.

"Talk to me, Frankie."

Pollock dunked a slice of garlic bread into the tomato sauce. "I had a drink last night with an old friend of mine, a guy who used to be a cop in this precinct. He retired on disability about seven or eight years ago, and now he's head of security at one of those big co-op complexes over in Manhattan. Lincoln Square Concourse, you know the place?"

"Is that relevant to what you have to tell me?" Major asked, popping a Rolaids mint into his mouth.

Pollock looked hurt. "Just wanted to give you some background on the guy. Anyways, we were reminiscing about the good old days and how things have changed in the neighborhood, all the drug deals, that sort of thing. So then he starts telling me what I already know—that you always have your rotten apples, and they aren't just the drug dealers, either. Sometimes, it's the cops, sometimes even the lawyers who are on the take."

He pushed the soggy paper plate away from him and wiped his face with his handkerchief. "Geez, I wish you'd have brought me a beer. A cold Bud would really hit the spot right now."

"Next time. So what do rotten cops and lawyers have to do with Paul Murray? Was he on the take?"

"Paul Murray? Nah. But didja' know he has a brother?"

"Jimmy Murray," said Major with growing excitement. "He used to be a cop, right here in the Bronx, wasn't it?"

Frankie Pollock burped. "Bingo," he said.

At 3:25 A.M., Rizzy Riznicki put down her red pencil and looked up from her copy of the brief.

Bernard Odette had finished proofreading his copy a few minutes before. "Done?" he asked.

"Done," she said. "I caught about six or seven typos plus five skipped sentences. How about you?"

"Something like that." He slumped against the back of the couch and yawned. His bones were aching with weariness, but the results more than justified the effort. "God, it's been a long day."

"And it ain't over yet. Not till the fat lady sings the corrections into the computer." Rizzy pulled herself out of the chair to pour another cup of coffee. "I'm really going to regret this in the morning," she murmured.

"It already is the morning. How soon can we get these changes inputted?"

"We've got a secretary coming over at five. It won't take long to revise and reprint. Do we have to show the final copy to Valentine and Spaulding before we file?"

"To what end?" Odette said scornfully. "They'll be lucky if I allow them to show up in court with me. Valentine's nothing but a businessman who mistakenly believes he knows something about the law, and Spaulding's a lawyer who shares the same mistaken impression. You be at the clerk's office to file when it opens."

She scowled over the top of her coffee mug. "Now that's a truly delightful thought. The subway at rush hour on no sleep."

He took pity on her. "All right. If you're angling for a ride downtown, you can tell my driver to pick you up at eight-fifteen."

"What a guy," she said, grinning. "Bernie, you're all heart."

"You deserve it, Riznicki. You've done a good job."

Rizzy put her hand to her forehead and pretended to go into a swoon. "Alert the media. They said it couldn't be done, but the Michigan Assassin just paid me a compliment."

"Well, cherish this one, because I don't do it often."

But he had to admit that credit was due her for all

her hard work during the last couple of months. She had matched him hour for hour while they'd fashioned the brief into a document that even he could find no fault with. Credit was due him, too, for having had the good sense to hire her. Though he would never admit it, she was worth twice what she'd talked him into paying her.

Rizzy sank wearily to the floor, which was littered with crumpled pieces of paper and stacks of memos, as well as empty soda cans and unwashed dinner plates. "What do you think?" she asked him, pushing away a bowl of soggy Caesar salad.

"What do *you* think?"

"Maybe I'm easily impressed, but I think you've covered every possible base and then some."

Easily impressed were not words he would ever use to describe Rizzy Riznicki. She had surprised him with her bluntness, playing devil's advocate on every point he'd raised throughout the entire process. She hadn't known very much about corporate law when she'd come to work for him. But she was a quick learner who had asked the right questions and helped refine his arguments.

"Let's hope the judge agrees with you," he said, massaging his temples.

"Too bad we don't get to pick and choose the one we want."

He chuckled. "It would be nice, but not really necessary. You've got a couple of old-timers in the Southern District who are blatantly pro-government. But in a situation like ours, when it's corporation versus corporation, there's a better than excellent chance the case will be decided on its merits. And you can quote me on that to your friend Zelmanski the next time he calls."

"Zelmanski. . . ." She wrinkled her brow. "Oh, yeah. I remember him. Nice-looking reporter with an attitude."

"It never hurts to befriend the press. It can make for some very interesting pillow talk."

"You have a dirty mind, Mr. Odette. Why would you assume we've gotten that far?"

"I'd be disappointed if you haven't. *Carpe diem* is my motto. Seize the day."

"And here I thought one of the advantages of being an orphan was that I didn't have anyone keeping track of me anymore."

Odette smiled. "I wasn't born yesterday, Rizzy. I'd have to be blind, deaf, and dumb not to have noticed the phone messages. I approve, however. From the first day he interviewed me, I liked his questions, even if I wasn't prepared to answer them. The one about Crandell's financing, for example. I wonder where he's taken that?"

His question was not idly posed. If Zelmanski had turned anything up on Crandell, Odette wanted to know about it.

He studied Rizzy's face, trying to detect any hint that she was holding back information from him. "Rizzy?"

"What?" She sounded defensive.

"Before I pose this next question, I remind you that whatever romantic or sexual heights Zelmanski may have taken you to, I'm still the one who's paying your salary. Now, I ask you. What does Zelmanski know that you're not telling me?"

She squirmed under his sharp gaze. "C'mon, boss. Give me a break. You know I haven't seen the guy in at least two weeks. How would I know what he's up to?"

"Don't go soft on me, Rizzy. When I hired you, I believe I made it clear that I expected nothing less than total loyalty."

"Well, there was something he was working on that he told me about over dinner," she reluctantly conceded. "But I don't know how far he's gotten with it."

Odette listened as she sketched out Zelmanski's suspicions.

When she was done, he said, "Zelmanski's a prospector. He's going for the gold. By now he's probably pretty close to the motherlode. I want you to find out everything he has to date."

"I can't do that, Bernie. I'm not a Mata Hari kind of girl."

"Oh, yes you are," he said confidently. "To keep it fair, you can feed him some piece of information that we weren't planning to make public yet. Nothing major, just enough to make him happy. As a matter of fact, why don't you call him in a couple of hours to tell him you're filing the brief. He'll appreciate the scoop. You can even give him a ride to court in my car."

"I don't *think* so, Bernie," she said darkly.

He decided not to press the point. Eventually she would come around. The case had become as much hers as his; she wanted to win it as badly as he did. She was tough, a street fighter who would brawl in the gutter if that's what it took to win. That very quality was the reason he had hired her. He recognized the type. He saw it every day of his life whenever he looked in the mirror.

JORDAN CRANDELL LAY prone on the table, naked except for a towel around his midsection. "Fuck! You're killing me!" he yelled at the man who stood over him.

"That's what I'm here for," Marcus, his masseur, said softly as he deftly kneaded the necklace of knotted muscles strung across the top of Crandell's shoulders.

Crandell groaned in pain. Marcus Smith was a slimly built young man, a strict vegetarian with gentle manners and a soft-spoken voice. But he had fingers of steel that could punish with their curative power.

"Your back's a mess," Marcus said, reaching for the oil.

"Worse than usual?"

"Much worse. I can tell this takeover fight is really getting to you."

"It's almost over," Crandell said, sounding more optimistic than he felt.

"Yeah? That's too bad. My Starwares stock has been climbing through the roof."

Crandell twisted around to look at Marcus.

"You own stock in Starwares?"

Marcus nodded. "Sure." He pushed Crandell back down on the table. "It's a great company. Everyone says Eric Lynch is a genius."

"So they say." Crandell grunted as Marcus began on his back.

"Have you been staying away from red meat, like I told you to?"

"You're my masseur, not my nutritionist," Crandell snapped back.

Marcus was unfazed. He pulled at the wad of flesh just above Crandell's waist and pinched it between his thumb and forefinger.

"Ouch! What the hell are you doing?"

"Red meat," said Marcus. "That's what gives you these love handles. You've been pigging out on those thick juicy steaks, haven't you?"

Crandell buried his head between his folded arms and forced himself to keep quiet. Whatever happened to the old-fashioned notion of service people who knew their place? If he wanted to be nagged about his diet, he would have stayed married to his last wife.

Marcus had a bad habit of giving unsolicited advice. But at least he didn't insist on playing New Age music and burning incense sticks like the last person Crandell had used. He was also the best masseur in the city. Even *New York* magazine had said so. His schedule was so crowded that he saw clients beginning at 5:30 A.M. Crandell had a standing appointment for two mornings a week at 6:30, which gave him time for a quick workout before-hand.

Marcus was right about one thing, however. The damn deal was getting to him. It wasn't playing out the way it was supposed to.

Normally, he liked a good fight. But this one felt dif-ferent. It was taking too long, and it was too unpredictable. He'd had to keep raising the stakes to outmaneuver Valentine, who late last week had topped him again by two dollars. Crandell had decided to hold firm at eighty-nine dollars for 51 percent. He could only hope and pray that the bloom wasn't off the romance with Summit for Lynch and his directors.

Some days Crandell had to ask himself whether instead of investing in another company, he wouldn't be better off buying a nice secluded island in the South Pacific where he could permanently retire from the fray. He pictured himself swinging in a hammock between two tall palm trees, drinking a pina colada, watching the tide inch closer to the beach, with nothing more pressing on his mind than what to have for dinner.

It was a tempting fantasy, but he was missing one element. Groaning again as Marcus moved down his back to pummel his legs, he summoned up the perfect, gorgeous, sexy woman to share his Shangri-La. She floated into the picture, a Polynesian beauty wearing nothing but an orchid in her long black hair and a sarong that ended just below her thighs. She smiled at him and bent to kiss his lips.

Again, there was something wrong with the picture. The face on his Polynesian beauty belonged to Hope Scott.

"Jesus!" he exclaimed.

"Hey, I'm hardly using any pressure," said Marcus.

"No, you're fine. I just remembered something I forgot to do."

It made no sense. He could have any woman he wanted, and he was becoming obsessed with Hope Scott. Hope Scott Murray, he supposed she now called herself. Which reminded him to tell Donna to leave another message for Rick Major. He would keep after that jerkoff P.I. until the guy came up with a story on Paul Murray that revealed him to be as imperfect as every other mortal.

His fantasy destroyed, he picked up the TV remote control and switched on CNN.

"Bad idea," Marcus said. "I'm trying to release your tension."

"It relaxes me," he said, but he muted the volume. He turned his head to stare at the screen just in time to catch a clip of Lew Valentine and his wife in front of the Waldorf. "Bastard. Now what?" he mumbled. He restored the volume as the picture shifted back to Bob Cain in the Atlanta newsroom.

"This just in," Cain announced. "In overnight developments in the ongoing battle between Valentine Industries and the Summit Corporation for ownership of Starwares, the giant computer software company, Lew Valentine has announced an additional contribution to his war chest of five hundred million dollars from Blinkoff, Ltd., the Toronto-based magazine- and book-publishing empire. Although Starwares' board has already rejected Valentine's most recent high bid of ninety-one dollars a share for fifty-one percent of the stock, presumably this money would be available should the bidding resume between Valentine and his adversary, Summit's Jordan Crandell."

Crandell jolted upright to a sitting position. "I don't *believe* this!" he exploded.

Marcus Smith stepped back to retreat from the line of fire. Still keeping an eye on the news, Crandell grabbed for the phone and speed-dialed Ken Wolch's home number.

The lawyer answered almost as soon as the connection was made. "Yes, Jordan," Wolch said. "I'm watching CNN. Hold it a sec. Let me hear the rest of the report."

Crandell punched up the volume: ". . . that according to industry analysts, it's now up to the court to decide who will be the winner in this takeover struggle that has dominated the business news for the last six months. Papers are expected to be filed perhaps as early as today in Federal Court in New York City by attorneys representing Valentine Industries. Turning to other matters. . . ."

"Ken?" growled Crandell, muting the sound again. "Are you on top of this?"

Wolch laughed. "What do you think, Jordan?"

"I think I don't want any surprises, Ken."

"From the moment Lynch told us that the board had rejected Valentine's latest offer, I've had someone standing by at the court clerk's office. We'll know what Odette's up to as soon as the clerk does."

Somewhat mollified, Crandell said, "Then what?"

"Most likely Odette will be asking for preliminary injunction relief from the key provisions in Starwares' rights plan. I'm sure you remember the drill from our run-in with Selkix. Our case will get assigned to a judge, Odette will present his arguments, and Byron and I will demolish him."

"Demolish the Michigan Assassin?"

"Are you losing faith in my abilities, Jordan?"

Crandell lay back down on the table. Ken Wolch had never failed him in the past. There was no need to worry. Everything was under control.

"No, Ken," he said, silently signaling Marcus to resume the massage. "I have perfect faith in you. Call me whenever you hear something."

"You bet," said Wolch.

Crandell replaced the phone and turned to Marcus. "Everything you hear in this room is strictly confidential."

Marcus rolled his eyes. "You're not the only captain of industry in my appointment book. But thanks for the reminder. Now, can we continue?"

Crandell nodded and gave himself over to Marcus's probing fingers. Unbidden, the South Pacific fantasy floated back into his consciousness. The tropical breeze felt soothing against his face. Hope Scott had disappeared, replaced by a trio of beauties hardly older than his daughter, who were doing obscenely delightful things to various parts of his body.

He sighed with pleasure. Life was good. He would triumph. First, he'd buy Starwares, then he'd buy the island. Even if he couldn't spend a great deal of time there, it would make an excellent investment.

TEN

PAUL HEARD THE news first from his law clerk, Naomi Bowman, who walked into his office grinning gleefully.

He glanced up from the memo he was preparing. "You look like you just won the lottery."

"No, you did." She waved a message slip at him. "I just spoke to the court clerk. Your name came up for a complaint that was filed this morning."

"It must be a juicy one. I haven't seen you smile like that since I told you I got married."

She cleared her throat and held the piece of paper up with a flourish. " *'Starwares, Inc., Summit, Inc., Defendants,* v. *Valentine Industries, Inc., Plaintiff.'* Is that juicy enough for you?"

Paul put down his pen and sat back in his chair. He'd just been assigned one of the most highly publicized corporate cases ever to be heard in the Federal Southern District of New York. He'd been following the takeover machinations in the newspaper for weeks, wishing he could have a crack at the case.

"I guess I did hit the jackpot. What's Valentine looking for? A preliminary injunction?"

She nodded. "To halt Summit's tender offer."

He and the rest of the legal community had been expecting Valentine's complaint since the moment that

Starwares had turned down Valentine's bid. "We have our work cut out for us, Naomi. It's you and me versus Bernard Odette and Ken Wolch, neither of whom is known for his economy of words or documentation."

"I understand that document boxes are on their way over—by the truckload. And I remember Ken Wolch. You granted him a temporary restraining order last year in *Acker* v. *Chellis*. What about Odette? Do you know him?"

"The Michigan Assassin? Only by reputation. He's as famous for his elegant rhetoric as for his sartorial style."

"In other words, a ladykiller who slays dragons in the courtroom."

He laughed. "In a nutshell."

Paul's secretary knocked on the open door. "Excuse me, Your Honor. It's Jesse Rubin on line one."

"Thanks. I'll be right with him. Naomi, see if you can get a sense as to the scope of those documents, so we can figure out when to schedule the hearing. We should try to move quickly on this."

"Will do," she said and left his office.

He picked up the phone. "Good morning, Jesse. How are you?"

"You son-of-a-gun. Congratulations! Talk about beginner's luck!"

"How you'd find out so quickly?"

"Are you kidding? News travels fast, especially news about this case. I already got a call from a reporter at *The Wall Street Journal*. He wanted me to comment on your grasp of corporate and trade reg. law."

"What did you tell him?"

"That I'd taught you everything you know, so this case couldn't be in better hands."

Paul smiled. He could well imagine Jesse saying just that. "Is this the same fellow who's been covering all the developments?"

"Zelmanski, right, a real comer. He'll probably be

calling you in case they want to run a profile on you."
He hesitated, then said, "Paul? I'm sure you know what
you're doing, but do you mind if I give you some unsolicited advice?"

Paul glanced down and noticed that two more of his
phone lines were lit up. He was already behind schedule,
and he might have calls to return before court. But Jesse's
tone had turned so suddenly serious that he felt it important to hear what he had to say. "You've never steered
me wrong, Jesse. Go ahead."

"Zelmanski and a lot of other people are going to be
watching you closely during the next few weeks, Paul.
Your colleagues, the press, your friends, and your enemies. Be careful. Crandell and Valentine are not your average plaintiff and defendant. They'll both go to great
lengths to get what they believe to be theirs."

Paul didn't know what to make of Jesse's rather omi-
nous warning. "You make them sound like a couple of
gangsters."

"No, I'm not implying that at all," Jesse assured him.
"But neither are they your average businessmen. They're
extremely driven, highly competitive, and their lawyers
take no prisoners. I have every confidence in your understanding of the law, Paul. I know you'll reach the right
decision. Just don't underestimate those two. They've
been publicly slamming each other for weeks now, calling each other all kinds of names. If either of them feels
the need, they're capable of stooping to those depths with
you, as well."

"Hell, Jesse, I'm almost sorry I took your call." Paul
chuckled. "I was sitting here, pretty pleased with what
the roll of the dice turned up for me. Now you're making
me feel like I'm the sheriff of Dodge City, it's high noon,
and the bad guys just rode into town."

Jesse laughed. "I've seen you in action. You're one
hell of a sharpshooter. Just make sure you keep your guns
loaded and the sun out of your eyes."

Paul's intercom buzzed. "Jesse, could you hold it a sec? I must be getting another call."

"That's all right. Call me if you need anything. Until then, happy trails, pardner."

Smiling, Paul pressed the intercom. "Yes, Doris?"

"Mrs. Murray's on two, and a Kurt Zelmanski from the *Wall Street Journal* is on three."

"See if you can find out what Zelmanski wants, please, and take his number. I'll speak to my wife." He picked up line two and said, "Hope? Are you all right? Everything okay with the baby?"

She laughed, and he was instantly reassured. "Everything's fine, darling. But I just got off the phone with Uncle George, who told me about your fabulous new case. He's absolutely thrilled for you, Paul."

Again, he was surprised by how quickly the news was spreading. "How did he know?"

"I have no idea. Why? Was it supposed to be a secret?"

"No, not at all. I'm just surprised that he found out so soon."

"Well, I suppose he makes it his business to know such things. But I wish you could have heard him rhapsodizing about what a marvelously brilliant opportunity this is for you. He was hurrying off to a meeting, but he's going to call you later to congratulate you himself. Evidently, he's been following all the negotiations very carefully. He says that Summit's sure to win because—"

"Hope."

"What?" She sounded hurt. "Did I say something wrong?"

"Darling, George Osburgh is entitled to his opinion about this case, but right now I'd rather not hear it." Suddenly, he was hit by a troubling thought. "He's not involved in any way, is he? There's no Scott money backing either of the parties, is there?"

"I have no idea, Paul. It's a blind trust, remember? He would never tell me."

"Of course not." Besides, George Osburgh was much too prudent and conservative to consider investing trust money in a takeover battle. He glanced at the newspaper that lay open on his desk and noticed Jordan Crandell's name in a headline. "What about Crandell? Isn't he a friend of yours?"

"Well, not a friend exactly," she said, after a moment.

"But you grew up with him, didn't you?"

"Darling." She laughed. "I grew up with a whole crowd of people whose names are regularly mentioned in the press. That doesn't mean I'm *friends* with all of them. Not like I'm friends with, oh, Yvonna Carter, for example. Why? Why are you asking me these questions, as if I were up on the witness stand?"

"Is that how I sound? I'm sorry," he said contritely. "I was concerned suddenly about the possibility of having to recuse myself from this case."

"I don't understand."

"Let's say that one of us had substantial money invested either in Summit or Valentine. Or that we were close friends with any one of the principal figures in the case. An argument could then be made that I wouldn't be able to render a fair and impartial judgment. I might have to decide to step down from the case. Or one of the parties could ask me to step down. Do you see what I mean?"

"Yes," she said tentatively. "Yes, I do. People might think you were being influenced one way or the other. I never thought about that before."

"No, of course not. Why would you?" he said, remembering that in fact the subject had come up before their wedding, when they'd argued about the need for a prenuptial agreement. She'd been so upset then by the idea of the prenup that she must not have paid much attention to his explanation about conflict of interest.

"Well, don't worry about it," he said. "I'm being ridiculous. But I'm about to be sitting in the glare of a very bright spotlight and I guess I took a nervous spell, as my mother would have put it.''

"That's totally understandable. Uncle George said this was going to be a whole different experience for you, but he knew you could handle the pressure.''

"Well, I'm glad to know he has such confidence in me.''

His intercom buzzed again. "Hope, I don't mean to be rude, but I should get going.''

"Call me later,'' she said. "And darling? Don't worry about a thing. I know you're going to have an absolutely wonderful time with this case.''

He picked up his secretary's line. "Yes, Doris.''

"Ned Berger from *The New York Times* on line two, they're running a story about you tomorrow and he has a few questions. Ditto Kurt Zelmanski. You're due in court in forty minutes.''

"I'll have to get back to Mr. Berger, but I'll talk to Zelmanski now and get him out of the way. Could you dial him for me, please?''

While he waited for her to put through the call, his glance fell on the large package that lay on his couch. The package had arrived the day before by UPS. He'd been too busy to open it, but he knew from the return address that it contained the robe he'd finally ordered to replace the one he'd used for the past six years.

He'd meant to unpack the robe to wear this morning. Now he changed his mind. He smiled, remembering how his mother had always bought him a new pair of pants and a shirt to begin the school year. "It's important to make a good impression on your first day, Paulie,'' she had told him.

For the sake of tradition, he would wait to wear the robe for the first time at the Starwares hearing. With so many people watching him, he wanted to be sure to make a good impression.

*   *   *

"JUST MEET ME for coffee. You must have time for that."
Kurt Zelmanski heard himself pleading with Rizzy and
winced. He never begged women for dates. He never
begged, period.

It was this damn story. He had lost his sense of per-
spective over it. Or was it Rizzy Riznicki? The fact that
he couldn't say for sure which interested him more was
alarming.

He followed her down the stone steps of the Federal
Courthouse Building. "Tomorrow morning, as early as
you want to make it, anywhere you want." Pressing his
luck, he went on, "Or we could have dinner tonight *and*
coffee in the morning, and whatever you want in between."

"Nudge, nudge, wink, wink," she said, her lips moving toward what could be construed as a smile.

"Does that mean yes?"

"No." She stopped at the bottom of the steps and
yawned hugely. "Sorry, I'm absolutely exhausted."

He studied her face, noticing the dark circles under her
eyes. "Yeah, you look awful."

"Thanks, Zelmanski, what a prince you are."

"Seriously, I'm concerned about you. Are you getting
enough sleep?"

"Try two hours last night."

He considered telling her that was only three hours less
than he'd had but decided against it. Instead, he said,
"You're keeping a reporter's hours but making a lawyer's salary."

Ignoring him, she looked up the street, as if searching
for a cab, then waved at a black limo slowly moving
toward them.

"Whoa! Is that Odette's?"

"It ain't mine yet, baby."

The limo pulled abreast of them, and the driver rolled
down his window. "All set, Rizzy?" he asked.

"Yup," she said, opening the back door herself.

"Take me home, please, Gene, the fastest way you know how."

Zelmanski saw his opportunity slipping away. "Let me ride with you uptown," he begged. He pushed himself between her and the open door. "Rizzy, please. I really need to talk to you."

"Well, why didn't you say so?" She grinned and slid over, leaving plenty of room for him on the capacious seat.

She smelled good. Even though she hadn't managed much sleep, she'd found time to put on some perfume. "You haven't answered my calls, Rizzy," he said accusingly.

"I've been busy, Zelmanski. That wasn't chopped liver you watched me file at the clerk's office just now."

The glass panel that separated them from the driver was open. "Can I shut that?" he asked.

"Sorry, Gene," she called to the driver, pushing the button that shut the panel. "He wants privacy."

He reached for her hand. "I thought we had a great time that night I stayed over."

She slapped his fingers away. "Don't go making any assumptions about us." Then she smiled. "I guess you were all right. For a reporter."

He liked that she was so prickly. It intrigued him, kept him guessing about what she was really thinking.

"Is that what you were calling about?" she asked. "Because your ego needed stroking?"

He grinned and nodded. "And something else, too. I'm about this close to getting my hands on some papers that could actually prove my theory about Crandell and his shaky financing."

She turned and stared at him. "How'd you manage that?"

Finally, he had her full attention. "Ken Wolch, Crandell's lawyer, called me to complain that my coverage was too one-sided. I used that as my opening to get inside Summit and meet some people on the business side."

He shook his head, recalling how they'd almost given him the run of the place. "I got friendly with a junior comptroller who turned out to be a regular fount of information."

"Gave you a lot of help, did she?"

She was still staring at him, but now her expression seemed less sympathetic. He met her gaze and tried not to feel guilty. But he felt as if she could see right through him.

It wasn't, strictly speaking, his fault that he'd spent the night at the woman's apartment. The comptroller, whose name he had trouble remembering, had suggested they go to dinner. Likewise, the second bottle of wine had been her suggestion. True, he had encouraged her to open up to him about her job, which she hated.

Jordan Crandell was a fiend who tormented her and everyone else in her department with his incessant demands. The last few months especially, he'd been on her back because the woman who usually handled Crandell's discretionary fund was out on maternity leave and she'd gotten stuck with the account.

The discretionary fund was so named because Summit's board had given Crandell unusually broad powers to invest these monies as he saw fit. Ultimately, of course, he had to show a profit. But in the short term, he got to play with the several millions of dollars as if they were Monopoly money.

What puzzled the junior comptroller were three checks, totalling a half-billion dollars, that had come in from the Scott Trust. She had particularly noticed the checks because the funds had appeared one day, vanished the next. Terrified that she was somehow responsible for the discrepancy, she had gone searching for the paperwork. Maybe the amounts of the checks had been miskeyed into the computer. Or maybe someone had neglected to record the transfer out of the funds.

Because so much money couldn't simply disappear, could it?

Rizzy was intrigued. Zelmanski could see it in her eyes. "Did your friend find any of the backup?" she asked.

"Not yet. But she's still looking. She's scared that any day now Crandell's going to demand an accounting, and she won't be able to make good."

"She's wrong, isn't she?"

He nodded. "That money was meant to go missing."

"Right. Because any first-year law student could tell you that no trustee worth a damn is going to invest a single penny of trust money in any of Jordan Crandell's speculative ventures."

"A half billion adds up to a hell of a lot of pennies."

"Far too many to stash away in your ordinary piggy bank. So where do you suppose that money went to?"

"First stop, an offshore account that's hard to trace back to Crandell and Summit. Final destination, a tidy little piece of the package that pays for the Starwares deal."

"Interesting," she said. "Zelmanski, why are you telling me all this?"

He'd asked himself the same question. He gave her the only answer he had come up with: "Because I needed to talk it through with somebody, and you were the only person who came to mind."

"I'm going to tell Odette this whole story, you know."

He shrugged. "I figured you would. That's okay. Now he owes me one. And there's not much any one of us can do with it unless my comptroller friend finds me some documentation. Until then, it's what you lawyers might call idle speculation."

"What does your friend stand to gain by feeding you this information?"

"Moral satisfaction."

She shook her head.

"Revenge? A chance to expose Jordan Crandell for the corrupt bastard that he is?"

Rizzy raised an eyebrow. "A regular Deep Throat, huh? As it were."

He blushed for the first time since fifth grade, when Sister Stanislaw had caught him looking under Annie Lenchek's dress.

Rizzy rolled back the glass panel. "Gene? You can pull over at the next corner. Mr. Zelmanski's gone about as far as he can go with me today."

IT WAS A done deal. Of course, they would still have to go through the courtroom formalities, the hearings and motions and whatever else the lawyers deemed necessary to earn their bloated paychecks. But that would all be window dressing, a false front erected to hide the fact that His Honor Paul Murray had no choice but to decide in favor of Summit, Inc.

Jordan Crandell slapped his knee and laughed out loud. Except that it was ten o'clock in the morning, he would have popped open a bottle of champagne to celebrate.

"Do you want to let me in on the joke, Jordan?" asked Ken Wolch, who had arrived with Byron Babcock for their previously scheduled appointment bearing the news that Valentine had filed suit that morning and Paul Murray had already been assigned to the case.

Crandell chuckled. "I'm just relieved that we're finally going to have our day in court. This thing has been dragging on too damn long as it is."

He wished he could share the joke with Wolch and Babcock. But they wouldn't properly appreciate the astonishingly fortuitous coincidence that had just delivered Starwares into his hands. It was karma, fate, kismet, God's will. Some deals were simply meant to be.

"Let's call Lynch. He should hear this from us," he said. He buzzed his secretary. "Get me Lynch, he's probably at the office. And three coffees." He glanced over at the two lawyers, who both nodded that they would like a cup.

"So when's the hearing?"

"Murray hasn't given us a date yet. But based on his record in Supreme Court, my guess is he'll schedule it as soon as possible," said Wolch.

"We're ready to go, whenever it is," Babcock interjected.

Donna's voice came over the intercom. "Mr. Crandell, I have Mr. Lynch for you now."

"Eric?" Crandell put him on the speakerphone. "I have Ken Wolch and Byron Babock here with me."

"Good morning, gentlemen. I guess I know why you're calling," said Lynch.

"Oh? You heard already?" Crandell felt vaguely disappointed. He'd been looking forward to telling Lynch himself.

"Of course. Valentine's guys called us last night."

"Oh, that." In his excitement, Crandell had almost forgotten about the additional $500 million that Blinkoff had just invested in Valentine Industries. "What did you say to them?"

"That they could accumulate enough money to pay off the national debt, but the board had reached its decision. They're out of the game."

Crandell beamed. Lynch was inching back into his good graces. "So then maybe you didn't know that Valentine filed its complaint this morning."

"I have a message here to call our lawyer in New York, but I took your call first."

"We'll know shortly from Judge Murray's clerk as to when he can schedule the oral arguments," said Wolch. "I haven't yet seen the brief, but I'm sure Odette has asked for expedited discovery. Your board members should expect to hear from him shortly."

"I take it you're feeling fairly optimistic," Lynch said.

"Speaking for myself, I'm feeling *very* optimistic," said Crandell. "Ken, how about you?"

"Eric, I suggest you hop on a plane and come watch

the show in court. This is one you don't want to miss. And as soon as the decision is handed down in our favor, we'll head uptown to the Second Avenue Deli, our treat.''

Lynch laughed. "You guys know me pretty well by now. I'll hold you to that offer. You know where to reach me if you need me.''

Crandell turned back to his two attorneys. "Give me a realistic time frame for all of this.''

Wolch shrugged. "My educated guess would be three to four weeks.''

Crandell frowned. He'd been hoping for a speedier resolution. "That long? Can't you do anything to move it up?''

"It's out of my hands now, Jordan. At this point, it's Judge Murray's call. And for better or for worse, there's not a damn thing any one of us can do to influence him.''

How wrong you are, thought Crandell. All that was necessary now was to calculate when to be in touch with Hope. Timing was all. He wanted Paul to sit a while with his case, peruse the documents, taste the sweetness of his judicial power. Then he would pounce on his prey, exacting his due reward for a favor generously rendered. He would have preferred to come armed with some incriminating morsel of information, fed to him by Rick Major. But so far, Major had nothing. Nevertheless, he was asking for so little and he'd given them so much. They couldn't possibly deny him this one request.

He smiled at Wolch and Babcock as he stood up to indicate the meeting was over. "Gentlemen," he said, "something tells me we have this case all sewn up.''

"Milton Cohen, huh?'' said Rick Major. "You don't meet very many—''

"Jewish cops. Yeah. I know," said Frankie Pollock's ex-cop friend. "That's the first thing most people ask about when they hear I used to be a cop. There are more of us than you'd think. We even have our own organization, the Shomrim Society.''

Rick Major nodded. "Sure, I know all about it."

"Then they say, 'Funny, you don't look Jewish.' Because of my blond hair and blue eyes, I guess." He laughed, a short, dry rasping sound that ended in a smoker's cough. "They should have seen my grandmother. She even fooled the Nazis back in Hungary."

Major smiled. "Thanks for seeing me on such short notice."

He already liked Milton Cohen. For one thing, unlike most other sources, he hadn't hit Major up for a free meal. Nor did he seem interested in a payoff. Probably he was making a good salary, plus he had his police pension coming in. Still, everyone could use a few extra bucks. Why wasn't Cohen looking for an envelope of money that could go unreported to the IRS?

"Frankie Pollock helped me out a lot of times when I was working in his precinct," Cohen said, as if in answer to Major's unspoken question. "He thought I might be able to give you some information, as a favor to him."

"That's right." Major pulled out his tape recorder. "Do you mind?"

"No. Just as long as my name doesn't end up in any newspaper stories or anything like that. I like my job. I wouldn't want to jeopardize it with any kind of bad publicity. Even by association."

"Sure, no problem," Major said. "I guess Frankie didn't tell you very much about me. I'm not a reporter, Mr. Cohen."

"Please, call me Milt."

"Okay, Milt. Anyway, I'm a private investigator."

"That right? I thought about going into that end of the business when I retired from the force. But my wife wanted me to keep more regular hours. So for the sake of keeping peace in the family. . . ." Milton Cohen shrugged. "She was probably right. This is a nice setup here. I negotiated a free two-bedroom apartment as part of my package. We love the location, just three blocks away from Lincoln Center. There's even a backyard with grass for residents only behind the building across the street.''

''Nice,'' said Major. ''Just out of curiosity, how many guys you got reporting to you?''

''Twelve, which isn't a lot for a six-building complex like this. But I run a tight ship. Maybe you could have guessed that from my office.'' He pointed to his desk, which was clear except for a memo pad and the stack of papers neatly piled in a wire basket labeled ''in-box.'' ''We manage to keep things pretty well covered. So, as you were saying, Rick?''

''Frankie mentioned you used to work with someone named Jimmy Murray.''

Milt Cohen nodded. ''Mind if I smoke? My wife's trying to get me to stop, but it's not easy.''

''Sure, go ahead.''

''Yeah, Jimmy Murray,'' said Milt Cohen, lighting a cigarette. ''A real likable kid. What's that expression? A face like the map of Ireland. I took a special interest in him. He kind of reminded me of my younger son.'' He paused and stared at the tip of his cigarette.

''Is he a cop, too?'' asked Major.

Milt Cohen inhaled and looked at Major. ''He died of leukemia when he was nineteen. He was sick five months, then he was gone.''

''I'm sorry,'' Major said. He waited for Cohen to continue.

Cohen stubbed out his half-smoked cigarette. ''So. Jimmy Murray. I met him when he was a rookie, must have been no more than twenty years old. Big smile. Very friendly. Smart, too . . . a real quick learner. I always thought he could have made detective. If he'd stuck around long enough.''

''What happened?''

''This is only because you're a friend of Frankie's, right?''

"Right."

"Because I'm not really keen to see this story in the paper or on some TV investigative report."

"Milt, my client feels the same way."

"Right." Cohen sighed deeply. Then he said, "Jimmy loved being a cop. He had this very old-fashioned idea about police work, about serving the community, keeping the streets safe and clean. He could sniff out the perps. Some months he made more collars than anyone else in his squad. You should have seen him with the Puerto Rican hookers who hung around Yankee Stadium. He was always trying to talk them into giving up the life and going straight. He had a lot of sisters, I can't remember now how many."

"You said he didn't stick around very long."

"Three years. Then he was out." Cohen snapped his fingers. "Like that. Just suddenly disappeared. I heard he started his own security consulting company somewhere outside the city."

Major nodded. He'd interviewed people like Milt Cohen before, people who had a story to tell that they'd kept bottled up inside them a long time, until one day someone came along to ask the right questions. But the habit of holding the story back was so strong that often it took them a while to get the words out. They needed priming, like a pump that hadn't gotten much use.

If he sat still and patiently, nodded where it seemed appropriate and pushed Cohen ever so gently, eventually the story would come spilling out. Major had a sense that it would be a good one—and that afterwards Milt Cohen would feel a whole lot better for having told it to him.

"They said he couldn't take the pressure, that he was getting bad ulcers." Cohen shook his head. "But they were lying to protect him. He had to quit. Otherwise, he was going to be arrested."

"Arrested? For what?"

"Jimmy had a friend, an assistant D.A. named Brendan Connor whom he knew from his old neighborhood in Brooklyn. The guy was a few years older than Jimmy, but I guess they hung around together a bit when they were kids. I never liked Connor very much, he was a real know-it-all, always trying to tell us how to run our business. Sometimes I'd bump into him on the street and he'd go off about all the muggings and B&E's, and why couldn't we ever track down any of the perps. A very aggravating guy. I'm sure you know the type."

Major nodded, thinking of Crandell. "Oh, yeah. I do."

"So I wasn't real distressed to hear that Connor had been arrested for accepting payoffs, tampering with evidence—all that good kind of stuff. He'd been under investigation for a couple of years."

Major was itching to ask how Connor's story tied in to Jimmy Murray. He knew the answer would come eventually, so he smiled encouragingly at Cohen.

Cohen pulled out another cigarette and gazed at it longingly. Then he gently put it down on his desk, and said, "This is the part that kills me. Mind you, I would never swear to any of this in court. I only know what I know through hearsay and rumor."

"I understand," Major said.

"Connor had a thing going with one of the biggest dealers in the neighborhood. This punk thought he *owned* one long stretch of the Grand Concourse and Walton Avenue. He was paying off Connor to go easy on his foot soldiers, plea-bargain them down to probation or minimal time. And Connor was such a smart-ass it never occurred to him that after a while the people upstairs might start picking up on his pattern. Then they found two small-time drug dealers who decided it was smarter to turn state's evidence against Connor than go to jail for life. But hey, if you're really looking to convict, you want to do better in the witness stand than a couple of pishers with mile-long records. That's when they really got lucky. Because it turned out that that bastard Connor couldn't leave well enough alone. He had to go and drag Jimmy into his stinkin' pile of shit.''

"How was that?'' asked Major.

"Supposedly, Jimmy needed some extra money. I don't know why, I heard he had a gambling problem.'' Cohen shrugged. "He must have mentioned it to his good pal Connor, and Connor tells him he has a great get-rich-quick scheme. All he has to do is *not* arrest certain guys who work for a friend of his. I think Jimmy took at least one payoff before the trail led to him. Maybe he even wore a wire to get more evidence on Connor. I'm not sure about that part. All I know is Connor gets his ass hauled into court, and Jimmy's off the force and into security systems.''

"Did you ever try to get in touch with him or talk to him after he quit?''

"No.'' Cohen spat out the word. "I wouldn't have been able to look him in the eye. Pissed me off what he did, a good kid like that.''

"Where's Connor these days?''

"Poor bastard.'' Cohen sighed again. "He got a light sentence, under the circumstances, only three to five. A couple of months after he got out, he died of a heart attack. Wasn't even thirty years old.''

"No charges were ever brought against Jimmy?''

"Nope.''

"Do you have any idea why not?''

"I have some ideas, but I bet you do, too.''

"Is there anyone else I could talk to about this?''

Cohen scribbled a couple of names on his memo. "Milly was a secretary at our precinct. She might be able to help you out if you can find her. Angie's her daughter in Port Chester who she used to go stay with on weekends. Tell her hello from me, and you could say I'm doing well.'' He hesitated. "If she asks, that is.''

"Thanks. You've been a great help,'' said Major. "Let me just ask you one more thing. You sound pretty sure that the story about Jimmy is true.''

Cohen tapped his index finger against his nose. "You're a P.I. You know how it is. You develop a sense for the stench of corruption."

Major nodded. "Right." Then, imitating Cohen's gesture, he tapped his finger against his nose. "And maybe the stink of strings being pulled?"

"I wouldn't know about that," said Milton Cohen.

ELEVEN

KEN WOLCH STRODE angrily down the hall to Byron Babcock's office and shoved open the door without knocking.

Babcock looked up, surprised by the sudden intrusion. "Hi, Ken—"

"What the hell did you think you were doing here?" Wolch demanded. He brandished at Babcock the transcript he had just finished skimming, the transcript of a deposition taken two days earlier at which Babcock had been present.

"What's the problem?" Babcock laced his hands behind his head and smiled.

Wolch dropped the transcript onto Babcock's desk. "Are you nuts? Since when does a member of this firm turn a deposition into an occasion to take potshots at a witness?"

"Just taking a cue from our client."

"Well, don't," Wolch said curtly. "Jordan Crandell can do as he pleases, but you and I have to answer for our behavior to the Bar Association and the court. Neither of which is likely to applaud your loose-cannon performance at this deposition. And you better believe that Odette will make sure they both know about it."

Babcock shrugged. "I felt that Valentine's attorney

was harassing our witness. I couldn't let her get away with that.''

Wolch seated himself across the desk from Babcock and glanced back at the transcript. "Rizzy Riznicki. I don't recognize the name.''

"No reason you should. She's just an inexperienced kid. God knows where Odette dug her up.''

"She may be a kid, but you seem to have overlooked how damning this deposition is to our side. For someone as inexperienced as you say she is, Ms. Riznicki managed to pose some very astute questions.''

"Oh, come on, Ken.''

"Stuff it, Byron.''

Wolch was worried. Normally, he micromanaged every detail of Crandell's affairs. This time, however, because of the complexity of the case and the time constraints, he had entrusted important pieces of it to Babcock. Based on what he'd read of the transcript, he wondered whether his confidence had been misplaced.

"I asked you to carefully prepare each one of our witnesses. Did you do that, Byron?''

Babcock leaned forward and glared at Wolch. "I resent that question, Ken. I'm your partner, not some second-year associate who doesn't know his ass from his elbow.''

"Did you prepare the witnesses, Byron?'' Wolch repeated. He pointed to the offending transcript. "Specifically, this witness?''

"Of course I did!'' Babcock picked up his calendar and tossed it at Wolch. "Look for yourself, if you don't believe me. Peter Gearing: April 24, five o'clock. If I recall correctly, I spent two hours with him. The guy's amazing. He has a brain like an adding machine.''

He smiled, but Wolch was not yet ready to forgive and forget. Peter Gearing was a superb numbers cruncher, but he was also a drunk. At five o'clock he was likely to be found at Harry's, the crowded Hanover Square bar around the corner from his office. On April 24, Byron Babcock had probably been sharing his table.

"Byron, you were right there beside Gearing at the deposition. You heard his responses to Riznicki's questions about how he'd arrived at his figures for the comparative earning potential of a Starwares-Summit merger versus Starwares-Valentine. He left a big hole in our argument, wide enough for Odette to crawl all over us."

"You're exaggerating wildly, Ken. Okay, maybe it wasn't the strongest testimony, but those figures are simply one tiny, insignificant part of the whole."

Wolch slammed his palm against the top of the desk, hard enough to rattle the top of Babcock's jelly-bean jar. "You buffoon!" he exploded, shocking himself as much as Babcock. "Starwares' amended Merger Rights Agreement depends on Summit's offer holding up as the better alternative. Those damn figures are integral to our case."

Babcock had turned pale. "Ken, I think you're overreacting. No need to panic."

"Mr. Wolch?"

"Yes?" He turned to face Babcock's secretary.

"Mr. Crandell wants to speak to you. Should I tell him you're on the way back to your office?"

Wolch shook his head. "I'll take it in here." He looked at Babcock. "You may as well hear what I have to say to him."

"Ken—" Babcock began.

Wolch waved him into silence and picked up the phone. "Hello, Jordan. I'm in Byron's office. Do you mind if he listens in? Hold it, let me get you on the speaker. Okay, what's up?"

"You tell me," Crandell barked. "It's a new day. I want all the latest developments. What happened with those depositions?"

"So far, I've read only one of the transcripts, and I have to level with you, Jordan. I'm not happy."

"I don't pay you to be happy, Ken. What the hell's that supposed to mean?"

"Simply this. At least one of our experts may not have been adequately prepared."

There was a long pause. Then Crandell said, "How badly do you think it went?"

"It's certainly not irreparable, but I'm afraid we might have handed Odette an unexpected gift."

Wolch and Babcock looked at each other, waiting for the inevitable outburst.

"That's not good," said Crandell.

Wolch thought that perhaps Crandell hadn't understood him.

"But as you say, it's probably not irreparable."

Babcock quickly wrote something down and held up the paper for Wolch to read: "I don't get it."

Wolch shrugged. He didn't get it either.

"You guys better get your act together and not screw up again."

Babcock held up another note: "Uh-oh. Here it comes now."

"Listen, I have to go. Get back to me on the rest of those depositions," said Crandell calmly. "I'll speak to you later."

There was a click, then the hum of the dial tone replaced his voice on the speaker. It took a moment for Wolch to recover from the shock of Crandell's reaction.

Babcock smirked at him. "Maybe he got laid last night."

"For Jordan Crandell, life's all about winning. Sex rates a distant third in his book."

"Then I guess I was right. You're making too big a deal out of Gearing."

Wolch saw no point in addressing Babcock's comment. He had known and represented Jordan Crandell for almost thirty years—the man simply didn't tolerate mistakes. He wondered whether he should call him back for clarification. There was something very wrong with his reaction. Wrong, but altogether refreshing.

Wolch smiled. Let sleeping dogs lie, he decided.

JORDAN CRANDELL HUNG up with Ken Wolch and sat back to plot his next move. This was not the time for him and Hope Scott Murray to be seen together in public. He couldn't risk Lew Valentine or Bernard Odette reading about them in some gossip column, then demanding to have Paul recused from the case. As he so often did when he needed to think through a problem, Crandell spun his chair around to stare out the window.

People were out in droves, reveling in the good weather after what had felt like endless months of snow. The temperatures were rather low for the end of April, with a wind that felt more like March. But the sun was shining and the sky was clear. Spring was coming. The downtown trendsetters were in a hurry to shed their winter clothes and get back to their basic black leather jackets and jeans.

He could call Hope, have the conversation over the phone. Somehow, that didn't feel quite right. He wanted to see her face while he explained what he needed of her. He wanted to see her smile, and say, "Of course, Jordan."

But how to make that meeting happen?

Across the street at the Guggenheim shop, a banner flapped in the wind, advertising an exhibition on industrial excellence. Crandell had ducked in one afternoon long enough to inspect the show, which touted elegantly designed objects, from toasters to telephones to clock radios.

But wasn't elegance all in the eye of the beholder? One person's idea of good taste was another person's definition of vulgarity. If you gathered together a panel of people, all of them noted for their sense of style and grace, could they ever reach a consensus as to what belonged in the elegance Hall of Fame?

The question amused him. It could make for an inter-

esting magazine article. He should pass the idea along to
Bebe Weiss. He picked up his dictaphone and suddenly
laughed aloud. He had found his solution. It was simple,
yet elegant.

THE INVITATIONS CAME hand-delivered on exquisitely
beautiful vellum paper embedded with delicate wisps of
dried flowers: "Bebe Weiss and the staff of *Pastiche* request the honor of your presence and the eloquence of
your opinions at a luncheon roundtable discussion entitled 'What is elegance?' "

Liz Smith received one of the thirty that were sent out
and was so charmed by the invitation that she wrote
about it in her syndicated column. Hope also received
one. She, too, was intrigued enough that even though it
was short notice, she called to say she would attend the
lunch on Friday.

It wasn't until her car pulled up in front of the building
and she saw the Summit, Inc. sign above the front door
that she remembered that Jordan owned *Pastiche*. Maybe
she would stop by his office and say hello after the luncheon. On second thought, remembering her recent conversation with Paul about Jordan, it would be better to
steer clear of him.

She identified herself to the guard at the security desk,
who checked her name against a list. "You can take any
of the elevators on the left to the fourth floor, then make
a right," he instructed her, picking up his phone as he
put a checkmark next to her name.

Two other women, both of whom looked slightly familiar, followed her into the elevator. "Are you here for
the luncheon?" one of them asked her. When she nodded, the other said, "Such fun, isn't it?"

They were already well launched into their discussion
about style and beauty when the elevator reached the
fourth floor. A young woman was waiting there to give
them their name tags and direct them to the conference

room. They could hear the voices of some of the other invitees as they walked down the hall and turned the corner.

"Hope?" Jordan Crandell strolled out of the office next to the conference room. "Are you here for the *Pastiche* lunch? Ladies, nice to see you, thank you for coming." He smiled at the other women as he deftly drew Hope into the office and closed the door. "I thought I might run into you today," he said.

For a crazy moment, until he dropped her arm, she had a flash of fear that he meant to harm her. But then he smiled, and she realized she was being ridiculous. This was *Jordan*, for goodness' sake. Whatever his many faults, he was no maniac rapist.

She caught her breath and smiled back at him. "How are you, Jordan?"

He moved away from her, closer to the desk, and she smiled again, knowing he wasn't comfortable standing so close when she had the advantage over him of several inches in height.

"I'm very well," he said, rubbing his palms together. "Very well indeed. I'm sure you've been reading the papers, so you know I'm involved in a big, big merger."

She nodded. "Who could miss it?"

He picked up a staple remover from the desk next to him and began playing with it. "Isn't it just my good luck that your husband's been assigned to the case?"

Now it was her turn to feel uncomfortable. "I guess so," she said. "He used to specialize in corporate law, did you know that? I'm sure he'll give your side a very fair hearing. And the other side, too, of course." She heard herself babbling. She couldn't seem to shut up. "But I'm sure you have a very good case, and probably the best lawyers money can buy—"

He laughed. "That's crassly put, but true. But even the best lawyers have their off days, and I don't want to take any chances with losing Starwares. Which makes this the perfect time to remind Paul about that little wedding present you and I arranged for him." He smiled and sat down on the other side of the desk. "Don't you think so?"

She stared at him, trying to convince herself that she had misheard or misunderstood. He was playing with the staple remover, clicking it open and shut like tiny mechanical jaws. He was playing with her, too, she decided. Toying with her for his own peculiar Jordan Crandell reasons.

"I don't get the joke, Jordan," she said. She looked at her watch. "I should go. I'm late for the lunch."

"This is no joke, Hope. I'm deadly serious. In the greater scheme of things, I'm not asking for very much. I'd probably win this case on its merits. But 'probably' isn't good enough. So fate has intervened in the form of your husband."

She swallowed hard. "Jordan, surely you don't expect him to rule in your favor just because you made a couple of phone calls on his behalf?"

"That's precisely what I expect him to do. I couldn't have phrased it better myself."

"You're out of your mind!" She glared at him, too angry to censor herself. "I thought you were doing me a favor. That you were my friend, someone I could trust. Now I find out you were laying the groundwork for blackmail!"

"Hope, please." His tone was soft and ingratiating. "I was happy to help you and Paul. It gave me a lot of pleasure to be able to do that for you. I assumed you'd feel the same way."

She felt the tears welling up but willed herself not to cry in front of him. "Jordan, that day at lunch, I asked you to keep our conversation strictly between the two of us. I told you then that Paul had no idea about any of this. He still doesn't and I would never dream of telling him."

"You're a clever woman. I'm sure you can come up with some way to tell him that won't shatter his ego. I hear he's crazy about you—and he should be. You're the catch of the decade, especially for someone like Paul Murray." He stepped toward her and patted her arm. "He'll understand. You'll make him understand."

She recoiled from his touch. "Forget it, Jordan! As far as I'm concerned, this discussion never happened. Because hell will freeze over before I'll say one word to try and influence my husband about you or anyone else. Is that clear?"

He laughed quietly. "You'll change your mind. Hope. I promise you."

She let him have the last word. There was nothing left to say. She pulled open the door and hurried into the hallway.

The same young woman who earlier had been handing out name tags was just walking into the conference room. "Mrs. Murray? Aren't you joining us for lunch?" she asked. "Are you all right, Mrs. Murray?"

"Sorry, I'm not feeling well." Hope's green eyes blurred with tears as she rushed past the woman.

She was trembling uncontrollably as she pressed the elevator button. Let it come soon, she prayed. She had to get out of there. She had to get home. She had to get as far away as possible from Jordan Crandell.

"ALL RISE! COURT is now in session! The Honorable Paul Murray presiding!" announced the clerk.

Paul walked in and took his place at the bench. "You may be seated," he said as he surveyed the courtroom.

He had expected the media to be present, but nothing like the crowd that gazed up at him. The spectators' section was jammed with reporters, not only from leading newspapers and business publications all over America but from major foreign publications as well. The takeover battle had international implications. His decision could well be a judicial earthquake, its shock waves reverberating through stock markets from London to Tokyo.

Law firms representing other commercial giants had assigned associates the task of watching the legal proceedings. Their corporate clients might eventually be affected, and they would demand instant opinions from their attorneys as to the case's long-range implications.

According to Jesse Rubin, the hearing had taken on the aura of a sports event, the legal equivalent of the famous Ali-Frazier "Thrilla in Manila." Bets were being taken as to the outcome, and there was even talk of smuggling in a minicam to create a bootlegged copy of the fight. Some of the top partners had managed to carve a few hours out of their schedules to hear the Michigan Assassin go up against Ken Wolch.

"In the matter of *Starwares, Inc., Summit, Inc.,* v. *Valentine Industries, Inc.,*" said the clerk. "Counselors, please make your appearance."

Both men looked armed for the fray. At the counsel table to Paul's right, Ken Wolch was flanked by Byron Babcock and Jordan Crandell. Next to Crandell sat Eric Lynch, who was accompanied by Bruce Einhorn and Jack Strawn, as well as his outside counsel, Morton Abernathy.

Bernard Odette was seated at the table to Paul's left. He was wearing his customary court appearance uniform: a dark blue suit with a faint white stripe, a lighter blue silk shirt, and a blood red silk tie. Joining him, all of them dressed very conservatively, were Rizzy Riznicki, Lew Valentine, and Walter Spaulding.

Just behind the front lines sat each team's battalion of associates, paralegals, and secretaries, prepared at a moment's notice to retrieve any of the well-indexed documents and affidavits from the stacks of cartons that had been hauled into court.

Paul had read through almost half of the affidavits. Naomi Bowman, who was also present in the courtroom, had perused most of the others and written him a lengthy memo summarizing their contents. They had spent many hours discussing the complaint, the legal points raised by each side, the previously rendered opinions that could apply to this case. Now he was eager to hear the oral arguments. From Odette's and Wolch's expressions, he guessed they were just as eager to present them.

Odette stood up. "Your Honor, Bernard Odette, representing the plaintiff, Valentine Industries, Inc."

"Go ahead, Mr. Odette," Paul said.

There was a crackle of excitement in the courtroom as the famous Michigan Assassin moved away from the counsel table to begin his presentation.

"Your Honor, I'm here today on behalf of Valentine Industries and its stockholders to apply for temporary and permanent injunctive relief from what I can only describe as a series of ill-conceived, unfair, and punitive provisions instituted by the Board of Directors of Starwares, Inc., in its attempt to prevent any and all suitors except the Summit Corporation from effecting a merger with its company."

He paused and looked at Paul.

Paul couldn't tell whether Odette was out of breath from his long-winded sentence or whether he wanted some acknowledgment.

"Yes." He nodded. "Continue."

Odette began to pace the front of the courtroom, articulating each of the points he'd enumerated in his complaint. His primary argument was that the deal pending between Summit and Starwares should be perceived as a sale, rather than as a strategic alliance, as Starwares was claiming it to be.

"Permit me, Your Honor, to explain why I believe this to be so. You have before you here the chairman of Summit, Jordan Crandell, who admits to being the majority shareholder in his company."

He stopped in front of Crandell and pointed his finger at him.

"Objection, Your Honor!" Ken Wolch shot to his feet. "This is a preliminary injunction hearing, not a murder trial. Counsel has no cause to gesticulate at my client as though he were a criminal."

"Your Honor," said Odette. "Counsel has no right to characterize my hand gestures—"

Paul had heard enough. "Gentlemen. May I remind you both that this is a court of law, not a junior dramatics society. Mr. Odette, we'll have no further finger-pointing. Mr. Wolch, keep your interpretations to yourself, please. All right, Mr. Odette. You may proceed."

"Thank you, Your Honor." Odette smiled at Murray, managing to convey the impression that the judge had ruled in his favor. "As I was saying, Mr. Crandell is the majority shareholder in Summit, so that should his proposed purchase of Starwares take place, he would perforce become the majority shareholder of Starwares."

He shrugged his shoulders, then walked closer to the bench. "Your Honor, you don't have to be a rocket scientist to deduce that this merger would give Mr. Crandell control of the new company. And as we know, Your Honor, a change of control would thus indicate a sale."

Odette thrust his left hand above his head. "As you can see, I'm not wearing a wedding band on my ring finger. There's a good reason for this: I'm not married. I'd like to be, and I admire those fortunate enough to have found the right life partner. But I value the state of matrimony too highly to enter into it lightly."

Thus far, the Michigan Assassin was sounding more like a media shrink than a hired legal gun. There had to be some point to his philosophizing, but Paul couldn't imagine what it was.

"Mr. Odette," he interrupted, "thank you for this discourse, but you're losing me. I don't think you want to do that. So tell me. What does all this talk about marriage have to do with your reason for being here today?"

Odette picked up a piece of paper. "Your Honor, I'd

like to quote from a transcript of a press conference held jointly by Mr. Crandell and Mr. Lynch at which they announced the acquisition of Starwares by Summit. On that occasion, Mr. Crandell described their deal as an 'irrevocable marriage that could not be torn asunder.' '' He turned his back on Murray and faced Jordan Crandell. ''A marriage, Mr. Crandell? Or a clever seduction of Eric Lynch that will only end in the rape of Starwares' shareholders?''

Ken Wolch jumped up. ''Objection!''

''Sustained.'' Paul glared at Odette. ''Knock it off, Mr. Odette. So far you haven't persuaded me of a thing except that you're trying to turn this hearing into a circus sideshow. Get down to the facts, or I'll order you to take your seat.''

''Yes, Your Honor,'' Odette said without a trace of apology in his tone.

He picked up a thin wooden pointer from the counsel table and strolled over to the large printed chart that was mounted at the front of the court. ''The facts are these. On November 27 of this past year, Eric Lynch met with Jordan Crandell at the headquarters of the Summit Corporation. According to notes taken at that meeting by an employee of Kraft, Wolch, Morad & Hathaway, Mr. Crandell offered to acquire Starwares for sixty-five dollars a share.''

Like a quick-change artist, Odette had suddenly recreated himself in the image of a dignified law school professor. Point by point, he led the audience through the maze of facts and figures that had culminated in Starwares' decision to reject Lew Valentine's most recent offer. His tone was dispassionate and neutral. For a few minutes, it was almost possible to forget that he was here to represent a client who stood to gain or lose millions of dollars, depending on the validity of Odette's argument.

Paul listened and watched as Odette wielded his wooden pointer down the length of the chart. He was an

artist, putting brush to easel, hoping to dazzle them all
with the brilliance of his creation. Most of all, of course,
he hoped to dazzle Paul Murray, to persuade him to see
the facts as he did. Knowing this, Paul still couldn't help
but admire the performance. Glancing at the opposing
counsel's table, he saw that Wolch, Babcock, Lynch, Abernathy, and the others were following Odette's show as
intently as he was.

Only one person seemed curiously uninvolved. Jordan
Crandell was leaning sideways in his chair, his back half-
turned to Odette, his eyes fixed on some distant point.
His lips were set in a half-smile, as if he were lost in a
daydream that was far more compelling than the drama
being played out in the courtroom.

Paul found Crandell's expression to be slightly unset-
tling. He couldn't ever recall seeing a defendant who
looked quite so blasé and unconcerned. True, this was no
life-or-death matter, and today's hearing was only the
first in what would probably be many rounds of court
battles. But like Valentine, Crandell had millions of dollars at stake. Like Valentine, he was not accustomed to
losing.

Paul turned back to Odette, then looked once more at
Crandell, who just at that moment shifted his gaze to
Paul. The half-smile became a full-fledged grin that
under the circumstances seemed wholly unwarranted.
Crandell beamed at him, apparently delighted with what-
ever thought was passing through his mind. And then,
Crandell did something no other defendant had ever done
in Paul's court.

He winked at Paul—a long, exaggerated wink that
could only be described as insolent.

Shocked by this lack of respect, Paul momentarily
looked away. When he looked back again, Crandell's
gaze was fixed on Odette. Paul could almost have convinced himself that he'd imagined the incident, except
for one thing. Crandell's mouth was still set in the same
shit-eating grin as before.

"So you see, Your Honor," Odette was saying, "my client has consistently matched or topped each bid made by Mr. Crandell. He has also conscientiously sought out and obtained ironclad financing commitments in order to make good on his bids. Yet the board of Starwares reneged on its fiduciary responsibilities by not giving Valentine's offer due and proper consideration."

He put down the pointer, sauntered back to his table, and took a sip of water. Then he said, "They did so by representing their association with Summit as a 'long-term strategic alliance' that had been arrived at after careful consideration of other potential suitors.

" 'Careful consideration,' " Odette repeated, gesturing with his forefingers to frame the words in quotation marks. "On November 26, just one day before his meeting with Mr. Crandell, Mr. Lynch met with Mr. Valentine here in New York. According to Mr. Valentine's sworn testimony, they spent five hours together, most of that time devoted to what Mr. Valentine thought was a fruitful discussion of a potential acquisition by Valentine of Starwares."

He turned to Lew Valentine, who nodded, as if to verify the truth of that statement. "This afternoon, Your Honor, I will call to the stand a witness who was present at that meeting. Then we'll hear the truth about Mr. Lynch's attempts to secure for his shareholders the best possible value for their money. We'll also scrutinize the provisions of the Merger Agreement entered into by Starwares, including the draconian defensive measures instituted by Starwares at Summit's express request to prohibit any and all other suitors."

Taking a few steps closer to the defendants' table, Odette glared at Jordan Crandell. "Finally, we'll examine the conscience of Jordan Crandell, the man who initiated this battle, who has spent his entire adult life buying and dismantling viable companies, and who himself has admitted that he's in the habit of destroying documents that he considers to be of no use. Of no use, Mr. Crandell?'' he demanded, once more facing his client's opponent. ''Or incriminating?''

Wolch was on his feet again to register an objection. But before he could say a word, Odette returned to his table and took his seat.

''Thank you, Your Honor,'' he said. ''I'm done for now.''

Although Paul was tempted to reprimand Odette for his gratuitous jab at Jordan Crandell, he decided to let it go rather than call further attention to the man's behavior. Instead, he nodded at the defense counsel. ''Mr. Wolch?''

''Thank you, Your Honor,'' said Wolch as he moved away from the table. ''Your Honor, I'm not going to bore you with any complicated charts or recitations of figures with which I'm sure you're already familiar. Nor am I going to assault the integrity of Mr. Valentine, as my esteemed colleague has mysteriously chosen to do to Mr. Crandell. My task today is simple: to remind the court that Eric Lynch and Jordan Crandell are seeking to enter into a partnership—a partnership that *unquestionably* should be designated as a strategic alliance—for only one express purpose.''

Pausing just a few feet away from Odette and Valentine, he nodded at them and smiled pleasantly, as if greeting two old friends he'd encountered while out for an afternoon stroll. Then he stuck his hands in his pockets and continued.

''Their purpose is to create more and better products. Their password is synergy . . . cooperation. Separately, these are two vigorous, prosperous companies that provide jobs for thousands of Americans. Together, united under one corporate logo, they will become an even more exciting and flourishing company, with the capacity to produce information systems, software and hardware, that boggle the imagination.''

Wolch shook his head and raised his voice. "No, make that *defy* the imagination. Because given the combined energy, brains, dedication, and financial resources of the men who head these companies, there's no limit to what they can—and will—create together. Because that's the kind of businessmen they are. They form a perfect fit."

He locked his hands together and held them up for everyone to see: "Like this. Like two matching pieces of a puzzle. A brilliant strategic alliance that will benefit thousands more men and women soon to be employed by the new Summit Corporation. That will benefit the stockholders. That will benefit the American economy."

He returned to his table and poured himself a glass of water. Paul would have bet money that Wolch wasn't thirsty. It was an old trick, one he'd used himself as a litigator. Take a moment to stop and drink the water in order to give the jury, or in this case the judge, time to digest all the verbiage he'd just thrown their way.

So far, Wolch's opening argument sounded like the chairman's address at an annual shareholders' meeting. Still, his evocation of the post-merger possibilities was compelling. There was no getting away from the facts of the case; but facts were subject to interpretation. It was Wolch's job to shed the best possible light on the steps Lynch and his directors had taken at Crandell's behest to forge a merger agreement. Paul felt the lawyer was doing his job, and doing it well.

"Your Honor," Wolch went on, "the so-called draconian measures undertaken by Starwares in its original Merger Agreement are merely your standard stipulations that have been commonly accepted by this and other courts across the country since the mid-eighties. The No-Shop provision, the Termination Fee provision, and the Stock Option Agreement were put in place to encourage Jordan Crandell in his acquisition of Starwares."

He began rocking back and forth on his heels. Paul recalled from Wolch's previous appearance before him

that the rocking was a kind of tic, a signal that he was
about to wrap up his argument.

"Mr. Odette would have you think that Mr. Crandell
and Mr. Lynch have joined forces to create the evil empire," Wolch said. "But I think that if you peel away his
rhetoric and uncover the reality of the situation, you'll
have to agree that what we're talking here about is good,
old-fashioned dealmaking, where two gentlemen hammer
out an equitable agreement, shake hands, and walk away
satisfied that they've done what's best for all concerned."

He hooked his thumbs under his red suspenders and
smiled amiably. "Thank you, Your Honor."

The law professor versus the country lawyer, thought
Paul. And behind both personas were two of the country's sharpest attorneys, worthy opponents who had just
delivered the bravura opening act that their audience had
come to watch and learn from.

It was a good point at which to break for lunch. "We'll
recess now until one-thirty, at which time Mr. Odette can
call his first witness," he said.

Just before he left the courtroom, he glanced back and
noticed Jordan Crandell, huddled with his lawyers, shaking his head in response to whatever Ken Wolch was telling him. He was no longer smiling, nor was there any
trace of his earlier smug expression.

Could he have imagined the wink? Maybe it was an
involuntary reaction to the stress of the trial. That must
be it, Paul decided. It was stress, not insolence. After all,
Jordan Crandell was as human as the next person.

THE DIRECTIONS MILLY Maniscalco had given Rick Major
to her daughter's place in Port Chester were precise and
easy to follow. As Milly opened the door of the modest,
two-story house, he remembered the brief hesitation in
her voice when he'd said he was calling at Milt Cohen's
suggestion. In that moment, he'd guessed that she and

Milt had had an affair, and that it had ended painfully for her. He'd held his breath, praying she'd agree to see him. Then she'd said, sure, he could come out and meet her.

She was a good-looking woman with dark brown hair that was teased into a bouffant bubble. Her large brown eyes were carefully made up, and she was wearing a short skirt that showed off a still shapely pair of legs. He figured she'd dressed up for him, hoping he'd go back and tell Milt that he was missing out on a good thing. He could smell the coffee brewing in the kitchen, and a plate of chocolate cookies sat on the coffee table.

"I baked them myself," she said, and he knew she'd never forgive him if he didn't eat at least a couple.

She brought them both coffee, settled herself in a chair across from him, and studied her nails, which were painted bright pink. "How's Milton?" she asked.

He sensed that he'd get more information out of her if he didn't paint too rosy a picture of Milt's current situation. "Oh, you know Milton."

She nodded. It was the right answer.

"The man has a problem figuring out what he wants in life. What a pity. He could have so much." She smoothed her skirt, then shrugged. "So what did you want to talk to me about?"

"I'm doing an investigation for a client of mine." He reached into his pocket and took out the tape recorder. "If it's okay with you, I'd like to record our conversation."

She stared at the machine, which he'd placed on the table next to the cookies. "Tell you what. Explain what this is all about, then I'll decide."

"Fair enough. Milt said you worked at his precinct house."

"That's right. I was a secretary, a civilian employee, for twenty-six years. My whole family was cops. My father, my brothers, my husband."

She took a cookie and dipped it into her coffee. "My

husband got shot and killed on duty. My daughter Angie was six, just starting school. I couldn't see sitting around all day, thinking about Dominick, and I needed the money. So I took the civil service test, and boom! Suddenly, I'm a career girl. By the time I retired, I was working for the head of the precinct. My boss just about cried when he said goodbye to me. I would have stayed on, but Angie worried about me traveling to the Bronx every day."

"Do you remember a cop named Jimmy Murray?" Major asked.

"Jeez, I haven't heard his name in the longest time. Is that why you're here?"

He nodded.

She leaned forward, her eyes animated with interest. "Let me ask you something. Was that Jimmy Murray's brother who married Hope Scott? The one who's the judge?"

"That's right."

"Holy Christmas! I knew it had to be the same one."

He put two cookies on his plate and, following her example, dipped one into his coffee. "Mmm, this is delicious," he said. "I keep asking my wife to bake more, but she's always dieting, so she doesn't like to have them in the house."

Milly Maniscalco clucked sympathetically. "I'll wrap you up a little package to take home with you."

"Milly, is it okay if I turn on the tape recorder?"

"Oh, I guess so," she said. "It's been so many years. Did Milton talk to you about Jimmy?"

"Yes, but I had a few more questions, so he sent me to you."

She shook her head. "Such a shame. I just never knew what to make of the whole thing."

He pressed the record button and waited for her to continue.

"He was a terrific cop. Everybody said so. And so

sweet. Poor kid lost his mother when he was so young. He had all those sisters taking care of him, but it's just not the same.''

"Milt thought that Jimmy should have been arrested along with Brendan Connor.''

She dabbed her lips with her napkin, taking care not to mess up her lipstick. "No. That's not exactly true. Milton thought it was *strange* that Jimmy wasn't arrested. He wanted to talk to me about it, but we . . . we had kind of a falling out right then.''

"Didn't you think it was strange?''

"Yeah, well. . . .'' She stared at the tape recorder.

He could feel her struggling to decide whether or not to confide in him. *Tell me, Milly,* he thought, willing her to speak. Most people he would have offered money as an inducement to get them to talk. Milly would be offended if he waved a large-currency bill at her. For her, it was a question of honor.

"This don't feel quite right to me,'' she said.

The policeman's code of ethics. You didn't breach the blue wall of silence.

"I'm not out to get anyone in trouble,'' he said. "Somebody protected Jimmy, and I'm not saying that shouldn't have happened. I'm just looking for a piece of information, is all. I only want to know how it happened.''

"Most cops are honest, you know.''

"I know,'' he said gently.

"It about killed me that Jimmy got himself messed up like that. I had great hopes for him. So did Milton and a lot of other people. To be honest with you, I was just as happy not to see him go to jail. I think we all were.''

"What saved him, Milly?'' He took a stab in the dark. "Did your boss decide to protect him?''

"My boss? Are you nuts?'' Her reproving frown made him feel like a guilty schoolboy. "It came from way higher than the precinct.''

But the call must have come in to her boss. She would have answered the phone, maybe even taken some kind of message. It took all his self-control to sit absolutely still and quiet and wait for her to supply the missing piece.

"Listen," she said, twisting the napkin into a ball. "I'm only doing this because you're a friend of Milton's, and he already talked to you."

"I understand."

"Awright then. So we all knew Jimmy was in some kind of trouble, but we didn't know exactly what, just that he'd done something he shouldn't of. One day I answer the phone, and it's my friend Antoinette from the D.A.'s office, and she tells me her boss wants to see my boss ASAP. This is a little unusual, you understand. I mean, spirit of cooperation and all that, but my boss doesn't usually get summoned over there at a moment's notice. So I figure something's up, and sure enough, ten minutes later, Antoinette calls back and says she's dying to tell me something but it'll have to wait until we take the subway home together. So then a while later my boss comes back, and he's not saying a word, except that he calls Jimmy into his office and closes the door."

She sighed and pointed to his coffee cup. "Can I get you some more?"

"No, thanks, I'm fine."

"I'm in the middle of typing up a memo, but I stop when Jimmy walks out of there, and he don't look too well at all. I ask him, 'Jimmy, are you okay?' And he kinda of mumbles that, yeah, he's feeling sick, and he's gonna go home. Now, this is *very* unusual, because Jimmy was never one to be taking any sick days unless he's practically dying. So that afternoon, I get the rest of the story from Antoinette, which she swears me to secrecy, because her boss will kill her if it gets out."

She looked away for a moment, then turned back to Major. "This isn't gonna get Jimmy into trouble, is it? I heard he's doing real well now, and what's the point in disturbing his life after all this time?''

He shook his head. ''My investigation isn't even about him.''

''Okay. So I don't think they had a lot on Jimmy, but it was enough to make him wear a wire when he went to meet with Brendan. But then someone high up in the Manhattan D.A.'s office called and asked Antoinette's boss, as a favor, to keep Jimmy out of it. So they did. Anyways, Antoinette said they were happy for the excuse not to prosecute Jimmy, because there was this big campaign going on to clean up the image of the Bronx, so they didn't want no big headlines about corruption in the D.A.'s office and the police department. So everything worked out for the best, right?''

''Right,'' said Major, though he didn't mean it the way she did. ''Did you ever find out how or why the Manhattan D.A. got involved?''

She shrugged. ''Aw, c'mon. Somebody knew somebody who knew somebody who didn't want Jimmy Murray's name dragged through the mud. It's all politics.'' She pointed her chin toward the tape recorder. ''Can we turn that off now?''

''Oh, sure,'' said Major. He had enough. He had more than enough. Never mind the cookies. Milly's story was so hot and delicious it almost made his mouth water. He couldn't wait to get to his car and call Crandell.

''I don't want you using my name for anything,'' she said. ''You swear?''

''Of course. Like I said, this is for background purposes only.''

Reassured, she nodded. ''One more thing. I would of broke my promise to Antoinette and told Milton, but we weren't really on speaking terms just then. That was the hardest part of the whole thing, not telling him.''

She stood up and headed for the kitchen. ''Here, I'm going to pack you up some of those cookies. I'll even make up a package for Milton that you could drop off with him, if it's not too much trouble.''

''Sure,'' said Major. ''I'd be happy to do that.''

After what she'd given him, it was the least he could do.

TWELVE

Bᴇʀɴᴀʀᴅ Oᴅᴇᴛᴛᴇ's ꜰɪʀsᴛ witness of the afternoon had been sworn in and directed to take his seat on the witness stand.

Jordan Crandell watched as the man, who'd given his name as Douglas Gardiner, eased himself into the chair and folded his hands in his lap with the air of a person supremely confident that what he was about to say was, indeed, the whole truth and nothing but the truth.

"Mr. Gardiner, thank you for joining us here this afternoon," Bernard Odette said. "Would you please tell us what you do for a living?"

Douglas Gardiner was a tall, stoop-shouldered man in his mid-forties, who regarded Odette as if he were studying a specimen under a microscope.

"Certainly," he said, speaking in a low monotone. "I'm a partner at the law firm of Gardiner & Gladstone in San Diego, California."

"Do you specialize in any particular area, Mr. Gardiner?"

"My area of expertise is bankruptcy law."

Odette smiled. "You must be doing very well in these troubled times."

"Yes." Gardiner nodded. "Fortunately or unfortunately, depending on your point of view, we've had an upswing in bankruptcy filings among major corporations in our area over the last ten years or so.''

"Do you belong to any professional associations, Mr. Gardiner?''

"Objection, Your Honor." Ken Wolch stood up. "Counsel seems to have embarked on a fishing expedition. I don't see the relevance of any of this.''

"Your Honor, the relevance of this witness's testimony will become clear in short order,'' said Odette.

Paul Murray nodded. "Very well. But don't keep us guessing very much longer. I don't want this to drag on.''

"Thank you, Your Honor,'' said Odette. He turned back to Gardiner. "As we were saying, do you belong to any professional organizations?''

Crandell stifled a yawn as Douglas Gardiner droned on about his various affiliations. The back-and-forth between him and Odette seemed like a colossal waste of time. All those questions and answers in order to establish that he was a second-rate lawyer whom Odette had dug up somewhere, probably to testify as an expert witness that Valentine was solvent.

He glanced sideways at Ken Wolch. His lawyer appeared to be absorbed in the exchange. He peered over at Paul Murray, who likewise seemed to be hanging on Gardiner's every word. He noticed that Murray wasn't casting any glances his way, and no wonder. His Honor had looked as shocked as a preacher at a peep show when he'd winked up at him this morning. Obviously, the guy had no sense of humor.

Had Hope followed up yet with Paul on their little discussion? He was inclined to think not, which was too bad, because Ken Wolch had seemed troubled by something Odette had said before the lunch break. He would call Hope this afternoon, after court was adjourned for the day. This time, he would leave no room for doubt that if she didn't raise the matter with her husband, he would contact Paul himself.

He yawned again. Wolch elbowed him in the side. "Pay attention," he whispered. "This is important."

Paying attention to Bernard Odette was why he paid Wolch big bucks. His job was buying, selling, and running his companies. He'd remind him of that as soon as he had the chance. Crandell tuned back in and caught Odette in midsentence.

"—first heard that Mr. Lynch was in negotiations with Mr. Crandell, as best you can remember?" Odette was asking.

"Objection!" Wolch said, standing up. "Hearsay. Counsel is asking Mr. Gardiner for his secondhand knowledge as to when my client was first in touch with Mr. Lynch."

"Sustained," said Paul Murray. "Do you want to re-phrase the question?"

Odette smiled. "No, Your Honor. Let's jump ahead here. Mr. Gardiner, were you present at the meeting of the San Diego County Bar Association on May 4 of last year?"

"Yes, I was."

"What was the main topic of discussion at that meeting?"

"The role of the company chairman in terms of corporate accountability," said Douglas Gardiner.

"At that meeting," Odette began, then stopped and cocked his head to one side. "Excuse me, Your Honor, but I could swear I just heard a telephone ringing."

"I heard it, too," said Ken Wolch. "There it is again."

Crandell suddenly realized where the sound was coming from. "I'm sorry, Your Honor." He smiled as he bent to retrieve his briefcase from under the table. "It's my phone. There must be an emergency."

"Well, go ahead and answer it, Mr. Crandell. But take your call outside the courtroom, so we can get on with our business here," Paul Murray said.

"Thank you, Your Honor," said Crandell. He grabbed

the phone from his briefcase and turned it on. "Hold it a second," he muttered and hurried out of the courtroom, followed by waves of barely suppressed laughter from the spectators' section.

He found a quiet corner at the end of the corridor that gave him some privacy. "This damn well better be important, Donna," he growled at his secretary.

"I have Rick Major on the other line. He says it's urgent. Do you want me to patch him through?" she asked.

"Yes, of course."

After a moment's pause, Major came on the line. "Mr. Crandell? You got a minute?" He sounded breathless, as if he'd been running hard. His voice was taut was excitement.

"What is it?" asked Crandell.

"Mr. Crandell, I think I got what you wanted on Paul Murray."

He listened as Major quickly sketched out his story about Jimmy Murray. He asked a few questions, but the P.I. was well prepared with all the right answers.

"You sure about this?" Crandell demanded when Major had stopped talking. "You have it all on tape?"

Major's reply was music to his ears. "Yes, to both questions."

Crandell saw the courtroom door open, and people begin to spill out. He glanced at his watch. Ken Wolch had said there'd probably be a brief afternoon break. Douglas Gardiner must have finished his testimony. Wolch was just coming out now, accompanied by Byron Babcock. Wolch waved at Crandell and started down the hall toward him. Crandell nodded and held up one finger to signal that he'd be with him in a minute.

"Get those tapes over to Donna now," he instructed Major. "Tell her I don't care how she does it, but I want them transcribed by the time I get back to the office this afternoon. Make sure she has the names and background on all the people you interviewed. And Major?"

He smiled. He could afford to be magnanimous. The guy had just delivered to him the best insurance policy he ever could have imagined, an ironclad guarantee for success. "That was good work. You just earned yourself a tidy little bonus."

He was still smiling when his two lawyers caught up with him.

"I hope it was good news, because we could sure use some," said Wolch.

Crandell clapped him on the back. "Ken, I don't know what's happening to you. You used to be such an optimist. Now you're turning into a regular prophet of doom."

"Too bad you had to leave when you did, Jordan. You missed the best part of the testimony."

Crandell studied Wolch, trying to read his tone. "The guy was a clown," he scoffed.

"Maybe so, but he had a great punch line. You really should have been there to hear it."

"I'm running a company, Ken. I had urgent business to take care of. It's your job to sit in court and listen to that crap."

"You're right, Jordan," said Wolch. "It was crap. It's hard to believe anyone with a scrap of intelligence would allow such stuff to come out of his mouth."

"Well, there you are," Crandell chuckled. "Just another small fire for you to put out. That shouldn't be a problem."

"You never mentioned that you gave a talk to the San Diego County Bar Association last year."

"Ken, I give a lot of talks. It's good for the company's image. What's this all about? What the hell do you care, anyway?"

Wolch turned to his partner. "You tell him, Byron. I have to go take a leak."

Crandell stared after Wolch. "What bug got stuck up his ass?"

"That clown in the courtroom," said Babcock. "In addition to being an attorney, he also happens to be a major shareholder of Starwares' stock. And he happened to attend the Bar Association meeting where you gave that speech. Odette had him read from the transcript of your remarks. Jordan, they were pretty damning."

"What did I say? Remind me."

"You told that roomful of lawyers that you have a shredding machine in your secretary's office. You said that any documents, memos, whatever, that you decide you don't need, you have your secretary put through the shredder. You laughed—it says so in the transcript—and added that you keep that shredder pretty well fed."

"Maybe I said that. So what?"

"Those sorts of statements don't do much for your image."

"I'm trying to buy a company, Byron. I'm not running for office."

Babcock shook his head. "But it gets down to the same issues. Trust and honesty. We can guess what questions Odette's going to be posing. If you're in the habit of regularly destroying documents, what have you gotten rid of that's relevant to your negotiations with Starwares? And how can we argue that you can be trusted down the line to do what's best for the shareholders if you're out there advertising that you do what you please and cover your tracks?"

"Did you say trust and honesty?" Crandell roared with laughter. "That's a good one, Byron. Trust and honesty!"

Babcock frowned. "This is serious, Jordan. I was watching Judge Murray's face. He was lapping it up like a cat with a bowl of cream."

"I could use a good joke, Jordan," said Wolch, rejoining them. "Why don't you let me in on it, too?"

"Something Byron said tickled my funny bone. You had to be there." He put one arm around each of his lawyers. "Cheer up, boys. It's all going to work out just fine."

"I hope so," Wolch said grimly. "Just promise me there aren't any other incriminating transcripts you've forgotten to mention to us."

Crandell smiled and straightened his tie. "No more transcripts. I promise. You have my absolute word of honor."

"NICE GOING, BOSS," said Rizzy Riznicki.

Court had adjourned for the day. The attorneys for both sides were holding court with public postmortems for the benefit of the press.

"I thought it went very well. My friend Ken Wolch was looking nervous this afternoon," Bernard Odette agreed with Rizzy, in a voice meant to carry over the heads of the reporters to his opponent at the opposite end of the corridor.

"As usual, Mr. Odette is so preoccupied with grandstanding for me and the court that he's failed to assess the true impact of the afternoon's proceedings," came the answering volley from Ken Wolch.

Odette smiled. Wolch's comeback would make for a great sound bite on the evening news. But they both knew the extent of the damage his witness had inflicted this afternoon on Wolch's case. And on Jordan Crandell.

"Mr. Odette?" A familiar voice rang out from the crowd.

"Yes, Mr. Zelmanski?" He turned toward the *Journal* reporter.

Zelmanski thrust his tape recorder in Odette's face. "I noticed you didn't raise the issue of financing in your opening argument. Are you going to address that question tomorrow? Or after examining Summit's affidavits are you satisfied about the solidity of Mr. Crandell's loan commitments?"

"Mr. Zelmanski," said Odette, mugging for the television cameras, "I'm *never* satisfied."

"So the ladies tell us," yelled one of the cameramen.

Odette grinned. "That's why they call me the Michigan Assassin. But seriously, if I were Mr. Lynch or a member of his board, I would have grave concerns about Mr. Crandell's financing. They seem to have closed their eyes to some important discrepancies in his accounting, but that's all I choose to say on that point at the moment."

He nodded at Ned Berger. But before the *Times* reporter could ask his question, he turned back to Zelmanski. "What about you, Mr. Zelmanski? You've been doing some pretty good in-depth coverage of this case. Are you satisfied?"

Because the cameras were pointed at Odette, they missed the sight of Rizzy Riznicki, covering her face with her hands as her shoulders shook with laughter.

For once, Kurt Zelmanski was at a loss for words.

Odette smiled. "Next question?"

JORDAN CRANDELL PUT in a token appearance on his side of the corridor and mouthed some platitudes about having every confidence in his legal team and knowing he would be vindicated. Then he rushed past the crush of press, impatient to get to the solitude of his waiting car.

He was prepared to leave a message on Hope's answering machine. He preferred not to. He wanted the instant gratification of this time hearing her promise that yes, she would speak to Paul. She would tell the Honorable Judge Paul Murray exactly what he had to do.

Even before his chauffeur had shifted into gear, he was dialing Hope's number on his car phone. She picked up almost immediately, and he guessed that she was waiting for her husband to call to report on how his day in court had gone.

"Hope?" he said. "It's Jordan."

He heard a sharp inhalation, then nothing.

"Hope, please, don't hang up. I need to talk to you."

Still no response from her end.

"To apologize."

There was a whoosh of air, as she let out her breath. "Go ahead. I'll listen," she said, playing the ice princess.

He did feel genuinely regretful that he'd made her so angry. They'd been good friends for such a long time. He didn't want to lose her friendship. On the other hand, he couldn't afford to lose Starwares.

"I'm sorry about that incident the other day. Afterwards, I realized I'd probably frightened you. Maybe I wasn't making myself clear. I wasn't trying to blackmail you. I was only asking for your help."

"I've never seen that side of you before, Jordan," she said. "The ruthless businessman."

He laughed. "Without that side, I would never have become the person I am today."

"Well, I don't like it. And you did scare me. You sounded so threatening."

"I do apologize, then."

He heard her sigh. "All right. I accept."

He looked out the window. They were stuck at a red light on Canal Street, in the heart of Chinatown. It was one of his least favorite parts of town—crowded, noisy, dirty. Filled with people who couldn't speak a word of English. He shuddered and felt grateful that his money protected him from having to rub shoulders with so many strange-smelling foreigners.

"I spent a fascinating day in court. Your husband is very impressive."

"I'll tell him you said so."

"Will you?" he asked.

"What's that supposed to mean?" she shot back.

He balanced the phone against his shoulder as he lit up a cigarette. "Please listen carefully, Hope, because I wouldn't want any further misunderstandings between us. I only want to do what's best for all concerned—you, Paul, myself. Do you hear what I'm saying?"

"I'm not deaf, Jordan. But I have no idea whatsoever what you're trying to tell me."

"I inadvertently got hold of some information that I don't think Paul would want released to the general public."

"Information." He heard the tremor in her voice. He had her hooked. He knew she wouldn't hang up on him. "What sort of information?"

"It's of a very sensitive nature." He paused, allowing the words to sink in. "You've already seen how effective I am about making things happen. All you had to do was ask, and there's your husband, sitting on the federal bench. I can do that again for you—and for Paul. I can make sure this information doesn't do him any damage."

He puffed on the cigarette and wished there was a bottle of scotch in the car. They covered the distance of a full city block before Hope responded. Her tone was calm and cold now, and she spat out each word as if she were rationing them.

"Blackmail does not become you, Jordan. Nor do I even believe you. I don't want you calling me again. Is that perfectly clear?"

"We're talking about friends helping friends, Hope, not blackmail. And I resent your implication that I'm lying to you. I'll send you a package of audiotapes first thing tomorrow morning. Listen to them at your leisure. But I wouldn't wait too long. This is a matter of some urgency, for both of us." He chuckled. "All three of us, I should say."

"I don't believe you, Jordan," she repeated, but now she sounded less sure.

"Just listen to the tapes. Then call my secretary. She knows how to reach me, wherever I am."

There was a hum at the other end. She had already hung up. He was talking to dead air.

HOPE AND PAUL had gotten into the habit of eating breakfast together in the airy, plant-filled conservatory off the dining room. Usually, this was one of Hope's favorite parts of the day, when she got to stare at Paul over her coffee cup, exchange sections of the newspaper as they went through them, read aloud whatever little news item struck their fancy.

Today, she felt as if there wasn't enough air to breathe in the room. Iron fists were twisting the insides of her stomach, making it impossible to eat or drink anything but a few sips of water.

She couldn't have slept more than an hour or two all night. The digital clock on her side of the bed had seemed to mock her every time she turned over and saw its face glowing in the dark. At four-thirty, when the birds began to sing outside their window, she had gotten up and crept off to read in the library. Paul found her there, dozing on the couch, when he got up to get ready for court.

"Are you all right?" he whispered, kneeling next to her on the floor. "Go back to sleep. I'll call you later."

She sat up and shook her head. "I need to get up. I have a lot to do today. I'm going to come in and have breakfast with you."

But every time she thought about Jordan's call—and she couldn't seem to *stop* thinking about it—it was all she could do not to push her plate away like an unhappy child. More than anything else, she was furious with Jordan. For years, she had risen to his defense whenever people had criticized him. She had always been kind to him, offering her friendship.

Whether or not he actually possessed information that could be harmful to Paul was irrelevant. He had threatened to betray her. He had proven himself to be every bit as loathsome as people said he was.

She was furious with herself, too. Thanks to her stupidity, she had created a situation that could prove dangerous to Paul. She no longer trusted Jordan. There was no telling what he might do in order to get what he wanted.

How could she have been so naive? She wanted to reach across the table to Paul, who was deep into the Sports section, and cry out, "I'm sorry. I only meant to help. Can you ever forgive me?"

It had seemed like such a wonderful idea at the time. Even Uncle George had thought so. In fact, as best she could remember, it had been Uncle George who had put the idea into her head. He might even had been the one who suggested she speak to Jordan.

Not that she blamed Uncle George for what had happened. She had to take full responsibility herself. She should have known better. Sneaking behind Paul's back, even for the best of reasons, was hardly the way to begin a marriage.

Hope was woefully short of experience in that area. She had only the most fleeting memories of her parents' marriage, most of them based on pictures in the photo albums she'd turned to for consolation after her mother's death. There were endless glamorous shots of her mother and father, laughing over their drinks and cigarettes, dining out, dancing, waving at the camera from yacht decks, tennis courts, and ski slopes.

In the pictures they always looked so happy together, so much in love. Now she wondered. Had her mother felt about her father the way she felt about Paul? She wished there was someone she could ask, but she didn't trust Aunt Grace's perceptions, and it wasn't the kind of question she could comfortably discuss with Aunt Connie.

Her own first marriage had been a near-total disaster, and she had stumbled frequently along the way to meeting Paul: the brief fling with Jordan, other missteps with men who ultimately meant nothing to her. For a while, she had collected men and dispensed with them in much the same way she ran through the fall and spring collections.

Most of them were interchangeable—handsome, successful men who used their wealth to find what passed in their circle for peace of mind. She understood them too well; until she'd met Paul, she had drifted from one affair to another, from one project and interest to the next, well protected by the safety net of her social standing and her trust fund. Money couldn't necessarily buy happiness, but it could certainly ensure that all her wants, needs, and desires were met.

Except for one. A relationship with a man for whom she'd be ready to make sacrifices, even change her life, if need be. A man who made her feel so loved and wanted that everything else paled by comparison.

She had found that man in Paul. Might she lose him now because of Jordan's perverse desire to extract his pound of flesh from her.

"Hope?"

She turned to Paul and realized that he must have been looking at her for some time.

"You were staring at that ficus tree as if you wanted to kill it," he said.

"Really? I guess I was wondering why so many leaves keep turning yellow and fall off. I'll have to go to the nursery the next time we're in the country and ask them for advice."

He didn't look convinced. "Hope, what's wrong? You didn't eat much dinner last night, you hardly slept, and you look like you're about to burst into tears. Has Aunt Grace been bothering you again?"

"I must have had something that disagreed with me for lunch. My stomach's just a bit off," she said.

"Shouldn't you call the doctor?"

"I will if I don't feel better by noon. I promise." She forced herself to smile and changed the subject. "Is there anything interesting in the paper? Any mention of your trial?"

He nodded and handed her the first section. "It made the front page. Crandell and Valentine are big news."

"Who cares about them? What about you? Do they

mention that you're the sexiest judge in the federal court system?" she teased.

He laughed. "Oddly enough, that didn't get reported."

She glanced at the article, and the accompanying photograph of Lew Valentine and his lawyer, surrounded by boxes of documents. "How is it going?" she asked, as casually as she could manage. "We got so involved talking urban politics over dinner with Yvonna last night that I never did ask you about the trial."

"The lawyers put on a great show for me. They're evenly matched, I think. I'm looking forward to Act Two today."

She pretended to take a sip of her orange juice. "Who's winning?"

"Too soon to tell."

"I was at one of my committee meetings yesterday, and everyone was talking about this case."

He nodded. "It's gotten a lot of press coverage."

"Most people think Crandell's sure to win."

He put down the newspaper and smiled. "Is that your subtle way of asking me whether I think Crandell's going to win?"

"Don't be silly. If I wanted to know, I'd ask you straight out," she said, suddenly very intent on spreading just the right amount of cream cheese on her toast.

"I know you would," he said. He gulped down the last of his coffee. "I better go. I have some reading to do before the fun begins again."

She followed him out of the conservatory and walked him to the door. Reluctant to see him leave, she said, "You look so handsome today. Does your new robe fit?"

"Like a glove. You take it easy, okay? And call the doctor if you're not feeling better by lunchtime."

"I'm sure I'll be fine." She handed him his briefcase. "This could use a good cleaning. Or maybe I'll buy you a new one. Why don't I do that? I could go to Mark Cross today."

He put his arms around her. "Hope. Stop fussing over me. I've had this briefcase since I started working at Goodstein & Carney. I like it just the way it is. More importantly, I love you. I want you to relax. Maybe we should go up to the country this weekend. Could we manage it?"

She tried to remember whether they had any weekend plans. Whatever they were, she decided, she would cancel them. They hadn't been up to the house for a month. A weekend alone there with Paul was precisely what she needed.

"That's perfect. We'll get away from everyone and everything. I'd love it. And I love you, too. Very, very much," she said, kissing him.

He grinned and put his arms around her. "This feels too good. If we don't stop now, Odette and Wolch will have to go on without me."

"Stay," she murmured into his neck. "You can always read the court reporter's transcript."

He laughed and pulled away. "Oh, sure. And give them grounds for a mistrial? No, thank you, ma'am."

A mistrial—the solution to her problems with Jordan. If only it could be arranged, she thought as she watched Paul turn to go.

He opened the door just as a young man in spandex bike shorts and a helmet got off the elevator. "Mrs. Murray?" said the young man.

"Yes?"

"I have a package for you."

The package from Jordan. Too panicked to speak, she stared dumbly at the messenger, who stood just inches away from Paul. Finally, she recovered enough to say, "The doorman is supposed to buzz up first."

He nodded. "Yeah, he spoke to your maid. The service elevator's out, so he told me to take this one."

"Oh." She stared at the brown manila envelope, thinking, *That bastard! He couldn't even wait until Paul had left for the day.*

"Could you sign here first?" asked the messenger. "They hate it when I don't get a signature." He fumbled in his bag for a pen, balancing the envelope under his arm.

"Let me help you with that," said Paul, as the messenger handed his receipt pad to Hope. Paul glanced at the return address. "*Pastiche.* Are you writing an article for them?"

"No, of course not," she said quickly, taking it out of his hand. "I went to one of their luncheons last week. This must be some sort of thank-you present."

"Well, enjoy," he said, kissing her once more. "I'll call you later."

She stood frozen as an ice sculpture, still clutching the package, until she heard the elevator close on the other side of the door. Then she sank down on the nearest chair and tore open the envelope. Inside, just as Jordan had promised, were two cassette tapes. As well, he had sent along several typewritten pages, which she knew without even looking at them to be the transcript.

She sat staring at the pages, unable to bring herself to read the words. She refused to believe that Paul could ever have done anything to be ashamed of, anything that could possibly do him any harm. What was the word Jordan had used to describe whatever was on the tapes? She tried to remember, and then it came back to her: "sensitive." He'd said the information was of a sensitive nature.

She couldn't imagine what that was supposed to mean. Of course, she didn't have to imagine. She could listen to the damn things.

Or she could: toss them down the compactor, to be ground to pieces and thrown into a landfill somewhere on Staten Island. She pictured the yards of shredded black ribbon, buried at the bottom of a mile-high pile of garbage. It was a satisfying picture, one she was tempted to put into effect.

Common sense got the better of her. Jordan obviously would have kept the originals. He'd probably had multiple copies made by now. He could start sending them to her by the dozens, instead of long-stemmed roses.

She stuck the transcript back in the envelope and went into the bedroom to find her Walkman. She wanted to hear the voices of whomever Jordan had spoken to. She wanted to hear whatever crazy lies they'd concocted to please Jordan Crandell and relieve him of some of his money.

She sat down on the bed, inserted the tape that had been neatly labeled "PM, #1," and turned on the machine. Two men, neither of them Jordan, were having what seemed to be a friendly chat. One of them mentioned that he was a private investigator. Who worked for Jordan? she wondered, and immediately knew the answer must be yes.

The thought of him deliberately sending someone out to poke around in Paul's private life horrified her. She turned off the tape and lay back on the bed until she felt calm enough to listen to more. The second man, named Milt, was a former policeman who was giving the private investigator an enthusiastic description of his new job.

Jordan really was crazy, she decided, fast-forwarding the tape. None of this had anything to do with Paul. She tuned in again in time to catch the private investigator in the middle of a sentence that ended with ". . . someone named Jimmy Murray?"

Paul's brother, Jimmy? She turned up the volume and listened closely. The man named Milt took a long time to spin out his story about Jimmy Murray. When he was finally done talking, she felt sick to her stomach. It had to be Paul's brother they were discussing.

Her hands were shaking as she snapped the second tape into the machine. She desperately wanted not to listen, but she had to know how Jimmy's story ended.

One thing she already did know. Whatever was recorded there could only mean trouble for Paul. But Jordan still had her confused with the lonely, grief-stricken divorcee who'd turned to him for comfort after she'd buried her father. She'd grown up considerably since then. She was no longer so easily impressed—or intimidated. If Jordan had his way, the results could be devastating for Paul, as well as for herself and their unborn child. Her happiness was too hard won to allow that to happen. She prayed that Paul would decide the case in Jordan's favor. If he didn't, she would have to find some other means to beat Jordan at his own best game.

KEN WOLCH HAD just finished questioning his first witness of the day, a director of Starwares named Harold Shaw, who was the first senior vice president of the Marbury Group, a Rhode Island financial services company. Paul waited as Bernard Odette slowly rose to his feet to take his turn with Shaw.

The courtroom was again filled to capacity. Naomi Bowman had told Paul that ten or fifteen would-be spectators had been turned away for lack of room. It was rare that a preliminary hearing in a civil suit attracted such a crowd. But the already-strong interest in the case seemed to be growing in direct proportion to the play it was receiving in the media.

Thus far this morning, the audience had not been disappointed by the interplay between Wolch and Odette. Like two veteran sparring partners, they had feinted and parried above the head of the increasingly bewildered witness, until Paul had finally declared, "Gentlemen! I would strongly advise you to knock it off. We're getting nowhere fast."

Summoning the lawyers to approach the bench, he sternly admonished both of them. "Mr. Odette, you're making me dizzy with all your objections. Stop popping up and down like a jack-in-the-box and allow us to move forward."

Next, he quickly dispelled Ken Wolch's look of self-satisfaction. "As for you, Mr. Wolch, you know what to do in here. Phrase your questions properly, or I'll have this witness dismissed."

They seemed to have taken his rebuke to heart, at least for the moment. He hoped the truce would last. If not, he was prepared to bring the hearing to a speedy close.

"Mr. Shaw," Odette began his cross-examination, "you testified that in your capacity as a member of the Starwares Board of Directors, you attended all the board meetings held over the course of the past six months."

"That's right," said Shaw, who kept taking off his glasses and wiping the lenses with his handkerchief.

"You also testified that you were kept abreast of the ongoing developments in the merger talks between Starwares and Summit, as well as Valentine's unsolicited bid for Starwares."

"That's also correct."

Paul leaned forward, ready to intervene if Odette didn't soon come to the point.

Odette seemed to sense his restlessness, and moved forward. "Mr. Shaw, at the board meeting you attended on October 28 of this past year, what kind of information were you given regarding the comparative value of the two competing offers?"

"I'm sorry, Your Honor"—Wolch had risen from his chair—"I must object. Counsel is asking the witness to characterize various forms of information. This kind of overly broad question can only lead to confusion."

Paul nodded in agreement. "Sustained. Please rephrase the question, Mr. Odette, and make it as specific as possible."

"Certainly." Odette pursed his lips, paced the length of the room, then began again. "Mr. Shaw, at that meeting, did you receive a report prepared by the management consulting firm of Coffey, Wilcox & Associates?"

"Yes, I did."

"In your opinion, what was the conclusion of the consultants who prepared the report?"

Harold Shaw adjusted his glasses on the bridge of his nose and said, "It was quite clear that the report unequivocally rated the Summit-Starwares alliance as being far superior to that of Starwares and Valentine."

"There was no question in your mind?"

"None whatsoever."

"On what did Coffey, Wilcox base its quantitative analysis of the merits of the two bids?"

Wolch was on his feet again. "Objection, Your Honor. The witness—"

Paul cut him off. "Sustained. He's right, Mr. Odette. Mr. Shaw isn't here to testify about the methodology employed by Coffey, Wilcox. Please confine your questions to the issue at hand."

He saw the trace of a frown on Odette's face. He was apparently not used to such strict guidelines. But with so much attention focused on the case and all the players involved, Paul could not permit any lapses in the courtroom procedure. There was almost sure to be an appeal. He wanted the upper court's decision to be based on the merits of the case, not the administrative aspects of the hearing.

"I'll rephrase my question, Your Honor," said Odette. "Mr. Shaw, according to the deposition I have here of Benjamin Coffey, a principal at Coffey, Wilcox, the sole quantitative analysis undertaken for this report was based on the market prices of the shares at that point in time, rather than on the future anticipated value of the shares, at the point they would be received by the stockholders. In your opinion, Mr. Shaw, do you consider that an adequate measure of the actual value of the securities?"

Harold Shaw squirmed in his chair.

Odette stepped closer to the witness stand. "I might remind you, Mr. Shaw, that this is sworn testimony. You're under oath to tell us your true, considered opinion."

Shaw removed his glasses and began polishing the lenses again. "Well," he said, "I suppose that, strictly speaking, it would not be an adequate measure. That's only my opinion, of course. I'm no expert."

"No expert, Mr. Shaw?" Odette, who had walked back toward the lectern, suddenly whirled around and pointed his finger at Shaw. "I would think that the clients who avail themselves of the financial services offered by the Marbury Group might be surprised to hear you make such a statement."

Shaw flushed.

"Objection. Counsel is badgering the witness," Wolch interjected.

"Overruled, Mr. Wolch," Paul said. "I'd like to hear Mr. Shaw's response."

"Thank you, Your Honor," said Odette. "Mr. Shaw, a moment ago you used the phrase 'strictly speaking.' It strikes me that in a transaction that involves millions of dollars and will affect the lives of thousands of people, one would want to be strict in one's assessment. Wouldn't you agree?"

"Yes, I suppose so," said Shaw.

"Then would you also agree that because of the constantly varying market prices of both Summit's and Valentine's stock, Coffey, Wilcox might have better served the directors of Starwares, as well as the stockholders, had it taken into account the future value of the securities?"

"Yes, I would agree."

"Then is it fair to say that you and the other board members were not sufficiently diligent in exercising your fiduciary duties as regards this decision?"

"Objection!" called Ken Wolch.

Paul nodded. "Sustained." Odette had crossed the line again into the area of speculation. Nevertheless, he had made a good point. It was one that deserved further thought and investigation.

"No further questions, Your Honor," said Odette.

The Michigan Assassin was living up to his reputation.

KURT ZELMANSKI GRABBED Rizzy Riznicki as she was walking out of the courtroom to go to lunch. "I have to talk to you," he said.

She shook her head. "Some other time, Zelmanski. I have a date with my boss."

He read her brusqueness as a positive sign. She was still angry that he'd slept with the junior comptroller. If she was jealous, she must be interested in him. That realization was both scary and exhilarating.

"Break it. This is important," he said.

She was walking so quickly that he had to hurry to keep up with her. "I'm in the middle of a trial. In case you hadn't noticed."

Odette was a few feet ahead of both of them, giving an impromptu interview to the circle of reporters who were trailing in his wake.

"Mr. Odette?" Zelmanski raised his voice to be heard above the shouted questions of his colleagues and waved his arm.

Odette turned and saw him waving. He stopped and waited for Zelmanski to catch up with him. "Yes, Mr. Zelmanski?"

"I know you need some time with Rizzy to prepare for the afternoon session, but I have to talk to her. Could you spare her for forty-five minutes?"

He didn't dare look at Rizzy as he waited for Odette's answer.

"Sure," said Odette. "It shouldn't take long for us to review whatever we have to. Go ahead, Rizzy. I'll see you back in the courtroom."

"How dare you?" she demanded as Odette was swallowed up by the crowd. "I'm not some damn peasant girl who's at her master's beck and call."

"Calm down. This will be worth your while."

"I didn't say I was coming with you."

"I'll buy you lunch. I'll even apologize." He sneaked a peak at her face. She seemed to be softening. "Hey, you're cute when you're angry."

"Don't start with me, Zelmanski." She marched out the door, then stopped short as the sun hit her face. "What a beautiful day," she said. "All right." She pointed to the fast-food vendors who had set up their wagons in the plaza to the right of the courthouse. "You can buy me some sushi."

"Sushi?" He made a face.

"I'm on a diet, Zelmanski. Take it or leave it."

She didn't know it, but he was about to do her a favor. So why was he putting up with her evil temper? Because he liked her, dammit. He even liked her evil temper.

"Fine. Sushi it is," he said.

Juggling their cardboard trays, they found a place to sit with a view of the Brooklyn Bridge arching across the East River.

He pointed toward Brooklyn. "I used to live in Greenpoint."

"I know," she said, squinting into the sun. "You told me the first time we had dinner."

"I was just checking to see if you were listening."

"So, make it worth my while. What was so important that you had to tell me?"

He reached into his jacket pocket and pulled out the copies he'd made for her. "Take a look at these."

"From your friend at Summit?"

He nodded. "She turned up dynamite stuff." He showed her the papers, explaining as he handed them to her. "First, the computer-generated receipts for the date on which the three Scott Trust checks were received into the discretionary fund. Second, the regular next-day report, which should show the half billion still sitting in the fund, because no way the checks could have cleared yet. But those checks aren't showing up, which is what got Ms. Comptroller crazy in the first place. This leads us to incriminating document number three: the backup for a transfer out of the discretionary fund, dated the day after the checks came in, for exactly that same half billion.''

He waited for her to examine the various pages. Then he said, ''And where's it all going to? The White Lake Investment Group, a Bahamian-registered corporation of ambiguous origins and ownership.''

''But what's all this got to do with Starwares?''

''I'm glad you asked that question, madam.'' He grinned at her. ''I'm still working out this part of it, but I wouldn't be at all surprised to discover that White Lake shows up somewhere in Crandell's SEC filings for the merger.''

She shook her head. ''I don't know. It could all be just a coincidence. What's the connection between White Lake and Crandell?''

''Check this out. Where do you suppose Crandell spent every summer when he was a kid?''

''I'm not into playing guessing games, Zelmanski,'' she said.

''At his grandparents' summer place in White Lake, Vermont. The house burned down when he was fifteen, and his grandparents sold off the land. He mentioned it once in an interview he gave years ago to *Esquire*.''

''Omigod. It's his Rosebud.''

He nodded. ''You wouldn't take Crandell to be such a sentimental guy, would you?''

''Yeah, but he's still a crook. What are you going to do with all this?''

''I'm going to turn it into the best damn piece of investigative journalism you ever read. But not until I have all the evidence. Plus I want to talk to George Osburgh. Give him a chance to explain those checks.''

''So why confide in me, Zelmanski? Why not one of your reporter friends?''

"Because if you haven't already told Odette any of this, I want you to tell him now. I want him to let me see whatever you have that might confirm Crandell's creative banking procedures."

And because he liked her better than any of his reporter friends. Being with her felt like coming home.

"You're crazy. Why would he let you do that?" she said.

"Tell him I'll show him mine if he shows me his."

She stood up to leave. "Zelmanski, I've seen yours, and it's nothing to brag about."

He smiled as he got up to follow her back to the courtroom. He was finally getting somewhere with her.

THIRTEEN

Hope? Hope, where are you?"

Paul's voice, thick with sleep, preceded him as he came around the corner of the house and found her sitting by the pond, watching the sun sink into the horizon. She rubbed her eyes to wipe away any trace of tears and smiled as he put his arm around her.

"I woke up and you were gone," he said. "What happened?"

She curled herself tightly against him. "The phone rang, remember? After that I couldn't fall back to sleep."

"You should have just let it ring. Who was it? Someone worth getting up for, I hope."

She wasn't about to tell him it was Jordan Crandell who had called, harassing her with threats of the damage he could do if Paul didn't rule in his favor. She was sure he was fully prepared to make good on his threat. In his own peculiar way, Jordan was a man of his word. He'd always kept his promises to her in the past. Judging from his tone, she had every reason to assume he would do so now.

After she'd hung up the phone, she'd gone back to the bedroom to check on Paul. He was fast asleep, oblivious to the potential firestorm that Jordan was planning to unleash. She'd kissed him gently so as not wake him and pulled up the covers that were tangled around his legs.

She wished that she could nap, too. But Jordan's call had destroyed the few fleeting moments of peace she had given herself after she and Paul had made love. Throwing on one of Paul's sweatshirts and a pair of his sweatpants that fit her now that her belly was beginning to swell, she had wandered outside to warm herself in the lowering sun and to think about what she should do.

She knew Jordan had to be right: Paul must have intervened on Jimmy's behalf. She could imagine how conflicted he must have felt about pulling strings to prevent any charges from being brought against Jimmy. It couldn't have been in his own best interests to make that decision. If only she could tell Paul that she loved him all the more for stepping in to save his brother.

How ironic that Jordan was now presenting her with a similarly difficult choice: to stay silent and possibly allow her husband to lose everything he'd worked for, or to tell Paul the truth about Jordan and risk losing his trust in her.

In *Now, Voyager,* Bette Davis had sacrificed true love for honor. Could she bring herself to do the same? Or was she giving Jordan too much power by believing it could come to that?

Jordan had said that his lawyer thought Paul would rule in their favor. He was just "looking for a little insurance policy," he'd said.

Paul's reputation was his insurance policy. Jordan Crandell was about to become the beneficiary of her naivete. Or was it stupidity?

"Hey," said Paul. "You look like you're a million miles away. I bet you didn't even hear me ask you who called."

"It was nobody," she lied. "A wrong number."

He picked up a pebble and tossed it into the pond. The pebble skipped once, then disappeared beneath the water.

"Well, I slept like the proverbial log. I didn't realize how tired I was from refereeing Odette and Wolch."

"Are they done with their arguments and witnesses?"

He nodded. "Now the real fun begins. I told them I'd give them my decision within one week."

"That sounds like an awfully short time to review all those documents and testimony."

"Short for me, an eternity for the parties involved. Lynch, Valentine, and Crandell have millions of dollars at stake. These guys aren't known for their patience. You've heard of the Type A personality? Valentine and Crandell especially are Type A plus."

She got up and walked a few feet away, suddenly very interested in the yellow rosebush that was on the verge of blooming. "I think you should decide in favor of Crandell," she said.

"Okay, I'll take that under advisement," he said good-naturedly.

Her nerve almost failed her. But she was determined to finish what she'd begun. She had to, for both their sakes.

"Don't humor me. I mean it. I've been following the case in the papers, I've been reading all the coverage," she said, trying to sound convincing. "It sounds like Crandell has much the stronger case."

He threw another pebble into the pond, this time managing to make it skip twice before it sank. "Hope, I appreciate that you're taking an interest in my work, but I thought we came up here to get away from everything. I could really use a break from Crandell and his cohorts."

"You never want to discuss your cases with me," she said petulantly. "I bet you and Helen always talked about your work."

"Excuse me?" He sounded as surprised as she was by her complaint.

The words had sprung to her lips from someplace within herself she hadn't known existed. They'd burst out before she'd had the chance to censor them. She was speaking out of desperation. Of course, she didn't really believe those things. Or did she?

"You don't seem to respect my opinion," she forged on, determined to finish what she had begun. "You treat me like a child. You pat me on the head, hand me my glass of milk, and tell me to go lie down. But I know much more about how corporations are run than you ever give me credit for. I know Jordan Crandell. I know the kind of person he is. He's a brilliant businessman—"

"You said you didn't know Crandell. That he wasn't a friend of yours."

His voice cut through her. He'd never spoken to her so coldly. That they were arguing about Jordan Crandell, of all people, made her heart ache with grief.

Cornered in a trap of her own making, she lashed out at him. "Don't you dare call me a liar, Paul! I told you he was part of my crowd. And in my opinion, he deserves to buy Starwares. He's worked hard to be so successful. Nobody handed him anything he didn't earn." She glared, daring him to contradict her.

"You say that as if you're not sure the same is true for me."

"Don't be ridiculous. You're deliberately twisting my words."

Paul shook his head, looking more hurt than angry. "I don't understand what's happening here," he said. "Why are we fighting?"

Because I'm trying to save your reputation, she wanted to cry out to him. *Because I love you and I don't want to see you destroyed.*

Instead, in a tone that rang too loudly in her ears, she said, "Because I want you take me seriously, and you don't. I know all about Lew Valentine. He's a nouveau upstart who pulls businesses apart as if they were Tinker Toys. People like him are destroying our economy. You're always going on about the tragedy of unemployment. Well, what about all the people who've lost their jobs because Valentine downsized their companies?"

The set of his jaw frightened her. She almost didn't recognize the man who stood staring at her.

"I'm sorry if I've bored you with my opinions about unemployment," he said stiffly. "And as far as downsizing companies is concerned, your friend Jordan Crandell has a track record that's just as bad, if not worse, than Lew Valentine's. But then, of course, he's not nouveau. His family's blood is almost as blue as yours, isn't it?"

"It's not about that!"

He shrugged his shoulders, turned his back to her, and trudged up the path to the house.

"Paul, you don't understand!" she called after him.

He ignored her and kept on walking until she couldn't see him anymore.

"You don't understand," she whispered, as the tears began to fall. She slid to her knees and hugged her belly, fearful of what she might have done to their unborn child. "I did it for you, Paul. Because I love you."

But what if he never came back? How would she ever be able to tell him the truth?

GEORGE OSBURGH HAD inherited from his father a deep mistrust of journalists that went back three generations. Even reporters from *The Wall Street Journal* were not to be trusted. Especially reporters from *The Wall Street Journal*. Fearful of seeing himself misquoted in print, he avoided giving interviews. Occasionally, however, a situation was simply too important—or the reporter too persistent—to dodge the encounter, in which case Osburgh set the terms.

The meeting had to take place in his office and could last no more than one hour. He had no qualms about stopping in midsentence. No matter was so important that it couldn't be covered in exactly sixty minutes, preferably fewer. The reporter could tape the interview, but Os-

burgh protected himself by making his own recording.
And no questions allowed about his personal life, thank
you very much.

All this was negotiated through Osburgh's secretary in
order to limit his direct contact with the reporter. When
he finally sat down to talk, however, he prided himself
on being courteous and forthcoming in his responses.

Osburgh had never met Kurt Zelmanski, but he'd read
his articles, particularly those he'd written about the
Starwares merger. If he wasn't mistaken, he detected
somewhat of a pro-Valentine bias in Zelmanski's tone.
He couldn't understand why Jordan Crandell hadn't
whipped the pup into shape, but there was a great deal
that he didn't understand—and didn't care to understand—about Jordan Crandell. All that mattered was that
Crandell win in court and the deal be consummated.

He'd had only two brief conversations with Crandell
since the complaint had been filed. Crandell sounded absolutely confident of victory, and Osburgh hadn't pressed
him to elaborate. He could read between the lines well
enough to guess the origins of Paul's judgeship. He'd
played his own part in that venture, planting the idea in
Hope's pretty head.

He didn't normally subscribe to Machiavelli's belief
that the ends justifed the means. These, however, were
special circumstances. Though he didn't want to know
the specifics of what Crandell was up to, he prayed for
his success.

If he could do his small part to influence Zelmanski's
understanding of the facts, he was willing to cooperate.
An hour of his time was a small sacrifice indeed compared to what he stood to gain.

The two tape recorders—his and Zelmanski's—sat
side by side on his desk. His secretary had brought him
his tea, and a cup of coffee for Zelmanski. Osburgh
smiled at the reporter. He was ready to begin.

"You told my secretary you wanted to get my reaction
to the Starwares merger," he said, sipping the tea.

Zelmanski nodded. "That's right. Your opinion still carries a lot of weight on Wall Street. I'm curious to hear who you think is a better match for Starwares from an investor's point of view."

Osburgh's smile faded. He didn't appreciate Zelmanski's use of the word "still," implying that he was some sort of antiquated Wall Street fossil, to be trotted out for newspaper filler.

"Young man, did one of your editors send you over here? Or did you deduce for yourself that there's something to be learned from three generations of experience on the Street?"

Zelmanski grinned. "I figured it out for myself," he said, seeming to miss Osburgh's point entirely. "So which would you choose, Summit or Valentine?"

The fellow wasn't worth bothering with, but Osburgh felt he could ill afford to waste this opportunity to speak out. At this very moment, Paul Murray was probably considering the pros and cons of the case. Judges were like everyone else. They made up their minds based on a hundred different factors other than the court documents or arguments. Depending on how they'd slept, whether they'd made love the night before, what they read in that morning's newspaper, they could just as easily lean one way as the other.

"My choice is not the issue here," he said. "However, if you're asking me for whom I think Judge Murray will find, I'd have to say that Summit's case is far stronger than Valentine's. I believe that the directors of Starwares made a fair and accurate assessment of the two offers and were right in voting to ally themselves with Summit. Moreover, I think that Summit's overall financial picture is much more attractive than Valentine's."

"So you like the financing package Jordan Crandell put together?"

Osburgh could see that he'd caught Zelmanski's interest. He'd probably come expecting to find a doddering old fool, past his prime and kept on only for the sake of his name. No doubt he was getting much more from this interview than he'd bargained for.

"From everything I've read about Summit's backing, I like it very much. There's money, there's commitment, there's an exciting vision for the future. The bottom line is I feel extremely positive about the merger."

Zelmanski leaned forward to check his tape recorder.

"Are you getting all of this?"

"Yeah, this is great."

Warming now to the subject, Osburgh said, "I'm happy to be of help. Anything else I can tell you?"

"I do have a couple more questions."

Osburgh glanced at his watch. "Go ahead. We have time."

The reporter pulled out a sheaf of papers and slid it across the desk.

"What are these?" asked Osburgh, reaching for his reading glasses.

"They're copies of Summit receipts for three checks you drew on the Scott Trust in the amount of a half-billion dollars. Is that why you're feeling so bullish about Summit's financing?"

Osburgh stared at the papers, pretending to study the figures printed there. "I have no idea what you're talking about," he said finally, putting them down and removing his glasses.

"Really?" Zelmanski pointed to the sheets. "Then maybe you'd better take a second look. It's all pretty straightforward."

Osburgh's heart was pumping at twice its normal rate. He took a deep breath and said, "What kind of game are you playing, Mr. Zelmanski? Because you know as well as I do that I never wrote any such checks."

"I think you did, Mr. Osburgh, and I'd like to know why. I'm sure Hope Scott Murray would like to know the same thing. I'm also curious about what part that money is playing in Jordan Crandell's bid for Starwares. And I'm that close"—he snapped his fingers—"to coming up with all the answers. Is there anything you want to say about that?"

He had to get Zelmanski out of his office quickly, before he said anything to betray himself, so he could think about what to do next. But he was afraid to open his mouth. The slightest word misspoken could be his undoing.

With all the calm and dignity he could muster, George Osburgh said, "I should have expected nothing less from a piece of scum like you. Valentine's probably paying you for that garbage you churn out. But now you've gone too far. The next call I make is to your boss at the *Journal*, to notify him that I'm going to sue you, him, and your paper if so much as one syllable of this garbage gets printed. Do you understand me?"

Zelmanski turned off his tape recorder and stuck it in his pocket. He put his business card on the desk and stood up to go.

"I'd love to hear your explanation," he said. "You can call me anytime, day or night. But don't wait too long. This story's aching to be born, and I'll write it with or without your input. Oh, and here." He tossed his handkerchief to Osburgh. "A present. To wipe those beads of sweat off your forehead."

Zelmanski left the office, whistling. Osburgh heard him saying goodbye to his secretary.

He picked up Zelmanski's handkerchief with the tips of two fingers and threw it in the wastebasket. He tried to stand up but couldn't because his legs had turned to rubber.

He wanted to run to Nancy's office, bury himself in her arms, beg her to say that everything would be all right. But she was away on business. Besides, he couldn't bear to admit to her what he'd done. And it wasn't going to be all right. His life was over. Soon all of New York would be laughing at his expense.

He was sure that Zelmanski had seen through his empty threat to call his boss. What was the point? There was no stopping the bastard. Zelmanski was intent on ruining him and dragging Crandell down along with him.

Crandell. Of course. Osburgh picked up the phone.

Jordan Crandell wouldn't let any little two-bit reporter destroy his deal. He would take care of everything. Jordan would know just what to do.

"JUDGE MURRAY? JUDGE Paul Murray?"

"Yes, this is Paul Murray," came the voice at the other end. "Who am I speaking with?"

Jordan Crandell put his feet up on his desk and smiled. "This is Jordan Crandell," he said.

The silence that followed lasted a solid thirty seconds. In that space of time, Crandell amused himself by wondering whether Hope had done what he'd asked her to do. It would be better if she hadn't. Now that he had Paul on the line, he wanted to be the one to break the news to him.

Paul cleared his throat. Then he said, "You shouldn't be calling me."

Crandell's smile broadened. "I know that. But we have to talk."

"Mr. Crandell, it's absolutely out of the question for us to have a conversation. I can't imagine what's on your mind, but I'm going to hang up and—"

"No," Crandell quickly broke in. "Don't. This is very important. It's about Hope."

"What about Hope?"

His question was tinged with anger. Crandell couldn't place its source. The edge in his tone had changed too suddenly.

He said, "There's something you should know, Paul. Unless Hope's already told you herself."

"Told me what?"

Now Crandell thought he heard fear in Paul's voice,

and he played on it. He knew what he would have thought, under similar circumstances. He waited, allowing Paul to consider all the sickening possibilities, giving him ample opportunity to develop the image of Hope in bed with him.

"Told me what?" Paul repeated more loudly.

Crandell had hooked his fish. Slowly, he began to reel him in. "Hope and I have been friends for a very long time, Paul. Since childhood. I'm sure you're aware of that."

There was another long pause, during which it occurred to Crandell that perhaps Hope hadn't told Paul how well they knew each other.

"What's your point, Mr. Crandell?" Paul asked, his fury barely concealed.

"Please, call me Jordan," he said. "We're not in court now. There's no need for such formality. After all, we're almost family."

He wished he had a videophone to see the expression on Paul's face.

"Crandell." Paul's voice was low and harsh. "You have exactly ten seconds to say whatever the hell is on your mind. Then I'm hanging up and calling your attorney to advise him that you've been in touch with me."

Crandell chuckled. "I don't think you'll do that, Paul. But we're both busy men, so I'll cut to the chase. I've been watching you during the hearing. You're very good. I know you'll make the right decision. I'm pleased I had a hand in getting you that judgeship."

"Mr. Crandell—"

"No need to thank me. I did it for Hope. How could I say no to her after all she's done for me? She's a special lady. I was happy to do her the favor."

"What are you saying, Crandell?" Paul's tone had gone flat, as if he were fighting to keep himself under control.

"She never told you? Dammit, I'm sorry. Now I've

gone and ruined her surprise. But since the cat's already out of the bag, you may as well hear the whole story. We were having lunch, just the two of us, and she asked me to help her give you this wonderful wedding present. It was no big deal for me, a well-placed word at the top, a couple of phone calls. The next thing we knew you were being sworn in.''

''You're lying.''

He feigned hurt. ''That's no way to express your gratitude, Paul. Of course, I realize you're under a lot of pressure right now with this case.'' Crandell chuckled. ''I empathize. I'm feeling the pressure myself. But as I told Hope when we spoke on Saturday, I'm sure you know how the system works. You scratch my balls, I scratch yours back. So stop worrying about making the right decision. Repay my favor, and we'll call it even. I would deserve to win even if you didn't owe me one.''

He lit a cigarette and waited for Paul's response. It wasn't long in coming.

''You're a sick bastard, Crandell,'' said Paul, and then he hung up.

''Maybe so,'' Crandell said to his empty office. ''But I'm having one hell of a good time.''

The taste of victory was sweet.

PAUL PUT DOWN the phone and realized he was still clutching the apple he'd been about to bite into when he'd taken Jordan Crandell's call. His appetite gone, he dropped it on the table and looked around the room, as if seeing it for the first time. He'd chosen the room for his office at Hope's urging, because it was so quiet, isolated at the other end of the hall from the master bedroom and main living quarters. It was the largest of the four spare bedrooms in the apartment, facing East 63rd Street and the brownstones across the way.

Hope had insisted on completely redecorating it, installing wall-to-ceiling bookcases, an antique mahogany desk, and a handsome pale green carpet. The overall effect was beautiful, if slightly too grand for his taste, though he never would have told her so. He still didn't feel comfortable working there, although he'd added his favorite books, reading lamp, and knickknacks from his old apartment.

Hope had placed an armchair at right angles to one of the windows, so that he could look up from his reading and enjoy the quiet, tree-lined elegance of the street below. Now, as he replayed in his head the conversation with Jordan Crandell, he stared out the window, blind to everything except the nightmarish picture Crandell had drawn for him.

With sickening clarity, he realized that Crandell must have put Hope up to discussing the case with him over the weekend. He'd said they'd talked on Saturday. Saturday—when he and Hope had been at the country house. When the phone had rung after they'd made love, and she'd told him later it was a wrong number, and they'd had that terrible argument.

They had made up eventually. But things hadn't felt quite right between them since, though both had pretended the fight was forgotten. He understood now why she'd been looking so tense and unhappy. She was caught in so many lies that he couldn't imagine how she was keeping it all straight.

She'd lied to him about her friendship with Crandell, lied about Crandell's phone call, lied about how many other things Paul could only begin to guess. Suddenly, he remembered the hand-delivered package she'd received the other morning from *Pastiche*. He hadn't given it a second thought; there'd been no reason for him to be suspicious. But now it hit him that, of course, *Pastiche* was Jordan Crandell's magazine.

What else was she hiding from him?

The very fact that he had to ask himself that question propelled him out of his chair and sent him pacing the room, trying to find the truth among all of Hope's deceptions. Had she slept with Jordan Crandell? Was she having an affair with him now? Was it all a sham? Their marriage, their whole life together?

And could Crandell be telling the truth about helping him get the federal appointment? That question was as painful to contemplate as the doubts about his marriage.

He felt as if he were stuck in a labyrinth of distorted mirrors, forced to face one monstrous possibility after another.

He needed answers, no matter how cruel they might be. Reminding himself that she was innocent until proven guilty, he went looking for Hope and found her in the nursery, sorting through samples of wallpaper.

She glanced up as he walked into the room. "I was just about to come interrupt you. I think I found the paper I want," she said. "What do you think?"

"Hope," he said, his anger rising, "I just spoke to Jordan Crandell."

The blood seemed to drain out of her face. "You did?"

"What the hell's going on with you two?"

"Nothing," she said. "There's nothing between us."

"Goddamnit, Hope! Stop lying to me!" he yelled, giving vent to all his frustration.

Her eyes got very round, and he saw that she was about to cry. "Please, I'll tell you whatever you want to know," she said, her voice trembling. "Just don't scream at me."

"Tell me the truth," Paul said, making a conscious effort to speak in a normal tone. "Are you having an affair with Crandell?"

"No, of course not." She stared at him incredulously. "Did he say that?"

"Not in so many words, more as an implication. But he did say that you asked him to use his influence to get me nominated to the bench."

She looked away from him, biting her lips.

"Did you do that, Hope?"

"So what if I did?" she blazed. "People do that all the time, ask their friends for favors. And you deserve to be a federal judge. Everyone said so."

"Who's everyone?"

She shrugged. "Uncle George, Aunt Grace . . . everyone."

"In other words, all your friends and relatives who didn't approve of you marrying a poor Mick immigrant's kid? A nobody with a low-status, low-paying state court position?"

"Do you think I give a damn about whether or not they approve of the man I love?"

"I don't know, Hope. You have me too confused. You went behind my back to Crandell, then you pretended to be as surprised as I was when I got the nomination. In my book, that's called lying. I don't expect my wife to lie to me."

"Well, I'm sorry if I don't live up to your expectations," she cried out.

She looked away again, and when she turned back to face him, the tears were spilling down her cheeks. "No, that's not what I mean," she said, speaking so softly he almost couldn't hear her.

As angry as he was with her, he loved her, and it hurt him to see her so distressed. But he wasn't ready to take her in his arms and say all was forgiven. He wasn't sure he could ever forgive her.

"I was only trying to help you," she said, weeping. "Because I thought that's what you wanted. I never should have gone to Jordan. It was stupid. I didn't realize then how evil he is."

"Well, I'd hardly call him evil. But you've put me in an extremely awkward position, you understand." Concerned now about the baby, he took a step toward her, but she waved him away.

"He's a terrible man. Did he tell you about the tapes?"

He shook his head.

"He hired a detective to find out about you. He knows what you did for Jimmy. He has it all down on tape." Hope sank down on the bed and began to sob.

She must be mistaken. It had happened too long ago, and too many people had a stake in keeping the story untold. He sat down next to her and handed her a tissue. "Shh," he whispered, "don't cry. It's okay."

She dabbed at her eyes, which were red and puffy from crying. "He sent me copies of the interviews, to convince you to rule in his favor. I'm scared he's going to blackmail you, Paul."

"Do you have the tapes here?"

She nodded. "And transcripts, too."

"All right, then," he said. "Let's hear what Mr. Crandell thinks he knows about me."

It must have been his Irish Catholic upbringing that made Paul feel as if he were coming to "Father" Jesse Rubin to confess his sins. He had to talk to someone he trusted—someone who would listen, advise without judging, keep his secret. That was asking a lot, and Jesse was the only one who fit the bill on all three counts.

"Thanks for letting me drop by on such short notice," Paul said, when Molly let him into their apartment.

Her expression made it clear she was dying to know why he'd rushed over at nine o'clock at night to see Jesse. But she was tactful enough not to ask, and he appreciated her discretion. Perhaps he'd tell her later; for now, he preferred to speak to Jesse in private.

"Jesse's in the den," she said. "Can I bring you something to drink in there?"

"Thanks, no," he said, then he changed his mind. "On second thought, how about a beer?"

"Beer it is," she said, and went off to the kitchen.

He followed the sound of the television to the den, where Jesse was stretched out on the couch, watching a baseball game.

"Sit down," Jesse said, pulling himself upright and muting the sound on the TV. "Make yourself comfortable."

"Sorry to break in on you like this," he said.

"Just as well. Those damn Mets break your heart every time."

Paul glanced at the set and saw that the Mets were up at bat. "What's the score?"

"They're behind by two." Jesse shook his head. "Just blew a four-run lead."

"Knock-knock." Molly appeared in the doorway with Paul's beer. "Anything for you, Jess, before I make myself scarce?"

Jesse grinned. "She's putting on a show for you, Paul. Usually, I'm on my own when it comes to bar service. Thanks, I'm fine, hon."

Molly put her hands on her waist and pretended to glare at her husband. "What an ingrate. I wait on him hand and foot, and he says I'm putting on a show. He's a bad role model, Paul. Don't you start taking Hope for granted the way he does me."

He felt a pang of envy for their easy warmth and affection, and wondered whether he and Hope could ever achieve a similar relationship.

"Come say goodbye before you leave." She smiled as she closed the door and left him alone with Jesse.

Paul removed the cap of the bottle of Heineken and tilted it in Jesse's direction. "Cheers," he said, taking a long swig.

"You don't sound convinced," said Jesse.

He knew that Jesse would leave it to him to begin the conversation. But he needed a few moments to gather his thoughts and summon the courage to explain what had brought him over here.

"How's Hope? Is she feeling okay?"

"Yeah, fine. She's just beginning to show."

"That's great. It's exciting, isn't it?"

Paul nodded, there was a pause, and suddenly he couldn't wait another moment to unburden himself. "I have a big problem, Jesse. I couldn't think of anyone else to talk to."

"Hey, I'm honored."

Quickly, before he could censor himself, Paul spilled out the whole story, starting backwards from Jordan Crandell's phone call. He spared nothing and offered no excuses for his behavior. The only dispensation he allowed himself was to periodically avert his eyes from Jesse's steadfast gaze. By the time he was done speaking, his beer had turned tepid. He slugged it down anyway, as much to wet his mouth as to reap the numbing effects of the alcohol.

"Is that it?" asked Jesse.

"Yes," he said, thinking, *Isn't it enough?*

Jesse smiled. "Why do I have the feeling you want me to tell you to say three Hail Marys and five Our Fathers?"

Though he never would have thought it possible, Paul somehow managed to produce what could have passed for a smile. "Because you know that once a Jesuit, always a Jesuit."

"Do you want to hear what I think?"

"Yes." He steeled himself for Jesse's disappointment.

"I think you made a mistake."

He nodded, almost eager to be rebuked. "I know. A big mistake."

Jesse held up his hand. "Hold it a minute. You're rushing to sentence yourself without the benefit of a fair hearing. You said you called a friend at the Manhattan D.A.'s office to see what he could do for Jimmy. How did you find out he was in trouble? Did he come to you himself?"

"No." He hesitated. After so many years, it was still hard for him to think about that afternoon. "My father called me. I was working with you on that big Japanese antidumping case. Do you remember it? *Shiozaki* v. *Panorama*?"

Jesse chuckled. "How could I ever forget it?"

"He was in a panic. I could tell from his voice, plus the mere fact of his phoning me at the office. Normally he wouldn't have wanted to disturb me. But this was urgent. Jimmy had just showed up at the house, scared shitless. Internal Affairs had him wearing a wire, and he'd gotten some very incriminating evidence on Brendan Connor. But it wasn't enough to save him from being arrested. You've met Jimmy?"

Jesse nodded. "Sure. He seems like a good, solid guy."

"Good, yes. Solid, I'm not so sure about. He's the baby in the family, and he got a little spoiled by all of us, especially my sisters. He was always the one who had to be bailed out of scrapes. Then he became a cop, and he was doing a terrific job. But some things don't change. He couldn't keep himself out of trouble."

"So your father asked you to help out?"

"In his whole life, my father never asked me to do anything except go to church and get myself an education. And there he is, almost crying because his baby's going to go to jail, saying, 'Help him, Paulie. You're the only one who can help him.' "

He shrugged. "I felt as if I had no choice. Of course, nobody was pointing a gun at me. Nobody told me what to do. I didn't feel good about myself, making that call. But for my father's sake, I did it."

"I'd say those were mitigating circumstances."

"I don't mean to be making excuses."

"You're not," said Jesse. "Nor am I. I'm simply bringing a measure of humanity to the table. Judging you the same way I've seen you judge others."

"What's my sentence?" Paul smiled grimly. "What do you suggest, Your Honor?"

"For starters, given Crandell's backing of my appointment, I'll have to recuse myself from Starwares. Then, I should report myself to the Bar Association for malfeasance. I guess I should also step down from the bench."

"God spare us from a hanging judge! Don't you think you're being rather hard on yourself? So what if Crandell brought your name to the senator's attention? He didn't buy you the President's nomination or the Senate's confirmation. Those you earned on the basis of your reputation. Starwares is a big, tough, complicated case. You've spent hours reading the briefs and declarations. You've listened to two days' worth of testimony. It would be a terrible waste of the taxpayers' money if you stepped down now."

Paul stared at him in astonishment. "But what if I decide against Crandell, and he comes forward with the information?"

"That's a risk you'll have to take, and the consequences could be devastating. But leave it to the Chief Justice to decide, if it comes to that. If you step down now, you'd be as much as admitting to Crandell that he has the upper hand. Don't give him that power. He already has enough."

"This is about the last thing I expected to hear from you."

"It's important to forgive," said Jesse. "Yourself and others."

"Hope?"

Jesse nodded.

"I know." He sighed. "Helen and I never had these sorts of problems."

"But you had other problems, ones you've forgotten," Jesse said gently. "Every marriage has its pitfalls. The key is to move past them, to learn from your mistakes, the way you did with Jimmy. Maybe that's one of the reasons your decisions are so fair and well reasoned. Because you understand firsthand how a person can screw things up for himself."

The grandfather clock that stood just outside the door began to toll the hour. Ten o'clock. He was exhausted. He'd taken up more than enough of Jesse's time.

"Thank you," he said, wearily pulling himself to his feet. "For everything."

Jesse stood up to walk him to the door. He said, "There's a wonderful Yiddish word you should add to your vocabulary. *Rochmones*. It means compassion."

"Rochmones." He tried to mimic Jesse's pronunciation.

"Not bad," said Jesse. "Take it home and keep practicing. You'll get it right eventually."

FOURTEEN

THE CALL FROM Naomi Bowman had come in to Bernard Odette's office just five days after he and Ken Wolch had made their closing arguments. Judge Murray's decision would be available for distribution that afternoon at three o'clock. By three-fifteen, Odette was back from lunch and seated in Lew Valentine's office, along with Walter Spaulding and Rizzy Riznicki, waiting for the messenger to arrive with the ruling.

"I think it's a good sign for us that Murray only took five days," Walter Spaulding said for the third time in as many hours. "Don't you think so, Bernie?"

"Walter, would you shut the fuck up?" Valentine snapped. "We'll know for sure in about fifteen minutes. What's the point of speculating?"

"Sorry, Lew," said Spaulding. "I just think that if he were finding for Crandell, it would have taken him a lot longer to put all his ducks in a row."

"Walter, bag it!" Valentine shouted.

Spaulding hung his head. "Sorry, Lew," he said again. "It's just so nerve-wracking, after all the hard work we've done."

Odette and Rizzy exchanged looks of amusement. Spaulding had done precious little on the case, except to call them periodically with urgent messages from Valentine that bordered on harassment.

Spaulding turned to Odette. "So what do you think, Bernie?" he asked.

"I think we did a good job. Beyond that, I agree with Lew. There's no point in speculation." Odette lit up a cigarette and glanced around. "Excuse me," he said. "I'm going in search of an ashtray."

Anita, Valentine's secretary, welcomed him with her generous smile as he approached her desk. "Do you want some M&M's?" She held up an open, half-empty bag.

"They'll make you fat," he said.

"More of me to love," she said, handing him the ashtray. "Pretty tense in there, huh?"

Odette shrugged. Whichever way Murray came down, the decision would be appealed. Win or lose, they were only at the halfway mark. "Dinner tonight?" he asked.

"Sure." She smiled again, flashing her dimples. "Only this time, let's eat first."

"Envelope for Mr. Valentine." A lanky young man in a T-shirt and chinos ambled through the door that separated Valentine's suite from the rest of his employees.

Odette caught a glimpse of the return address as the messenger handed the envelope to Anita. "I'll take it," he said, intercepting the package, which was thicker than he had expected.

"Good luck," said Anita, as he tore open the envelope.

She was sweet. Sexy, too. He wondered if she would ever consider relocating to Detroit.

By the time he stepped back inside Valentine's office, he'd scanned enough of the decision to know that he and Anita would be celebrating that evening.

"Judgment for plaintiff." He read the words aloud to his anxious audience. "Congratulations, gentlemen. And you, too, Ms. Riznicki. I couldn't have done it without you."

She blushed. He wouldn't have believed it if he hadn't seen it with his own eyes.

"Son-of-a-bitch!" Valentine whooped. "I *knew* it!"

"I told you it was a good sign," crowed Spaulding.

"What did Murray say?" asked Rizzy, coming to read over Odette's shoulder as he skimmed through the pages.

"Basically, he agrees with the arguments we made. He considers the deal with Summit a sale." He flipped to the next page. "He faults Starwares' board for failing to fulfill its fiduciary responsibilities by improperly analyzing our bid."

"What about the poison pill?" she asked, referring to the provision that gave Starwares the right to flood the market with newly issued stock in the event of an unfriendly offer.

Odette grinned. "Out. He also struck down the lockup provision and the other consolation payments Starwares would have had to pay to Summit if the board had voted to go with Valentine."

Valentine threw open his door and called to Anita. "We need a bottle of champagne in here and some glasses." Then he turned back to Odette. "Go on. Let's hear the rest."

"We scored points with Harold Shaw's testimony. Murray says that Starwares didn't properly assess the strengths and weaknesses of our offer. He's pissed off that they refused to meet with you, Lew, except for that initial meeting you had with Lynch in November."

"I *love* this! What a vindication!" Valentine gloated. "Give me more."

Odette skipped to the last page. "Here, this is juicy. He says, 'The Starwares board, by its actions, has prevented shareholders from choosing between Summit and the higher immediate value offered by Valentine. Indeed, by its discriminatory assignment of the poison pill and various other antitakeover features that give preference to Summit, Starwares' board would in effect compel its

shareholders to accept the lower-valued bid offered by
Summit.' ''

"Put simply," said Valentine, "we win, Crandell takes
a hike."

Odette nodded. "That about sums it up. Of course,
he'll appeal. But Paul Murray's a good, careful judge,
with an excellent record on the state level. I have to read
this carefully, but at first glance, it seems much stronger
and broader than I had even hoped for."

"Jordan Crandell must be pissing blood," said Spaulding.

"I wouldn't count on it," Valentine said. "Crandell
has ice in his veins. He's already plotting his next move.
But this is one time none of his tricks will save him.
Starwares is mine, and I have you to thank for it, Bernie.
You're damned expensive, but you're worth every
penny."

Odette smiled. "That was never in question."

DARKNESS WAS FALLING across the city. Paul absentmindedly gazed out the window as a sprinkling of lights came
on in the building across the street from the courthouse.
Most of the offices were dark and empty, their occupants
having left for the day. Normally, he too would already
be gone, but this evening he was in no particular hurry to
leave.

Hope would be waiting for him at home, wondering
why he was late. Torn between not wanting her to worry
and wishing he didn't have to speak to her just now, he
sighed and reached for the phone. Then he remembered
she had a late-afternoon class today and probably wasn't
home yet herself. It was just as well. After this grueling
day, he needed some time to be alone with his thoughts.

For better or for worse, he had reached his decision
and handed down his ruling. It remained to be seen what
the fallout would be. His messages were mostly requests
from the media for interviews and comments. Several of

his colleagues had also phoned, including Jesse, who had merely said, ''I'm here if you need me.'' But Jordan Crandell, the one person he had most expected to hear from, hadn't yet seen fit to be in touch.

Paul briefly tried to imagine what Crandell's next move would be, then banished the question from his mind. Second-guessing would get him nowhere. He rubbed the back of his neck, kneading the tension knot that had developed as he had worked through the Starwares decision.

The process had taken him longer than usual, not because he was unclear about the facts, but because he was determined to make certain he was being absolutely fair to both sides. This was one case where he couldn't afford even the slightest shadow of a doubt to be cast over his thinking. Whatever might happen down the line, he wanted no one accusing him of faulty reasoning or insufficient regard for precedent.

Both Odette and Wolch had offered sound arguments on their clients' behalf. The issue for him had come down to one relatively simple point. No matter what vision of the future the Starwares board had in mind for the company when it voted on the merger with Summit, as the new majority stockholder, Jordan Crandell could single-handedly alter that future with his own vision of the company's structure and direction.

Starwares stockholders would have little if any voice in the long-term financial rewards available to them. In Paul's view, the board owed the stockholders either some sort of protection against their potential loss or the opportunity to secure the greatest possible return on their investment by offering the company for sale to the highest bidder.

Everything else followed from that. Normally, he would have enjoyed fashioning his opinion, citing relevant case law, building his argument point by point, trying to anticipate any questions or objections that might be raised on appeal. But each sentence was punctuated by one thought: He was as guilty as Jordan Crandell of flouting the law.

Jesse had offered him the freedom from guilt he thought he craved. Now he realized it wasn't absolution that he wanted but rather the chance to finally serve the punishment he'd been waiting all these years to receive.

Over time, he had managed to bury the incident so deep in his subconscious that he rarely even thought about it, except occasionally, after seeing Jimmy, when his guilt would surface in his dreams. It was a relief to bring his memories out into the open, where he could examine his conscience with the same mixture of trepidation and sense of imminent release that his schoolboy self had brought each week to confession.

Though still confused as to what he should do, he had followed Jesse's advice and applied himself to the case at hand. It was entirely possible that Crandell would take the initiative and force the issue so that the decision about whether or not to step down from the bench would not be his to make. In the meantime, again at Jesse's urging, he was also trying to practice compassion. He had struggled to come to terms with what Hope had done and to forgive her.

Forgiving himself, however, was a far more difficult proposition.

Kurt Zelmanski was just leaving the office to meet Rizzy Riznicki when the call came in from Jordan Crandell. It took him less than a nanosecond to decide to stick around. Rizzy would understand if he showed up late.

"Mr. Crandell," he said. He flipped on his computer and pulled up the file he'd named "Cranfund." "Thanks for getting back to me."

"Hell, why not?" Crandell's voice boomed at him. "You want a quote, right? A snappy line to show your readers you can go right to the top? I'm happy to oblige."

"Really?" Zelmanski didn't bother to hide his surprise. This was a different, seemingly more cooperative Jordan Crandell than he'd anticipated.

Since yesterday, when Valentine had won the first court round on Starwares, Crandell had been uncharacteristically restrained in his reaction. Except for a brief press release issued through his corporate spokesman in which he'd denounced the inequity of Judge Murray's decision and proclaimed his confidence that the Starwares-Summit alliance would be vindicated on appeal, he'd refused to make any statements. Zelmanski and everyone else had been forced to get their information from "well-informed sources within the company" who had insisted on anonymity.

It made for flabby stories, which would have bothered Zelmanski more were he not so close to a wrap on the Osburgh-Crandell connection. All that remained was to try for a comment from Crandell, who most likely had already been warned by Osburgh.

"As a matter of fact, I have something I thought might be of interest to you."

"Same here," said Zelmanski.

"If you mean that wacko fairy tale you fed to Osburgh, forget it. Osburgh's a nervous old lady whose wife has been carrying his balls around in her purse for years. You scared the shit out of him, Zelmanski. I don't know what he told you, but you have a wild imagination. You should be writing novels, not business pieces that are supposed to be based on facts."

Zelmanski had expected Crandell to put up a bluff. "Are you denying that you received money from the Scott Trust to help finance your acquisition of Starwares, Mr. Crandell?"

"Get real, Zelmanski. That statement is too preposterous to even deserve a denial."

"I'll fax you some of the evidence I've collected that proves my allegations."

"Fine, whatever. I'm not worried."

Crandell sounded so convincing that for a moment, until he glanced at the pile of documents on his desk, Zelmanski was almost prepared to believe him. The facts were all there, including the proof of the loss Osburgh had taken on a savings and loan deal. He had to remind himself that Crandell was a master bullshit artist.

"Make sure you read the *Journal* on Wednesday morning, Mr. Crandell, particularly if you like to see your name in print."

"Thanks for the free publicity. My lawyer will be calling your lawyer on Wednesday afternoon. Now, you listen to me. I've got a story you're going to love. I've done all the legwork for you. All you need is to write it and get it printed."

Crandell was an operator, but he was damn smart. Zelmanski couldn't afford not to listen. "Go ahead," he said.

"I got Paul Murray his federal judgeship. So what the hell's he doing, ruling against me? Why didn't he recuse himself when he first got the case? Good questions, huh? And wait, it gets better. This guy's passing judgment on honest businessmen like myself, but he's got a secret from his past that's about to blow up in his face."

"Uh-huh," Zelmanski muttered, wondering whether Crandell was on drugs.

"Are you paying attention? Here's the best part. He used his connections to protect his cop brother from being arrested on corruption charges. What do you think about that?"

What he really thought was that maybe Crandell had snapped under the tension of the last few months. The story was too preposterous, and Crandell's attempt at revenge was much too transparent. For all his influence and wealth, he was only human. Zelmanski had seen it happen to other corporate giants. At a certain point, they started buying all the hype, all the bull, all the rumors

THE HEART OF JUSTICE

their PR firms put out about them. Or maybe the devil got the better of their souls.

"It's not my kind of story, Mr. Crandell. I'm more interested in what you're going to see on Wednesday's front page."

"You're making a huge mistake, Zelmanski," Crandell snarled.

Zelmanski clicked off his computer. Rizzy was waiting. "Tell it to the *National Enquirer.*"

IT HAD BEEN a week since Paul had confronted Hope about Jordan Crandell, a week since he'd heard the tapes and gone to Jesse Rubin for advice. Afterwards, he hadn't told her much about his old mentor's reaction, except to say that Jesse believed there was no reason for him to recuse himself from the Starwares case. Whatever else he'd said, Paul seemed terribly preoccupied, as if he were grappling with a heavy bundle of problems. She sensed that he was trying to be kind to her, that it would take time for him to overcome his anger so they could get back to their normal existence.

They were living under an uneasy cease-fire. Things were so strained between them that she'd learned about his Starwares decision by reading about it in the *Times.* She didn't dare raise the subject with him, for fear he'd again suspect her of plotting to influence him. It didn't surprise her that he'd ruled in favor of Valentine. She was proud of him for doing whatever he thought was most fair.

But with each passing hour, her terror—and her rage— about Jordan's reaction was growing more intense. She felt as if he held in his hand the stolen key to her family's future happiness, and she couldn't let him throw it away in order to punish Paul. She was so proud of Paul for finding in favor of Valentine, regardless of the consequences. Taking heart from his example, she learned a lesson in courage that helped her decide what she had to do. On Wednesday morning, two days after Paul had handed down his ruling, she realized she had no choice but to appear unannounced at Jordan's office, catch him off guard, and somehow force him to leave Paul alone. She would have preferred to face him with an already formulated plan of attack, but none had yet come to her, and she didn't want to wait another minute.

The guard at the elevators remembered her from the luncheon. "Go right up to the tenth floor, Mrs. Murray. Ask for Donna," he said, holding the door of the elevator next to his station so she didn't have to wait for another one.

Finding her way to Jordan's office was simple. She followed the sound of his voice, screaming abuse at some hapless soul who apparently hadn't followed his orders. After a few minutes, when the shouting had stopped, she stiffened her back and marched down the hall to brave the enemy.

"You must be Donna," she said to the harried-looking person seated at the desk outside Jordan's office. "We've spoken by phone. I'm Hope Scott Murray."

"Of course, Mrs. Murray. It's nice to match the face to the voice," said Donna. She frowned. "Do you have an appointment with Mr. Crandell? I don't see your name in his calendar."

Hope smiled, determined to charm her way into his office. "I happened to be in the neighborhood and thought it would be *such* fun to drop in on him. He's invited me so many times, but I rarely get down here. Could I just tiptoe in and surprise him?"

Donna hesitated. "He's not in a very good mood today." She lowered her voice. "It's this Starwares thing. You can imagine how he feels. . . ."

"That's precisely why I was hoping I might be able to cheer him up," she said brightly.

Donna nodded. "Sure, you're right. He has a meeting in twenty minutes, so why don't you go in right now?"

"Thanks, Donna." Ignoring her pangs of guilt for having tricked the woman, she quietly opened Jordan's door, stepped inside, and closed it firmly behind her. He was on the phone, his back to her, his feet up on the windowsill.

"Jordan."

He turned around and stared at her. "I have to go," he said into the phone and hung up abruptly.

"What are you doing here?"

"I lied my way past Donna. I have to talk to you."

"You *had* to talk to your husband, but you didn't. Thanks for nothing."

"I couldn't help you, Jordan, but you refused to believe me. Paul's far too ethical a person to make his decision based on anything but the facts as he sees them."

He started laughing before she had a chance to finish the sentence. "If you still believe that, I can offer you a great price on the Brooklyn Bridge. I assume you listened to the tapes. Perhaps I should put you directly in touch with those nice folks who took the time to talk to my investigator."

His arrogance pushed a button in her that let fly the anger she'd been harboring toward him since he'd first turned on her with his sick threats.

"Don't you *dare* speak to me like that, you disgusting little prick," she hissed, hardly recognizing her own voice. "You're a loser, Jordan Crandell, and I'm not afraid of your pathetic attempts to intimidate me *or* my husband! You may think you have the upper hand. But if you *ever* release those tapes, or do anything to hurt Paul, I will make sure you suffer for it. I have enough money to see to that."

He looked stunned by her outburst. "Are you threatening me, Hope?"

"You're damn straight I am," she said. Clenching her fists by her side to keep from slapping him, she marched herself to the door. "And you better take me seriously, because I never, ever go back on my word."

Her mother had taught her that a lady never slammed a door in anger. "Sorry, Mama," she whispered, as she broke her mother's rule.

Jordan Crandell had to understand she meant business.

She was still fuming when she reached the lobby and stopped at the newsstand to buy some mints. She glanced down at the stack of *Wall Street Journals* and a headline leaped up at her: "SCOTT TRUST FUNDS ILLEGALLY USED FOR STARWARES BID."

She grabbed a paper, slapped her money down on the counter, and devoured the story. Halfway through, she had to stop and take several deep breaths. The article claimed that her uncle George had written illegal checks to Summit, totaling a half-billion dollars, drawn on Scott Trust funds. *Her* trust. The story went on for several more paragraphs, with mentions made of bad investments by George Osburgh and offshore umbrella corporations, all of which ultimately seemed to link Uncle George to Jordan Crandell.

The details were too much to take in. She would read the rest of it at home, where she could properly digest all the facts. She folded the paper into her bag and went outside to hail a cab. It wasn't until she reached 42nd Street that she realized she'd left her car and driver sitting in the middle of SoHo. And it wasn't until the cab pulled up in front of her building that she thought to look at the byline under the article and suddenly remembered that a Kurt Zelmanski had called several times the previous month, urgently requesting an interview.

A pile of messages was waiting for her at home—from Paul, Uncle George, Aunt Connie, Winthrop Harding, Harry Matheson, friends and family she hadn't heard from in years, newspaper and television reporters. The list went on and on. Everyone who had seen or heard about the *Journal* article wanted to talk to her about it and get her reaction.

Before anyone else, she wanted to speak to Paul, but

his message had said he would be in court until noon, and it was just eleven-fifty now. The others could wait. She needed time to sort out the jumble of emotions cluttering her mind and keeping her from thinking clearly.

She lay down on her bed and pressed her face against Paul's pillow, inhaling the faint trace of his scent, wishing he were there to comfort her. Her world was turning upside down. If the *Journal* story were true, Uncle George, her father's oldest and dearest friend—one of the people she trusted most—had stolen money from her and given it to Jordan. The layers of deceit went so deep she couldn't begin to trace them.

The enormity of her uncle's betrayal struck her now like a fist in her gut. How could he have done such a thing? How could he face her, invite her to dinner, come into her home, knowing he had used her father's money for his own illegal purposes? And how Jordan Crandell must have been laughing at her, when all the while it was Scott Trust money that was helping to make his deal possible.

"Bastards," she muttered, the anger rising in her.

But poor Aunt Connie. What must she be thinking? And her daughters, Hope's childhood playmates—how would they feel to know their father was a thief?

What could have led him to turn to Jordan for help?

She immediately had the answer to that question: the same impulse that had led her to Jordan. He was a genius at manipulating reality, so that it seemed as if all you had to do was ask and the most difficult problems got resolved. If only she had understood the price he exacted for providing those solutions.

She felt the wetness on her cheeks before she realized she was crying. She was sobbing aloud, weeping as she hadn't wept since the day her father died. She couldn't stop, nor did she want to. Her anguish was too great.

Then, suddenly, she felt a pair of arms around her and turned to find Paul there, just as she had wished for, his blue eyes tired and worried. "Shh," he murmured. "We'll get everything straightened out. I promise."

She clutched at him. "What are you doing here? I thought you were in court."

"I was too worried about you to concentrate, so I called an early recess. The Osburgh thing . . . did you read about it?"

She nodded. "I can't believe it. Do you think the story is true?"

"Possibly. Kurt Zelmanski is usually a very careful reporter. He wouldn't write a story without getting his facts straight."

"What's going to happen to Uncle George?" she asked. "What do we do?"

"Charges will be filed against him on behalf of you and the trust. He could face a stiff fine, probably a prison sentence."

"Prison?" She stared at him in shock. "But why? Can't he just repay the money?"

"Maybe. But he committed a pretty serious crime. I assume George will testify against Crandell. If the evidence is strong enough, he'll be charged, too, for promising George a kickback, and he'll be the one to repay the money."

"I'm so sorry, Paul," she whispered, starting to cry again.

"Why? This isn't your fault."

"I'm sorry I went behind your back to try and fix things for you. I should have asked you first."

He sighed. "Yes, you should have. I would have said no. Would you have listened to me?"

"I don't know." Hope smiled weakly. "I hope so. But I was so determined to make everything perfect and wonderful for you."

He took her hand. "I see that now. Stop beating yourself up. I forgive you."

"I can imagine how hard these last few days have been for you," she said.

"No, you can't," he said with a trace of bitterness. "Holding on to that case was the single hardest choice I've ever made. But I couldn't run away from it. That would have felt as if I'd let Jordan Crandell win as surely as if I'd decided in his favor. I've thought long and hard about all this, Hope. Part of me believes those tapes are my punishment for breaking the law. Maybe I deserve to be found out. How can I judge other people for their crimes when I've committed a crime myself?"

"But you didn't!" she cried. "It was Jimmy who broke the law. You were just trying to help him."

"I've told myself that very thing a thousand times." He shrugged. "That still doesn't make it any easier for me to decide whether or not I have to resign my appointment. Of course, the choice may not be mine to make, if Crandell has his way. Besides, it was wrong. I did it for my father and my family, but it was still wrong, and I knew it."

"It was a good thing you did. Look at Jimmy now. He's no criminal. Who knows how it would have turned out for him if he'd gone to jail?"

She sat up suddenly, feeling her way toward the answer to their problem. "Wait a minute. We could do the same thing for Jordan. You said charges would be filed against him. Don't I have a say in that? What if I offer not to press charges if he gives us all the copies of the tapes and promises to forget what he knows?"

Paul smiled at her like an indulgent parent. "You can't do that."

"Why not?" she asked with growing excitement. The tables were turned now. She held the weapon that could badly damage Jordan's empire. "This is perfect. I'll offer to let him keep some of the money. A hundred million should be enough to buy him off."

"Don't be ridiculous, Hope. It's not only your decision. Harding and Matheson, as the two other trustees, will never agree to your giving up that kind of money. Nor should you give it up."

"They'll have to agree. Otherwise, I'll sue them for not properly looking out for my interests. As for the money, believe me, I have more than enough. It's a good investment if it keeps our lives intact."

He shook his head. "This doesn't feel right to me. You're bribing Crandell so I can keep my seat on the court. I'm being rewarded instead of punished for my mistake."

"You've punished yourself enough. Your life and career shouldn't be ruined because of an act of kindness you committed for someone you love. My life shouldn't be ruined by Jordan Crandell's greed. Maybe he'll even learn a thing or two about how decent people behave if he sees how little that money matters to me compared to your happiness. My father, for all his faults, loved me more than anything in the world. I bet he would think it's money well spent."

"I don't know," Paul said slowly. "You'd really be prepared to sacrifice that much money to save my career?"

She reached for the phone. "Just watch me."

FIFTEEN

THE FIRST SKI run of the season held its own special magic that was unlike anything else Eric Lynch had ever experienced. Perhaps it was because it made him feel a bit like a kid again, discovering the sport for the very first time. Or maybe it was because the snow was so clean and pure, the lifts and slopes still relatively empty, that he could close his eyes all the way up to the top, then fly down the trails pretending he owned the mountain.

Buying his own mountain was, in fact, Lynch's greatest—and most secret—ambition. Not even his closest friends were aware of his fantasy, which he had nurtured from the moment he'd made his first million. Robert Redford, who owned the mountain where Lynch had his home, was his inspiration, but Lynch planned to do Redford one better. *His* slopes would be closed to all but a few select friends and business associates who had earned the right to share his private domain.

He had personally scouted almost a hundred potential sites from Utah all the way up to British Columbia. He had surveyed remote Rocky Mountain peaks and valleys via helicopter, often landing under conditions that would have made his stockholders shudder in fear, had they known the risks their CEO was exposing himself to. But Lynch knew he had already survived the greatest risk of all—the sale of Starwares, which had provided him with enough cash to make his dream come true.

Five months had passed since the New York court had ruled in favor of Valentine Industries, thus forcing Starwares to reconsider Valentine's bid. Just days after that had come the bombshell revelations about the illegal payments by George Osburgh to Jordan Crandell and Summit, which had knocked Summit off the map, as far as Starwares was concerned.

Lynch's bankers had quietly scoured the corporate woods for other suitors, but no one was prepared to take on the mighty team of Lew Valentine and the Michigan Assassin. The headline in *The Wall Street Journal* had proclaimed Valentine Industries "the Ultimate Victor in Starwares Battle." The untold story behind the headline was that Lynch would end the year a much wealthier man than he could ever have expected to be.

Lynch was laughing all the way to the bank, but the ultimate joke was on Valentine, and only Lynch knew the punchline. Starwares was worth much less than it seemed on paper, and Valentine had way overpaid for a company that was actually nothing more than a very good, medium-priced property. Victory was sweet, very sweet, now that Lynch's wallet had been fattened by the man who'd once fired him.

Both Crandell and Valentine had taken at face value Lynch's demands for ongoing control of the company, never guessing that he was fully prepared to leave and start anew. The fact was that Starwares was only as strong as its chief executive's concepts. Research and development were lagging far behind the competition. It was only a matter of time before the companies ranked number three and four in the software race would overtake Starwares in new product development, unless Eric Lynch downloaded the cache of ideas he had stored in his brain.

If he and Valentine could work together, well and

good. Meanwhile, he would caretake the company while he searched for the perfect ski slope to conquer. The waiting game was all the more delicious because of the power he now had over Valentine. Everything depended on how Valentine treated him in the coming months. One false move, and Lynch would remove himself to the mountaintop of his choice to plot his next venture.

"HEY, BOSS, GOOD to see you." Rizzy Riznicki grinned at Bernard Odette and bent to kiss his cheek before she sat down across the restaurant table from him. "Mmm, nice aftershave. What is it?"

"For your information, only impoverished reporters wear aftershave. Inordinately rich lawyers wear eau de toilette, and the more expensive, the better," Odette said, smiling at his former employee.

"I'll remember that," said Rizzy. She glanced around the bright airy dining room, decorated in simple but elegant French country style. "Great place. I bet it's terrifically expensive."

Though they'd kept in touch by phone, they hadn't seen each other since the end of June, when Odette had closed down his office in Trump Tower. Rizzy's hair looked less tousled than usual, and her suit jacket was cut to deemphasize her broad shoulders. He wondered whether it was Zelmanski's influence or her new job that was responsible for the changes she was making in her image.

He suddenly realized that he'd missed her. He wished she'd accepted his offer of a permanent position with him. But that would have meant her moving to Detroit, and she was too stuck on Kurt to leave New York. Besides, who would ever leave New York for Detroit?

"You mean Zelmanski's never taken you here?" he teased. "You have to find yourself a guy who can give you the lifestyle to which I got you accustomed. Dump him, Rizzy, before it's too late."

"That's not what you told me last spring," she said.

"Last spring we needed him for the case. What damn use is he to you now?"

"You'd be surprised," she said with a wink. "So, what's good here?"

"Everything's delicious, but the chocolate dessert soufflé is outstanding. Oh, good, here's the champagne I ordered."

"Champagne, huh? You ought to come to town more often." She bent her head to study the menu as their waiter uncorked the wine and poured it for them.

"Cheers," said Odette, lifting his glass and touching it to hers.

"To many future successes." She took a sip and smiled appreciatively. "Damn, I could really get used to this stuff. How's life in the Motor City, boss?"

"I haven't spent more than four days at a stretch in Detroit since we finished up Starwares. Business is booming. What about you? How does being an associate at Kraft, Wolch compare to working for me?"

"A piece of cake. I never imagined myself as a law firm slavey, but it sure beats waiting tables. Thanks for the recommendation."

"My pleasure. How's my friend, Ken Wolch?"

"Fine. I bumped into him in the hall today and told him we were having dinner. He sends his regards."

The waiter reappeared at their table. "Ready to order, Mr. Odette?" he asked.

Odette nodded. "Rizzy?"

"I'm outclassed here. I'll leave it to you to decide."

"Smart woman. We'll both have the 'tasting menu,' " he told the waiter, opting for the seventy-dollar, fixed-price dinner. "And I'll look at the wine list again."

He glanced around the room, pleased to see that people were noticing him. The publicity generated by Starwares had made him a celebrity in New York. Court TV had asked him to appear as one of their expert commentators, and he'd been approached by another of the cable networks about doing his own talk show. As much as he'd disliked Valentine, he was almost sorry that the case hadn't gone any further. There was no telling what could have happened after he won the appeal.

"Is Jordan Crandell still keeping Ken busy?"

"Our number one client? You better believe it."

"After your boyfriend's article last spring, I'd have thought Ken would be spending the fall in court, defending Crandell's honor." He lit a cigarette. "Funny how that whole mess with Osburgh and the Scott Trust money just vanished into thin air. What does Zelmanski make of it?"

"He thinks it's pretty damn weird that the Trust didn't press charges against either Osburgh or Crandell. He went back to all of his sources, followed up every lead, and kept coming up with nothing. What got him most suspicious was that neither Osburgh nor Crandell sued him or the paper."

"Did he talk to the two other trustees or Hope Scott?"

"He tried. No one would answer his calls. It was like a goddamn news blackout. One thing he did find out was that Osburgh had a stroke three weeks after the story ran. The poor guy's paralyzed on one side."

Odette shook his head. "That's tough."

"Yeah, Zelmanski's feeling just a tad guilty. He thinks maybe it happened because Osburgh got so upset by the article. *I* think he got too excited in the saddle."

"Osburgh?" Odette chuckled. "I doubt it. Have you seen pictures of his wife?"

"Zelmanski talked to the EMS medic who brought Osburgh to the hospital. He was in bed with his girlfriend, a sweet young thing with a Harvard B.A. in economics, a great bod, and hair that never gets frizzy, no matter how high the humidity."

Odette whistled. "Son-of-a-gun. I wouldn't have guessed he had it in him. What was Mrs. Osburgh's reaction?"

"She must have forgiven him, because she took him down to Florida to recover. I guess she's the understanding type."

Rizzy stared over his shoulder, then leaned forward and lowered her voice. "Speaking of the Scott Trust, don't look now, but here comes Judge Murray and the primary beneficiary herself."

Odette sipped his champagne as he watched the maître d' lead Hope and Paul to a quiet spot at the back of the room.

"She's pregnant," whispered Rizzy.

"So it seems," said Odette, amused to discover that even Rizzy could get excited by a sighting of Hope Scott Murray, who looked beautiful as always, despite the fact that she was obviously close to delivery.

He caught Paul Murray's eye across the aisle and nodded a greeting. The judge nodded in return, then helped his wife make herself comfortable at the table.

Rizzy shifted slightly in her chair to get a better view of the couple, who were holding hands and smiling at each other, seemingly oblivious to all the attention they were attracting.

"They look so happy together, don't they?" She sighed.

Odette shook his head. He'd mistaken her for a bona fide cynic, like himself. Any minute now she'd be telling him she, too, wanted to have a baby. "I'm surprised at you, Rizzy. You're getting goofy and sentimental. What you're looking at is the face of money. You'd be amazed how a few billion dollars can keep the bloom on a romance."

She glanced at them again before she turned back to Odette. "Boss," she said, "for once, your cynicism has led you astray. That's the face of love all right. Even a blind man or a lawyer could see that."

ABOUT THE AUTHOR

WILLIAM J. COUGHLIN was a prosecutor and defense attorney in Detroit for twenty years. At the time of his death, he was Senior United States Administrative Law Judge. The father of six children and author of fifteen previous novels, he lived with his wife, Ruth, in Grosse Pointe, Michigan.

Elizabeth Daren is in dire straits. With evidence missing and key witnesses changing their stories, the battle for her dead husband's fortune is turning ugly. Someone is out to get her, and only Jake Martin, one of the country's shrewdest, most battle-hardened lawyers, can save her. If he can trust her.

IN THE PRESENCE OF ENEMIES

WILLIAM COUGHLIN

A beautiful young woman's corpse is found along a highway. There's not a mark on her and an autopsy can't determine the cause of death. Rumor says her boyfriend, a prominent surgeon, will be charged with murder...unless defense attorney Dan Sheridan can stop the indictment.

THE INDICTMENT

BARRY REED

THE INDICTMENT
Barry Reed
_____ 95416-6 $6.99 U.S./$7.99 CAN.